throne of truth

THRONE

OF

TRUTH

by

New York Times Bestseller
PEPPER WINTERS

THRONE

OF

TRUTH

by

New York Times Bestseller

PEPPER WINTERS

Throne of Truth
Copyright © 2017 Pepper Winters
Published by Pepper Winters

Published: Pepper Winters 2017: **pepperwinters@gmail.com**
Cover Design: by Cover it! Designs
Editing by: Editing-4-Indies (Jenny Sims)

DEDICATION

To every person I've ever had the honor of meeting, talking to online, passing in the street, or looking up to. We might have met for a second, but it's those seconds that make me who I am.

PROLOGUE

PENN

LIES.

They have a life of their own. They multiply, divide, and conquer—not just the listener but the liar, too. They infiltrate the truth. They twist words until false is truer than reality.

I should know. I'd become a master at them.

For a while, lies had been my saving grace. They'd kept me warm on the coldest nights and kept me sheltered when only darkness remained, but now, I have wealth and family, and my lies aren't giving me power anymore…they're stripping me of it.

Stripping me of her.

She ran away from me.

She ran before I could tell her the truth.

It didn't matter the truth wasn't what she wanted to hear. It didn't matter I had so many confessions and only the guts to reveal a few.

She ran.

And then she vanished.

CHAPTER ONE

ELLE

"GET OUT OF the fucking car, Elle."

I cocked my chin, glowering out the window.

Get out of my life, Greg.

The slur scalded my tongue, but I didn't have the balls to say it. My cheek still hurt. Fear still sliced my insides. The view outside the car was foreign and unwanted.

I was kidnapped, hurt, and pissed off.

I hate you, Greg.

I'll make you pay, Greg.

My lips pulled into a sneer of contempt.

You won't win, Greg.

"Elle!" He thumped the roof of his graphite Porsche for the third time. The rattle shook the interior, making me flinch. I'd done well for most of the journey.

He'd prattled on while miles slowly crept between me and my home. I'd remained stoic and deathly silent—I didn't wince when he shouted for a response and didn't cower when he raised his hand in threat.

I refused to let him affect me, even though I couldn't ignore my body's discomfort anymore. My bound hands were numb from the twine around my wrists. My shoulders screamed for mercy, and my butt was flat from the long drive.

For five hours, I'd tried to come up with a plan to either talk Greg out of whatever manic idea he'd concocted or figure out a way to incapacitate him.

My mind kept me entertained with images of knocking him out, leaving him tied to a tree, and stealing his car. I'd drive myself back to New York. It didn't matter I hadn't driven since I got my license—*all David's fault for driving me everywhere.* It didn't matter I barely knew how to operate a standard rather than an automatic gearshift. And it definitely didn't matter I had no idea how to knock out a full-grown male with my hands tied behind my back.

I would do whatever it took to get free from this lunatic who I'd been raised with.

Starting with refusing to cooperate.

"Elle…" Greg growled, thumping the car one last time before ducking to shove his face into mine. The night sky bled with shadows and gloomy clouds. Not one star; no sliver of moon. It was as if we existed in a dead end while the roads of the world were back at a U-turn somewhere.

"I won't ask again."

I forced every inch of authority I could into my glare. "I don't want to be here, Greg. Take me home."

He laughed, rolling his eyes. "Too fucking bad. We're here. *Now get.*"

I didn't let him undermine me. I didn't let him see my fear or frustration. "I'm not getting out of the car because you're driving me home. Right now."

"Oh, I am, am I?" He laughed harder, this time with a sinister echo. "That's what you think." He undid my seat belt and placed his fingers on my thigh. "I'm going to count to five." He squeezed. Hard. "I suggest you get out before I hit five.*"

My heart coughed.

Greg dropped all pretenses and ripped off his mask. He was done masquerading as the boring son of my father's best friend and my employee. Out here (alone), he showed who he truly was, and I *hated* him.

I hated him more than I feared him.

But the longer he squeezed my thigh, the stronger my fear grew. I trembled with disobedience, cursing him, wishing the ground would grow teeth and chew him alive.

"One." He smiled, his fingers climbing up my leg toward my core.

I gritted my teeth. I didn't let him see how much my skin crawled to have his touch so close to where I vehemently didn't want him.

"Two." He crept the final distance, cupping me roughly with a harsh glint in his eyes.

I shivered as he let me go as quickly as he'd grabbed me. His touch slithered upward, stroking my belly, my hip, my waist. "Three."

I shifted despite myself.

My legs bunched to obey—to climb out on my own willpower to avoid whatever nastiness he had planned. But he wedged himself in the door, not giving me any room to exit.

He knew that.

He nodded slyly, knowing I'd figured out that he'd blocked me. That I didn't have a choice in what would happen next.

"Four." His touch switched from my waist to my breast, tweaking a nipple before climbing the rest of the way to my shoulder. His fingers dug into me like barbwire, sharp and steely—ready to rip me apart.

I braced for pain.

I sniffed in retaliation.

Not that it did any good.

"Five." The grasp he had on my shoulder became a throbbing anchor. Digging his fingernails into my flesh, he yanked with all his energy.

With nothing holding me in the car, I toppled sideways.

I had no way to fight or stop my sideways motion.

I fell out, landing painfully on my shoulder with my legs still in the Porsche and my arms tied behind my back. Sharp gravel dug into my cheek. Wind whooshed from my lungs.

With my face wedged against the ground, I had a perfect view of Greg's black loafers as he squatted over me. "Well, that's one success. You're out of the car." He nudged me with his toe. "Now, get up."

I squirmed, wincing as every joint and ligament squealed in pain. My spine hated the way my legs pretzeled above while my shoulders slam-dunked into the earth.

Terror sprouted like weeds in my veins as Greg took a step back. I tensed for a kick or reprimand, but he placed his hands on his hips, waiting.

If I'd climbed out like he'd asked ten minutes ago, I could've avoided the shrapnel to my cheek and the new contusions to my body.

You were stupid, Elle.

Was it wise to refuse everything out of principle or obey to save my strength?

I knew the answer even though I hated it.

Doing my best to stifle my moan, I slowly unhooked my ankles from the Porsche and wiggled forward to give my legs room to drop down. Slowly, achingly, I figured out how to slide sideways and push off the ground with my hands behind my back—granting just enough leverage to sit upright.

It took a while, but the moment I sat up, Greg clapped condescendingly. "Finally, you listen to the boss."

I spat out a mouthful of acrid dust. "You're not my boss."

"Wrong, Elle. I am. You've been in charge for far too fucking long. Things are gonna be different now."

I clamped my lips together. I wouldn't antagonize him further. He was delusional. There was nothing I could say to a crazy person. Let him think he was my commander. I'd correct him when he was in jail.

We held a staring war like children until I cocked my chin and ignored him.

He didn't speak as I navigated my sore body into movement.

It took a few minutes to figure out how to shuffle my legs beneath me and push off on numb tingling feet to trade driveway for standing, but I managed.

The second I succeeded, Greg captured my elbow. "About time you got up." Pulling me toward a large cabin resting on the boundary of a dense forest, he added, "Wasting my time, Elle. Gonna pay for that."

"You could've helped me. Better yet, you could take me home."

He chuckled. "Funny girl."

The cabin reeked of disappearing CEOs and illegal activity. In any other situation, the cute windows with yellow and brown trim would've made any guest feel welcome. In this situation—when I'd been stolen against my will—it was a coffin I had no desire to enter.

Every inch of me did not (with a thousand *did nots*) want to go into that place. But I was tired, hungry, and emotionally wrung dry. My head still throbbed from his punch at my apartment, and my heart still panged for the lies Penn had told. The glittery blue of my sapphire star dangled in my mind, destroying Penn's fibs over and over again.

Where had that necklace come from?

Was it true Penn was Baseball Cap or Adidas?

Regardless of the truth, I knew one thing for sure.

All men are assholes.

And unless my father or David could figure out where Greg had taken me, I was on my own.

I glanced out of the corner of my eye at Greg and his pompous face. Everything about him irritated me to the point of sheer rage.

He's a moron.

A moron who can kill me with no one here to stop him.

Despite running from Penn and cursing him forever, I wouldn't be opposed to him hunting and freeing me. He was the lesser of the two evils tonight.

Climbing the porch steps, our footsteps echoed on a stained wooden deck, weathered with a stylish décor.

Greg let me go, fumbling in his pockets for a key.

I didn't run off or try to bolt into the forest.

My hands were still tied, and I had no idea where I was. I'd never been good at hikes in school and would rather deal with Greg than a bear in the wilderness while incapacitated.

I kept my voice icy. "Where are we?"

Greg grinned as he slotted a key into the antique looking lock. "My father's cabin."

I vaguely remembered Steve bragging about buying a vacation place before I took over Belle Elle. He and Dad had gone away for a weekend to do manly things.

I hadn't asked what those manly things had entailed.

It's true. He is a moron.

I blinked, forcing myself not to roll my eyes at Greg's stupidity.

He'd kidnapped me and taken me to a location that his father knew about.

I wanted to thank the nonexistent stars.

Bless him for his small brain. It would only be a matter of time before the cavalry came for me.

I kept my conclusions to myself, nodding respectfully as Greg opened the door and held it wide for me to enter. He followed, leaving me standing in the foyer as he turned on lights to reveal wooden walls, cathedral ceilings, and timber flooring.

It wasn't called a log cabin for nothing—every single inch, including the kitchen counter, was made out of sacrificed trees.

It was wood overload with a plaid couch, rustic dining room table, and a window seat that could fit ten children more inclined to read than explore the sinister forest waving its shadowy branches by the windows.

The place was big with hallways leading off to bedrooms and a second lounge down a few steps with a giant log fireplace.

Greg shrugged off his blazer, throwing it haphazardly on the back of the couch. He smiled. "Come here."

I wanted to kick him in the balls, but slowly, I inched closer.

Once I was standing in front of him, he spun his finger in the air. "Turn around."

I swallowed a retort and did as he asked. Instantly, my spine crawled. I didn't like having him behind me, unable to see.

His fingers latched around my wrists.

I tensed, then relaxed a little as the tight twine slowly loosened, sliding off one wrist altogether.

I looked over my shoulder, waiting to be freed completely, but he tied a new knot around one wrist, tugging it until I turned back around to face him.

His teeth flashed in the golden light bulbs. "Can't have you running now, can we?"

I glowered at the leash he'd formed, binding my arm into his control, tethering me to him while giving my other arm the relief of coming forward and working out the kinks in my shoulder.

"I won't run." I itched with the need to undo the knots imprisoning me.

"Don't take it personally, but I don't believe you." Pulling me forward, he grinned as my body pressed up against his, my arm forced around his waist with the aid of the rope.

Lowering his head, he nuzzled my neck.

I shuddered with repulsion.

"Now that I've got you, I'm not letting you go, Elle."

Doing my best to breathe slow and steady, rather than give into the overwhelming desire to scream, I said, "You don't have me, Greg. You'll *never* have me."

"Well, I don't see anyone else here claiming you." He kissed my cheek. "You're mine, and you're not going anywhere."

"I don't need someone to claim me. *I* claim me." The CEO in me came out. I looked down my nose with arrogant authority. "What do you hope to achieve here, Greg? You can't keep me prisoner for long. They'll find me. Whatever sick and twisted idea you have of marrying me to gain access to Belle Elle is riddled with flaws. Even married to me, I'd never give you part ownership of my company, and no judge would ever grant you my property if I said you forced me."

My mouth ran away with things I'd promised myself I wouldn't say. "And what about our fathers? Do you honestly think they'll let you get away with this? My dad will either have you murdered in your sleep or thrown in jail, and your dad will have to live with the shame of what you've done."

My free hand swooped up. I tapped him in the temple as if he were a simpleton and needed a good slap to wake up. "Think this through, Greg. Release me now, and I won't press charges. I'll tell our fathers to let it go. I'll inform everyone that you had to get whatever jealousy you felt about Penn out of your system and then everything can go back to normal."

His face didn't change from the cordial playboy I knew and tolerated. His dark blond hair cascaded over one eye, giving the illusion he was easy to play and manipulate. "Normal, huh?"

I nodded. "With no repercussions. Think about it." I tugged my wrist, jiggling his hand where he held the other end of the rope. "Release me, take me home, and we'll forget about all of this."

He pursed his lips as if contemplating my proposal. Then a dark veil fell over his eyes. "Too bad for you, I don't like normal."

Stomping forward, he jerked me through the kitchen and out the backdoor. Stumbling down the steps toward the forest edge, I swallowed my fear as his stride headed straight toward the looming forest.

What the—

Where is he taking me?

The cabin wasn't wanted, but it was a damn sight better than traipsing through a jungle late at night.

"Greg—"

"Shut up, Noelle. You've had your little speech; now, shut the fuck up." He yanked a small flashlight from his pocket and turned on the ray of illumination as we crunched through bracken, entering the world of looming leafy giants. "You think you have me all figured out, huh? Bet you thought I was a fucking moron for bringing you to my dad's cabin." He laughed coldly. "Bet David is already on his way here. Too bad for him."

He laughed harder as he broke into a jog, dragging me behind him. "I'm not a fuckwad, Elle. I've been planning this for months." Beelining toward an old shed tucked up against ancient trees, he skidded to a stop.

Looking back with victorious smugness, he wrenched the unlocked padlock off the rickety doors and slithered the chain from around the wooden handles.

The rope leash lashed tight around my wrist each time he moved, giving me no slack to run. Cracking open the doors, he pulled me through and shone the flashlight onto the one thing I didn't want to see.

Another car.

Clean and new—something that would guarantee to work and not break down in exhaustion.

A black Dodge Charger.

Pulling me around to the passenger entry, he opened the door and shoved me inside. "We're only half-way there, Elle. This was the decoy. The real destination is where no one will guess. A place only I know. A place where we'll finally get to know each other."

My heart switched from pissed off to manic.

Greg slammed the door in my face, locking me inside.

Oh, God, what should I do?

Jogging around to the driver's side, he hopped in as if we were honeymooners about to explore. Inserting a key into the ignition, the car woke up with a loud grumbling growl.

He placed his hand on my knee. "A place where we'll get to know each other *very* well." Throwing the car into gear, he shot forward and rammed the shed doors wide, not caring about marking the vehicle or ruining his father's retreat.

We fishtailed on the mulchy ground as the engine roared. He stomped on the accelerator and drove rocket-ship style through the small trail, past leering trees, over broken branches, and exploded onto a dirt track, leaving all phones, cars, and well-known cabins behind.

Penn wouldn't find me.

David and Dad wouldn't find me.

I truly was on my own.

CHAPTER TWO

PENN

I THOUGHT THE night couldn't get any worse.

I was wrong.

Served me right, seeing as my entire life I'd had the shittiest luck of anyone. If I took a risk, it backfired. If I spied an opportunity, it was a con. If I saw hope, it was always false.

So why I thought tonight couldn't get any worse after Elle ran from the charity function, didn't answer her phone, and refused to come to the door when I drove over to her place, I didn't know.

This was my normal. I had to get used to it instead of being constantly surprised.

I'd returned home confused and fucked off with the entire world. I'd entered my building and climbed the steps to the renovated unit that I'd keep as my own while doing up the rest of the apartments for people transitioning from an existence on the streets back into the rat race we called life.

I had great plans for this place.

The chipped walls and leaky pipes didn't faze me. I had the funds to invest in its foundation and décor, and I couldn't fucking wait until the building crew had finished their current project in lower Manhattan and could work exclusively on mine.

My thoughts bounced between my past and Elle as I stalked into the kitchen and grabbed a glass of vodka on the rocks.

Carrying my drink to my bedroom, I didn't bother to undress. I merely kicked off my shoes, shrugged out of the silver blazer, and unbuckled my belt. The rest—a white shirt, silver tie, and metallic slacks remained on as I climbed onto the bed, sipped a sharp mouthful of liquor, and pulled the bag containing Elle's lingerie and sex toys from our first night together toward me.

I couldn't fucking wait to use the toys on her, but now, she'd run away. She'd run before I could tell her, then refused to have anything to do with me. Her door remained closed, her phone unanswered.

If I was honest, the anvil wedged where my heart should be made me ache. But I'd known we couldn't have a future. I'd banked on it. I'd hunted her knowing full well I would take what I wanted and then leave.

But that was before the chocolate mousse and the limo and the gala.

Each time I saw her, it got harder and harder to keep my emotions from spilling.

The fake engagement, the bullshit…all of it was gone. Just like Elle.

Fuck.

Exhaustion from all the years I'd been planning this finally caught up with me. I swigged the rest of my drink before my eyes could close.

I would rest tonight.

Tomorrow, I would apologize, accept her verbal lashing, and then walk out of her life for good.

The plan wasn't a good one but having it helped calm my messy thoughts.

I reclined against my pillows and vanished into sleep, just as Elle had vanished from my life for the second time.

* * * * *

Sleep began quickly and ended suddenly.

Just like I should've expected more shitty things to happen, I should've seen this coming.

But I hadn't because I was a fucking idiot.

I woke to a fist to my jaw, jarring me from chaotic dreams into manic reality.

Another fist landed on my solar plexus, stealing my oxygen, making me gasp.

Another fist to my jaw followed by a double jab to my stomach.

What the fuck?

Two men, four pummels, one of me.

I curled up on the mattress, protecting my head while they fucking beat me. Hip, chest, ribs, temple.

Wash and repeat.

I lost count how many blows they delivered or how many aches flared into being from new injuries and old. My past meant I'd taken a beating a few times while others I'd done the nasty work.

Bones never forgot, though.

They heated some nights in remembrance. They ached on others in punishment.

I was a walking shambles of bones and lies, and these cunts had let themselves into my place to attack me while I was unconscious.

There was no way to retaliate without being knocked out. So I waited, grunting with agony, as they struck again and again.

Finally, when I didn't move or threaten to kill them, the bastards stopped their rain of pain, whispering to each other as I lay in my stupid little ball.

Spying an opportunity to fight back, I pushed aside the blazing discomfort and launched upright.

I always could move fast.

They didn't see it coming.

I landed an uppercut on one asshole's jaw and a side-kick

to the other dickhead in the groin. "You fucking come into my place and hurt me?"

They stumbled backward, holding body parts.

I half-leapt, half-collapsed off my bed, fists raised. "Who the fuck are you and what are you doing in my apartment?"

The bigger guy of the two cracked his neck, rearranging his beefy body. He swiped at his lower lip where his teeth had sliced him from my uppercut. "You'll pay for that." He launched himself at me.

I met him head-on, fists to fists, kicks to kicks, but they'd already stripped my strength, and there were two of them.

His punches landed too often, whittling away my power.

"Hey, fucker," the smaller guy said with a balaclava over his face. "Lie down, or we'll knock you out."

The larger grunted something I couldn't hear, his face covered with acne scars and a chin strap. He decked me hard, ringing my skull with church bells, swiping my balance until the room spun.

I wobbled backward against the mattress.

I tried to blink it away—to keep fighting. But a solid punch to my chest sent me soaring into horizontal.

The smaller guy leapt on top of me, his knees pinning my chest to the bed. "Gonna stay down?"

I kicked, but the big thug grabbed my legs. "I wouldn't if I were you."

I glowered. "Get the hell off me."

"Say the magic words."

No fucking way was I being polite to these bastards.

"What do you want?" I spat. "Money? Too fucking bad, I don't have any here."

"Oh, we're not here to steal from you." The big guy chuckled. He motioned for his minion to get off my chest then planted a meaty hand on the same place he'd punched just a few seconds ago.

My ribs screamed as he pressed heavily, activating bruises. "Now that we have your attention, I'll give you the message."

"What message?"

He tapped my cheek in warning. "Ah, no talking back, got it?" He glanced at his buddy, rolling his eyes. "They never learn."

I bit my tongue with all the hate I wanted to spew. They broke into my place, beat me up, then had the motherfucking audacity to roll their eyes at me as if *I* were the idiot.

The second they left, I'd have them arrested, then ask Larry to ensure they never left the penitentiary system.

Assholes.

"Nope." The balaclava dude laughed. "I can hurt him more, if you want?"

"Nah, the orders were to rough him up not hospitalize him." The brute climbed off me, brandishing his fist in my face. "You have a message."

"From who?"

"Not gonna say who." He smirked. "Message is to stay away from her. She's mine. She's left you to marry me. So fuck off, and screw some other blonde." He cracked his knuckles. "Got it?"

Oh, hell yes, I got it.

That bastard Greg Hobson.

The guy I'd hated from the moment I first met him and not just because he was the competition. I despised the way he watched Elle. It bordered on obsessive.

"He hired you to scare me off." I laughed, hacking up a mouthful of crimson spit. "He's fucking delusional."

"Don't care what he is. Those are the terms."

I pressed my bloody nose, checking for a break. My eyes watered. "She'll never agree to be with him. He'd lost before I took her."

The big goon crossed his arms. "Don't care about the fine print. We've done our job and delivered the message."

My mind raced, boycotting the image of Elle ever agreeing to be with Greg. She wouldn't. She couldn't.

Unless…

Shit!

I stood up. The room swam. My head pounded.

What if Greg hurt her? What if that was why she hadn't answered the door or picked up the damn phone?

Elle.

Shooting forward, I dodged the guys as they tried to hit me again.

"Hey!" They gave chase, but even bleeding and beaten, I had a lifetime of running on my side. Years of sprinting to save my skin. Decades of avoiding death.

I didn't look back.

Bolting from the bedroom, I skidded into the living room and slammed into the sideboard where I'd tossed my car keys.

My bare feet slapped on the hardwood, my trousers loose from no belt. But thank Christ I never undressed.

What I was about to do would've been severely inconvenient while naked.

My fingers hooked over the key chain as I propelled myself forward, ducked under a swinging fist, and bowled out the door before they could catch me.

I was gone before they managed to huff down the second flight of stairs.

CHAPTER THREE

ELLE

FROM ONE CABIN to another.

The décor and building materials were the same (pine everywhere), but this was smaller with a cozy living room, tiny kitchen, and narrow hallway to the bedrooms. However, judging by the car headlights that'd glinted off a body of water as we pulled down the long drive and stopped outside the quaint dwelling, we were now on a lake rather than buried in a forest.

The clock over the higgledy-piggledy stone fireplace said we'd been here an hour. A full hour since Greg tossed me onto the red and navy plaid couch, grabbed a bottle of gin from the fridge, and made us both a cocktail.

I'd accepted it and actually drank the sour liquid, doing my best to relax and let the liquor take away my fear so I could concentrate on the best way to get free.

My attention refused to leave the clock.

Four a.m. yet my eyes were wide and brain zapping with awareness rather than scratchy with sleep. We'd been traveling for hours. It felt like days since I'd seen Penn or Larry or Stewie. Months since I'd heard my dad or stroked Sage's soft fur.

Too damn long being Greg's little captive.

Greg groaned as he reclined on the single seat next to the couch; the twine from my wrist dangled over the arms of the chairs, forever joining me to him. "God, it's good to sit down."

"You've been sitting while driving."

He sipped his cocktail. "Driving is tiring."

"And kidnapping is wrong."

"Who said anything about kidnapping?" He smirked, bringing the glass to his lips again. "Last time I checked, you weren't a kid anymore." His gaze dragged up and down my body. "In fact, you're very grown up."

I fought the desire to slap him. My hands curled around my drink.

We stared for the longest minute, full of war and battle for authority.

Breaking the contest, I threw back the rest of the gin and planted the glass loudly on the wooden coffee table. "I need to go to the bathroom."

"So demanding." He stood, waiting for me to pull my aching body into standing. "But I can't have you being uncomfortable now, can I?"

"Just being in your company makes me uncomfortable."

His forehead furrowed. "Careful, Elle. That tongue of yours is going to get you into trouble."

Yanking on the rope, he marched forward, dragging me with him. He escorted me (for lack of a better kidnapping word) down the hallway to a single bathroom with a shower over the bath, an autumn leaf decorated shower curtain, and shell basin that had seen a few decades too many.

He sidestepped, letting me overtake him. "Don't try anything." Shoving me toward the toilet, he grinned and waved the string, pulling it with him. "I'll be right outside."

With his threat lingering, he shut the door.

If this had been a ploy to climb out the window or find a weapon in the medicine cabinet, the leash and my bladder would've made it impossible. The twine barely gave me enough room to fumble with my dress and back up onto the toilet to do my business.

My arm remained speared in front of me, doing my best to keep the rope from cutting off my circulation.

Once done, I washed my face in the basin. With droplets raining down my forehead, I glared at the whiteness of my cheeks from anxiety, the purple of my temple from his punch, and the redness in my left eye from his smack. My blonde hair mimicked a mini tornado with out of control curls, and my makeup had smeared beneath both eyes making me look like a haggard aging rock star.

I hated the reflection.

Turning away, I sucked in a deep breath, preparing to tolerate him again. But I paused, eyeing the mirror.

I can't go.

Not without checking.

Pulling open the medicine cabinet, I tried not to give into the despondency of finding nothing of use. No toe-nail clippers, no scissors, not even a Q-tip or floss.

The cupboard was bare, just like the water-swelled drawers beneath the sink.

Not one piece of human mess that I could use to saw at the rope or puncture Greg's jugular.

He smirked as I stepped into the corridor. "All done?"

I didn't reply.

He marched forward, tugging on the string. He didn't guide me back to the living room. "I think we've done enough for the night. I'm fucking wiped."

So he's taking me to bed.

This is it.

This was where my one-man experience became an unwanted two.

At least, he won't steal my virginity.

How would it feel to be taken against my control? Would I maintain my calm annoyance or break into pleading tears.

I don't want to find out.

He carted me into a bedroom, and turned on the bulb that hung in a sad tasseled shade above the queen-sized bed with a patchwork quilt, ancient wooden side tables, and wrought-iron bedside lights.

My skin crawled at the thought of sharing that mattress with him.

"Here, let me help you." His hands landed on my shoulders, spinning me around to undo the invisible zip of my silver dress.

"No, wait—" I darted forward, but he jerked the tiny zipper and yanked at the heavy satin on my shoulders.

"I've waited long enough." He tore the gorgeous garment off me, pushing it over my hips until gravity puddled it to the floor. Turning me around, he groaned.

The slinky silver and white lingerie I wore had been for Penn's benefit, not his.

Penn—the man who'd lied to me about everything. The man who didn't deserve me, just like Greg didn't deserve me.

I clamped my free arm over my breasts, hating that so much of me was exposed. I loathed the way his gaze latched onto my skin; how his hand came up to hover over my breast as if fighting his desire to touch me.

His eyes met mine as he licked his lips. "I was going to make us official tonight, but I've waited so fucking long to have you, Elle, I've become a bit of a sadist."

He leaned in, brushing his mouth over my bruised cheekbone from the driveway gravel. "I'm so hard for you, but the anticipation of what I'm going to do to you is almost as good as doing it."

Letting me go, he unbuttoned his shirt and tossed it on the floor, followed by his shoes, socks, and jeans. "For the next few hours, we'll rest. And then...we'll have some fun."

He wasn't lying that he wanted me. His cock stood proud in white boxers, mimicking a totem pole and flagstaff.

I tore my eyes away in disgust.

He chuckled under his breath. "Time to sleep, Elle.

Tomorrow is a new day, and we have a shit-load of things to do." Pulling the twine around my wrist, he guided me to the bed and pulled back the sheets. "Get in."

My throat swelled with tears. The scream inside wanted to erupt and destroy—to summon help even though Greg had successfully laid a red herring and driven in a car I'd never seen before to a cabin he'd never mentioned.

We'd cut through forest and roads and small townships.

We were well and truly gone.

No one would come if I cried for help.

No one could save me but me.

When I didn't move, he pushed me onto the mattress. I fell forward, flopping angrily onto my side and curling my legs up to hide as much of my lingerie-clad body as possible.

Greg stared down like a doting lover, running his finger over my jawline, tucking in a curl. "I can't believe we're here. Together."

I arched away from his touch, trying to kill him with my stare. "We're not together. I don't want this. You're forcing me. Don't ever forget that I don't want you. I never have and I never will."

He stiffened. "You'll take that back. You'll see."

"Wrong. It will only become more and more real the longer you keep me. I liked you before, Greg. I thought you were a nice friend. But now…now, I *hate* you."

Clenching his jaw, he swiped the comforter from beneath my legs, making me roll a little. "Your lies are almost as bad as his were."

The painful barb wriggled inside me as he gently placed the linen over me. His footsteps fell heavy on the floorboards as he turned out the light and climbed into bed.

I remained stiff and unyielding, but he spooned me, gathering me tight in his arms.

His erection prodded my ass, making me sick.

The memories of sleeping with Penn and the chemistry between us tried to replace my current situation. But even that wasn't comforting. Penn had destroyed what I'd felt for him by being so terribly linked to my past.

He'd proven I couldn't trust anyone.

Only my cat.

Thank goodness, Dad had taken Sage home tonight; otherwise, she'd be unfed and unloved.

God, Dad will panic when I don't show for work tomorrow.

Fear about his heart pushed through me, ignoring my situation, tearing me into pieces about what this would do to him.

I swallowed my loathing, whispering in the dark. "Greg?"

He snuggled closer, his hips jamming forward. "Yes, baby?"

I shivered. "I'm not your baby."

"You are now."

I wouldn't let him distract me with an argument I couldn't win. "I need to call my father. You know he has heart issues. He needs to know I'm okay."

His nose tickled the back of my neck. "He'll survive."

I tried to wriggle away, but his arms looped tighter. The damn rope around my wrist kept me pinned. "He'll panic."

"Not my problem."

I shoved backward, rocking the bed. "It *is* your problem. And I'll tell you why. If he dies because of the stress of what you've done, I'll never stop trying to kill you. You have my undying promise that I will—"

He slapped a hand over my mouth, dragging my head backward until my skull wedged against his chin. "Hush. I'm trying to sleep." His cock thrust against my ass. "If you're a good girl, I might let you call him tomorrow. If you agree to our agreement."

I tensed.

No way in hell would I willingly sleep with him, but if he held my father's health as bribery, I would do what he wanted. I'd obey because I could never live with myself if Dad had another heart attack.

I hate you, Greg.

He kissed my cheek. "Now, no more talking." Wrapping the string from my wrist around his fingers, he stroked my hair with a threat disguised as tenderness. "Goodnight, Elle. Tomorrow is going to be so much fun."

CHAPTER FOUR

PENN

"SHE'S GONE, LARRY."

I fought every instinct to crush my phone with furious fingers.

My heart, my blood, my motherfucking breath raced with adrenaline from bolting from my place to Elle's and grabbing the security guard with the threat of a lawsuit if he didn't let me into her apartment to make sure she was safe in bed and not taken as I feared.

He'd done what I asked.

Her bed was empty.

And now, I stood in her kitchen where red wine stained the floor, her phone and silver bag from the party—the same bag I'd shoved off the limo seat to pull her into my lap—sat sadly on the counter.

A drawer hung open, the pantry unclosed.

Signs of an evident struggle made me fucking wild with rage and worry.

I'll fucking kill him.

He'd taken her.

He'd hurt her.

And I hadn't been there for her.

She'd run home because of me. She'd had to put up with that bastard for years because of me.

I have to fix this.

Larry cleared sleep from his throat, slipping into the authority figure I knew and respected. "Gone? Who's gone?"

"Elle," I snapped. "That idiot she works with has taken her."

Larry didn't ask how I knew or if I was sure. He'd never been suspicious of me because I only ever told him the truth.

He was the exception to my rule.

Mainly because he'd trusted me before I gave him reason to. After hearing my tale when we first met, I'd expected him to scoff and roll his eyes like all the others. But for the first time, someone believed me. He'd stayed by my side and done what he'd promised. He gave me a second chance when no one else would.

His voice lost its haze. "What are the details?"

"Greg came in and abducted her then sent his fucking goonies after me to scare me off."

"Time-frame?"

"Who the fuck knows." I paced the kitchen, ignoring the security guard who'd let me in and who was on his phone to the police. "Could've been the same time the assholes came to ensure I had bad dreams or could've been the moment she left the gala."

"Have you called her father yet?"

"No."

Rustling happened in the background as Larry no doubt clambered from bed. Waking him when he needed his rest was not a good thing, but I couldn't do this on my own. I'd tried to navigate life without leaning on anyone and look where that got me. The day Larry found me was the day I learned how to share and let good things happen to me and not just the bad.

"Hang up and call her father. Tell the police, get all the information you can, then come here. We'll go after him together."

No, we won't.

"Okay." I cut the call before I could tell him that I'd get Greg's whereabouts, but I wouldn't take him as reinforcements. His health had only just improved. I wouldn't risk him as well as Elle.

I'd go after her on my own. I'd chased her for my own selfish reasons. I hadn't cared about her mental state when she found out who I was.

Most of the time, I'd convinced myself that I would walk away before it got to that stage.

Shit, it had already gone on too long.

I'd tried to end it.

But each time, she revealed a little more of herself, gave a little more, and fucking stole everything of mine in the goddamn process.

And now, I'd get her back—even if it was stupid to go alone.

I'd always done things the hard way.

I left the security guard to welcome the tardy police and stalked into her bedroom to call the brownstone where Elle used to live.

I knew the number by heart, just like I knew what window was hers, what her favorite food was (blueberry pancakes), how many times she'd snuggled with that damn cat (over six hundred since I'd starting watching), and how hard she worked for Belle Elle (every hour of her life), which was what made my guilt so much worse.

Guilt compounded on guilt for every awful thing I'd thought about her over the past three years.

The phone rang.

I paused with my fingertips tracing her pillow, noticing the pristine sheets with no feline ball indenting the mattress. Sage hadn't attacked me when I arrived, which made me suspect the cat was either with Elle's father or Greg had taken it when he'd taken Elle.

"Hello?" A groggy voice finally came on the line.

Thank Christ for landlines and the non-ability to silence them at night.

"Mr. Charlston? It's Penn Everett."

Joe Charlston cleared his throat. "What do you need at five o'clock in the morning that couldn't wait for normal hours, son?"

My heart did a weird flip at the endearment. He was nothing like I thought he'd be. I'd despised him almost every day for three years. I'd misjudged him just like I'd misjudged his daughter. "I need all the information you have on Steve Hobson's son, Greg. Any real estate purchases or favorite locations."

His voice whipped sharp. "Why? What's happened?"

I braced myself. "Greg has taken your daughter."

"What?"

I pinched the bridge of my nose, dislodging dried blood and activating bruises. I'd forgotten about my bare feet and bloody face when I'd shoved the security guard into the elevator. I must look fucking awful. "Elle has been taken by the cocksucker Greg Hobson. Her apartment is empty. There are signs of a fight. I need to find her. Immediately."

Otherwise, who the fuck knows what he'll do to her.

Joe barked, "Stay there, I'm coming over."

"No—just tell me—" The phone went dead.

I growled into the empty room.

Goddammit.

More time wasted. More people involved.

I had to leave. I'd call him from the road.

I wouldn't wait any longer than I had to.

Elle was mine.

I would bring her home on my own.

* * * * *

As planned, my cell-phone rang fifteen minutes later when Elle's father arrived at his daughter's apartment only to find me missing. "Where the hell are you?"

"Driving."

"You should be here helping me look for Elle."

My fingers tightened on the wheel. "I *am* helping look for Elle."

"By what? Driving in circles?"

I didn't bother telling him that Larry had contacts in the NYPD—that he could help me with phone records and credit card statements. I'd wanted a faster way, hoping Joe could provide, but if he was going to slow me down, then so be it.

He'd get left behind.

"Tell me everything you can about Steve and Greg."

Joe sniffed. "Greg lives with his father a few blocks over from me. However, he's not there. I called Steve, and he's as freaked as I am about all of this. He said Greg never came home last night—but that's nothing new. He has girlfriends who he stays with periodically."

I ignored the fact that the slime ball slept around all the while trying to get Elle into bed.

I'd kill him just for that.

"Any other property? Known addresses he'd go to on his own?" My car broke the speed limit as I weaved down Broadway.

"Steve bought a log cabin a few years ago out in Rochester. He said Greg might've—"

"The address. Now."

"It's off the beaten track. Look for a creek called Bearfoot Rapids. The house is tucked away with a carved lumberjack holding a mailbox at the start of the driveway."

"No street name or number?"

"No, that's what made it appealing. It can't be found easily."

Fucking brilliant.

Holding back my curse, I gritted, "Thanks. I'll call you when I'm there."

I hung up and tossed the phone onto the seat beside me.

Rochester was a good five-hour drive away.

Christ, he could do anything to her in that time, and I'd be too late.

The Mercedes snarled as I stomped on the pedal, forcing gas to feed its greedy engine.

Hold on, Elle.

This time, I wouldn't let her down.

CHAPTER FIVE

ELLE

SUNSHINE.

A new day.

No sleep.

No rest.

Only panic.

Greg shifted, his arm still locked around my middle, his skin against mine, his body sickeningly close.

Dawn had arrived, and I'd watched every painful minute of it as the sky switched from black to pink then pink to gold, basking the cabin, glittering on the lake through the windows.

It took all my willpower to stay calm and not give in to the panic gnawing at my bones.

How many more mornings would pass before I could get free?

Greg rolled over; the leash tethering me to him jerked my wrist. My skin was red and irritated from rope burn.

I grunted as he forced me to roll over, tucking me against his body. "Morning, beautiful."

I bit my tongue and didn't reply.

If I did, I'd spew curses and commands—neither of which would do me any good.

I had to hope that if I remained silent and obedient, he'd let me call Dad and ease his worry, so I remained parented and not an orphan.

The only good thing about Greg taking me was I didn't have time to stew about Penn and his deception. I only had the brain capacity to currently hate Greg.

Penn will come later.

"I don't care if you don't speak, Elle. I rather like quiet women." Unraveling the rope from his fist, he stood up and stretched. Morning wood once again speared his boxer-briefs.

He smirked, catching me looking. "That's all yours the moment you've had a shower." He bent over me, pressing his hands into the pillow on either side of my ears. "Can't fuck you without washing you first. Who the hell knows if that bastard touched you last night."

I fought the reply plastering itself over my face.

Penn *had* touched me.

He'd fucked me in the limo before I knew the truth. I'd believed he felt something for me while I felt something for him. I was excited, thinking he'd be honest and forthright and all the mistrust and lies would vanish like mist fading over the lake.

I'd begged for clarity.

Just not the clarity I'd been given.

My necklace had ruined those fantasies.

Grabbing my hand, Greg pulled me from the warm covers and into the crisp morning air. No heating meant goosebumps scattered over my flesh then layered with more as he leered at me. "All this time and we could've been waking up side by side, instead of working on different floors at Belle Elle." His fingers traced my belly button. "Isn't it nice?" He leaned forward, brushing his lips against mine.

I ripped my face away, not only because I had a phobia of morning breath but because he had no right, *none*, to kiss me.

"Let me go, Greg." The first words I'd spoken in hours.

He grinned. "You mean untie this?" He tugged the twine,

making my arm bounce.

"You know what I mean. Everything. Cut me loose, drive me home. This has gone on long enough."

He shook his head. "You're not leaving until you understand your place is by my side."

"My place is running Belle Elle. With you in a prison cell."

He chuckled, mirth bright in his green eyes rather than retribution. "You'll change your mind the more you get to know me."

I highly doubt it.

Carting me from the bedroom, he guided me into the bathroom and undid the rope around my wrist. "Get in the shower."

I rubbed at my sore skin, backing up against the sink. "I'm not washing with you in here."

"Oh yes, you fucking are." He grabbed the edges of his boxer-briefs, pulling them down his legs. His cock sprung free, heavy and hard with red veins bulging on the sides. He wasn't as big as Penn, but it looked angry.

Before I could move, he grabbed my shoulders and spun me around. With quick fingers, he unhooked my bra.

My arms slammed over my chest, covering myself.

It didn't do any good.

He snatched my arms away, making me teeter, bruising me as he ripped the straps down and tossed the bra into the hallway. He spun me back to face him. "Now the rest."

"Go to hell." I kept my arms over my chest, defending my modesty.

His gaze fell to my panties, a heated smirk on his lips. "Are you going to remove those or shall I?"

I backed up. "Greg...don't."

"Greg, don't," he mocked with a sneer. "Do you know how many years I've had to listen to you giving orders? Smiling at me over the dinner table with your holier-than-thou bitch face. Giving me commands at work when all I really wanted to do was fuck you." He loomed over me. "You thought you hid

41

your true feelings, but every time you looked at me, I knew. I saw your disdain. I knew you believed you were better than me—"

I slapped him.

I didn't think it through. I just did it.

We both froze, equally shocked.

I hissed, "If that's the bullshit you're feeding yourself, then you're completely screwed up. I never looked down on you, Greg. For most of our childhood, I enjoyed playing with you. But then you went and let jealousy corrupt—"

He grabbed my jaw, squeezing my sentence to a stop. "*Jealousy?* You think this is about jealousy?" He laughed with utmost frustration. "I'm not jealous of you, Elle. I don't envy what you have."

He brushed my lips with his thumb. "I don't care that you're one of the richest women in the world. That doesn't intimidate me. What *does* intimidate me is some fucking loser thinking he can lie about being engaged to you just to get access to what you have."

I fought in his hold, lashing my fingers around his wrists to get free. "That wasn't why he lied."

He did it to sleep with me after a three-year promise in an alley.

"Don't care. He's gone now. I merely want to be with you, to share in what you have. Is that so wrong?" His voice lowered. "I don't want to take it away from you, Elle. I only want to enjoy it side by side. I'm willing to be a good husband, hard worker, and loyal father to any kids we have. This isn't about me stealing from you. It's about me giving you what you deserve."

I snorted. "What I deserve? Do I deserve to be kidnapped and held against my will?"

Please, he was moronic.

"Until you listen to me, yes." Shoving me away, Greg ripped at my silver and white panties and jerked them down my legs.

One arm stayed glued to my chest, and the other darted

between my thighs to hide the trimmed curls and smoothness I'd taken to maintaining ever since I met Nameless and became a slave to my libido in an open park. I'd never wanted to be unprepared for a moment where sex could be a possibility—even when my life had been chained to work with no time for pleasure.

Until Penn.

My heart threw up then did an odd pirouette. Part of me was repulsed I'd slept with him knowing what I knew now, while the shallower, less cohesive part of me couldn't care less. He'd been a crook three years ago—could he have changed? Could he be a good person after being so bad?

You're talking gibberish.

I blamed it on Greg.

I only accepted Penn's lies and who he was hiding because even in that dark alley with his awful fingers shredding my clothes and stealing my money, he still wasn't as bad as Greg was. Sure, he would've scared me and stolen what he could. But Greg thought he could keep me in a lifetime of servitude, believing we were equals all while he suffocated me in a marriage I resented, revoked, and wanted to rip to shreds.

Grabbing me around the waist, he lifted me over the edge of the tub and held me until my feet gained traction on the slippery bath.

Climbing in behind me, I shivered with repulsion as he reached around my nakedness and turned the tap on.

I gasped as icy water spewed from the single showerhead directly onto my chest.

Greg wrapped his arms around me, keeping me under the glacial torrent, breathing hot breath into my ear. "See how cold you are on your own, Elle? How hard it is to get warm?"

Moving closer, his front pressed against my back, wedging unwanted but much-needed body heat against my back.

His cock thickened, pulsing against my lower spine as he cradled me. I hated that he offered shelter from the cold spray, twisting my mind as the protector when he'd been the one to turn on the water in the first place.

"Let me go." I reached behind to dig my fingernails into his hip. Shivering hijacked me until my teeth rattled. "Dammit, Greg. Stop!"

He flinched but only held tighter. Reaching with his left arm, he swiveled the tap to hot, and I waited with goosebumps and trembles as the liquid ice slowly switched to tepid waterfall to steamy stream to scalding tempest.

I winced as my skin turned lobster red. "Ouch!"

"Whoops. Can't have you burning up now, can we?" He twisted the tap again, finally finding the right hot to cold ratio.

My flesh no longer tried to turn into an ice-berg or melt with magma, but I didn't relax. Not one little bit.

Turning me around, he barely noticed my resistance. My feet slipped with no effort on the bath, my body stiff as a sword. When I stood facing him with my arms acting as my underwear, he grinned. "Back you go." He pushed until my head vanished under the shower, drenching my long hair.

The water offered a reprieve, filling my ears and eyes and senses with cleansing rushes rather than reveal the tiny bathroom in the tiny cabin with the madman I was currently with.

After I was sufficiently drowned, he pulled me forward and opened a bottle of shampoo on the ledge of the bath. "I'm going to show you how supportive and kind I can be, Elle."

He licked his lips, tipping synthetic berry bubbles into his palm. "I'm going to make sure you're squeaky clean, and then we're going to have a chat about our new life together."

I bit my tongue.

Words didn't work on him, and I refused to stoop to a level where I begged or pleaded for some rationality. There was no rationality left. I was in a shower naked with Greg while he promised to care for me after I'd promised I'd kill him if my disappearance hurt my father.

He either believed in his delusions or was so twisted, he honestly thought I wanted him and was merely playing hard to get.

His hands landed on my head, rubbing the unwanted bubbles into my strands, coating me with a foreign smell.

I missed my bathroom and honeysuckle body-wash.

I missed Sage and her morning meow and head-butt.

I missed my father and his gentle smile.

Hell, I even missed Penn even while hating him.

"The silent treatment won't work on me forever, you know." Greg gathered my wet tresses, plopping them onto my head where he massaged more suds.

I refused to enjoy his fussing. My skin crawled rather than relaxed with the soft pressure.

I put my chin in the air, glowering.

We'll see.

"If you're going to be like that, turn around." He pushed my shoulder, swiveling me in place. I wobbled on the slippery surface, refusing to unlock my arms from protecting my decency to act as balancing rods.

His fingers trailed from my hair down my back, spreading more bubbles. My teeth chattered in horror as he hooked his hands under my arms, washing me intimately, cleansing me of my past life for whatever he meant to do to me in this twisted present.

"I can't wait until you're clean, Elle," he murmured as his fingers drifted to my ass. "Once he's washed away, I can replace every memory with me."

I swallowed a moan as his touch pressed into my crack.

I spun around, not caring anymore if he saw me naked as one arm swung up to punch him and the other gripped the white tiled wall for balance. "Don't fucking touch me!"

He caught my arm mid-swing, holding me steady. His gaze locked onto my breasts then to my core.

A blackness I instantly feared cloaked him. His cock grew harder as he captured my nipple, tugging hard. "Fuck, you're stunning."

"Let me go." I tried to fight, but he kept my wrist

imprisoned and deliberately pushed me sideways against the wall to keep my other arm pinned.

"In another few days, you'll wonder why you fought this, Elle." His voice grew husky with desire. "I'll show you how good we can be together. You'll see." His hand dropped from my breast, trailed down my stomach, and cupped my core.

I fought harder, slipping and forcing him to take my weight to keep me standing. He balanced me but never let go where he held between my legs. His fingers remained on the outside, merely a dominating reminder that he believed I was his now and everything about me was his, too.

"This is the part of you that needs washing the most." He gathered more bubbles, pressing them into my short curls. "Fucking asshole needs to be deleted."

I tore my eyes from his, glaring at the ceiling while furious tears sprang. He washed me slowly, possessively, with so many threats and promises.

I couldn't stop the tears overflowing, mixing with the shower, rolling down my chest.

He caught one with his finger, bringing it to his lips. "Don't cry, Elle. You're clean now. What happened is in the past, we have a brand new future to look forward to." Pushing me under the spray, his hands trailed over every inch as he rinsed away the soap.

Cuddling me into him, his embrace reeked of contempt for Penn and lust for me.

A recipe that would end up ruining me.

"Are you hungry?" He kissed my wet scalp. "Come on, let's eat. And then…we'll get to know each other exactly the way we should've years ago."

CHAPTER SIX

PENN

I PARKED AT the top of the long, sweeping driveway that disappeared into dense trees.

A stupid carved lumberjack with an axe and overalls decorated with peeling paint offered me a mailbox to place friendly correspondence, not deliver war on the inhabitants.

I wanted to hack it to pieces.

No lights glimmered apart from the fresh pink of dawn. No signs of habitation apart from recent tire tracks down the gravel.

But I knew.

They're here.

Leaving my Merc, I grabbed my phone and jogged down the driveway. I wanted to sneak up and surprise Greg, rather than drive and give him notice.

He'd already taken what was mine. I wouldn't give him the opportunity to hurt her, too.

My shoeless feet glided lightly as I ran, trying to make as little noise as possible. Pebbles bruised my soles, but I didn't stop.

Goddammit, how long is this driveway?

The gravel kept going, deeper into woodland. If this wasn't a rescue mission, it would've been a nice place to bring Elle. To get away from the city and relax together. And by relax, I meant fuck until we both couldn't walk.

There was something about her I couldn't fight. When I was around her—shit, all I could think about was touching, kissing, and being inside her.

Three years' worth of blue balls. Three years of waiting since the first time we met.

My gut clenched at the thought of her with Greg. I hadn't been nice or even kind to her ever since I plotted the moment in the gin bar with her father. Everything about our 'convenient fate-designed' meetings had been meticulously planned.

I hadn't let my guard down once.

I'd taken what I wanted from her as I believed she owed me that after what had happened.

But now, I felt fucking sick that I could be such a bastard—especially since she'd been taken by someone she trusted, all while being lied to by me.

I was an asshole.

I admit it.

The sky slowly grew lighter as a cabin appeared in the forest. A small clearing with a homely retreat nestled in the foliage.

Greg's car sat out in front with the twinkling of dew on the gray paint.

My heart raced, preparing for a fight.

Keeping to the trees, I skirted the front porch, making my way to the side.

Ducking low, I charged toward the house and pressed against the timber siding. Twigs jammed into my bare feet but I ignored the pain. A bay window sat above me, taunting me to look.

My ears strained for noise. For footsteps or voices.

When nothing came—no creak of floorboards, no flush of

water—I stood upright and peered into the dim cabin. Birds slowly woke up, their morning song the only sound apart from my shallow breathing.

The window looked into the kitchen, the kitchen opened out into a living room, the living room funneled traffic to the hallway.

Empty.

Every room.

No signs of life at all.

Shit, where are you, Elle?

Moving around the property, I peered into more windows, searching.

The bedroom with plaid blankets: nothing.

The office with overflowing bookshelves: no one.

The side living room with an ancient video cassette player and TV: empty.

Moving toward the front porch again, I forced myself to remain calm even while I fought panic.

Joe gave me this address.

Greg's car was here.

Yet him and Elle were gone.

Fuck!

Leaping off the stoop to continue my hunt, my eyes caught the displacement of gravel.

Footsteps.

One big with boot tracks.

One small with no tracks.

Was Elle barefoot?

Like me?

My feet had not appreciated the jog down gravel or looked forward to the pokes and pinches from more twigs in the forest. Knowing she'd felt the same discomfort didn't make me happy—it made me fucking furious.

Clutching my phone, I followed the prints into the trees, willing the sun to wake up completely and chase away the remaining shadows. I hadn't had quality sleep, I'd been beaten awake as my alarm clock, and twitched on an overload of adrenaline and rage, but my hands were steady (if not bloody), and my eyes were narrowed (if not blood-shot).

I was ready to attack.

No mercy.

Breaking into a jog, I followed the small path, hoping against fucking hope that Greg hadn't marched her into the undergrowth to shoot and bury her. Images of finding her corpse haunted me in ways I couldn't admit.

I thought I'd protected myself from her this past month. I thought I'd steeled myself against feeling anything.

I'd done a shitty job with the way my heart pounded with terror. I'd wasted so long, fantasizing about her being mine. And she'd been mine—for a brief moment. If I couldn't have her again…what the fuck would I do?

Leave?

Say goodbye?

How could I?

I forced my mind back to facts rather than idiotic matters of the heart. If Greg had wanted to kill her, why not just do it at Belle Elle—somewhere her father would see and destroy the company from the inside out?

He's an asshole, but he's not mentally disturbed.

Why would he kill her where he could be questioned? Much better to do it where no one would see, and he had a better chance of denying his involvement.

Even if this is his father's cabin.

Breaking through the tree line, my heart sank as a shed with open doors and an empty interior beckoned me closer.

Tire marks led from the gloomy cobwebbed shack, footprints in the dust showing Greg had been here with Elle.

And now, they were gone.

CHAPTER SEVEN

ELLE

"YOU KNOW HOW to cook, right?" Greg asked, twirling the steak knife tip on the countertop.

For the thirtieth time, I tugged on the gold negligée he'd made me slip into. Where he'd gotten it from, I had no idea—it wasn't a Belle Elle brand, and the satin slipped over my nakedness in the most awful way—but he'd been extremely incessant I wear it.

I hate you, Greg.

The spaghetti straps barely held the material over my nipples while the hem skimmed my ass cheeks, leaving so much of me nude and available for his ogling attention.

I stood in the middle of the kitchen glaring at the knife, wanting so much to pluck it from his hand and plunge it into his leg.

I didn't want to kill him—just incapacitate him until I could get free, call David to come and break me out of here, and then press charges like a sane person would.

Greg is not sane.

You have full reason to join him in that insanity and kill him.

I didn't doubt I would if it came down to his life or mine. But call me old fashioned, I couldn't kill someone I'd known all my life. I couldn't switch off like that.

He slammed the knife down. "Better answer me, Elle. I've been kind and gentle, but if you don't start talking to me, I'll have to show a different side of me, got it?"

I planted my hands on the counter, bracing myself. "It's not a different side to you. I know that side better than you think. I've seen it in your eyes for years."

He grinned. "Great, so you know I'm telling the truth."

I swallowed as he moved toward me and stroked my cheek, his eyes dropping to my chest. "I showered you, dressed you, and now the least you can do is cook us a lovely meal to celebrate our new future together."

I cringed, stepping away from his touch.

His face shadowed. "I almost forgot." Clicking his fingers, he turned and disappeared into the living room where a duffel bag sat on the couch. Placing the knife on the coffee table—away from my eager fingers—he unzipped the bag and checked the contents.

Greg had many faults, but I'd never known him as so meticulous.

He'd planned my abduction flawlessly.

Clothes for me hung in the wardrobe right alongside clothes for him. The kitchen was stocked with delicacies and staple requirements, and hygiene products such as toothbrushes and toilet paper were in ample supply.

The bathroom had been bare when we'd arrived, but that was before he'd returned to the Dodge and emptied the trunk.

How long had he been concocting this?

How long is he planning to keep me here?

Greg returned with the bag, placing it with a loud clunk on the kitchen counter.

My hair was still damp from the shower, my skin still warm despite the lack of thermal properties of the skimpy negligée. Once he'd turned off the water, he'd dried me (despite my fight and refusal), then dragged me into the bedroom where he'd shoved the gold satin over my head.

He hadn't let me go until I stood in the middle of the kitchen and he'd grabbed the knife. The sharp blade didn't scare me, but the lack of warm clothes and shoes did. Even if I did spy an opportunity to run, I wouldn't get far unless I dressed appropriately.

Greg patted the duffel. A smirk spread his lips. "I brought these as a last resort, but after having the convenience of the rope around your wrist, I think they'll come in handy." Pulling out a leather cuff, the heavy clinking of chains sounded.

My mouth shot dry as his bicep bulged, hefting the weight from the bag to the counter.

He'd dressed in a white t-shirt with faded jeans, his dark blond hair swept back, drying from our joint shower, while the odd droplet turned his t-shirt translucent on the shoulders.

He looked innocent…familiar. The contents he'd just dumped into view were the exact opposite.

I backed away, bumping into the oven. "What the hell is that?"

He chuckled. "Gifts for you, of course."

"I don't want any gifts."

"Believe me, you'll change your mind soon enough." Unbuckling the leather cuff that attached to the glinting chain, he carried the metal across the living room to a sturdy looking hook. A fire poker and small shovel hung for cleaning out the ashes in the grate.

Removing the poker, he secured the chain and locked it with a small padlock before making his way back toward me, letting the links slip through his fingers to stain the floorboards with imprisonment.

The length kept going from the living room to where I stood petrified in the kitchen.

Dropping the remaining chain by my feet, he said, "Until you behave and stop looking at the door to run, I'm going to ensure you stay here with me, okay?"

"No, not okay. You've already squirreled me away where no one can find us." I darted backward, trapped by cabinets. "I don't like being tied up, Greg."

"Too bad." His eyes narrowed. "I didn't ask your opinion or permission." He held up the leather cuff. "Now, come here."

I shook my head, my eyes flickering to the knife on the coffee table over his shoulder.

If only I could reach it. "I won't run."

"I know you won't. This system will make sure of it." He advanced.

I pushed harder into the cabinetry but had nowhere else to go.

Only a foot separated us.

Greg smiled then dropped to one knee as if to propose. I held my breath, shock and horror crawling over my insides as he reached for my ankle and latched his heinous fingers around my leg.

The moment he caught me, he wrapped the leather cuff around my limb, pulling tight before running the chain through the small hook at the top and securing it with the aid of another padlock.

The second I was locked in place, he stood with a triumphant look on his face. "You should be able to go anywhere you need in the cabin but not outside." Returning to the bag, he pulled out another chain, this one shorter with two cuffs on either side instead of one. "Give me your hands."

"What?"

"Your hands, Elle."

"You can't be serious."

"I'm deadly fucking serious." He came forward, letting one cuff dangle while he reached for my wrist—the one with rope burns from the stupid twine he'd used.

What the hell is he doing?

"I'm not your prisoner, Greg."

"I beg to differ." His fingers bit into my arm as he

wrapped the cuff around me and once again secured it with a tiny padlock. At least the leather was soft and supple rather than coarse and prickly. It looked expensive with gold stitching and faux fur trim. Not the cheap kink sold at wannabe sex shops.

Not that I know what cheap or expensive sex toys look like.

A memory of the Seahorse and other dildo samples from Loveline reminded me Penn still had my property.

He has my underwear, too.

At the time, it hadn't bothered me. I thought I'd be back for more sexcapades, and he would use the toys on me. But that was before he let me walk home and I was almost molested; before he scooped me up and washed my feet. Before his lies came crashing down and burst into fiery flames.

Capturing my other arm, Greg growled as I wriggled and tried to break free. "Stand still."

He grunted as he tucked my arm against his body and circled my other wrist with the last cuff. The soft snick of the fourth padlock shattered my thoughts of strangling him for my freedom.

"There, nice and secure." Greg kissed my forehead, pulling me forward thanks to the looping chain now permanently present.

I deliberated punching and kicking and screaming and *cursing* him, but what would that achieve? My leg was tethered to the fireplace, I was practically naked, and my arms were now joined like an inmate on death row.

He wouldn't let me run. He wouldn't let me go.

He'd only pay me back if I hurt him. And I already knew how painful his punches could be.

My temple throbbed in agreement.

Had it only been last night he'd hit me in my apartment garage?

It had to have been centuries with how tired and stressed I was.

Even the thought of having sex in the limo with Penn

didn't affect me the way it had before.

The tummy moths were dead, their paper wings dissolved in bile.

I'd gone from liking Penn to hating him, and it was *exhausting* hating two people at the same time for entirely different reasons.

Greg released me, inspecting his handiwork. "You look hot in chains."

"You'll look hot behind bars when the police catch you."

"There'll be no crime once you come around to my way of thinking."

"I'll never come around because I don't want what you do."

He chuckled under his breath. "So argumentative. I don't remember you being like that in the past."

I tried to plant my hands on my hips, but the chain wasn't quite long enough. I settled for threading my fingers together and holding tight with all the aggression I wished I could throw at him. "That's because you don't know me. You never knew me. You never *tried* to get to know me."

His brow settled angrily over green eyes. "I'm trying now. So give me a goddamn break and give me a chance."

I laughed, rattling the chain in his face. "This is not trying. This is kidnapping. Release me."

"Still used to barking orders, huh, Elle?" He padded barefoot from the kitchen. Hoisting himself onto a bar-stool, he added, "I'm hungry. Let's get back to the topic of food."

I moved to face him, glad that the counter now separated us even if he was demanding I cook for him like some slave. I moved my right leg, testing the weight of the chain locking me to the fireplace across the room.

God, that's heavy.

The metal loops weren't light nor were they easy to step over or kick away as I did a small circle, testing how fast I could move. The chain around my wrists was lighter, with just enough room to scoop and handle things but not enough to stab him with a knife or swing a skillet on his head.

My shoulders rolled, finally understanding that this wasn't just a game to him.

This was serious.

"What do you want, Greg?" My bravery faltered. "Tell the truth. I'm done playing."

He slid off the bar stool, came back into the kitchen, and hoisted himself onto the counter in front of me. "I'm glad you're finally ready to be sensible." His dangling legs thudded against the dishwasher as he pulled another knife from the butcher's block and twirled it tip first again. "But I've told you what I want. You just keep ignoring me."

"No, you haven't." I spread my hands, giving him the space to speak. "You haven't set your terms; you've merely demanded what you expect. They're different." I did my best to ignore the skimpy nightdress and leather cuffs, draping myself in an imaginary suit with bodyguards and personal assistants ready to do whatever I commanded. "Pretend we're in a business negotiation at Belle Elle. What would you say?"

He smirked. "I'd say this was a takeover."

"A hostile takeover, don't you mean?"

"No, Elle, a partnership. A new director of the board buying fifty-one percent of the stock but letting the old manager keep forty-nine."

Oh, how generous of you.

"That's not a partnership. It's a dictatorship."

"Wrong again. It *is* a partnership with the smallest amount of authority."

I would never sign Belle Elle over to him. Even if he killed me. The company wasn't mine to give. It was my family's—it belonged to my future children. The Charlston legacy would only go to a man worthy of serving by my side.

"If it's about the money, I'll give you some. What do you want? A million? Two?"

He threw his head back, laughing hard. "Oh, I knew your anger was cute, but you're just adorable when you try to bargain with chump change."

"A million isn't chump change."

"It is to you."

"Ten million." I pursed my lips. "Ten million and you walk away." I flung my hands in the air, hating the weight of the chain and the jingle of the links as I moved. "Walk away from this, from me, from Belle Elle, and I'll wire the money to you right now."

"We don't have reception out here. No Wi-Fi."

"Fine, take me back to the city, and I'll do it there."

Where I can call the police, not the bank.

"Nice try, Elle." He tapped his nose with the sharp blade. "I much prefer our current situation." Leaping off the counter, he inhaled my neck like a grizzly bear. "Ten million is still chump change. You can't buy me off. The only bribe I'd accept would be..."

He deliberately left me hanging.

I hated myself, but I took his bait. "Would be?"

"You." His eyes flashed. "Marry me, give me fifty-one percent of Belle Elle, fifty percent of the contents of your bank accounts, and then divorce me for all I care."

My eyes flared. "You're saying if I married you and gave you half of everything I own, that you'll walk away?"

He cocked his head. "Maybe."

"Maybe isn't an answer I can agree to."

"Guess you'll just have to make us dinner and stop trying to barter then, huh?" He ran the knife around my belly button, pressing the gold satin against my skin. "Cook me something, wife-to-be, then we can finally see if we're as compatible in the bedroom as we are in the boardroom."

"We were never compatible in the boardroom. You were never *allowed* in the boardroom."

"Precisely. You were boss there." His teeth glinted. "But here in my bed, in my cabin—I'm the boss.

"And I can't fucking wait to show you what I can do."

CHAPTER EIGHT

PENN

"HE'S NOT FUCKING here," I growled into the phone. "Does he have another property?"

Joe Charlston cleared his throat, the sound of an engine loud on the line. "No, that's the only one that Steve—"

"Everett? Is that you?" Steve Hobson's voice replaced Joe's. I envisioned him snatching the phone, either to stand up to me and beg me not to hurt his cocksucker of a son or help me find the woman who was like a daughter to him.

"Tell me where I can find him." I paced the woodland where the car tracks vanished onto a road. I had no clue what direction they'd gone in, no more hints or clues to chase.

Elle was still out there.

A new day had replaced the night, and I was fucking raging at the thought of her still with him.

"He's not at the cabin?"

I ground my teeth. "He was. His Porsche is here, but they're not. He had another car. They're still missing."

Steve cursed something I didn't catch. "I don't know what else to tell you."

"Tell me something helpful. Tell me you know your son. Hotels he prefers, locations he likes."

Steve paused then rushed, "I know he was thinking of buying a fishing lodge. I don't think he did, but then again, I had no clue he had another car up at the cabin." His voice turned despondent. "This entire fiasco is showing how little I know my own flesh and blood."

Another man came on the phone. A man I remembered vividly for multiple reasons. And he remembered me. "Everett, David speaking. Elle's bodyguard."

"I know who you are."

I remember the night we first met when your judgment stole all my joy at being with Elle and reminded me I was scum who doesn't deserve her.

"I'm driving Mr. Charlston and Mr. Hobson to the cabin. Wait there, and we'll track them down together. I'll do some digging with my contacts and see if there are any other assets under his name."

Contacts.

Digging.

Of course.

I had someone better to call.

Urgency to hang up on such a pointless conversation made me snarl, "Come here, I can't stop you. But I won't be here when you arrive. I'll find her on my own."

I hung up, not caring I'd given Elle's father shit-loads of reasons why he should ban his daughter from ever seeing me again—if she ever let me in the same room as her, of course.

But I didn't care about family dynamics and winning favors.

All I cared about was finding Elle and making sure she was safe.

If she tried to kill me after I told her who I was, then I would accept that. At least she would be back home where she belonged.

My chest tightened at the future conversation we would have. The explanation about why I had her necklace, why I'd done what I had that night in the alley, and why I'd tracked her down (thanks to her I.D card) then taken things she wasn't ready to give.

But first, I had to find her.

My fingers shook as I punched a well-used number into my phone.

He answered on the first ring.

The man who I turned to for everything.

The man I called my father and friend.

"Larry speaking."

"You still have that Meerkat in your zoo?"

First thing Larry had taught me: people were always listening. The higher in society you climbed, the bigger your bank account grew, the more people eavesdropped on every part of your life.

Meerkat was code for cops and zoo was code for payroll. Larry was a lawyer. And a damn fine one. But it didn't mean he didn't use extra tools when it suited him—all in the name of defending the innocent, of course. The same method had helped free me, revealing what I'd sworn under oath to be true even when the jury didn't believe me.

Even when I'd been thrown away to rot in a cell for something I didn't do.

"Yes, my zoo is always full."

"Great, I need some apples."

Stupid code for information. We need to change that one.

"Name it."

"You know the animal in question. I need bucket monitoring for any large refills in the last few years. Track down his zookeeper and any cage cleaners. See if he's left his comfy pen and suddenly taken a liking to the wild or has any other nests tucked away. Got it?"

I hoped he did because my mind hurt remembering how to vaguely insinuate he look up Greg's credit card statements (bucket monitoring) for any out of place shopping sprees such as cars or rentals. And to research his mortgage documents (zookeepers) or line of credits (cage cleaners) for hotel statements or house purchases.

If Greg had planned this…something damning would appear.

It always does.

"Consider the report in progress." Larry cleared his throat. "He's still got her but—"

I knew he wanted to reassure me, but I didn't have time. "He might for now—" I crunched the phone tight in my hands "—but not for much longer."

"Give me twenty. I'll call you back."

I hung up.

Gritting my teeth against the cuts on my feet and the seizing of bruised joints from the beating, I jogged through the forest and up the driveway to my Merc.

The minute Larry called with new information, I would find her.

And this time, I wouldn't fail.

CHAPTER NINE

ELLE

COOKING IN CHAINS wasn't something I was used to.

It was awkward, heavy, and I positively hated the clinking as I shuffled toward the pantry and grabbed ingredients for a simple tagliatelle with basil pesto and parmesan.

I had to hand it to my prison guard—he'd brought flavorful things that were easy to turn from separate food groups into a main course.

Normally, I wouldn't obey him out of principal—no matter he kept twirling the knife with a gleam in his eyes as if daring me to speak out. But normally, I wasn't starving. My stomach constantly grumbled, empty and ready to eat.

I told myself this meal was for me, and my unfortunate companion would have the leftovers.

Greg sat on the counter, occasionally kicking his leg out to prevent me from moving past, stroking my shoulder and tucking a blonde strand behind my ear.

"You ever think of giving up the corporate world and becoming a stay-at-home mom?" His touch dropped to my breast, squeezing it before I could swat him and continued to the sink to drop the cooked pasta into a colander to drain.

His touch made my heart quake, but I had to remind

myself he was just a man. My flesh was just a body; it was repairable. Yes, he'd violate every commandment by taking me forcibly, but I couldn't focus on that yet.

Only when it happens.

I hated that my mind had accepted *when* not *if.*

"No. I've been too busy with Belle Elle." The hot water splashed from the pan down the drain.

Besides, I'm still young. I want to see the world first. I want to explore and be reckless and fall in love.

My insides knotted.

Penn.

Could I have fallen in love with him if he hadn't lied?

Could I have given up the idea of Nameless to find happiness?

Now, I would never know because I'd never see either Penn or Nameless again.

"You should. Domestic chores suit you."

"That's such a sexist thing to say."

"No, sexist would be that house chores suit all women." He smirked. "I just said you."

I rolled my eyes and returned the now drained pasta to the pot where I added sautéed mushrooms, parmesan, and pesto to stir through and warm.

I found comfort in cooking. The method hadn't changed even if my circumstances had. The recipe still worked even if I was chained in a nightgown waiting to be raped and my business stolen.

"Fuck, watching you cook for me makes me hard." Greg grabbed his erection. "See what you do to me?"

I had no desire to look. "It makes me sick."

"That's because you're still brain-washed by that bastard, Everett."

Goosebumps erupted on my skin.

I didn't know if it was Penn's domination over my body and the lust I still felt (no matter I wanted to murder him) or the belief that, in some strange way, he would save me even if he was a criminal.

Don't be so ridiculous.

I didn't reply, focusing intently on folding in the pesto sauce.

Greg huffed, pushing off from the counter to grab the chain around my wrists and pull me forward. "Come with me."

"What? But I'm not finished."

"Doesn't matter. Two minutes won't hurt it."

I had no choice as he pulled me from the kitchen and down the small hallway to the bedroom we'd shared. The bed clothes were tangled; my underwear still on the floor from where he'd kicked them from the bathroom.

He let me go, stepping over the chain wrapped around my ankle (that now snaked down the hallway back the way we'd traveled) to open the wardrobe door. Hanging inside were an array of lingerie and negligées—all completely impractical for making an escape. No shoes, only stockings. No jackets, only bras.

I sighed heavily, fighting depression and tiredness.

This strange role-play helped delete some of the immediate worry I had about my situation. Cooking in chains? It was odd, but at least I wasn't being hurt. Being washed and cuddled in bed? Awful on many levels but still not pushing the boundaries into horror.

What is he doing?

Why is he dragging this out?

Not knowing was the worst part. I didn't know when he'd pounce; when he'd demand me to open my legs and let him have me. I didn't know how much longer I could stay alert and constantly ready to fight.

Eventually, I would tire. I would sleep. And then I'd be at his mercy.

Greg pulled out a small turquoise bag with Tiffany's logo.

Oh, no.

My heart scrambled into my throat as he placed the bag into my hands. "Open it."

I backed away, tossing the offending gift onto the bed. I didn't need to open it to know what was in there. "I don't want it."

His jaw clenched as he scooped up the bag, tossed the ring box into his palm, and cracked it open. "Yes, you fucking do, Elle." Plucking the one carat diamond from the plush box, he grabbed my left hand and jammed the ring onto my engagement finger.

It fit perfectly.

Of course.

Instantly, I wanted to get it off. I'd cut off my own finger to be free of it.

"You're going to marry me, Elle. You're going to change your last name to Hobson. Belle Elle will be mine."

He slithered his arms around my waist, tucking me tight against him. "You're going to give me a daughter or son, so our families will forever be joined, and Belle Elle will always be mine by right, and then, once you've given me everything I want, I'll let you divorce me."

His teeth flashed as he chuckled. "But only with a hefty settlement for being the best husband ever. We'll spread a rumor that you cheated and the sympathy vote will ensure everyone will be on my side while you fade into obscurity."

He captured my chin, kissing me quick. "Or you could stay married and be my dutiful wife and share in everything I give you."

I wanted to disinfect my mouth, tear out my tongue, and zip up my lips so he could never kiss me again. But then I wouldn't be able to tell him what I thought about his ludicrous, monstrous plan.

I laughed in his face, shaking with rage. "Do you believe in fairies, Greg? Because you have to if you think that will ever come true." I shoved him away, swelling with pride as he stumbled. "Ten million is all you'll get out of me, and that offer is only valid for the next five minutes. I don't even know why I'm offering that." I shrugged, waving the damn chain between my arms. "Who knows? Perhaps, I still see the Greg who helped me pick the right bike when I was eight, or the Greg who helped me move into my apartment."

Stomping toward him, I stabbed my finger into his chest. "Ten million for the past we share and not a penny more. I'm not marrying you. I'm definitely not bearing your children. And no way in hell are you getting Belle Elle—"

I went to tear the ring off but he clamped his hand over mine. "You remove that diamond and I hurt you." His threat wasn't idle. It reeked with cold-hearted promise.

I gulped, letting him pull my fingers away, leaving the ring ensnaring me.

Then, as if he hadn't just petrified me, he cupped between my legs, his fingers bruising me. "Are you sure I won't get Belle Elle? Are you sure I won't get *exactly* what I want? That I won't get to fuck you, keep you, steal everything from you? Because it feels like I'm winning."

Hitting his arm, I scooted backward. My toes landed on the chain, making me wince. "Get away from me."

He walked with me, his fingers never loosening, curling tighter around my core beneath the stupid negligée. He didn't let go as I scratched his wrist, tugging for him to let me go.

I repelled backward so fast, I slammed into the wall, giving him the perfect purchase to slap his free hand onto the upright surface by my head and press a finger inside me.

I shuddered in grotesque denial.

I was dry. It hurt. It was brutal rather than blissful.

My mind shattered, begging for Penn and the wizardry of his touch. He made me wet even while he confused me with stories. He made me come even while I denied how much I liked him.

Penn was a master manipulator.

Greg was just the devil.

I wanted him out of my life and far away from me.

I want him dead.

I shoved him, the chains around my wrists clinking loudly.

He grabbed the metal, hoisting it up, giving my arms no way to disobey before being yanked upright and pinned against the wall.

"This…Elle, your fucking pussy is mine." His voice became thick and cruel. "I'm going to have you. I'm going to fuck you. I've waited as long as I can. You wear my ring, you've slept in my bed, I've washed you in my shower. You no longer belong to him but me, get it?"

His finger hooked inside, his nail scraping delicate flesh. "I'm going to fuck you the minute lunch is finished."

Withdrawing his touch, he let me go and pointed at the kitchen. "Now, get in there and finish making me food like a good little wife."

CHAPTER TEN

PENN

THE MERC'S ENGINE snarled as I pressed the accelerator as far to the floor as possible.

Thirty-two minutes and Larry still hadn't called.

But I didn't care.

I had to stay on the move. Otherwise, I'd fucking take my rage out on an innocent tree and end up hurting myself in the process.

And I was hurt enough.

I didn't know if I was going in the right direction or wrong. I had no clue if Elle was still safe or if Greg had done something un-fucking-forgivable.

All I had was the hope I'd be on time.

Tearing down a country road, I jumped as my phone ring-tone split the air.

Answering with hands-free, I grunted, "Where am I going, Larry?"

"Cherry Cove, Medina."

"Hotel or private house?"

"Fishing chalet."

"His?"

"Not sure. Couldn't find any records of him buying

---

another property."

"How do you know she's there then?"

"He bought another car—under a friend's name, but he helped secure the finance. The Dodge Charger is equipped with antitheft GPS. I had someone who owed me a favor switch it on. The car is outside the address I've sent to your inbox. I used Google maps to see what sort of abode it was."

"Your sleuthing never fails to impress me."

Larry's voice hid a smile. "You can tell me how great I am later. Get her back, Penn, and then you're fixing this. You're telling that poor girl everything. You're going to be honest."

I bared my teeth but nodded reluctantly, knowing she'd never want to see me again. "Fine."

I pressed end, downshifted, and grinned at the growling engine as I cannon-fired after Greg.

According to my GPS, I was just over an hour away.

A mere hour until Elle was mine again and then all my lies would be revealed.

But, at least, she would be safe.

I would be fucking heartbroken, but she would be back where she belonged.

Without me in her world.

CHAPTER ELEVEN

ELLE

THE PASTA SAT like glue in my stomach.

I'd eaten because I was hungry, but the much-loathed company made nutrition unwanted by my body.

Greg slurped at the tagliatelle, swiping at globs of pesto sauce that splashed against his cheeks.

He grinned as he swirled more pasta onto his fork. "You really are a good cook, Elle."

"You're lucky I didn't poison you."

He chuckled. "There's nothing here to poison me with." He took another bite, eating with his mouth full. Steve would swat him if he saw—he'd been trying to break him of that habit since Greg was little. "No bleach, no cleaning products. Nothing that can harm."

I reached for my water glass, hating how the links clinked over the table and threatened to slide through my lunch. Hoisting my other wrist, I balanced the foot of chain above the plate and awkwardly took a drink.

Greg never took his eyes off me.

Bastard.

I glanced out the window at the sparkling lake and sunshine. If I were here with any other person, it would be the perfect vacation away from working so hard. A vacation I'd never had. I would walk around the lake, have a picnic, read a book beneath a tree, and then come back and make love to whoever had brought me here.

Penn.

You would've made love to Penn.

I shut down my thoughts.

I didn't want him in my head.

He wasn't allowed or permitted inside my mind anymore. Twenty-four hours ago, I would've given him the benefit of the doubt and listened to what he had to say.

That was before the necklace.

Now, I would tell him to go away—no matter what explanations he formed.

Greg finished his last mouthful, smacking his lips and pushing the plate away. He nodded in appreciation. "Best lunch I've had in a while."

"You obviously don't get out much then."

"I work for you." His eyes narrowed. "I normally work through my lunch break because you expect so much from your staff."

I couldn't let him get away with that bullshit. "Whatever, Greg, your executive assistant does her job and yours combined. You're never in your office; you're always off site."

His lips tightened.

"What? You think I don't notice? That I don't keep an eye on my *employees?*" I dragged out the word, enjoying the way he shifted full of annoyance in his chair. "It's my company. Of course, I'm aware of who's doing a good job and who isn't. And I hate to say it, but you've never done a good job. Even from the first day Steve asked Dad to give you that position. You've taken your salary and done nothing for it."

I wiped my mouth with my napkin, no longer hungry. "In fact, I've been claiming your salary as a charity donation on our tax returns because I have to pay your executive assistant twice her normal wage so she doesn't walk out and leave your department in shambles."

His mouth hung open. "You truly are a bitch."

"And you're just a bastard. Guess we're even."

He crossed his arms while I let the chain fall into my lap, the cuffs heavy around my wrists.

"What a way to ruin a nice lunch, Noelle." He stood, snatching his plate before storming to my side of the table and grabbing mine. "Does it make you feel good to think you're still so high and fucking mighty?"

I didn't let his shadow looming over me intimidate me. I straightened my back, glowering directly into his eyes. "First, it's Elle. I never have, and never will like Noelle. And second, yes it does make me feel good to point out your flaws and show you that whatever this is—" I flashed the engagement ring sparkling on my finger—the same ring I'd tried to pull off for the second time only to earn a slap so hard, I suspected his handprint still glowed on my cheek "—is a sham."

Furious tears and racing heartbeats wobbled my words. "You're just like him. You force an engagement on me and expect me to go along with it!" I laughed with disbelief. "I was an idiot where Penn was concerned. I should've stood up to him more. Should've dug into his background sooner, but I didn't because beneath his lies, I actually *liked* the glimpses of normalness."

I sneered at Greg. "But when I look at you, all I see is rotten greed. All I smell is hunger for things you haven't earned and never will."

My hands curled just before his fist connected.

It crunched against my cheekbone, layering upon the last punch, no doubt turning the faint grayness under my eye into a full-on black spot.

My head snapped to the side, my chin lolling on my chest as my arms shot out to grip the table. I teetered on the edge, only a fraction away from falling out of the chair and puddling at his feet.

I'd known it would come to this, yet I couldn't help

myself. I had to tell him off like a silly little child because that was what he was.

A child.

An ignorant little boy who needed a good spanking.

"That's the last time you'll *ever* talk to me like that." His breath smacked my hair with fury. "Hear me?"

I blinked and dared to shake my head a little. The world righted itself. The pain dimmed. I sat firmer in the chair, planting my elbows on the table and cradling my head. The chain and cuffs hindered me as I hid behind a curtain of tangled hair and pressed exploratory fingers to my puffy, hot cheek.

Ouch.

God, it hurt.

My tears were from physical pain instead of emotional frustration this time. I didn't bother to stop them as they splashed sadly against the tabletop where my lunch had been.

Greg stomped into the kitchen and tossed the plates into the sink. China cracked with a loud splinter, but he didn't care. Marching back toward me, he hoisted me to my feet with biting fingers around my elbow. "You want to fight, Elle? Fucking fine, we'll fight." Dragging me into the living room, he pointed at the hallway. "Choose, right now. Bed or couch."

I squinted, doing my best to ignore the pain throbbing in my head. "What?"

"Bed or couch."

"I don't know what that means."

He pressed his nose against mine. "I'm going to fuck you. Would you prefer over the couch like a whore or in the bed like my fiancée?"

Everything went black and cold.

So, so cold.

I squirmed in his hold; stepping backward the cuff around my ankle jingled and I stepped on the chain looped behind me for the thirty-seventh time, hurting yet another piece of me. "Greg, stop. I don't want either."

"Too fucking bad. You need to learn your place. You're no longer my boss or the CEO, Elle." His voice lowered to a hiss. "I am."

Grabbing a handful of my hair, he threw me onto the plaid couch. The scratchy material stuck to my gold negligée like Velcro as I scooted sideways, trying to reach the other end and climb off.

He grabbed the chain around my ankle, hoisting me back.

The satin rose up my hips, exposing between my legs.

His eyes latched on greedily before I slammed a hand over myself with as much decency as I could muster. "Don't touch me."

"I'm going to do more than that."

"I'll scream."

He smirked. "No one to hear you."

"I'll kill you."

"I'd like to see you try."

My fury turned caustic, burning me up inside. I shook so hard my teeth chattered.

He leered over me, keeping his hold on the chain, giving me nowhere to go. Bending down, he grabbed me by the throat, pinning my body against the couch.

My legs stayed tight and crossed, hand wedged low.

"Kiss me. Show me that you can be nice, and I'll be gentle our first time."

I spat in his face.

Wrong move.

Seriously wrong move.

But it was the only move I had because I couldn't kiss him. I could never give anything of me willingly because the hate I had would transfer into hatred for myself.

Time slowed down.

His hand came up, rubbing at the bead of saliva I'd put there. Never looking away from me, he wiped his hand on his jeans, shaking his head. "You'll pay for that."

His face turned nasty, his fingers grabbing my elbows and

plucking me from the couch as if I weighed nothing.

"No!" I pummeled his chest as he hauled me against him, marching me backward until my legs pressed against the couch end.

"Yes." Spinning me around, he pressed me over the rolled armrest, running his hands down my spine to my ass.

"Get ready to be nice to me, Elle. 'Cause I'm sure as shit not going to be nice to you."

CHAPTER TWELVE

PENN

THIS CABIN HAD lake views, not forest.
This cabin had a Dodge, not a Porsche.
This cabin held Elle, not empty.
This place ricocheted with a scream, not silence.
Fuck!

I cursed that I'd left my Merc at the top of the driveway again, hoping for the element of surprise. I'd taken my time sneaking through the bushes and shadows, staying out of sight.

The occasional smell of cooking had carried on the breeze the closer I got.

The electrical tingle of being close to Elle revved me the nearer I sneaked.

But that was before the scream.

Forgetting stealth, I bolted forward from gloomy undergrowth to gleaming daylight. All instincts told me to barrel through the front door and tear Greg fucking apart.

But the sensible part of me—the part that'd kept me alive for decades on the streets—whispered patience.

What if he had a knife to her throat?
What if he had a gun ready to kill me?
I had to know where they were, what they were doing—

then I could win.

Ducking, I snuck around the perimeter of the house. My ears strained for another scream, but nothing came. Ice water washed my spine. No scream could be good, could be bad.

I couldn't see inside the dim interior with the bright sunshine beating on my head.

I ran through the small garden with baby saplings swaying in the breeze and approached the side of the house where a bathroom window cracked to allow shower steam to dissipate.

No movement down the back of the cabin.

Pressing against the siding, I made my way back to the front where the living room and kitchen would be.

I kept my height beneath the window frames, listening for any hint of what room Elle was a prisoner in.

The sound of chains dragging on hardwood screeched in my ears from a cracked window.

He's chained her up?

That motherfucker.

He'd pay for this. Over and *over,* he'd pay.

He had his motherfucking hands on her.

Soon, I'd have mine on him.

Sounds of raised voices filtered through the afternoon, garbled and cut short as something thumped and then couch legs squeaked over floorboards.

I couldn't stop myself.

I stood upright, keeping my body low but my eyes above the trim. Peering through the glass, my heart fucking stopped.

Greg had Elle pinned over the edge of the couch. Chains on her wrists and ankle. A gold nightdress shoved over her hips, exposing her nakedness below.

I thought seeing her vulnerable with half-torn clothes in the alley three years ago was enough for me to turn rogue.

This…this was enough for me to commit fucking murder.

CHAPTER THIRTEEN

ELLE

I SCREAMED.

How could I not?

When a man who you'd just eaten lunch with, grew up with, someone you watched turn from boy to grown-up suddenly takes away all control and prepares to rape you—all common sense, conversation skills, and bartering flies out of comprehension.

I gave up pain and precaution.

I felt nothing but wildness and terror.

"Stop!" I kicked. I wiggled. I clawed at the couch.

"All it takes is for you to be nice to me, Elle. And this can go so much better for you."

The promise whispered in my head to do something. To be generous with compliments if it meant he wouldn't hurt me. But I physically gagged on such blasphemy.

He stroked my back, running his fingers over my naked hips as he wedged his jeans-clad cock against me. He didn't move to unzip, but it didn't stop his hardness from sending disgust gushing through my blood.

A shadow fell over the floor for the briefest second, wrenching my eyes to the window where sun spilled upon my ruin.

Perhaps a fellow vacation-maker had come to borrow a cup of sugar. Maybe a fisherman needed to dig in the garden for some worm-bait. Hopefully, some good Samaritan was here to save me.

I opened my mouth to scream again, but Greg slammed his sweaty palm over my lips.

"Be nice, and we go into the bedroom." He fumbled with his belt with his other hand. "Don't, and you're mine right here."

My heart atrophied at the sounds of leather unbuckling.

I'm running out of time.

Do something.

Think.

Kick. Fight. Bite. Scream.

Anything!

The shadow came again, quick and fleeting, but I caught what made it this time. The barest glimpse of an angel come to free me.

I didn't believe it.

I *couldn't* believe it.

It wasn't a fisherman or a bird or even a confused bear out for a stroll.

It was so much better.

So much worse.

My heart grew wings even as heavy tar coated it. Greg undid his jeans. The sensation of denim switched to bare male flesh.

I moaned behind his palm, tossing my head.

The figure in the window appeared again, this time closer to the front door. His tussled dark hair scattered stencils on the floor.

Him.

The liar.

The alley abuser.

The man I had feelings for despite everything.

He ducked again.

Did he know I'd seen him?

Did he know I was grateful?

What would he do?

How had he found me and not David or Dad?

My questions evaporated as Greg's hard cock lined up with my ass. He shuddered, his hand clenching around my mouth while his other yanked my hips into him.

He was moments away from taking me.

So I did the only thing I could.

I chose survival over pride.

I decided to lie just like Penn.

Letting my body go loose, I forced my ass against him, rubbing his erection, deliberately arching my back as if being fucked by him was exactly what I wanted.

My body hated, *hated* me.

My heart cursed, *cursed* me.

And my lips didn't know how to form the falsehoods I was about to spill.

His hand tumbled from my mouth in shock, giving me freedom to speak.

"Mmm, *Greg*." My sultry moan made my skin scratch itself with knives. "You're right... I'm so—" I rocked into him, making him groan and fingers spasm "—*so* sorry."

He froze, his thighs twitching against the back of mine. "What did you just say?"

I kept my voice slow and decadent—like chocolate and liquor and rich, rich coffee. "I said you're right. I should be *nicer* to you." I rolled my hips, dragging a revolting pant from him and a coil of nausea from me. "If you let me stand and face you, I'll show you how *nice* I can be."

My tongue burned with lies.

My throat slashed with fibs.

Was this how Penn felt every time he talked to me?

Greg nudged me with his hips, keeping me pinned against the couch. "Why should I trust you? You've been nothing but a bitch since we got here."

I jingled the chain around my wrists. "I'm yours, remember? I'm not going anywhere." I let my body go completely submissive. "It's time I listened to what you're offering rather than destroy what we could have together without giving it a chance."

Lies, lies, *lies*.

I wanted to vomit with lies.

I wanted to wash away the lies.

I wanted to bleach the lies.

Greg slowly relaxed. He stepped back, giving me room to stand.

I took one last look at the window. A slight shadow appeared closer to the door. Penn was many things, but I trusted him to help me. He'd come for me in his car that night. He'd fought for me in the club at the beginning. He would get me free, and then I'd politely thank him and walk away.

All I needed to do was keep Greg distracted enough, so it was an ambush rather than a full-on fight.

I didn't need more complications in my life by turning this abduction into death or bloodshed. Regardless of what Greg had done, the law would deal with him, not vigilante justice.

Standing upright, I pushed the negligée down my hips for coverage and turned to face him.

The only problem was he had a full view of the door where Penn would most likely come in.

I have to change that.

Placing my hand on Greg's chest, I disguised my shuddering fingers with a breathy laugh. "You know…I agree with something else you said, too."

His eyes widened then narrowed with suspicion. "Agree with me? That will be a first."

I nodded, licking my lips, taking a step to the left, doing my best to ignore the sound of the chain dragging on the floor behind me. "Belle Elle could be ours."

Another step, guiding his attention from the door. "You and me."

He followed, trying to sniff out my agenda. "What do you mean?"

"I mean if you'd work harder once Belle Elle was yours, then perhaps that's an option."

He smirked coldly. "And why should I believe this sudden change of heart?"

Another step, three-quarters turned from the door. He swiveled to follow me with every footfall I took.

"Can't I change my mind?"

"You can, but it's odd you change it now." His hand cupped my cheek, running his thumb over the bruise he'd given me. "Strange that you turn cooperative just before I show you how good we are together."

I swallowed bile as I stroked my finger down his chest, drawing a circle around his open belt buckle. "You scared me. But if you're nice to me—like you promised—I can be nice to you."

The sexual reference scalded my tongue, but Greg's eyes glowed. "Oh yeah? How *nice* are we talking?"

Another step and his back was toward the exit. Over his shoulder, I hid my victory smirk as the door cracked open with a sliver of warm sunshine.

Penn's livid gaze locked on mine.

I looked away, staying in character, and not giving in to the crazed patter of my heart.

He was bloody and broken. Smeared with rust and torn on the shoulder, he still wore his white shirt and silver trousers from the charity gala. He moved silently but with a stiffness that wasn't there before.

What the hell happened to him?

Doesn't matter.

Keep going.

Keep Greg distracted.

I moved closer to my enemy, tugging his belt, sliding it through his jean loops. "I can be very, *very* nice." I fluttered my eyelashes. "I've grown up a lot the past month. I know how to please."

Penn moved closer.

I daren't glance up. I couldn't afford to see how angry he was at my flirting or how angry I was at his fibs. We were furious with each other.

Good, fury is better than lust.

"That right?" Greg's hand landed on my shoulder, squeezing, adding downward pressure just like Penn did when he taught me a lesson and ordered me to suck him in my office.

I couldn't be on my knees. I had to watch Penn behind Greg's back, so I could get out of the way at the right time.

I giggled—I never giggled—but I amped up the flirt to terrible levels. "How about we discuss the terms first, and *then* I'm nice to you?"

"You already know the terms." He grabbed my hand, spinning the engagement ring on my finger. "This means you're mine. Everything you own is mine. That's the deal, Elle."

"And my body? Is that yours, too?"

He looked down at my breasts with a hungry glare. "Fuck yes, it is."

Nausea splashed my stomach as I stroked his chest, moving back up his body away from the hardness in his pants. "And your body? Is that mine in return?"

He licked his lips. "It is if you want it."

I dared look over his shoulder as Penn slowly slinked from the doorway into the living room. His eyes met mine again, narrowed and dark and full of murder. His fists clenched with no other weapon but his hate.

He was utterly sublime.

And totally terrifying.

My skin shivered with a mixture of frustration and appreciation. I'd felt something for him. I could've been happy with him. But the truth shattered that.

I was glad he was here, and this situation warranted gratitude, but after that…*I never want to see him again.*

Tearing my eyes back to Greg, I counted the seconds until I could stop this pantomime and let Penn incapacitate him.

Placing my hand over Greg's heart, the chain around my wrists dangled, nudging his erection with morbid jewelry. "Yes, I want it."

He wrapped his arms around my waist, wedging himself against me. "In that case, be a good girl and get in the bedroom. I'll make it good for you if you make it good for me. That's all I ever wanted, Elle."

I giggled again even though I wanted to strangle him. "Okay…"

Penn sneaked forward, his eyes darting between me in Greg's arms and his feet on the floorboards, searching for squeaky spots.

"Let's go." Greg moved forward, his head turned toward the kitchen. If his peripheral was any good, he'd see Penn and all my lying and touching would've been for nothing.

"Wait!" I grabbed his face, holding his gaze with mine. "Don't go, not yet."

His eyebrows knitted together, dark blond hair cascading over his forehead. "Why the fuck not?" Temper tightened his eyes. "If you're playing a game—"

"No game—" Panic made me blurt rather than hum with sexual intrigue.

Penn inched closer.

A floorboard creaked.

Greg's nostrils flared as he twitched to look over his shoulder.

I did the only thing I could.

The only thing I could think of.

Digging my nails into his cheeks, I wrenched his face to mine and kissed him.

The world screeched to a halt as my lips willingly found his and seduced him.

He tasted wrong.

He *felt* wrong.

He was *wrong*.

His body tensed.

For a second, I feared he'd slap me away and find Penn just a foot behind him. But then he relaxed, grabbing me close and spearing his tongue into my mouth.

I gagged as he kissed me deep, his hands tangling in my hair.

I hated every wet heat of it. I despised every swipe of his unwanted invasion.

Trying to stay in character, I did my hardest not to bite him. But I couldn't stop the moan of rejection or squirm of refusal.

He grunted, dragging me closer to him. The kiss turned brutal and basic. Teeth nipping at my lip, sharp and smooth.

And then…it was over.

Commotion, clamor, then Greg was torn from my arms and jerked backward. Instinct made him grab the chain around my wrists, yanking me with him.

A sharp gasp fell from me as we fell together, plummeting to the hardwood.

I landed with a bone-rattling jar half on him, half on the floor. I didn't have time to register pain as vicious hands wrapped around my waist, plucked me from Greg, and threw me to the side out of the way.

I rolled to my knees just in time to see Penn dive onto Greg as he pinned him to the floor and delivered two solid punches to his jaw. "You cock-sucking motherfucker!"

"What the——" Greg tried to protect his face, but Penn had the element of surprise.

"How dare you take her?" Penn rammed his knuckles into Greg's jaw.

"How *dare* you fucking touch her?" He hit his temple, his throat—his punches messy but swift.

"How dare you goddamn hurt her!" He turned diabolical,

hitting every part he could reach.

Greg whimpered, his voice punctured by punches and pain.

Penn didn't let up.

He didn't stop the violence.

He'll kill him.

"Wait!" I scrambled upright. "Stop!"

Penn didn't listen.

Greg's nose popped in a gush of blood. He groaned something incomprehensible.

Penn pushed up, towering over him. His chest heaved with breath, his body covered in stains and injury. "You're an asshole." His foot kicked out, connecting with Greg's side. "A creep who ought to be exterminated—just like all the other fucking creeps who think they can take what isn't theirs."

Even in the midst of a fight, I couldn't help my inner voice from whispering, *hypocrite.*

Penn was one of those creeps. He'd tried to rape me in that alley. He'd stolen my necklace.

I backed away, holding my stomach in revulsion.

Two emotions tangled and braided. They knotted together trying to confuse me. I liked Penn. I hated Penn. I wanted Penn. I couldn't forgive Penn.

The flash of his bare foot brought me back as he buried it in Greg's soft belly. A sickening thud made nerves tangle into sickness.

I couldn't do a damn thing.

Penn was a ruthless machine, utterly unstoppable. He was no longer the surly liar who'd enchanted me but a cold, merciless killer.

Greg grunted, curling up, protecting every part he could. "Stop! Fucking stop!"

Hot tears came from nowhere, brimming with betrayal and exhaustion. They spilled over, distorting the room, tickling my cheeks as Greg spat red saliva on the hardwood.

Penn didn't move back, but he didn't strike either. Greg's

blood covered his knuckles. His stance defensive and possessive. His intentions of winning blaring all around him.

He'd been in a fight before this one. He'd been hurt before he hurt Greg. Why? How? By who? Yet more questions landing on the unanswered hillside I already had.

I'd seen Penn in many moods over the past few weeks—sarcastic, protective, combative, and seducing. But I'd never seen him channel the wish of a murderer. He glowered at Greg with no compassion or belief he was even human.

Planting his foot on Greg's sternum, he pointed a finger in his face. "Go near Elle again, and you don't survive."

My chains jingled as I inched closer. I didn't know if I wanted to pull Penn away or check that Greg wasn't seriously hurt. I didn't want to be close to either of them.

Deciding they were both idiots and it was my turn to rule, I pushed Penn out of the way, yanked off the despicable engagement ring, and threw it on Greg's chest. "You can take that awful diamond back." The minute I was free from that shackle, I dangled the chain between my wrists over Greg's face. "Now, enough fighting. Where are the keys to the padlock?"

Penn blinked away his violent stupor, focusing on the cuffs around my wrist and ankle before focusing on the tossed away engagement ring.

His eyes turned black. "He fucking *chained* you." His fingers dug into my shoulder, holding me tight as he inspected me. His gaze flew over the gold negligée, down my chest, legs, and toes then spun me around and repeated.

His voice wobbled with fury. "He fucking tied you up, bruised you, forced his ring on you, and made you dress in whatever he damn well pleased?" He laughed with an iceberg in his throat. "He fucking *kissed* you? Oh, hell. Fucking. No."

Shoving me away, he launched himself on Greg for the second time.

Greg, to his credit, managed to land a decent head shot, rolling away and clambering to all fours. "Get off me, you son of a bitch."

Penn shook his head free from stars, dazed for a second. A second was all Greg needed to feed off adrenaline and stand.

"She's mine, asshole." He leapt on Penn.

Chaos erupted. Elbows. Knees. Fists and curses. They were no longer two men but one mass of punching arms and striking kicks. Their centrifugal force shoved furniture this way and that, their bodies crashing into a side table and sending a swan-shaped lamp smashing to the floor.

Greg tackled Penn into the couch.

Penn struck the back of Greg's head, getting free.

While Greg shook away the pain, Penn kicked him straight in his ribs then delivered a lightning-fast punch to his belly.

With fists up and biceps bulging, Greg attempted to strike again but Penn was too nimble. He landed a perfect uppercut to Greg's jaw all while quiet fury rippled off him.

His experience in fights was alarming. His past was the perfect training course for such systematical punishments, reminding me I knew nothing about him or how far into lawlessness he'd fallen.

He'd mentally disconnected. Focused entirely on winning.

"Stop! Both of you!" I screamed.

It didn't do any good.

They attacked with vigor born from survival.

The sound of a roaring vehicle outside wrenched my head up just in time to see the black Range Rover I knew so well hurtle down the driveway and slam to a stop. The windows revealed David leaping out with the engine still roaring, charging toward the cabin with his gun free from its holster.

"Quit it! Right now!" I darted to where Penn and Greg rolled. Someone's leg struck out, hitting my cuffed ankle.

I tumbled to my knees, a pained gasp falling.

Penn made eye contact with me just as his fist slammed into Greg's temple. "Shit."

Greg toppled sideways, his eyes rolling in the back of his head. Out cold.

A second later, the front door ricocheted open, and David stood braced with his weapon raised. "Everybody freeze."

I held up my hands, hating the chains so damn much. "It's okay, David. I'm fine."

"Ms. Charlston?" He stomped forward, his finger never pulling away from the trigger. His ex-Marine gaze swept the room, taking in the carnage, and understanding without being told the gist of what'd happened.

His attention latched onto my face where a black eye had formed and tear tracks painted me as exhausted and strung out. His gun pointed away as he came to my side. "Who did that to you?" He swung around as Penn stumbled away from Greg's unconscious form and stood on wobbly legs. He winced a little as he put weight on his right ankle.

David immediately trained the gun on Penn's chest.

Penn put his hands up in surrender, but his body still carried the remnants of battle.

David growled, "I knew you looked like a trouble-maker the first time I saw you."

Penn spat a mouthful of blood by Greg's prone body. "I don't care what you think of me." Stalking toward me, Penn grabbed my hand and wrenched me forward. "Come on, Elle. I'll take you home."

Home?

Was he insane?

He needed to go to a hospital. Greg, too. The police would be involved. Not to mention, I never wanted to be alone with him again.

"I'm not going anywhere with you." I tugged on his hold, looking down at Greg. "Do we need an ambulance?"

Penn chuckled coldly. "Doubt it. He's better off than he would've been if your fucking driver hadn't turned up."

David hoisted the gun higher. "Keep talking like that, and we'll have an issue. Let Ms. Charlston go."

Penn wrapped tight fingers around the chain joining my wrists. "No, she's coming with me."

My bare feet dug into the floor. "No, I'm not. I told you. I'm not going anywhere with you."

"Yes, you are. We need to talk about this." He swiped a swollen hand through dirty hair, letting me go. "Tell me where he put the keys and I'll free you. Then we're leaving."

I shook my head. I wouldn't go with him. I didn't trust him. I didn't like him.

I don't even know him.

But answers...they were the only thing that made sense in this screwed-up reality.

Maybe I should go...

End this like adults.

David fought on my behalf, giving me time to weigh the pros and cons. "Don't move, either of you." Moving toward Greg, he ducked and put his finger on his pulse.

Greg didn't twitch. His legs splayed, arms spread, blood everywhere. It looked like a murder scene.

David muttered, "You're lucky he's still alive. Otherwise, I'd shoot you for killing him."

Penn snorted. "And I suppose that's fair justice to kill the man who rescued the head of Belle Elle?"

David stood, holstering his weapon with angry jerks. "I was about to rescue her."

"Yes, but I beat you." Staying close, Penn didn't touch me, but his eyes captured mine in a way that sent my tummy mimicking baby birds clumsily learning how to fly. He'd never looked so rough and dangerous but beneath the bloody smears was passion and desperation. "Elle, please. We need to talk."

I backed up. "Maybe in a few days. Once I'm home, and this is behind us."

"I don't have a few days."

My voice sharpened. "Why not?"

Penn shook his head, a sad smirk on his lips. "You'll find out soon enough."

Is he leaving?

Why would he say that?

Something about the way he shrugged tugged at me to know. He looked resigned. Pissed off and full of injustice but grudgingly accepting whatever he knew that I didn't.

He knows many things you don't.

He must've thought I was so stupid that day in Central Park when I'd asked where he was on the 19th of June three years ago. He would've known I'd refused him and his asshole friend in the alley but got it on with Nameless an hour later.

Was that why he came after me?

Because he thought I was easy?

I shivered, hugging myself. I wanted to know, but mostly, I just wanted this over with. For the first time, I missed the simplicity of my life before sex. I missed knowing what my day would entail: working, hugging my cat, and reading in bed.

There was comfort in blandness. I wanted that comfort back.

"No, Penn. I'm going home."

His eyebrow rose as if expecting an invitation.

My chin came up. "Without you."

I needed time to put aside this awful event with Greg and remember I was in charge, not these men in this tiny cabin.

Me.

"Let's go." I looked at David, seeing as Penn hadn't budged and his jaw worked as if chewing on things he didn't know if he should say.

David nodded. "Right away."

I held up my wrists. "Uncuff me and take me home. Please."

David immediately strode back to Greg, dropping to his haunches and rummaging in the unconscious man's pockets for keys.

Penn glowered at my bodyguard. "You're not taking her. Not until we've had a chance to talk."

"Another time, perhaps," David snapped. "We're leaving. Right now."

Penn's temper morphed into something calculating.

Placing himself in my view, he scooped up the metal links between my wrists and tugged gently. "Do you trust me?"

That phrase again.

"No."

His voice softened. "You're safe. Just…come into the kitchen."

"The kitchen? Why?"

"Trust me." Pulling me forward, I swayed backward for a second, fighting him.

David looked up, unsuccessful on the key hunt, his eyes narrowed on Penn.

David was here. Penn couldn't hurt me.

When did he ever hurt you? You were alone with him often.

I punched common sense in the mouth.

Allowing Penn to guide me forward, our matching bare feet padded over the cabin's floor. I wanted to ask why he wasn't wearing shoes, but if I asked one question, I wouldn't be able to stop the avalanche.

Penn led me into the kitchen then let me go. He watched me warily as if unsure I'd stay or bolt away from him.

I gave him a slight nod, showing I was relaxed and had no intention of running. Yet.

His lips quirked at the corners, his gaze skating over my body, filling with desire. Clearing his throat, he pulled open a drawer and pushed aside a few utensils until he found what he was looking for.

A meat pulverizer.

I backed away. "What are you going to do with that?"

"Come here, and you'll see." Leaning over the bench, Penn pulled out a knife from the same butcher's block that Greg had taunted me with while I'd cooked lunch.

Dirty pans and plates sat in the sink, ready to be washed. What would Penn think of that? Would he think I'd played house with Greg? Get jealous that I'd cooked him lunch even though it was under duress?

Somehow, I got the feeling Penn wasn't petty or stupid.

He held violence in his palm, ready to unleash it on his enemies but he also allowed kindness.

I took a step closer, warily.

"May I?" He pointed at the chain with the knife.

I swallowed, nodding.

Taking the links, he jammed the knife tip into the loops and placed it on the counter. Twisting the blade, he added pressure until the link refused to bend anymore. Picking up the meat pulverizer, he struck the metal with an awful *whack*. The noise vibrated through my limbs as well as my ears.

Tossing the pulverizer away, he pulled out the knife and with another twist, broke the link.

The chains fell apart, no longer together but still cuffed to my wrists by soft leather.

"That wasn't exactly worthwhile. I'm still—"

"Trapped, I know. You have a choice." He scowled. "Either come home with me where I have a lock picking kit and can undo the cuffs like I would with a key. Or…"

I ignored his comment about going home with him. "Or?"

"Or I use this." He held up the knife. "I can't exactly use the same method with the pounder, but the padlocks look flimsy enough to break with a blade."

David came forward. "The keys won't be far. Be patient and help me search."

Penn didn't look at him, keeping his eyes on me as he said, "By all means look, but she'll be free before you find them."

I quipped, "So arrogant."

He chuckled. "Only just noticed?" Pulling me forward by the dangling chain, I refused to let the shiver of lust infect me. The longer I was in his presence, the more I fought an unwinnable battle between my heart and body.

Penn wasn't good for me. He was a liar. But my body truly didn't care.

He stepped closer—closer than necessary—and hugged my arm close. "You have to stay still. I have a knife against your delicate skin. Don't move."

His voice licked down my spine. My nipples that had no right to be a part of this conversation tingled.

"I won't move." I couldn't really see as he hooked the knife into the small padlock and with a savage corkscrew, smiled triumphantly as the soft sound of something plopping against the floor came a second later.

"Free." Unwrapping the leather, his fingers feathered over my wrist with affection, protection, and most of all, a request to hear him out. To give him a chance.

The cabin vanished and all that remained was us.

The mystery.

The falsities.

David and Greg.

All gone.

Penn had a magical way of capturing my every sense and keeping me locked in whatever world he created.

Licking his bottom lip, he gently let one wrist go to manhandle the other.

I held my breath as his touch skimmed down my arm then a sharp tug and knife on metal freed me from the second cuff.

Not saying a word, Penn tossed the leather away, looped his fingers around my wrist and guided me from the kitchen, past David who didn't stop glaring, and toward the fireplace where the chain around my ankle locked to the hook.

His forehead furrowed, contemplating if he should break the chain or not bother and just undo the imprisonment around my ankle.

He chose the more streamlined option.

Ducking to one knee, he looked up as his touch landed on my calf.

I flinched as his breath fluttered the gold negligée and heat erupted between my legs. Black desire coated him as he glanced at my breasts then inserted the knife tip into the tiny padlock and jerked.

The final tether fell away, leaving me unbound by chains but unable to move from his hold. He massaged my ankle, rubbing me gently. "Elle, please. Let me take you home."

"I—"

David barged into our little moment. "You already know you're not taking her anywhere."

Penn ignored him, his chocolate gaze locked with mine. "I'm not taking no for an answer."

"Like hell you aren't. We're calling the police and getting this settled." David reached for his phone.

Yes, the police.

I had to report Greg. I had to ensure he didn't try something like this again.

But Penn turned cold, standing from his one knee pose. "Don't."

"Don't tell me what to do." David stalked away, already punching in the emergency number.

I wanted to ask him where Dad was, if he was okay, but Penn's stiffness and the way he inched subtly toward the door made me focus.

He's nervous.

As well he should be. He was a criminal who'd done time before.

He was right to be worried but not because of what he'd done to Greg. He'd gone a bit far, but he'd done it in my defense.

They can't arrest him for that. He was the hero in this scenario not the villain.

He rolled his shoulders as if it wasn't a big deal. "I'm not waiting around for paper pushing idiots. He's the one who needs to be arrested." He pointed his chin at Greg still passed out on the floor. "And he's not going anywhere."

David scowled. "You knocked him out. The police will want to talk to you, too."

"Well, I don't want to talk to them." Penn marched back toward me and took my hand. "Elle, please. Come with me."

My conviction wobbled. He looked so young, so pleading, so lost. But he was also the man from the alley.

"I—no, I don't think—"

Penn heard my uncertainty, my lack of absolution.

His fingers looped with mine, pulling me forward with a sudden burst of power. "Before you say goodbye, just hear me out. That's all I'm asking."

The instinct to fight his unwanted coercion made me dig my heels into the floor. "No. Not today. Come to my office in a few days and we'll—"

"No. It has to be now." He stormed forward, dragging me behind him with no effort.

David leapt into action, abandoning the phone call where he'd been murmuring details to the police. He grabbed my other hand, using me as the rope in a tug of war. "You're not taking her, Everett."

"Goddammit!" Penn threw my arm away, severing all ties. For a second, it looked as if he'd run and never look back.

But then he spun around, seething with restraint, itching to leave. "Fine." Ever so slowly, he let his tension uncurl, holding his hand out to me like a lover asking me to go on a hot air balloon ride at sunset. "Elle, it would mean a lot to me if you came with me."

He lowered his head, watching me with hooded eyes. "One conversation. In private. And then you can leave. You have my word."

David relinquished me, so I stood on my own, no longer trapped by any of the three men currently surrounding me— even though one was still in la-la land.

"Ma'am?" David played with his gun holster, touching the handle of his weapon. He kept his gaze on Penn. "Let me take you home. Your father and Steve are on their way here. I dropped them off at a local establishment before finding you. I refused to let them come to the crime scene, in case—" He coughed. "Anyway, the important thing is to call him and say you'll meet him back at home. I'll arrange transportation for him to meet us there."

Dad.

I needed to check his heart was okay from this stressful night. I needed to do a great many things. I should nod and follow David to the Range Rover and never look back. I should file a police report, tell Steve as gently as I could that Greg was fired and if he ever got within a few hundred feet of me he'd be arrested, and spend the evening soothing my dad's nerves.

And Sage—I need to feed Sage.

But something about Penn bewitched me once again. He stood there with his hand shaking slightly, his invitation unanswered.

I tilted my chin, ignoring David and asking questions of my own for once. "Why should I go with you, Penn? You've done nothing but lie to me. I've been so stupid up until now not to dig into who you truly are. To force you to tell me what you're hiding."

He didn't move, merely cocked his head in agreement. "You're not stupid. You trusted me. There's a difference."

"I never trusted you."

"You did. Just like I trust you to come with me now and give me the courtesy of letting me explain myself."

"The courtesy? Where was your courtesy when you hid who you truly are?" I moved closer, rage replacing my fear from the past few hours. "Where was your courtesy when Stewie dropped my sapphire star necklace at the charity gala and told me he'd kept it for you to reduce your robbery sentence?" My voice rose. "Where was your courtesy when you hurt me in that alley?"

David stiffened, his weapon coming back out as my voice throbbed with unresolved hatred and pain.

Penn didn't move. His hand stayed up, waiting for me to accept him. His eyes remained unreadable, but his lips softened as he murmured, "My courtesy is now. I came for you, Elle. I didn't save you from Greg so I could leave and never see you again. I came for you so you could give me a second chance."

I huffed. "I've already given you a second chance. You blew it."

98

"Third chance then."

Shaking my head, I wrapped arms around myself, suddenly cold in the ridiculous negligée. "I'm done with lies."

"Good, so am I." Penn stepped closer. "I promise you on that alley three years ago that I won't touch you, I won't hurt you, and I'll drive you home the moment we've talked."

"So you admit you were there. On the 19th of June."

David glanced at us, watching our conversation with steely concentration.

Penn nodded. "I admit it. Just like I want to admit all of it. If you agree to come with me."

Answers were so close. I was desperate for them. Hungrier for closure and truth than I'd ever been. It didn't matter he was just as handsome as when he'd taken my virginity. It didn't matter he was just as silver-tongued as when he'd coerced me to say yes to his seduction.

All that mattered was ending this, finishing the clues, and closing the story on this so-called romance.

David stepped closer, already knowing my decision before I did and ready to change my mind. "You can talk at a later date. Let me drive—"

I held up my hand, never looking away from Penn. "All right. I'll go with you, Mr. Everett, if that is even your real name." I stormed toward him, not caring he was dressed in blood and gore and so many unspeakable things from his past. A large bruise marked his cheek, his nose slightly swollen, his lip cut on the bottom. Despite all that, he was just as pretty as that night in the club when I'd said yes. "But the minute you've told me, I never want to see you again."

His jaw clenched. "Understood."

He moved toward the door. "Let's go. The sooner I tell you, the better."

I cringed at the bitter nastiness in his voice.

I couldn't help the sting.

He wanted to put this behind us, too. Whatever physical connection we shared wasn't enough to climb over the chasm of misdirection between us.

Good truth or bad.

Penn and I were over before we even began.

CHAPTER FOURTEEN

PENN

AN HOUR INTO the drive and we hadn't said a word.

I had so many of the bastards to say yet not a single sentence formed in my head.

Elle didn't help matters.

David had given her his blazer to sling over the gold thing she wore, and she sat with her arms and legs crossed, glaring at the road, the trees, the passing cars—anything but me.

Stopping for gas didn't make it any better.

While I pumped fuel into the hungry vehicle, she climbed out and entered the service station—not caring what she wore, making me fall even more with the aloof beauty she wielded.

Once I finished filling the Merc, I found her slipping into a pair of pink diamanté flip-flops and braiding her tangled hair with a rubber band. She stood in perfection, surrounded by chip packets, cold drinks, and smutty magazines.

Such a mundane store in a mundane world but Elle fucking took my breath away. She stood so strong, even after what that cunt had done to her. She still moved with authority even though I'd done my best to strip her of it.

She was older, wiser, and more supreme than she'd been that night in the alley but just as intoxicating.

I should probably buy some shoes too, but all I could think about was her.

Unable to tear my eyes off her, I walked into a display holding promotional chocolate bars, dislodging a sign and splattering it to the floor.

Her head jerked up, her lips pulling into half a smile as I spun around and marched to the counter to pay for the gas.

Shit.

The attendant swiped my card just as her electrical presence appeared by my side. My skin instantly rippled with chemistry, need, and heavy frustration that I'd been with this woman. That she'd let me into her body and started to open her heart, and now, I had no claim on her.

She wasn't mine standing in the middle of the gas station in a nightgown and bodyguard's blazer. She was free to be looked at, flirted with, and seduced.

I punched the credit card machine with fury.

"Can you pay for these, too? I don't have my purse with me." She dropped the price tag of the flip-flops and a bottle of water onto the counter, giving me a pointed look. "I'll pay you back."

I knew she'd pay me back. She was generous that way.

"I don't want your money. Call it a gift."

She shook her head. "No, it's fine."

How was she supposed to know buying her something— even something as simple as shoes and a drink—gave me more fucking pleasure than I'd had in years?

I wouldn't let her take that pleasure away from me.

I nodded, allowing her to think she'd won, not trusting my voice. Not trusting my body when she was around.

Every inch of me craved to grab her and just hold her. I didn't need to fuck her to feel close to her. I didn't need to kiss her to feel the supernova sensation I already drowned in.

Smiling at the attendant, Elle took her bottle of water and

padded out of the station in her new shoes. I watched her go, drinking in the sight of her toned legs and the way the blazer skimmed beneath her ass.

The cashier cleared his throat. "You'll have to swipe your card again. I've put the new amount in."

It hurt to trade the vision of her with him, but I did and paid the eight dollars she'd cost me before pocketing the receipt and leaving the store.

Elle had already climbed into the passenger seat, sipping on her water.

The way her throat moved.

The way her hair fell over her shoulder.

Goddammit, I needed to get myself under control so I could have a civilized conversation with this woman. Knowing Greg had touched her—*kissed* her—caused a dominating urge to crawl through me. I had to replace the last man who'd had his hands on her with me.

But what was the point?

She's going to leave the moment she knows anyway.

Then there'd be other men. Men much better than me in every way.

Hiding my sigh, I yanked open the Merc's door and slid behind the wheel.

I needed to let her go once I'd found a pair of balls big enough to tell her who I was. But sitting with her in the small space, inhaling her smell, wishing I hadn't been such an asshole...it hurt.

She wasn't wearing perfume but her natural scent alone was enough to make me rock fucking hard and going out of my goddamn mind.

Turning the key and throwing the Merc into gear, I revved the engine and rejoined traffic.

Glancing at her, I said, "Are you going to be silent the rest of the drive or are you going to talk—"

She held up her hand, taking another sip of water before screwing the cap on. "Not a word, Penn. Not one word until you can give me your undivided concentration."

"I can talk and drive at the same time."

"But can you tell the truth and look me in the eye?" A droplet lingered on her lower lip, making me suffer with the desire to wrench her close and kiss her so fucking hard she only felt lust, not anger.

But I kept my hands to myself—just like I promised and fell silent.

She wanted to wait?

Fine.

I would wait.

The next few hours would give me time to formulate how best to·tell her everything that'd happened to me, everything I was, and everything I would never be.

And I hoped to fucking God she didn't walk out the door the moment I'd finished and refused to see me again.

* * * * *

The drive that'd taken me all night and most of the day to find Elle only took a few hours in the opposite direction. Mainly streamlined by knowing the address and direction and going a more direct route.

New York glittered on the horizon, welcoming me back with hardship, promise, destitution, and wealth. I'd lived on two extremes. Poor and rich. Lost and found. Safe and scared. Most of the time, my new world was a thousand times better than my old one.

But that was before Elle.

Before I fucked everything up.

Pulling into the parking space attached to my apartment block, I turned off the engine and gripped the steering wheel with all the frustration and regret I couldn't show. Emotions I couldn't let her see if I was going to be honest tonight.

She had to think I had no shame. That I had accepted the consequences and wouldn't beg like a pussy for forgiveness.

The sun had gone down.

I couldn't remember the last time I'd slept, and I doubted

Elle had managed any either.

She'd been kidnapped and mentally tortured. If she wasn't so damn strong, I would've expected her to cry and nap the entire journey home.

But she hadn't.

She'd watched the view but never relaxed. Not once. Then again, neither had I.

Fuck, I really should've driven to her apartment and allowed her to take a shower, have some painkillers for her black eye, and rest before I dumped this shit on her.

I wasn't any better than Greg was by holding her hostage at my place.

However, Elle didn't seem to care. Climbing out, her pink flip-flops smacked the pavement in the direction of the front entrance. She hadn't waited for me to hold her door. She didn't need my help in any way.

I followed, making sure to lock the Merc, glowering at the tire marks on the street from the night I'd peeled after her when that bastard jumped her.

I knew his situation was a shitty one. I understood his pain.

But that didn't give him the right to touch what was mine.

I'd thought sleeping with her wouldn't change my steadfast plan to taste her and then move on. That was why I'd kicked her from my place only moments after being inside her. I needed space to clear my head and school my stupid fucking heart.

But that was before I found out she was a virgin.

Before she trusted me enough to give me that first time.

In an odd way...she'd waited for me.

And fuck, that twisted me up inside.

I hadn't deserved that gift. Not in the slightest. If she knew what I'd done, who I truly was...she wouldn't have let me anywhere near her, let alone inside her.

You didn't give her a choice. You stalked her. You infiltrated her life. You befriended her father. You're the worst kind of bastard.

I jogged (painfully) in front of her before she got to the front door. Inserting the key, I didn't make eye contact, didn't reach out to touch her.

I couldn't.

My bones bellowed from Greg's henchmen beating me awake and the recent fight with Greg himself. I suspected a rib might be broken, and my nose had definitely earned a new bump.

I was sick of the crusty blood on my knuckles and the throbbing in my joints. I wanted to rip off my dirty clothes and have a long hot shower, a triple shot of expensive vodka, then pass out cold in my bed.

But I couldn't do that either.

Because Elle came first. Just like she always had and always fucking would. She didn't have a clue what she meant to me and how much I'd thought about her, cursed her, and bargained with my fate over her.

For years, I'd hated her. I'd planned ways to make her pay. But now that she'd been in my arms, now that I'd tasted her, listened to her, fucked her...that hate? Shit, that hate had turned into something so much worse.

Elle didn't look over her shoulder as she entered the building. Her footsteps were weary as she placed one on the flight of stairs, preparing to haul herself to the twelfth floor.

"Wait." I strode to the left where the foyer bent in a crescent, hiding the two elevators that served the building. I'd had them repaired and ready to use. "This way."

She huffed but followed. The slap of her flip-flops sounded like an accusation.

Pressing the button, an elevator opened, and I held the doors while she ducked under my arm and jumped in. She kept her gaze on the old-fashioned round buttons as I stood beside her and pressed my floor.

The only floor renovated so far, and the one I would move out of once the building was ready for inhabitants. I'd rent each apartment and buy another for myself.

The doors closed, and the clunking of mechanisms filled the space.

Elle stiffened.

The atmosphere around us thickened. If there weren't so much unsaid shit between us, I'd shove her against the wall, haul up that ridiculous nightdress, and sink inside her. I'd force her to say hello to me, to see me, to truly listen.

But I'd lost that right.

I merely clenched my hands and counted the eternally long seconds in my head, so I didn't terrify her by slapping the emergency stop and forcing her to listen to me with no way out, nowhere to run, and no way to ignore me.

She shot out the second the elevator stopped and the doors slid open with rusty groans.

I followed, ducking around her to unlock the door. Stepping inside the art deco delight, I had no sense of comfort or relief at being back. My blood decorated the floor from the nosebleed I had as I barreled from the bed with thugs chasing me. The interior design company who'd modernized and styled the place had bought the furniture, so there was nothing of me in the walls or appliances. Nothing of me in anything because I'd been taught to be so transient in my world. To only covet that which I could carry. To only steal that which I could use. To only befriend those who wouldn't kill me.

The three cardinal rules.

Too bad, I broke all three the night I met Elle three years ago.

I'd coveted her when she wasn't mine to take. I'd stolen pieces I wanted because I had no choice. And I'd befriended her even when I should've kept my distance.

Elle kicked off her flip-flops by the door and padded barefoot to the black couch on chrome legs that made it look as if it hovered in the living room.

She sat demurely, her legs crossed, eyes narrowed with focus. She didn't ask to use the bathroom or beg to rest before we began.

She was all business.

"We're here. We're alone. Speak." Her chin came up. The loose braid she'd done in the gas station looped over her shoulder, begging me to fist it and drag her upright to kiss me. To take what I was desperate to take before she walked out the door and disappeared.

Not replying, I headed into the kitchen, grabbed two glasses, and filled them with water. Popping a few Advil—two for her, two for me—I took my haul to where she sat and waited until she held out her hand for the drugs then took the water.

We sipped silently, swallowing the painkillers as I sank into the chesterfield armchair at a right angle to where she sat on the couch.

She reached forward to put her half-empty glass on the coffee table, watching me carefully.

I didn't give up mine.

I kept it as physical support, tracing the droplets on the sides, smearing it with grime from my hands. I needed something to hold. Something to touch. I just wished it could be her.

"Are you going to spit it out, Penn, or do I need to leave?"

I brought the glass to my lips, buying another few seconds as I swallowed a cold mouthful.

She shifted impatiently, her thighs tight and fingers clutching the couch.

Wiping my lips with the back of my hand, I said quietly, "Where do you want me to start?"

She flinched as if I'd shouted. Her shoulders stayed around her ears as she snapped, "How about the beginning?"

"There are too many beginnings to know which one you mean."

She rolled her eyes. "Stop with the riddles and spit it out."

I inhaled hard. "You want to know about the alley."

She nodded, her tone sarcastic. "Obviously. If that's where you want to start."

I risked looking at her. Our eyes locked, heat and fire and brimstone. Passion and lust and denial. So much denial. She looked at me as if I wasn't worthy of being close to her even though I'd saved her life.

Twice.

"I was there."

"I know." She crossed her arms. "What part did you play?"

"Part?" I frowned.

"Were you the one to rip my clothes, steal my necklace, or try and force me to give a blowjob?"

I winced, gripping the glass too hard. Any harder, it would splinter. Placing it on the table, it wobbled in my haste to be free of it.

Elle flinched; her nostrils flared, waiting for my damning response.

Familiar anger toward her rose. Anger I was more acquainted with than whatever I felt now. Shoving myself off the chair, I slammed to my knees in front of her.

Grabbing her face, I held her firm as she shied backward, trying to get free.

My fingers dug into her cheeks, holding her even as she latched her fingers around my wrists and scratched me hard. "Let me go."

I didn't answer.

I couldn't answer.

My lips sought hers.

I dragged her forward, our mouths connecting in a vicious kiss.

She cried out as I held her close. My tongue licked her seam, begging for entry but not forcing, even though every cell in my body demanded to shove her back, climb on top, and show her in actions not words who I was.

It fucking hurt that she had to ask. That she looked at me and wasn't convinced. That she could think such awful things about me. That she couldn't *see*.

Her tiny fist connected with my sternum. If I hadn't been punched there a few times already, it wouldn't have registered over the sex haze in my brain. But she prodded a deep bruise, stealing my air, making me pull back.

"Stop touching me." Her voice was a hiss, a threat, a plea.

I didn't let her go, drinking in her rage, sinking into the vulnerability in her gaze. "How can you ask that question?"

She coughed in surprise. "What question?"

"Who I am?"

She bared her teeth. "Because I don't know."

"You do know. You've known all along."

"Wrong. You've lied to me from day one."

I shook my head sadly. "I never lied to you, Elle. Not once."

She swatted away my hands, sucking in a breath. "You lied about *everything*."

"Did I lie about how much I want you? Did I lie how much I—"

"You're going to sit there and claim whatever it was between us was purely physical?"

"*Is*. Not was. It's not past tense." I took her hand, my cock hardening against the intoxicating buzz between us.

"Answer the question, Penn." She tried to untangle her fingers from mine.

I didn't let her.

I wanted to nod with conviction. To say the connection linking and pinging and zapping like nuclear energy was nothing more than shallow lust. But we both knew emotions had crept their sneaky asses into our lives long before we'd acknowledged it.

They'd been there since that very first night.

They'd been there every day for three goddamn years.

I'd hunted her down, invaded her life, and befriended her father because of emotion. To deny that would be the worst kind of lie because it would mean I'd have to lie to myself.

"I won't say that because it's not true."

"Oh!" She rolled her eyes. "You're finally going with truth."

I scowled. "I promised, didn't I?"

She laughed, hard and brittle. "Sorry if I don't believe you. That I don't believe you're going to answer me honestly for the first time—"

"You dare lecture me on honesty?"

"You dare deny you've been anything but a liar?"

"Elle," I snarled. "Don't start an argument you can't win. You want the truth. I'm giving you the truth. You've known the fucking truth all along."

She stood up, knocking me sideways. My arm flew out, smashing her glass of water off the coffee table. Liquid spilled in a waterfall onto the brown and turquoise retro rug but I didn't care.

She charged for the door.

Launching upright, I chased after her. My body hurt, my head pounded, but I caught her arm, spinning her to face me. "Stop."

"Let me go." She kicked my knees, anger painting red spots on her cheeks. "I don't want to be here."

"You do. You have to listen."

"I don't have to do anything." Her chest puffed as she inhaled hard. "Let me go, Penn, or whoever you are." Her face turned nasty. "Or should I say Gio or Sean."

The world froze.

She remembered?

Christ, three years and she remembered.

Her father had said she was intelligent and I'd seen first-hand how capable and strong she was but to remember…fuck.

My heart raced. "My name is Penn."

"But what was it three years ago?"

Passion raged through me. I wanted nothing more than to hurt her the way she'd hurt me. To force her to be honest the way she was asking me to be. Couldn't she see she stabbed me with a blade each time she believed I wasn't who I said?

"It's always been Penn."

Does that answer your question? See me. See who I am.

It would be so easy to come out and tell her. To wrap my lips around the words and reveal my secret. But just as I hated her three years ago, I hated her now for doubting. If what'd happened that night was real she shouldn't have to ask.

She should know.

Just like I knew.

She should hurt as much as I did.

I'll show her.

The ridiculous idea popped into my head. Wrapping my fingers around her throat, I marched her backward toward the kitchen wall. She stumbled, her hand coming up to fight against my hold. "Let—let me go."

I didn't stop, not when she tripped and I had to pluck her feet from the floor and hoist her into my arms, not when she kicked my shins as I crashed her against the wall, and not when I grabbed her chin, held her firm, and kissed her like she ought to have been fucking kissed for the past three years.

She was a virgin.

She'd waited.

I liked to think she'd waited for me. That her body had always been mine just like her heart. But I was in the habit of lying to others, not to myself, so I wouldn't believe such fantasy.

Her tongue tangled with mine. Her breath feeding my lungs as I devoured her.

Her sharp moan made me pull back. Panting hard, I murmured, "I was there. I'll tell you even though you already know. I'm—"

A fist hammered on my door. "Police. Open up."

Elle froze in my arms.

My muscles atrophied in horror.

Shit.

Shit.

Shit.

I thought I'd have more time.

I thought I'd tell her. Explain why I'd acted the way I had, and then either win the lottery by having her forgive me or drive her home, so I knew she was safe.

It's too soon.

I haven't finished.

I knew they'd come for me. It was a risk I'd been willing to take. A chance I had to take to save her. But not so soon. Not before I could fix what I'd ruined.

"Elle, I'm—"

Her eyes flared wide as the pounding came again. "Penn Everett, open this door. Immediately."

"Fuck." I raked a hand through my hair, stepping away from Elle, seeing all my dreams and wishes evaporate into dust.

Elle slipped back onto her toes, smashing a hand over her mouth. "Oh, my God."

I didn't know if her sudden profanity was at our interruption or my roundabout confession. Her face shot white. Her eyes searching for something real, something she could latch onto and find—

"We know you're in there. Open up!" the police barked, destroying everything—just like they'd destroyed the first night we met. Just like they destroyed my entire fucking life before I ever found Elle in that alley.

My gaze danced around my apartment, looking for something, *anything*, that I could use against what was about to happen.

But I was at a loss.

All because I'd let the violence in my blood carry me away.

My shoulders sank with depression. There was no getting around this. Unfortunately, this time, I deserved what would happen.

Larry is gonna be so pissed.

Swallowing hard, I glanced one last time at Elle and stalked to the front door. I opened it just as an officer raised his hand to thump again. "It's open. Calm the fuck down."

One moment, I was a free man standing in my own apartment trying to repair the damage with a girl I would never admit to caring for.

The next, I was a prisoner held between two officers, brute force yanking my arms back even when I offered no retaliation.

"Penn Everett, you're under arrest."

I laughed.

It was the only fucking thing I could do.

That night.

That field.

That kiss.

Elle lost her shock, dashing forward and hanging on the arm of the officer who snapped the metal restraints over my wrists. "Wait, you can't do this."

A female rookie with a fresh uniform, polished buttons, and a never-been-used weapon stepped forward and pulled her back. "Ma'am, don't touch the arresting officer."

Elle whirled on her. "Don't touch him? Well, tell *him* not to touch him." She pointed at me, her hand shaking. "We're not done. I need to talk to him."

"He's done." The officer who caught me grinned with smugness. His ginger hair prickled like a hedgehog with his buzz cut. "Guess you're going home, huh?"

I glowered.

Elle shook her head. "What's that supposed to mean?"

The officer replied, "It means I've followed his record, and it was only a matter of time until he slipped again. They always do." He chuckled, motioning to the rookie to grab an elbow and march me toward the door.

I went with them. I offered no resistance.

Things would only get worse if I did.

"Wait. You can't do this. Release him." Elle stayed by my side, fighting all over again for me.

Does she remember that night?

Did she remember the way she begged for my freedom in

the park? The way she'd run as hard as she could and offered herself as a sacrifice when she couldn't run anymore? The way she'd kissed me breathless and frantic in the bushes while I waited for the police to take me because I didn't want her to hurt or fear anymore?

I'd fallen for her for that.

I'd fallen so fucking hard in only a heartbeat. She'd been the only good thing in my world. The only light after so much darkness. How could I control my free fall when she treated me with such kindness? When she'd kissed me. When she'd trusted me. When she'd given me half the chocolate bar I'd stolen from the convenience store only an hour before meeting her?

Christ, I'd fallen so damn hard, I hadn't recovered from the bruises even years later.

It was only till after I was freed from prison did my infatuation with the princess I'd met that night turn to malice. Such simple adoration twisted the more I learned about her. The more I researched and grasped at fragments of information widely available online and in newspapers.

She was rich.

She was powerful.

She could've helped free me.

But she hadn't.

She'd left me to rot.

She'd lied to me that night about feeling something. Because if she'd felt half of what I had, she wouldn't have left me behind bars without doing everything in her goddamn power to find me.

But I'd grown up since then.

Since Larry found me and did what I'd hoped she would. I finally had someone on my side, and it wasn't her.

I wasn't proud, but I'd let the snowballing hate smash through whatever ground I'd stood on. I'd fallen harder for her but the wrong way this time. I'd allowed my stupid sleuthing to tarnish the only good thing in my world and turn it into the chalice of everything I despised.

I'd never felt like that before.

Never been so livid against injustice and frustration and anger. I'd known weakness and helplessness. I'd know destitution and abandonment. I'd known terror and shame and respect and confusion and every fucking emotion on the roulette called life.

But I'd never known love until her.

And I'd never known hate until her.

Never laid awake at night with my guts churning and heart burning and a paralysis that kept me stuck forever thinking about her.

Her out there. Free.

Her out there. Rich.

Her out there. While I was inside trapped and crippled by a system that'd failed me in every fucking way since I'd been born.

I had nothing to say as the officers led me from the apartment I'd paid for in cash—cash I'd earned the right way, not the wrong way—and crammed me into the hallway.

Elle chased us.

Her face alive. Her eyes disbelieving that once again, the law would tear us apart. She didn't even know. She didn't trust, even now. She believed I was Gio or Sean.

How fucking could she?

How could she kiss me and not trust in that?

How could she think I was a rapist when I had so much I wanted to fucking say to her but never would?

You hurt me, Elle.

More than anyone.

In a strange way, I was glad I wouldn't be allowed to see her again. It made this so much easier. I wouldn't have to deal with the betrayal or spill everything I'd done to make amends.

I wouldn't have to admit I was wrong.

That she was rich and powerful and above most rules, but she hadn't forgotten me. I knew better now. She would've come for me. If only I'd told her my goddamn name that night instead of keeping it secret—terrified she'd be embarrassed by me. That she'd go from thinking I was a down-on-his-luck passerby and know the truth. The truth that my bed consisted of cardboard and donated blankets. That my meals consisted of charity and theft.

It was my fault.

And hers.

We'd fucked up together.

All this time, I thought I would be begging for her forgiveness. That she would walk out of my life once she knew I'd lied to her and I admitted just how much my hate navigated my actions.

But in reality, I would leave her and the justice system would banish her from my world.

"Stop!" Elle stood to her full height in her ridiculous gold negligée, wrapping herself in authority not many excel at and few are born with. "Let him go. I won't ask again."

"Ms. Charlston?" David, her driver, bodyguard, and fucking nuisance, climbed the stairs with his arms loose by his sides. He seemed to have a knack for turning up at the wrong time.

Did he not trust me with his employer?

That made two of them.

His languid steps didn't fool me. He was packing and just itching to draw. He'd wanted this ever since he recognized me the night I picked Elle up at the Blue Rabbit and took her back to my place to fuck her the first time.

He'd glared into my eyes, and in that glimpse, we'd both relived that night in Central Park. The night when he'd come to claim sweet nineteen-year-old Elle and left me on my own. I'd expected him to say something. To say more than 'he looks familiar' but he hadn't. He'd zipped his lips and let Elle decide who to believe I was.

I had to give him credit for that, at least.

"David, tell them to let him go." Elle whirled toward him, looking to him to fix this. He might've stopped Elle from being arrested three years ago, but he hadn't done it for me then, and he wouldn't do it for me now.

His jaw tightened, his dark skin hiding stress and anger better than Elle's pale complexion as he moved to her side. He didn't touch her. Professional until the end. "Greg woke up and pressed charges. Mr. Everett hurt him. He'll have to suffer the consequences."

Elle growled, "Greg kidnapped me. He was seconds away from raping me. Penn stopped him."

The officer with red hair mumbled, "Greg will be taken in for questioning, too, once he's been cleared at the hospital."

"Hospital?" Elle threw her hands up. "Are you kidding me? He'll have a few bruises. He's over-acting the entire thing."

The office shook his head. "Reports of a bruised larynx and broken ribs have been confirmed by the doctors. It's a serious matter, Ms. Charlston, and both parties will be dealt with."

At least I'd hurt him.

He deserved to be in pain.

The rookie sidled up to Elle. My hackles rose as she said, "When you've returned home and eh, recuperated." She looked at the state of Elle's undress. "You're required to come to the station to submit your statement about how Greg Hobson took you, what his intentions were in the cabin, and any outstanding issues we need to be aware of."

Elle spasmed with anger. "I can tell you all that right now. In exchange for letting Mr. Everett go."

I chuckled. "Come on, Elle. You know from experience they won't do that. Just leave me like you did the first time."

Her hands wedged in her stomach as if I'd physically hit her. "Do you think I'm that heartless?" She moved closer, dragging my gaze to her perfect body and just how fucking much I suffered when it came to her. Love her. Hate her. Adore her. Abhor her. I could never win.

Because I wasn't telling the truth.

The truth was I'd never felt like this for anyone.

Ever.

I'm in love with you, you chocolate-kissing, night time stealing, gorgeous girl. And I'm pissed as hell about it.

My shoulders straightened. I would never tell her because she hadn't earned my truth. The only person who had was Larry.

Fuck, Larry.

I had to talk to him the moment I was allowed a phone call.

The ginger officer guided me toward the stairs. "Time to go."

"Penn, please!" Elle wrung her hands. "I believe you. Don't punish me for fearing the worst."

Was it wrong of me to want her to hurt just a little? To make her feel how awful it was not to have someone trust you.

Tears brimmed in her blue eyes, begging me to relieve that hurt.

I cursed her. But I couldn't let her suffer.

Tugging against the cop's pressure, I said, "Go into the kitchen. Above the fridge is a safe deposit box. Combination is 0619—19th of June."

Elle half-gasped, half-sobbed.

Before she could say anything, I added, "Inside, you'll find things that will answer some of your questions, but you'll also find my emergency details. Call Larry Barns."

"All right, enough chitchat." The officer pushed me.

My feet descended the stairs. "Tell him I need his services again. Tell him I know I fucked up but he better come."

Elle nodded, her hands grasping the banister as she stayed on my floor, and I slowly headed below. "Can you say it out loud? Admit what happened between us that night. Please…I need to hear that, Penn…"

Even now, she still had a splinter of doubt puncturing her trust.

Fuck, that hurts.

I smiled harshly. "The fact that you have to ask is all the

answer I'll give you." I glanced down, judging how many steps to go. How many steps before I was trapped behind barbwire and bars again.

Tears welled in her gaze. "So you *are* Nameless?"

I shrugged. "I've never been called Nameless. But if you're asking who I am? How can I tell you? How can I make you see what you don't want to see?"

"But I *do* want to see. I've been dying to see for three years. I've been trying to find you, Penn. I—"

"Stop, Elle." I didn't want to hear her declarations of hardship. Of the occasional half-hearted search while she lived in her crystal tower and I rotted in a cell.

We reached the landing, ready to turn and vanish from Elle's line of sight. I gave her all I could. I finally admitted my truth. "I can't tell you who I am because I never told you my name. I could give you any name, and you would never know it was real because you never knew me."

The officers prodded me. "Get going."

I ignored them. "All you need to know is how I made you feel. What did you feel when I kissed you on that baseball field? How did you feel when I gave you the only food I'd had in days? How did you feel when you walked away from me and didn't look back?"

Her tears broke her disciplined wall, turning from sorrow to sob. "God, I felt something huge, something I'd never felt before. I fell for you when I didn't even know what that was." She whirled down a few steps, only for David to stop her from chasing me. "Penn, I'm sorry. So sorry."

Her apology didn't fade the pain I'd carried for so long.

I sighed sadly. "Glad to know it wasn't just one of us who fell that night."

The rookie shoved me forward.

I didn't look back.

Just like she hadn't three years ago.

Chapter Fifteen

Elle

APARTMENT HALLWAYS HAD a habit of causing damage to furniture edges and being scuffed by human traffic, but I never thought it had the power to hurt knees and palms.

Until I slammed to all fours under the colossal weight of despair.

"I can't tell you who I am because I never told you my name."

How many words in that single sentence? How heavy the truth in that string of confession? Enough to steal the remaining energy in my limbs and throw me headfirst into faintness.

I wasn't a woman anymore. I was sharp breaths, swirling thoughts, and lost bearings. Falling forward as if in prayer, begging the world for a better answer delivered in a kinder way, I pleaded for a do-over.

I'd dreamed of finding Nameless. I'd had fantasies of loving him, saving him, proving to myself that what I'd felt that night wasn't some silly teenage fling but the start of something raw and terrible and utterly undeniable.

But that was before he'd looked at me with pain so deep-seated, so long lived with, he couldn't stop the flash of disgust in his eyes.

He *blamed* me.

He blamed me for not finding him, for not doing exactly what I'd promised myself I'd do and didn't.

Oh, God.

I hugged my waist, ignoring the bruises from Greg and focusing on the bruises on my heart. I needed to touch him, promise him that I believed now. That I *trusted* now.

But how flimsy was that?

How awful of me to doubt and accuse, unable to see that my wishes had come true and I'd done nothing but fight against him since he came for me.

To finally find Nameless.

To come face-to-face with him and put aside the three years and pick up exactly where we left off—with passion and purity and no lies or worries.

That was the stupid teenage ideal, not the night we met. The belief that years later it would still be unsullied and ready to morph into something true.

It's ruined.

It's over.

My life had gone the exact opposite of everything I'd wanted.

Did young-hearted idealism make him my perfect other? Or fate?

Was he right to look at me as if I was a coward?

Penn had stared at me, not with happiness and satisfaction at finally reuniting, but with regret and disappointment. He acted as if he couldn't forgive me for not trusting the nudgings of my heart that his secret was one I'd wanted, not one I didn't.

How did I think he was Baseball Cap? How could I ever call him Adidas? Why was I so *weak*?

A soft gray blanket fell over my shoulders, smelling of Penn. David crouched beside me, rubbing my back with a warm, heavy hand. Slowly, he took my weight, plucking me from the dirty carpet of the hallway and onto my feet.

The minute I was standing, he guided me into Penn's

apartment and motioned for me to sit.

To sit in the exact same place where Penn had sat just moments before. The place where my heart had started to unravel, already hearing Penn's truth but somehow unable to let go of my anger and finally believe.

He'd lied.

He'd been an asshole and covered up any sweetness that existed inside him.

Why?

Why be a jerk when I would've leapt into his arms the moment he'd told me the truth?

Why the make-believe?

Why didn't I recognize him?

Why couldn't I see the similarities between Penn and Nameless?

Why couldn't I see past the beard and dirty hoodie?

Why couldn't I see past the suits and wealth?

Why?

Why?

Why?

Ignoring David's request to sit, I stood and beelined for the cupboard above Penn's stainless steel fridge. Reaching on my tiptoes, I was able to touch but not grab the small safety deposit box.

I can't—

I tried to manhandle it, but my stupid fingers couldn't reach. I turned to spy a chair to stand on, but David reached for me and placed the metal navy box on the kitchen counter.

I didn't like him all that much currently. He'd prevented me from chasing after Penn. *Nameless.*

All along, he's been Nameless.

My heart stopped skipping a beat and settled for a jangled symphony instead.

I might not like David at the moment, but I kept my manners. "Thank you."

"You're welcome."

The box was heavy but not one to screw into a floor or wall. This was movable, only opened by the combination.

The combination Penn gave me.

The combination of the night we met.

Was that an unnecessary stab at my romantic ideals or had he felt something so strange that night?

You know he did.

He admitted it.

His voice echoed in my head with such delicious words. Words that clenched my tummy, suffocated my lungs, and restarted my heart. *"Glad to know it wasn't just one of us who fell that night."*

And now, he'd been taken again. Locked up where I couldn't reach him.

Holding back more tears, I inputted the code and spun the dial. Holding my breath, I slouched in relief as the mechanism unlocked, beckoning me to lift the lid and learn its contents.

Cracking the top, I glanced at the treasure trove Penn had decided was valuable enough to keep safe.

Inside was his passport, a wad of one hundred dollar bills, an envelope marked stocks and bonds, and another one with the words: *'In an emergency.'* I opened that one, pulling out what I assumed was Larry's phone number.

David passed me his cell-phone before I could ask. His smile was knowing, his eyes obedient, even if he didn't necessarily agree with what I was about to do.

I took his phone but paused. "You knew. Didn't you?"

He clasped his hands in front of his belt buckle. "I had my suspicions when I recognized him outside the Blue Rabbit."

"Yet you didn't say anything?"

"It wasn't my place."

"Not your place to protect me?"

He smiled, chuckling softly. "My place is to protect your body. It was never in my contract to protect your heart." He motioned to the phone. "You already called me a meddler like your personal assistant. I wasn't about to risk my job by telling you who or who not to date."

Awkwardness fell between us. I'd spent years with David, yet we'd never had a truly frank conversation—especially about my love life.

"Just out of curiosity." I turned his phone on, typing in Larry's number. "Would you have protected my heart if I'd decided to date Greg like my father and Steve wanted?" My thumb hovered over the call button, waiting for David's answer.

He smiled, but it tinged with rage that Greg had taken me out of his custody and hurt me. "I would've fired myself if you'd announced you were with him." His lips twitched. "Respectfully, of course, Ma'am."

Despite everything—the lies, the police, the fact that Penn was Nameless and he'd just been carted away for the second time—I smiled. "That's what I thought."

I pressed the call button as David said, "For what it's worth, I do believe he's a good guy. If you read between the lines, that is."

"I know." I held the phone to my ear. A ring tone sounded. "I saw it that first night."

I just forgot to trust it and not let doubt and disbelief get in my way.

I knew Penn was a good guy—despite his jackass ways the past few weeks.

In his mind, I deserved that treatment.

In my mind, I kind of agreed with him.

"Larry speaking."

My questions snapped away, leaving more important things. "Larry, this is Elle Charlston. Penn's been arrested."

He reacted straight away. "Ah, damn, I feared something like this would happen."

"Something like this?"

"Him getting mixed up with you. It's not exactly good for his temper."

I agreed Penn had a temper, but he could also control it. He'd unleashed it twice since I'd known him and both were to protect me.

He had my back. I hadn't had his.

God, I had to stop tormenting myself and fix what was broken, not focus on the reason for it. "It would've been a lot simpler if he'd told me the truth from the beginning."

"I did tell him that." Larry sighed. "Did he tell you the truth now?"

"As the police dragged him away, yes."

"And?" Larry prompted.

"And what?"

"How do you feel?" His tone cajoled.

"I...I don't know."

Confused.

Annoyed.

Frightened.

Guilty.

"What does that mean?" He sighed again, heavier this time. "Look, when I first helped him, he kept his feelings for you a secret. He didn't tell me about the girl in Central Park. But after a while, he confided in me. When I managed to revoke his sentence and free him, he said he would track you down and see if what you had was a one-night spark or real."

He didn't continue.

I blurted, desperate for more. "What else...what else did he talk about?"

"He, uh—he found you."

"Obviously."

"No, he found you the night he was released." He waited for that bomb to destroy me. "He found you and then refused to contact you."

Tears puddled inside, growing wetter with every breath. "Why?"

"I'm guessing that's his part to tell." He cleared his throat. "I'd better go. I'll get my ass down to the station and start the proceedings to free him. Again." Something clattered in the background. "I don't know how things ended with you tonight, but if you want, call me tomorrow, and I'll arrange a time for you to see him once he's been processed."

My heart lurched. "Wait, he won't be released tonight?"

Larry laughed as if I'd told a hilarious joke. "No, my dear. Where Penn is concerned, the NYPD have a thing against him. They'll keep him locked up for as long as they can. And they'll succeed."

"Why?"

"Because they have history."

CHAPTER SIXTEEN

PENN

I FUCKING HATED bars.

I hated metal sinks and hard-ass beds.

I hated the men who were as corrupt as everyone else, getting high off shiny badges and getting hard on screwing over innocence.

Fair and just, my ass.

The short journey down to the precinct irritated me. The cops and their radios irritated me. Pedestrians and traffic lights irritated me.

Everything fucking irritated me because I knew I wouldn't be treated fairly.

The moment I was on their turf, I had no power.

None.

I sat in fury, listening to my heartbeat pounding and splashing around in pools of regret. For once, the regret wasn't toward Elle but Larry. I'd let him down. I'd promised him I wouldn't be in this situation again because it was too fucking hard to get free last time when I'd done nothing wrong.

This time...I *had* done something wrong.

I'd beaten up Greg.

They had reason to detain me, and the man out for my blood would fucking wring his hands in glee when I showed up. He would ensure Greg would elaborate and collaborate; he'd document my victim's injuries with pride, and he would once again take great satisfaction in fucking over my life knowing he had me fair and square.

It wouldn't matter Greg had been the kidnapper and about-to-be rapist. It wouldn't matter his crimes far exceeded my own. And it didn't matter I'd been taken shoeless, moneyless, and with dried blood and gore all over my body.

It would make an interesting mug shot.

It would only make his workday that much more enjoyable.

My head ached with the battle I was about to walk into. I wanted to rub my face, but the cuffs kept my hands tied. New York spat me out like a worm from the apple as the cop car slid through the reinforced gates and into Hell.

I didn't make eye contact or listen to the bastards who'd arrested me as they opened the vehicle, let me climb out with my motherfucking dignity, and didn't dare touch me as we stalked into the processing room.

And wouldn't you know? He was there already.

Him.

My nemesis.

His uniform, like always, was iron-creased with starched perfection. His salt and pepper hair cut short on the sides and balding on top. The paunch from too many years spent behind a desk and too much gluttony on the lost dreams of others thickened his middle.

His hands annoyed me.

His face annoyed me.

His entire fucking body pissed me the fuck off.

I stood tall, bracing my legs. "Hello, Arnold."

His chapped lips opened in undisguised joy. "Ah, hello again, Everett. Fancy seeing you here. This is my lucky day."

He bared his teeth with bipolar emotions. "By the way, it's chief of police to you."

"Chief?" I cocked my head condescendingly. "Seems, I owe you congratulations. Last time you fucked me over, you were only a captain."

He buffed his nails on his shirt, gloating. "Yes, well, I've moved up the ranks since then."

Not good.

Fucking so not good for me.

"So it's Chief Twig now?" I wrinkled my nose. "No better than Captain Twig, is it? An unfortunate last name you've got there, Arnie."

His face reddened with anger. "You honestly want to piss me off? You know what happened last time, boy."

"I do remember last time. Quite clearly, in fact." I smirked. "And I have no doubt being polite or begging for mercy will get me the exact same conclusion as being a fucking bastard. So do your worst."

I shifted on the spot, spreading my stance. "Oh, and I'm no longer a boy. Then again, keep calling me that if it make's you feel better, seeing as I could kick your ass back when I was thirteen."

The other officers stepped forward, one on either side to teach me a lesson in respect.

But Arnold waved them off. He enjoyed breaking me too much to let others do it. "I'll take it from here, ladies and gentlemen. Good work bringing in this violent repeat offender. Coffee's on me."

"Not a problem, Chief." The officers left, closing the door behind them.

I wished they hadn't.

If they'd stay for the show, they'd finally learn what a twisted, immoral bastard their captain, now chief, was.

The room turned stagnant with history, slurs, and a past both of us would like to delete.

"Don't you mean the donuts are on you?" I glared at his

waistline. "Put on a few pounds there, Arnie."

His hands clenched into balls, but he smiled tightly. "Keep being a dick and your rap sheet will just get longer and longer."

"I don't need to be a dick for that to happen. By the time I'm out of this place, the protection of a woman from an asshole about to rape her will have morphed into armed robbery, intent to kill, child molesting, and most likely a bank job and grannie murder." I smiled, even though I felt like tearing the room apart with rage. "Isn't that right, *Arnie*?"

He matched my smile, both of us using a normally kind human response to wield emotion filled with contempt and loathing. "You got it, my boy."

"If you're going to use a term of endearment, how about you choose a more appropriate one?"

Arnold grinned. "What would you prefer?"

"Oh, I dunno. How about the truth for once? Scapegoat? Fall Guy? Whipping Boy? Any of those work."

I'm the one you blame and take the rap for others, you lying sack. Might as well own up to it.

His face blackened. "Keep your voice down."

"Why? So your staff won't find out what a heartless cunt you are?"

He flinched.

I didn't stop.

"Five years of my life you stole on three different occasions—all for things I didn't do. And now, you're about to steal more. But this time, I'm not gonna be so silent. I have a family now. I'm rich. Charge me with whatever you goddamn like, but rest assured, I won't have some shitty state-appointed lawyer who's on your payroll to shuttle me off to the slammer and then be beaten by your men to keep me silent inside."

I took a step toward him.

It was a balancing act of pushing but not being an idiot. Any one of his officers could shoot me if they thought I was threatening him.

"I'm not afraid of you anymore." I lowered my voice. "Do

your worst. Let's fucking dance, Arnie. Let's see who wins this
time."

CHAPTER SEVENTEEN

ELLE

WAS IT WRONG of me that I'd taken Penn's box?

Was it immoral to sit on my bed after the longest bath in history, biggest dinner I could stomach, countless checks on my father and his heart, and endless cuddles from Sage to open his box of secrets?

For the past three hours, I'd assured Dad I was okay, made sure he was okay, answered his questions, dodged others, and then lamented with him while he directed his red-hot fury at Greg.

Steve called professing apologies, David stood guard at my door—even though I told him that wasn't necessary—and Sage wouldn't let me go even to use the bathroom on my own.

She curled up on a towel on the edge of the bath while I soaked away the aches and bruises Greg had given me.

Afterward, she swatted the belt of my Terry cloth robe as I padded warm, tired, and finally alone to my bedroom.

And there was Penn's box.

Begging me to read its contents.

To pry.

To sneak.

To steal everything I could about him.

I'd stared at it for the past hour while both angel and devil squatted on my shoulders, whispering to keep it closed, muttering to open it, murmuring to trust, nudging to search.

I'd failed him in the hallway when he was taken. I'd failed him when he'd kissed me, and I fought the knowledge my heart already knew.

Was I failing him again by picking apart his lies and seeking the truth without him here to fill in the blanks?

He's Nameless.

Wasn't that all that mattered?

I thought it would feel different to finally know.

To hear him admit that he was there, he was the chocolate kisser, he was the Central Park romance.

But his confession had split me. I couldn't add up the Penn I knew and the Nameless one I didn't. They didn't match. Why had he changed so much? *Had* he changed or was it all an act?

The stupid fantasy that I'd believed in of finding Nameless and picking up where we left off, faltered. What if that kismet attraction and instantaneous lust weren't enough to delete the mess between us and start afresh?

I'd slept with him. I'd lost my virginity to the man I'd been dreaming of for three long years.

I felt…ashamed.

I'm confused.

I'm angry with him and myself.

I didn't know how to make sense of anything anymore.

It made me doubt everything I'd felt that night and tarnished it because if I could be around Penn this long and not fall insanely in love with him, then what did that mean about that night in Central Park?

Open the box.

Stop wasting time.

Sage batted it with her paw, meowing softly as if she didn't approve of the foreign object taking up space on my lap. Her soft silver fur glowed warm like a tiny moonbeam, her tail flicking in impatience and curiosity.

"Don't look at me like that. Go. Fetch." I threw her purple mouse that was missing its tail and half of its whiskers.

She arched a kitty eyebrow as if pitying me that I thought she'd play catch like a dog. I merely held her stare until she scowled and leaped off the bed, hunting for the thrown toy.

While her back was turned and her judgy eyes were elsewhere, I cracked the lid and held my breath.

I held my breath until my head swam and my heart knocked on my ribs in a reminder that it needed oxygen to breathe.

I didn't want to breathe because beneath the emergency contact numbers was a driver's license of a man I wished I could forget; one I wished I could delete and pretend never existed.

Baseball Cap.

Gio...I believe.

I recalled the two men calling each other names but couldn't be entirely sure I'd remembered them correctly.

Then again, his name printed on the license told me I was right.

Why could I remember him so clearly when I'd struggled to place Penn?

My fingers shook as I plucked the laminated identification and stared into the heartless eyes of the man who'd tried to rape me. Without the cap, his hair was shaggy and unkempt, mousy brown with matching uneven stubble on his jaw.

He was nothing like Nameless.

Nothing connecting us enough to evoke the emotions Penn did.

How could I think Penn was him?

How could I have let the years erase the feeling of disgust and terror?

Penn wasn't Baseball Cap or Adidas.

He could *never* have been, and I must have known that all along.

Oh, my God.

Dropping the license, I clamped a hand over my mouth.

How insulting to him.

What a slap in the face for me to believe he could be as evil as those two bastards.

He was right to hate me.

Could he forgive me?

But why does he have Gio's license?

Gio Markus Steel according to his full address.

Steel…that name was familiar. It flopped around inside my head like a fish on a line, ready to reel in, but the string was too tangled to haul.

What was Larry keeping secret on Penn's behalf? Who *was* Penn? Where did he come from? His family? His past?

He'd given me a tiny part of himself, but I needed more.

So much more.

Steel!

I sat upright in bed, recalling the day Penn had ambushed me at work. The day I'd done my floor inspections and come upon a little boy having a suit made from a man's.

Master Steel.

Same last name as Gio.

Did that mean Stewie and Gio were related?

Argh!

How could I unravel this mayhem and make sense of it without Penn to guide me?

Penn had saved my life—multiple times—but now, I needed him to save me from my questions.

There was only one way for him to do that.

I have to see him again.

Chapter Eighteen

Penn

I KNEW THE process—I'd done it a few times before—but it didn't make it any easier.

The first time had been scary as fuck with a night in the station, arraignment with a useless public defender nodding to felonies I hadn't committed, and no cash to post bail. It took days to join gen pop before I settled in to serve time for a crime I hadn't done.

That night had also been the first time I'd had the joy of meeting Arnold Twig.

Fucker.

I'd served one year, one month of a three-year sentence—let off for good behavior.

The second time was unfortunate bad luck, but once again, Arnold was there to ensure I was the perfect scapegoat.

A night in the holding cells, another useless arraignment, another district attorney advising bail I couldn't afford, and then I was back in jail.

Once there, I enjoyed a two week stay in the infirmary after a vicious beating ensured my lips remained firmly shut about the secrets Arnold Twig had no intention of letting me spill.

I'd served three years, two months of a four-year sentence—let off once again for good behavior.

The third time had been the night I met Elle. The night when my heart was full and my head hurt, knowing if Arnold had his way, I'd be in prison for a lot longer.

He'd shuttled me back to Hell as fast as he could. The moment dawn arrived, he'd yanked me from the cell and sent me to the district attorney with yet another jaded public defender. By the afternoon, I was in a prison uniform and holding out a plastic tray for food.

Hey, at least I got to eat that day.

That night, though…fuck, that night I couldn't stop tormenting myself with memories of kissing the girl I'd rescued, imagining we'd been able to finish what we started— that in a better, kinder world, I would've asked to see her again and done my best to get off the streets so I could deserve her.

And now, while my bones still cried and my clothes hid a fight-sweaty body, Arnold once again expedited my case.

After our little chat, he personally escorted me to complete the sham of gathering my official information.

I refused to say a word apart from, "bite my ass."

Besides, I had no reason to give up my name, age, and entire autobiography. They had that information already.

My file listed exactly who I was and precisely what my past convictions entailed.

What was it again? Oh, yeah.

Incident number one—grand theft auto.

Two—aggravated assault and theft.

Three—aggravated assault and rape.

After that waste of time, he arranged for my transfer to central booking where they could keep me up to twenty-four hours in the cells affectionately called the tombs. The rank, filthy pens where homeless, drunks, and low-collar criminals were crammed together like livestock destined for the canning factory.

My statement consisted of, "Call my lawyer," and Arnold took great joy in repeating my Miranda rights as he slammed the bars closed.

Whatever evidence Greg had fed them while moaning and playing the victim at the hospital ensured my case was a special one. Not only did I have the chief of police ready to bury me in the system, but he also had the power to speed up or slow down my trial.

The meeting with the Criminal Justice Agency ensured a district attorney who bowed to Twig's every command, agreeing that I was too dangerous a flight risk to allow bond at any amount.

Unfortunately, my prior actions supported such a shitty denial because the last time I'd served in the great state's penitentiary, the moment I'd been released, I'd moved with Larry to LA to get my head on straight and the fuck away from New York.

Either Larry was too late to attend the hearing, or he was busy putting together my defense. Whatever the reason, I trusted him because he knew what I was up against. If he thought it was worth staying away for now, then fine. I had no doubt he'd file an appeal and request an early trial to set this long-winded, beyond-aggravating system into motion.

Greg had better get fucking arrested, too.

I wouldn't be able to stomach going to jail while the real perpetrator got away with it.

Again.

At least this time around, I wasn't a penniless, homeless throwaway.

I had money.

I had friends.

And that made it even more imperative in Arnie's corrupted mind that he control my reinsertion back into prison with utmost perfection.

I had no intention of keeping his secrets this time. Give

me a judge, a jury, a fucking court full of people and I'd tell them all about Arnold's precious son.

Unless I get shanked, of course.

Fuck, I missed Elle. I missed being free.

Hours had a tendency to blur together in this place. I had no idea how many had passed by the time I was collected in a minivan with bars on the windows and manacles on the floor.

Cuffed hands and ankles, I shuffled onto the vehicle and a clank of chains locked me into position. The noise of the links reminded me Greg had chained Elle.

That he'd hurt her.

Almost raped her.

My rage and desire to punch him all over again helped overshadow my fear at being trapped against my will. The incessant blistering fury fed me better than any food or liquor, and I didn't pay attention to the officer closing the door or the driver sliding the van into gear and taking me from police station to prison block.

At least, Arnold had retreated to his office like the scum he was.

* * * * *

Arriving at the Department of Corrections, I was finally given a shower to wash away the blood, a quick check up by the in-house doctor, who kindly prescribed more painkillers, and searched for contraband—which was the single most degrading thing a man could go through.

Once clean and dressed in a dark green prison uniform, I was met with the usual welcome of a blanket, pillow, and toothbrush parcel then ferried into the prison population where remanded felons were kept just in time for the warning bell for lights out.

For now, I had a cell with two bunk beds pressed up against the wall to myself.

I had no doubt that would change, but tonight, I'd enjoy the fucking privacy.

Choosing the top bunk, I spread out my blanket, fluffed

my pillow, and lay down to glower at the pockmarked ceiling.

Every inch of me hurt.

My head, my hands, my chest, my legs…*everything*.

But despite the heat and throbbing in my joints, I waited to feel something other than physical maladies.

To ache with unfairness and suffer discomfort at being somewhere foreign. To crave freedom and open spaces with the unsatisfied appetite of a drug addict.

And I did suffer.

But I couldn't fake myself into believing this place was foreign.

It wasn't foreign at all.

It was familiar.

A second home.

A well-known place I despised with every inch of my being.

Its welcome whispered over me, deleting the past few years where I'd been wealthy and cared for and obsessed with the girl who'd shared my chocolate bar, fell for me, and then looked at me as if I was scum even when she heard the truth.

Her apology echoed in my ears.

Her tears glistened in memory.

I'd hurt her, but she'd hurt me.

And now, I was here, and she was there, and there was no way to fix what was broken.

"Fuck." I punched my pillow, rolled over, and closed my eyes.

CHAPTER NINETEEN

ELLE

"I HAVE TO SEE him."

Another phone rang in the background, but Larry didn't make an excuse to end our call to answer it.

He sighed, but it wasn't cruel, more like lost as to what he could offer me. "I can arrange it but not for a few days. New prisoners are given a stand-down period before visitors are allowed."

"New prisoners?"

"He's being held without bail. I've already filed an appeal and fighting for a hearing date that isn't sometime in two years. We'll get him back, but the justice system is archaic. It'll take time."

"Time?" I sucked in a breath. "How much time?"

"Can't say. But it'll be as short as I can make it."

My heart plummeted, rolling in shame, coating in guilt until it sat tarred and feathered in my stomach. "But...he didn't do anything wrong."

"The previous times he was locked up, I would've agreed with you." His voice layered with tiredness, reminding me not so long ago, he was seriously sick, and Penn had been the one to look after him. Now, it was Larry's turn.

How many times has it been his turn?

"Previous times?" My voice was small, timid. My question hesitant.

Larry heard my uncertainty.

I hated myself for it. Here I was so close to the truth, and I wasn't sure I had the balls to learn any more.

The more I did, the more I cursed myself. Cursed myself for not trying harder to find Penn. For doubting him. For hurting him.

His arrogance and fine-edged cruelty had been the perfect mask to hide the loneliness and hardship of a life I could never imagine.

Fate had been so generous and kind to me. It had been an absolute bitch to Penn.

How can I make it right?

Once again, I had dreams of protecting him, cooking for him, caring for him the way I knew he would care for me if only he could forgive my doubting.

Sage waltzed over my desk, sprawling on her side on my notepad, unapologetically asking for cuddles while my mind whirled.

Automatically, my fingers sank into her soft fur. I blinked at my office in Belle Elle's tower, returning to the present rather than dwindling on awful, awful imaginings of what Penn was going through.

"Yes," Larry said. "The previous times he was arrested." Something banged as if he'd closed a desk drawer. "For example, the night in Central Park—when he was with you."

I froze. "What about it?"

"He was sentenced to eight years for aggravated robbery, armed assault, and attempted rape."

"But that's a lie!"

"Doesn't matter. He had no one to fight for him then. Neither did he have support when he was first arrested and

---

held in an adult penitentiary, even though he was a minor. He didn't commit the crime, but he paid—purely because of bad luck and similar facial features to another."

My mind cartwheeled, growing dizzy. "I don't know what you mean."

"I mean, Elle, the first time he served thirteen months and was out early for good behavior. The state didn't ask him if he had a home to go to, family to see, or a job to earn a living. They just kicked him out with nothing—not even the lint from his pockets because he didn't *have* any lint when they'd arrested him."

"That's...awful." I didn't want to hear anymore.

Tears wobbled in my gaze, making my office dance and Sage turn into a gray blob. Belle Elle suddenly wasn't a tower of servitude but a pillar of strength. This was my core asset. This company had made me rich and powerful.

It's time I used that wealth in other ways—freeing innocent men ways.

Larry chuckled with pride. "He made do. He's a resourceful lad. He stole—he's not innocent on that account—but he only did it to survive. The second charge was betrayal by a so-called friend and the result of bad luck, bad timing. He got time for theft and for knocking out the house owner and molesting his wife."

I gasped. "That can't be true. He would never—"

"Of course, he wouldn't," Larry snapped. "He was framed."

My fingers tightened on my phone, falling more into the tangled tale of Penn's past. "How?"

"Penn happened to be walking back to his current bed for the night when he saw his so-called friend entering the house in question. He followed. Tried to talk some sense into him, only for the wife to get confused and think it was Penn who'd touched her and the man to wake up groggy and brain-bruised and accuse him. The real perp had run before the police arrived. By the time Penn was processed, *he* had heard the news and personally oversaw Penn's arrest. By that point, it was too late."

Chills scattered down my spine. *"He?"*

Larry made a hate-thick noise in the back of his throat. "Arnold Twig."

The name alone made me shudder with anger and the need to scratch out his eyes for being the cause of Penn's misfortune. "And who is Arnold Twig?"

"Sean Twig's father. Penn's nightmare."

* * * * *

I couldn't stop replaying the strange conversation over and over.

Larry had been forthcoming but cryptic at the same time.

How had this Arnold Twig got away with framing Penn?

Why had nothing been done about it?

Why hadn't Penn himself been a whistleblower and shouted to the world what had happened?

Why had I never been contacted to testify about the rape and assault charge the night he was stolen from me?

The man in the hoodie from the alley had honor and backbone. He didn't let me get raped because he morally had to help. That strong ethic code would stand up for himself, too, surely?

With my questions keeping me constant company, the day passed like all the others.

But it didn't feel like the others.

It was different.

Strange.

However, the calendar hadn't changed.

I had.

The second I'd wandered into Belle Elle after heading downtown with David and Dad to answer police questions and provide my statement about Greg, I'd had no mental capacity to work.

Even Fleur had frozen in shock and demanded to know what I was doing there.

I'd given her the socially acceptable response that I was head of this empire and I'd already had a few days away. I wouldn't miss more.

That was a lie.

The real reason was I couldn't sit at home on my own anymore. I couldn't raid Penn's safety deposit box and stare at the handsome passport photo of a slightly younger man with aged wisdom and persecution in his gaze.

The same prettiness that had beguiled me now broke my heart that I couldn't pick up a phone and call him or knock on his door and hug him.

He was untouchable, unreachable, and it hurt so damn much.

The only good thing was the knowledge that Greg had been questioned. He was under arrest pending discharge from the hospital. On the flip side, Greg had submitted his own statement about Penn's treatment and wanted him punished to the fullest extent possible.

It's a damn racket.

Greed had caused this and greed could kiss my ass.

My stomach never stopped roiling at how vindictive Greg had become. How a boy from my childhood could become such a conniving, jealous asshole.

I had no idea if he'd end up in the same prison as Penn or what it would mean for Steve's future at Belle Elle, knowing his best friend's daughter had sent his only son to jail.

But it wasn't my fault, and I was too tired to worry.

* * * * *

Six p.m. rolled around, and instead of having a productive day, I couldn't remember where the time had gone.

My website browser had court processes and information on what happened to reoffenders. My history painted research on how unlikely a release was when the victim was pushing for full penalty.

Greg had not only tried to take Belle Elle away from me, but he also had the power to take away Penn.

The fermenting anger inside threatened to boil over. Nothing was simple all because of him. All because Greg thought he deserved something for nothing.

He can't get away with it.

I wished I had more knowledge on how to argue cases that weren't just black and white. But I was sheltered in that respect. I just had to hope Larry knew what he was doing— which drove me nuts, as I needed to do *something* to help.

Another kernel of loathing layered on top of my anger as I Googled Arnold Twig: chief of police, part-time volunteer at the soup kitchen, father to one son, and all-a-round good citizen. The scarce photos of him online depicted an older gentleman who preferred crisp ironed clothes and sensible shoes.

I couldn't see why he would be such a threat to Penn.

A knock raised my head.

I glanced at the door, yanked from my scattered thoughts. "Come in."

I expected Fleur. I smiled with kindness and welcome— grateful to see my helpful assistant and friend before she left for the night.

The true visitor turned my smile to marble. I hid my grimace behind it. "Steve…what a surprise."

I had no desire to see him. He'd done nothing wrong, he'd showered me in apologies, but I couldn't separate my fondness of him against the dislike of his son.

Steve lingered on the threshold. "Elle, I wondered…can I have a minute?"

My heart raced, noticing for the first time the similarities between Steve and Greg. Matching jawline, the way their mouth formed certain words, even their nose shared the same genetics.

It had never bothered me before, but that was before Greg punched me and drove me across the state to try to do what exactly? Rape me into falling in love with him? Arranging someone to marry us under duress and believing the marriage certificate would've held up against the lawyers I would've hired to bury Greg under litigation?

Idiot.

I stood, planting my hands on my desk. "I think you'll need more than just a minute to explain what the hell Greg was thinking, Steve." Nothing but swift authority was in my voice. No gratitude for his guidance over the years or friendship toward a father figure I'd grown up with.

I was his boss.

He was my employee.

He was also the father of the man I never wanted to see again.

He tugged on the bottom of his blue blazer, striding into my office. Wisely, he didn't close the door. Already I felt trapped, and the sounds of departing staff echoed in the hallway, inviting me to run with them.

"You have a point there." He stopped in front of my desk.

Sage, picking up on my vibes but not sure why, did what she always did and jumped to the carpet to wrap herself around his ankles in welcome.

He smiled sadly, his eyes welling with tears and more apologies. "Shit, Noelle. I'm so goddamn sorry." His gaze trailed over my bruises—the black eye of pain and memories of the short hostage situation I'd endured. "I never thought he'd do something so terrible. He's Greg." He shrugged. "He's never been violent. Greedy and spoiled, yes, but…" He spread his hands. "I don't know what to say."

"Tell me where he is."

"Still at the hospital. I think he's being discharged tomorrow." He looked at the floor. "Then he'll be transferred to the police station, I guess."

Tomorrow.

On the one hand, I was glad he would be dealt with so soon. On the other, it didn't give me much time to threaten him to drop the charges against Penn.

Whoa…you're going to do what?

The plan had come from nowhere, but…it made sense.

It's ridiculous.

But so what?

I had no other skill or way of helping Penn.

I have to do something.

Even something moronic.

Who better to help Penn than the woman who had power over the man accusing him? If I wanted to use that power, I had to be quick.

Steve didn't notice my hastily forming, crazily stupid plan, or the rush of heat over my skin at the thought of kicking Greg where it hurt and making *him* suffer for a change.

"I've arranged with human resources to create the necessary severance packets. He won't be coming back to Belle Elle." He ducked to pet Sage before she wandered off with her tail high.

"Thank you."

I was glad he'd taken care of it but annoyed that we had to tiptoe around contract clauses and fulfill our end of the bargain with vacation pay and remaining sick leave.

I didn't want to give him a penny more than he'd already squeezed out of me. But I wouldn't give Greg any reason to come after me again—suing me for incorrect dismissal or otherwise.

"Do you know what time he'll be collected by the police tomorrow?" I delivered my question void of emotion. However, it held two sides. One innocent. One plotting.

I wanted Greg behind bars.

But not before I had a few moments alone with him.

Don't do this…

It could backfire royally.

I told myself to hush up.

For three years, I'd done nothing to help Penn. There was no way I could do that again. I could never live with myself.

I kept my body stiff; my secrets hidden. Ever since I'd found Gio's driver's license in Penn's box, a seed had been planted. I didn't know what that seed had been or what actions it would have me take, but now it had sprouts, straining for truth like a flower strains for sunlight, giving me a blueprint of a plan.

I knew what I had to do.

Penn was Nameless.

Nameless was Penn.

That put me in an uncomfortable situation.

Nameless, I owed a debt. That debt was still unfulfilled and never paid. Penn, I owed thanks for repeating history and saving me, but it didn't wipe his behavior clean. If we were to have any chance at fixing this, I had to know the *real* him...not the many faces he hid behind.

Nameless—I'd fallen for him in a lightning strike of adolescent stupidity. Penn—I'd fallen out of love with every lie he'd told.

It looked as though the same had happened to him with me.

We both had grudges.

Perhaps, a third chance would fix everything that went wrong.

"No idea. Probably early afternoon?" Steve said. "I think he has a final check up in the morning."

It's now or never.

I picked up my turquoise fountain pen, tapping it against my palm. "I want to see him."

"What?" Steve gripped the back of his neck. "I don't think that's wise."

"Too bad. I want to."

His face scrunched up. "Uh, okay. I'll come with you and act as a mediator to ensure you're safe."

"No. I want to be on my own."

"But—" His skin turned a sick pallor. "Elle, you have every right to hate him. I know you gave your statement this morning, which you have *every* right to do. But please...you're better than he is. You've always been so much gentler and smarter than all of us."

His tone switched to begging. "I'm outraged with him and don't know how to call him my son after what he did, but I'm begging you on our friendship, please don't send him to jail."

A cold smile slipped over my face. "Do you honestly think I have any power over that? He has to answer for what he did."

His head hung. "I know. I just...shit, it kills me that it ended this way."

"It kills me that the man who came to my rescue is now in jail because of Greg's statement." I cocked my head. "Would you say that's fair?"

He gulped. "No. That's not fair."

"If David had been the one to knock a little sense into Greg in order to save me, do you think he'd be rotting in prison right now with no bail?"

He sighed heavily, air expelling from his body, knowing that whatever pleading he'd come to do had backfired. "No. He'd be justified."

"Exactly."

My hands curled as my temper worked through me thick and fast. "Greg has to pay for locking up an innocent man—not to mention answer for what he did to me."

Steve flinched. "As you have every right to do."

"You keep saying I have a right to do these things, yet your voice says otherwise."

He looked away, unable to keep eye contact. "It's hard for me, Elle. I love you both. I hate everything about this. I hate Greg for what he did, but I still have the inherent need to protect him."

"Just like I have the need to protect Penn."

"I know."

"I'm going to talk to your son, Steve." I leaned forward, my wrists aching from hovering my weight over my desk. "But like you just said, I'm better than he is. He's a greedy little bastard who thought he could take from me. I won't stoop to his level. I want Penn's freedom, and Greg will give me what I want. He owes me, Steve. I'll get what I want, one way or another, so if you can't handle that, I can arrange human resources to give you a comfortable retirement package and sever our relationship right now."

He held up his hands. "No, I can keep this separate from work." He lowered his voice. "I love your father almost as much as I love Greg. If Greg gets taken away from me, I need to have someone to support. Your father's heart—I'll watch over him."

I twitched a little at his audacity saying I couldn't look after my own father, but I knew the bond the two older men shared. He wasn't answerable to his son's actions. I had to remember that just because blood made family, family didn't necessarily share the blame.

Penn didn't share Larry or Stewie's blood, but they were family, and they would stand by one another regardless.

Just like I will.

Tomorrow, I would give Greg a little visit.

And just like I'd told Steve, I would get my way—one way or another.

CHAPTER TWENTY

PENN

TWO & A HALF YEARS AGO

"YOU HAVE A visitor."

I looked up from where I was reading. The Department of Correction's library had come a long way since the previous visits I'd enjoyed, but it still needed some TLC. The torn linoleum was ugly, and a lot of the books had missing pages from bastards not handling them with care. But at least, the government required certain books to be accessible to inmates.

For the past six months on my third stint here, I'd read most of the heavy volumes on law, company structure, and other mind-numbing jargon. Most of the time, they put me to sleep, making me wonder why I fucking bothered.

It wasn't as if I'd ever get out and have the money to either trade the same companies I'd researched or somehow build a community out of nothing for the homeless kids I'd met along the way.

But I never stopped reading because of that one chance in a million that somehow I'd win the lottery of life, and all of this would change.

It sucked 'cause a few months before I got locked up, I'd been introduced by accident to Gio's younger brother, Stewie. We'd met one night behind a pizzeria that donated their end-of-night waste to alley kids.

Gio and I didn't get along—mainly thanks to his friendship with the fuckwit Sean who used me as his 'get out of jail free' card, but Stewie was too young to get caught up in their world.

I had no idea how Sean and Gio became such idiotic friends. The son of a police captain and the orphaned, homeless kid. Just like most of us street rats, the young ones had no family to turn to.

Gio had successfully hidden Stewie and provided for him through crime. Sean was looking for kicks, and encouraged it.

I didn't approve, but I did approve of the love between the brothers and almost wished I had a sibling to care for like he did.

I liked Stewie. I enjoyed his juvenile naivety that life would get better.

But then I cursed myself for wishing such a shitty existence on anyone—even if it would mean I wasn't so damn lonely.

"Did you hear me?" The officer kicked the leg of my rickety chair. "Visitor."

I closed the book on truth and justice and what the court of law was *supposed* to do and not how it'd failed me, and looked up. "I don't have any visitors."

Any I wanted to see, anyway.

Sean I definitely didn't want to see. And Arnold Twig? Hell, fucking no. They were as bad as each other.

"Too bad. You have one, and they're not leaving."

I contemplated making a fuss, hitting this douche-bag over the head with the book to be reprimanded and not allowed visitors for a month. But I had eight years this time. I had nowhere else to be out there, but I was slowly fucking dying in here. I needed fresh air. I needed grass. I needed baseball fields and chocolate kisses with some girl who made my insides change owners and leap to belong to her.

Fuck…that girl.

She'd been a saving grace for me the past six months. I couldn't remember the last time I'd had something good to think about…but that kiss? Man, it warmed me on the nights I was coldest. The feel of her breast in my hand…wow, it gave me good dreams while I lived this fucking nightmare.

The officer rapped the table with his fist then walked away, pulling the proverbial leash that his uniform dictated over my prison overalls.

Reluctantly, I pushed the book away and followed.

Sean would be sorry if he ever showed up here again. Rules or not. I'd punch his motherfucking face in and screw it if it cost me an extra few years.

Punch Sean, and you'll earn life.

Punch Sean and Arnold would have exactly what he'd wanted since the beginning.

A reason to crucify me.

No, as satisfying as it would be to waste my life on one measly face smash, I had bigger plans.

Someone had to pay.

Somehow, the law had to work.

Otherwise, what sort of fucked-up society did we live in?

* * * * *

"Hello, Penn."

I scowled, shaking the hand of some old geezer with a canvas jacket slung over a shirt with a cravat and linen pants.

I'd never met him before in my life. "Who the hell are you?"

He grinned as we squeezed palms then separated. Motioning toward the metal table and chairs in a private room (not the welcome hall where normal inmates saw their loved ones), he sat first, waiting for me to join him.

"My name is Larry Barns. I'm your new attorney."

What the fuck?

"I hate to tell ya, but you're about six months too late." I waved around the space. "Look around."

Larry smirked as if he had a secret, pointing once again to the chair. "Please. Sit."

I paused for a second, weighing pros and cons, deliberating about being a dick or decent.

Ah, whatever…I have nowhere else to be.

The book would still be there. I was the only one who read them apart from Henry who got released last week.

The guy linked his fingers over a file with my name scribbled on the top.

Penn Michael Everett.

The only thing linking me to my dead father, Michael Everett. My mom died having me, and for twelve awesome years, Dad did his best to care for me, work, pretend to be normal, and hide the depression eating holes inside him.

In the end, the depression didn't kill him. It was the testicular cancer that he hadn't checked and never said a word about until I found him dead in bed one day.

Child Protective Services stepped in, and the same sob story that happened to most orphans began. I got shuttled around—different schools, different families—until one day, I never went back.

I vanished into the streets of New York and became an adult rather than a burden on people who didn't want me.

"I've been doing a case study on inmates here. Studying how long between arrest to jury hearings and paroles." Mr. Barns opened my file. "I noticed you haven't been granted the same courtesies as other inmates. Do you want to talk about that?"

I crossed my arms. "Nope."

The beating I'd received still acted as super glue on Arnie's secrets. I hated that asshole with my entire being. But I hated his son even more—the son I conveniently looked like, who shared my height and build, so I was the perfect fall boy for his crimes.

Captain Daddy Dearest couldn't have a criminal for a son, now could he? So he'd used his power to shift that blame onto me and keep good ole' Sean squeaky clean.

"You know, I'm not like a normal lawyer." Larry slid me an icy can of Coke that he must've grabbed from a vending machine outside.

Part of me didn't want to take it as I didn't want to owe him a dime, but then again, it had been so long since I'd tasted pure sugar.

Snatching it, I cracked open the drink and swigged.

Tart bubbles hit my tongue.

Christ, that tastes good.

Wiping my mouth with the back of my hand, I muttered, "Don't care if you're not a normal lawyer or not. Not gonna change the facts."

His eyes narrowed. "Yeah, about that. It's the facts that interest me." He lowered his voice. "There are discrepancies in your file that I want to know more about."

My heart pounded as I glanced at the camera in the ceiling corner. Was this a trap? A test? Was Arnold watching me, waiting for me to slip up?

Wouldn't fucking happen.

I bared my teeth. "Don't know what you're talking about."

"I think you do."

I stood. "Back off. Leave me alone."

He reclined in his chair, holding up his hands. "I'm not trying to make this harder for you."

"Well, you are, so beat it."

Larry slowly closed the file and matched me standing. His eyes were soft, kind, but sharp with intelligence. "You know, I represent another man who refuses to say anything, too." His head tilted. "You wouldn't happen to know a boy named Stewart Steel, would you?"

My knees locked. Violence filtered through me to protect Gio's little brother.

What the fuck happened to Gio?

Why is this guy representing Stewie?

He was just a kid. He couldn't be charged with shit like this.

"Why?" I forced between gritted teeth. "What's that got to do with me? Or you, for that matter?"

He smiled, knowing he'd hooked me.

Bastard.

"I'm representing his older brother. Turns out, Gio Steel was picked up for arson while trying to cover up a robbery. Stewart helped start the fire. It's a shame really because that kid is impressionable, and I don't want him to end up where you are."

You and me both.

"Tell you what." He clapped his hands. "I'll tell you everything I know in return for you telling me everything *you* know. Off the record, of course. Complete confidentiality. Tell me why Gio told me to talk to you. Why he seems to think there's some conspiracy going on and why he's begging me to take care of Stewie until you're released, so you can take care of him yourself. Help me help you, Mr. Everett, and we'll see where this road takes us."

"Why should I trust you?"

His eyes turned sad, serious, utterly honest. "Who else do you have?"

He had a point.

I hated it, but I made a choice.

I sold my soul for the truth.

I nodded at the stranger and accepted whatever mayhem he'd bring into my life.

Either the truth would kill me or the lies would suffocate me.

I'd die and there wouldn't be any fucking difference.

CHAPTER TWENTY-ONE

ELLE

CHAPTER TWENTY-ONE

ELLE

"MS. CHARLSTON IS here to see Greg Hobson." David eyed the police officer standing guard outside the hospital room we'd been advised to visit.

The entire drive here, I'd suffered David's disapproval. His posture said how stupid he thought I was being. My inner voice told me how stupid I was being. But all I could think about was wringing Greg's puny neck.

Parking and walking inside with me, David kept his mouth shut. Heading up in the elevator to the fourth floor, his opinions wafted full of frustration that he couldn't knock sense into me.

I'd watch what I said to Greg.

I'd be careful not to be overheard.

But if I didn't do this—after three years of not doing anything last time—I would literally have to smash every mirror in my apartment because I could never look at myself again.

As we stood in the linoleum-lifeless hallway, David pursed his lips, glancing at me quickly. That was the difference between a friend and employee. David was my friend, but he was ultimately my staff, and what I wanted…I got.

Just like I'll get what I want from Greg.

Because there was no other option. I couldn't fail.

I kept my hands folded in front of my black slacks and cream shirt, going for a somber uniform with my long hair curled in a knot at the base of my skull. It made me look older, stricter…cutthroat.

I wanted Greg to fear me.

I wanted him to quake knowing what he'd done and how hard I'd go after him to teach him a lesson.

The police officer stood from his plastic chair, hoisting up his utility belt. "I wasn't told—"

"You will. Expect a call any second." David smiled just as the officer's walkie-talkie crackled and a female voice alerted him to a visitor arriving at any moment and to clear access.

"That would be me." I nodded at the guard, moving to peer through the glass window of the door.

The officer stepped aside and then there he was.

The man I no longer understood or knew. The man who held the life of another in his rotten little paws.

"Five minutes," the officer said, dragging a hand through his short blond hair.

"Five minutes is all I need." Turning the doorknob, I looked back at David.

He ground his teeth, his head slightly cocked. "I'd ask if you wanted me to join you. But I think I already know the answer."

"You do." I patted his arm. "I want to be alone with him."

He scowled but accepted it. "Scream if you need me."

I laughed under my breath. "Got it."

Inhaling deep, I pushed the door and traded the sharp smell of disinfectant and giggles of nurses for the more subtle smell of a man I'd grown up with hidden beneath medicine and bleach.

Sudden gratefulness filled me. The last time I was in the hospital was to stay vigil at my father's bedside while he recovered from his heart attack. We'd walked out together, and I wouldn't be here today visiting Greg if it wasn't for him.

I'd called the police station and asked for a meeting but had been laughed off the phone.

I'd asked Larry to arrange it—believing he'd have contacts that would make it easy—but he had no jurisdiction over a felon who wasn't his client.

That left me near tears and furious when Dad walked in to bid me goodnight. I'd spilled my frustrations, and he'd mentioned he'd ask one of his friends to see if he could help.

Up until this morning, I had no hope that anything would come of it.

But the minute I walked wearily into my office, Dad had announced I had a meeting arranged thanks to Patrick Blake.

I hadn't managed to spend much time with Dad since my reassurance and the many hugs after my abduction, but I squeezed him so damn hard when he gave me the news.

Apparently, Patrick Blake—fishing buddy and fellow golf enthusiast—was actually a judge.

Belle Elle hadn't been free of its own lawsuits and court appearances over the last few decades and thankfully, Dad had befriended a few people along the way.

He fished with a high judge. He played golf with a district attorney. He had friends who had held his hand while grabby people tried to sue for ridiculous things like incorrect sizes offending their snowflake personalities.

He hadn't once asked for favoritism or help fighting such claims. But for me, he'd requested approval and managed to give me the five minutes I needed to try and save Penn's life.

Not that I told him it was for Penn.

He would've said no.

He'd approved of Penn before this nightmare, and I hoped he'd stand by him while incorrectly incarcerated for something as noble as saving me. However, what he wouldn't approve of was Penn's prior convictions or his unsavory background.

He was a good man, my father, but a snob through and through. Only the best of the best could marry his daughter and run Belle Elle. Which was hypocritical when he put so much energy into getting me together with Greg, only for him to be the worst of all.

Greg opened his eyes as I shut the door with a harsh slap, getting his attention.

"Shit…Elle?" He sat higher in bed, shuffling against the mountain of white pillows, his skin rosy with health not white with sickness. "Came to visit. You love me after all, huh?"

His smirk made me rage.

I hated that he was here being pampered while Penn was in jail going through who knew what.

My hands curled, holding back my temper. "Shut up, Greg."

His forehead furrowed. For a moment, it looked like he'd retaliate and a small frisson of fear bolted into my legs remembering how it felt to be washed unwanted by him. To be naked in front of him. Cook for him. Such normal things but it left a terrible taste in my mouth that could never be washed away by mint toothpaste.

He's a creep. Nothing more.

Stalking toward the bed in my high black heels, I stopped close enough to glower but far enough not to touch.

My eyes fell on his wrist on top of the starched sheets. A silver handcuff attached him to the steel frame of the bed.

That was karma. A few days ago, I was the one in cuffs. Now, he had the joy.

I smiled before I could school myself to be cold and aloof. "I see it's your turn to be imprisoned."

He bared his teeth. "It won't stick. I'll get a good lawyer. I'll—"

I held up my hand. "Stop. I don't want to hear any more of your delusions, Greg." Before he could launch into another tirade, I said, "I'm here for one thing and one thing only."

His eyebrow rose, his body relaxing into a flirt. "Oh,

yeah?" His gaze traveled over me. "Come to finish what we started?"

I hid my shudder. He wasn't worth my retaliation. "Withdraw your statement about Penn."

"What?" His green eyes flashed with surprise then darkened with anger. "No way. Look what that bastard did to me." He raised an arm, showing a few bruises. "He fucking broke me."

"I see nothing but a spoiled brat milking a stay in the hospital before he goes to jail."

He froze. "I'm not going to jail, Elle."

"I say otherwise."

The metal handcuff jingled on the bed frame as he shifted again—uncertain but still trying to dominate the situation. "He broke my ribs and bruised my throat. I've had a headache since—"

"Oh, spare me, Greg." I waved a hand at his prone body. "All I see is a boy who never grew up. You're an adult. You have to take responsibility for the things you've done and the people you've hurt."

Moving closer toward the bed, I growled, "I won't ask again. Revoke your statement about Penn. Drop the charges."

"Why the fuck would I?"

"Why?" I bared my teeth. "Because you kidnapped me, tried to rape me, and attempted to steal my company. Yet here I am being civil to you, asking you politely to be the bigger man and let Penn go."

His face turned nasty. "He's not going anywhere."

My skin crawled, fighting quicksand—a losing battle. Why did I think I could come here and negotiate with Greg like he was a sane, logical thinking adult?

He wasn't. He had a screw loose or ten.

Fine, you leave me no choice.

Looking over my shoulder at the door, I moved closer. Close enough that he could touch me if he wanted but close enough to hurt him if I did. "Drop the charges."

"Fuck off, Elle. If I can't have you, no one can—including that asshole."

I didn't respond, focusing on my task. "Drop the charges or *else*." My voice mimicked a general giving the orders on a firing line.

"Or else?" He laughed. "Who are you trying to be? A CEO who actually has the balls to threaten?"

"I'm being myself. And I *do* have the balls to threaten." I held up my finger. "I will *ruin* you—"

The door cracked open, followed by David's command, "Ms. Charlston, step back. You have two minutes remaining, according to our friend out here."

"Close the door, David." I didn't look away from Greg. "I know what I'm doing."

He knew better than to argue with me in public. The door clicked shut, leaving me alone once again.

I'd tried to do this kindly, but Greg was an asshole and left me no choice. "Drop the charges against Penn. Tell them you mistook everything that'd happened and no longer want to follow through with your statement."

"No way. They'll prosecute me for lying." His mouth twisted, knowing he'd just slipped into truth. The sticky substance had a way of coming to light beneath the slickness of lies. "Besides, I'm hurt. *He* hurt me. Bastard will get what's coming."

I breathed hard through my nose, doing my best to stay calm despite the overwhelming need to wrap the IV cord around his neck and strangle him. "Don't care. Be honest for once in your miserable life and accept whatever punishment is coming your way. Or…"

He still didn't look afraid, merely entertained—waiting to see what I would do. "Or?"

"Or I march back to the police station, and I tell them in *graphic* detail how you raped me. How you took advantage of me against my will. How after multiple times of hurting me, you planned to kill me."

He instantly froze, filling with doubt. "You wouldn't."

"I would."

"They'd prosecute you for filing a false report."

I shrugged. "If it's the price to pay to free a man who shouldn't be in jail, then consider it done. I would do it because he's right and you're wrong and I'm sick of not standing up for the truth."

"But that's a lie! You're insane. Why would you fucking do that?"

I shook my head, unable to believe he had no concept of loyalty or love. Did he even love his father like a normal son? Or was his selfishness a commanding passenger, making him only think of himself?

Time was running out.

Taking the final step toward the bed, I hissed, "So help me, Greg. I'll turn the kidnapping and Belle Elle takeover into a rape and attempted murder. I'll hire every lawyer I can and pay them to bury you in a life sentence. I'll do whatever it takes to make sure you're never a free man again." I glared with hooded eyes. "Who knows? Maybe I'll push for the death penalty."

He gulped. "You wouldn't."

"Wouldn't I?" I raised an eyebrow. "I tried to be nice to you, Greg. If you want me to play hardball, I will."

"You weren't even with that fucker." The handcuff screeched on the bed frame as he wriggled with anxiety. "It was a fake engagement. Why the hell are you—"

"Because he's worth it. He's decent."

"He's a liar."

"Not anymore."

Greg snarled, "You're completely batshit—"

The door opened; the police officer entered the room. "Ma'am, your time is up. I have to ask you to leave."

I looked over my shoulder, smiling demurely. "It's fine. I'm finished." My smile turned into a knife when I glanced back at Greg. "Yes or no. Tell me right now. Will you do what I asked?"

He pouted, yanking his arm, making the handcuff jangle once again. He wouldn't make eye contact, glowering at the drip, the heart rate monitor—everything but me.

I waited for some resemblance of contrition. That his money-hungry brain would put self-preservation first rather than screwing over another just because Penn had things he didn't.

For a second, I thought I'd won. His shoulders fell, his pout turned into questions.

But then he looked up, locked eyes with me, and something changed. Hard-edged contempt replaced his petty, childish greed. He snickered. "Oh, Elle."

It sent sharp claws down my back, shredding me.

He murmured soft and sultry as if we were in bed together. "Guess you'll find out in court. Won't you?"

The world slowed down.

I'd come for a conclusion. To free Penn and finally uphold my side of the debt. But instead, all I got was uncertainty. The open-ended, unresolved fear that Greg wouldn't do what I demanded. That he would willingly gamble with his life if it meant destroying Penn's. That he would force me to lie under oath and join him in his manipulative game. That it might all backfire and I'd be the one behind bars for committing a crime.

This *was* stupid.

I hate him.

"How dare you—" I seethed.

The police touched my elbow, making me jump. "Ma'am, time to go."

"This isn't over, Greg." Fury stole the rest of my voice as the officer guided me from the room while Greg blew me a condescending kiss.

I'd come to save Penn.

I'd failed.

I'd screwed up.

Again.

CHAPTER TWENTY-TWO

PENN

FOUR DAYS IN hell.

I still had the cell to myself, which at least gave me some privacy. Recreational time and meals, I kept my head down and behavior impeccable. I didn't brown nose or try to make friends, but I didn't answer back or act like a dick if someone spoke to me.

I knew the rules. I stuck to them.

Larry told me to hang in there and stay focused on getting out. He pumped me with confidence only he could—thanks to the previous miracles he'd worked on my behalf.

I didn't let the thickening anxiety drown me because he was on my side.

He said he was working on my case when I'd been given a phone pass two days ago. Visitation rights were still pending and probably wouldn't be granted for a while. Remand prisoners sometimes got better rights than our convicted cousins, but most of the time, we got worse.

They liked to claim visits and phone calls were detrimental to remand prisoners because evidence hadn't been provided to the court yet and no verdict had been granted. Documents and information pertinent to particular crimes had a way of going missing, but at the same time, fact building and truth collaborating stalled because communication was denied.

An unwinnable situation.

But hopefully, my lawyer and benefactor of not just money but friendship and happiness would find a way.

Like he always does.

Besides, phone calls were better. At least, I didn't have to sit across from Larry and see the fucking disappointment in his eyes. It would kill him to see me back here, and I'd already spent last year fearing he'd die. I didn't want to be the cause of his stress all over again.

Not to mention, I couldn't think about Elle in a place like this. I couldn't call her because it ripped my heart out knowing I couldn't touch her, kiss her, look her in the eye and tell her everything she wanted to know.

She knew who I was. She didn't know my past. Would she still apologize to me after I'd told her everything? Would she still trust me...or at least *learn* to trust me?

We were forced apart, and we would remain apart until I was a free man again.

And if that never happens?

I coughed with pain.

Well, I guess it's over then.

I wouldn't let her waste her life waiting for me while I festered in this hellhole.

Shuffling forward in the line for lunch, I handed over my tray as the men on kitchen duty slopped a runny taco with the barest amount of cheese. I pursed my lips in disgust then moved on to collect a bottle of water and a rosy apple.

Taking my food to the table squashed against the wall, I climbed over the bench and sat heavily. The prior times I'd been here, I didn't remember being so fucking down. Sure, I wasn't happy, but at least I still had a laugh with one or two of the guys I had become friends with.

I still had the motivation to go to the library or work hard on assigned tasks throughout the week.

This time? Fuck, I felt so *tired*. My body hadn't gotten over the beating. My joints were still hot and swollen, reluctant and stiff to move. I hadn't slept well with the occasional nap while glaring at the ceiling, and I had no desire to make friends, even while I knew it was safer to be liked than ostracized.

I just didn't fucking care about anything anymore.

Maybe it was because I'd tasted what true happiness should be? I'd been wealthy, working toward a good cause, and falling in fucking love with a girl I'd wanted for three very long years.

To have that stripped away…it hurt. A lot more than being told I had a bed and regular food after months of roughing it in a New York winter.

"Hey." A guy with black dreadlocks and a spider tattooed on his cheek sat opposite me. His long legs looked like a praying mantis as he clambered over the bench. "Name's Scoot."

I took a bite of my apple, extending my hand like civilized society demanded. "Penn."

We shook then released. Scoot dived into his taco while I worked my fruit.

"You in for long?" he asked.

I shrugged. "Could be."

"Me, I'm here for seventeen. Served three. Not even half-way there yet."

I nodded in commiseration, placing the apple core to the side.

As much as I should chat and get to know this new crew, I found my mind slipping backward to a few years ago.

To the day when Larry came for me and I was able to leave as a free man.

* * * * *

TWO YEARS, THREE MONTHS AGO

"We're leaving."

I did my best to control my heartbeat as it fucking leaped. However, I couldn't stop my mouth from hanging wide in utter fucking surprise. "Are you serious?"

For three months, Larry had been a regular visitor. Between representing Gio and me, I guessed he spent most of his life behind bars. The only difference was he got to go home at night, and we stayed inside.

I shook my head, not daring to believe. "How?"

"Lack of evidence and too much circumstantial hearsay. You're free to go." He grinned, waving with his briefcase to the door.

The door.

That was open.

The room where we always met had become a safe haven for me. I didn't know where in the prison it was located or how many steps I'd need to take before I traded locks for freedom but just the words *free to go* made my blood pump faster, feeding limbs speed and power, ready to bolt and never fucking stop.

"But—I have so much time left."

"Time that was never yours to serve." He leaned forward, whispering, "I wasn't able to point fingers at Sean Twig this time, but I'll continue to work on the case. I've had a few interesting leads pop up, so I'll follow those and see where they go."

I couldn't...

How the fuck did he do this?

Why had he helped me?

What made me so damn special?

Larry had achieved the impossible. Not only had he freed me but he'd also kept me away from Arnold Twig's hatred by not targeting his son. To this day, I had no idea why Twig hated me so much. Was it because I tried inherently to be good despite doing bad things? Because his son was a fucking idiot, who committed crimes because he was bored? Or had I mistakenly pissed him off at the beginning, and he'd had a grudge ever since?

Either way, it didn't matter anymore.

Free.

I'm...free.

I almost fucking came with how sexy that word sounded.

"What will you do with the information once you've got it?" I tried to keep my voice disinterested when really I panted for knowledge. Would he go after Sean? Would he give me an even greater enemy in Arnold?

He cleared his throat. "I guess that's up to you."

Most of me wanted them to pay. To do the time I'd been forced to and steal parts of their lives in return. But a part of me was still terrified of Arnold. He had the power to lock me up all over again.

I should run and disappear.

Leave New York.

So he could never touch me.

Larry followed my thoughts. "As far as I'm concerned, this is over unless you want vindication. You're free to do whatever you want." He grinned. "If in the future you want justice, and decide to go after Sean and his father, you'll have to promise me one thing."

After everything he'd done for me in the past few months? Everything he'd listened to? The judgment he didn't give? The kindness he delivered? The updates he gave on Gio in Fishkill? The visits he gave Stewie in Child Protective Services? The decision to apply for temporary custody of a kid who wasn't his just because he clicked with him and wanted to provide a better future than the one he had?

Fuck, I'd give him anything he asked for. "I promise."

"You don't even know what it is yet."

"Don't need to. You've done me a solid, Larry. Name it."

He smiled, and it was full of friendship and respect rather than demeaning and cruel. "Promise me you won't end up here again." His face shadowed. "If we do go after Sean and you end up back in here…God knows what Arnold Twig will do or how far he'll bury you."

Goosebumps spread under my prison uniform. That wasn't a hard promise to keep. I'd keep it for me, not just him. "I have no intention of ever ending up here again."

"Good. Keep it that way." Larry placed the paperwork I just signed, accepting my release and terms of my parole, back into his briefcase. "Let's go then. I think a burger and fries are the first points of business, don't you?"

My mouth watered to have junk food while surrounded by air and no bars in sight. "You're on."

Marching toward the door, I paused on the threshold, expecting a hand to clamp on my shoulder or an order to return to my cell.

Fear crashed over my thoughts of burgers, believing for a split second that this was a dream and I'd wake up in my cot with years left to serve.

But nothing happened.

No commands. No punishment. No opening my eyes and seeing the same gray cell.

"What are you waiting for?" Larry pushed past me into the hallway. "Come along, I'll have to leave you now while you're processed, but I'll meet you out front." He patted my back. "You okay, kid?"

I swallowed the nerves, excitement, terror, joy. "Yeah, I'm good."

* * * * *

This is all so surreal.

Eating in a fancy-ass dining room; listening to the conversation between Larry, my lawyer turned guardian angel, and Stewie, Gio's baby brother—I couldn't get a grip on reality.

I liked Larry. I loved him for what he'd done for me. But we were still lawyer and client, not friends—we were on our way, but people like me didn't let their guard down easy.

For years, I'd lived alone on the streets. Scrapping for safe sleep spots, fighting over good quality dumpster food, arguing over the best corners to beg at.

Making friends in that situation wasn't easy, so I avoided everyone. If someone smiled, I took that as a threat. If someone followed me, I took that as war.

For Larry to open his house to me—a fucking thief—and make me welcome. Well, that made me feel like a real shitty person that I didn't have his class and trust.

It also made me ache inside with a heart that'd long since stopped looking for affection when he and Stewie grinned at each other.

Their relationship was totally different from ours.

Theirs was pure and uncomplicated.

Man and boy. Tutor and student. Father and son.

They laughed with each other. Joked. Stewie giggled with intelligence that I'd never seen him show on the streets, and Larry poked fun at him, throwing corn kernels, not caring if he got food on his expensive dining room rug.

I didn't say much that first night.

I couldn't.

I just soaked it in, waiting for life to interrupt this wonder and say *'you asshole, get back on the streets where you belong.'*

Instead, Larry offered me a place to stay until I got on my feet. He told me I could earn my keep by helping him with other cases. That I could go with him when I was ready to visit Gio and maybe let bygones be bygones and become friends, thanks to Stewie.

To him, the offers were so simple. But to me, they were the motherfucking world.

Before retiring to the guest room where a queen-sized bed and navy striped linen invited me so much better than scratchy single bunks, Larry called me into the drawing room where he and Stewie were playing a game of Chutes and Ladders.

I doubted Stewie had ever played games, let alone board games with no other purpose than social fun. His fun had been lighting fires with Gio to destroy evidence. Probably a pickpocket or two.

"Penn, before you crash, Stewie has something to give you." Larry looked pointedly at the kid with slightly protruding ears who stared at the game board as if he could magically make the dice roll so he could avoid all the chutes and climb all the ladders.

When he didn't look up, Larry prompted. "Stewie, remember what you wanted to give Penn? You spoke about it this afternoon when I said he was coming to stay with us for a while?"

Stewie's head suddenly sprang up. "Oh, yeah!" Pushing up from the coffee table where he sat on his knees on the thick carpet, he bounced over to me, pulling something small from his pocket. "Here." Handing it to me, I flinched as the cold slither of a necklace fell into my palm.

A sapphire star.

It might've been nine months since I'd seen her, but I remembered everything she said. How Gio and Sean had run off with her necklace. How her father had given it to her as a nineteenth birthday gift and how she'd forgotten to ask for it back. She'd also said it wouldn't have been hers anymore but mine for saving her.

I'd told her no fucking way would I accept her charity. And yet, somehow, the necklace had ended up in my possession anyway.

It's not mine.

I'm not keeping it.

It has to go back.

"How?" I cleared my throat. "Why do you have this?"

Stewie dug his foot into the carpet. "Gio gave it to me when he got snatched."

Larry came over, holding a glass of amber liquor, looking content and completely relaxed even though he had two thieves living under his roof. "He asked Stewie to keep it for him, so he didn't get charged for the robbery and attempted rape *you* were currently serving time for." He lowered his voice. "That would've been highly inconvenient to Arnold Twig if evidence came to light, and the girl in question testified that it wasn't you who'd accosted her in that alley."

My heart pounded. This one piece of evidence could clear my record of that misunderstanding. All I'd need would be for Elle to collaborate my story. I could have vindication.

But then I'd also have two vicious enemies.

Sean was still out there…who the fuck knew what he would do if he learned I was free and ready to start fighting rather than remain the easy scapegoat.

"You didn't return it to her?" I looked up, fingering the sapphire as if the jewelry could magically transport her to me.

"No."

Stewie reached for it. "It's mine. I gotta look after it. Keep it safe."

It's not yours.

I held it up, just out of reach. "Do you mind if I borrow it for the night?"

Larry met my eyes over Stewie's short height. He tilted his head, trying to understand why I wanted to keep something so unusual and unimportant to me.

But he was wrong. It was important. So fucking important.

I wouldn't say it out loud. I wouldn't admit that the plan to head to bed and sleep safely for the first time in forever had been put on hold for a few more hours.

But somehow, he knew.

He smiled, full of secrets as if he'd stolen mine and made them his own.

I'd told him a little about Elle. It'd been a mistake. I'd been down one day and didn't want to talk court cases and potential freedom, so he'd brought up girlfriends. I'd snorted and said, of course, I didn't have one, but then slipped as I mentioned the girl who'd kissed me in Central Park.

The entire story had come out.

Including the saga about the missing sapphire necklace.

"Uh, I dunno." Stewie chewed on his lip. "I'm not

supposed to let it go."

I ducked to his height. "I know. And I won't do anything bad with it. I promise."

The lie burned my tongue, but I loved how easily it came. How swiftly I was able to bullshit. Was that my first real lie? The practice run for the torrent about to come?

Larry moved forward, placing his hand on Stewie's shoulder. "Let Penn borrow it. He's heading out, but he'll be back soon. Won't you, Penn?" His eyes were serious, intent on hearing my assurance.

How does he know?

"Upper East Side. Number twenty-two on Cherry Avenue."

I didn't need to ask who the address was for. Just like he didn't need to ask what I was about to do.

Not looking at Stewie—unable to see the unwillingness to part with the necklace—I nodded once at Larry. "I'm coming back. I promise."

"You'd better." He tipped his glass in a salute. "I'm counting on you to keep that promise."

"You can trust me, Larry."

With Elle's necklace clenched in my fist, I jogged to the front door and disappeared into the night.

* * * * *

Fuck, she's even more beautiful than before.

My heart hit a stop button and hung love-struck in my chest.

Noelle Charlston.

The girl from the alley.

The name seared into my mind thanks to her identification card with the logo of Belle Elle—the largest retail chain in the US.

She thought I hadn't noticed. That I didn't believe her when she said she was an office worker at the one place I could never enter without a security guard throwing me out. My wardrobe told them all they needed to know and the fact that the last time I snuck inside I'd taken a nap in the houseware department didn't help my case.

I found it sexy that Elle worked there. I had fantasies of her working hard, renting a tiny studio, making something of her life while I looked up from squalor below.

I respected her for her tenacity to better herself. I was attracted to her for her lack of confidence or willingness to talk about her life when minimum wage made her so much richer than I was.

I'd become infatuated with her from the start. It turned to an obsessive need to know her the longer we walked back to her home. And when she mentioned it was her birthday, and she wasn't even out of her teens yet, I had the disgusting desire to be the first to welcome her to adulthood.

I'd taken her to the park to see how far her limits would go. A sheltered little girl out for a thrill. But then she'd agreed to follow me.

To break into the park with me.

To *trust* me.

Then she fucking kissed me. And I no longer wanted to test her but steal her to be mine forever. I'd lived in pure happiness for an hour out of so many years of loneliness.

That was before the night ended, and I never saw her again.

Until now.

She sat in an overstuffed armchair with a gray cat on her lap, stroking it with languid pets while her shoulders remained tense. Her long blonde hair that I remembered filled with leaves and grass clippings from rolling around on the baseball field, draped over the back of the chair while her eyes locked on the three males in front of her.

Two older, one around her age.

Their lips moved, faces speaking with animation that I couldn't hear.

The closed windows were air tight; the occasional whir of traffic and murmur of dog walkers meant I couldn't distinguish any other noise but the city buzz.

The sapphire burned my hand, demanding I knock on the door and give it back. To say *'hi, do you remember me?'* To kiss her if she'd forgotten and remind her if she hadn't.

I wanted to give her the benefit of the doubt about why she hadn't come looking for me. Why I'd thought about her for nine long months, but she'd moved on and dismissed me.

But the longer I stood in the manicured bushes hiding me from the street and spied on her life, the more I understood why.

I thought we'd had a connection that night.

I thought she'd fallen down the same slippery slope that defied logic or reason as I had.

Turned out, it might've just been one-sided. Because there she was, smiling at the boy opposite with his sandy blond hair and a smirk that said he wanted to fuck her and she'd probably let him.

She wasn't surviving in a crappy apartment with annoying roommates and eating budget groceries to make ends meet. She wasn't dressed in cheap clothes and costume jewelry so common to girls her age.

Nope.

There she sat, leading a pampered life in a spoiled little world.

She was the daughter of a rich man.

She had a pampered kitten in a spoiled big house.

She was probably allergic to work and had servants for everything.

To prove my case, a woman in an apron trundled into the living room with a tray of baked goods and a teapot. Elle smiled at her but didn't get up to help pass out the sweets. She waited like the men until the woman had placed cupcakes onto glass dishes, accepting the food cordially but with the airs and graces of someone used to having things given to her.

This wasn't a recent climb up the monetary ladder. She wasn't poor and now suddenly rich.

She'd been born into wealth, and it *dripped* off her.

Why didn't I see it that night? Taste it? Smell it?

Fuck, I was so stupid.

For so long, I thought she was an employee. That she knew the value of hard work in a different capacity to me but still understood the cost of survival in a big city.

I gave her excuses about why she couldn't find or visit me in prison even if she didn't issue a statement saying I was innocent.

To her, I would've been an adventure, nothing more.

To me, she was untouchable, something I could never have.

Standing outside her castle, wrapped in the shadows I'd befriended, I gave up on my stupid fantasies. She was nothing more than an overindulged brat who ran away from her doting father to be something she wasn't for a night.

She wasn't who I thought she was.

She'd let me believe in a fairy-tale.

I had no time for brats.

The visions of returning her necklace faded.

She didn't need it.

She probably had thousands of replacements.

I wouldn't be lying to Stewie tonight.

He could have it back.

He was the rightful owner now, not her.

With a stupid heart that'd finally learned its lesson, I turned and walked away.

CHAPTER TWENTY-THREE

ELLE

TWO WEEKS PASSED.

An insanely long two weeks where I went to work but didn't manage to do even the simplest of tasks.

I constantly hounded Larry for updates on visiting hours for Penn and promised him unlimited funds to gather whatever information he needed to submit for Penn's case.

Dad kept popping in to check on me, but for his benefit, I kept my stress hidden.

He didn't need to know I hadn't slept properly since the night Greg took me. He didn't need to understand I couldn't carry a normal thought without almost bursting into tears thinking about Penn locked up while I carried on my life as if nothing had happened.

I couldn't shift the guilt.

The awful compounding guilt that history had repeated itself, and instead of banging down police doors and ramming a bulldozer into the prison for a jailbreak, I was twiddling my thumbs bound by bureaucracy and tied up with paper pushing.

Even Fleur hadn't been able to get me out of my depressive funk.

Thanks to her heart of gold, she picked up my slack and kept Belle Elle running. She told me what to sign and when. She helped prepare my notes for business meetings and ensured my wardrobe screamed CEO when really all I wanted to do was cry in the corner with Sage.

Enough with the pity.

You told Greg what would happen if he goes after Penn.

Hopefully, in another few weeks when he went to trial or Penn went to trial or whatever was supposed to happen next, Penn would walk free, and Greg would pay for what he'd done.

The last I'd heard, he'd been transferred from the hospital to some penitentiary system and processed. No mention of bail or whiff of him being released.

Would Penn and Greg see each other inside, or would they be kept apart, knowing the history and the reason for Penn's incarceration?

I had so many questions about the law and judicial system.

I hated being uneducated on topics I'd never had to know before.

Clicking open a new web browser, I typed in: *how to free someone framed for a crime they didn't commit.*

As the results loaded, my phone vibrated across my desk with an incoming call.

Sage tried to swat it before I scooped it up and looked at caller I.D.

Larry.

I couldn't answer it fast enough. "Yes? Larry. Any news?"

Poor guy called me every day and got the same panicked questions.

"I'm downstairs. They've allowed visitation. I'm heading over there if you want to come."

I stood up so fast my chair fell backward. "I'm on my way."

* * * * *

Willingly walking into such a clinical, terrifying place tied my stomach into unfixable knots.

My heart lodged in my throat as Larry guided me through the process of signing in, being searched, and given a visitor badge. The forms we had to sign, the rules we had to abide by—it all made me believe I was the guilty party and I'd never be allowed to walk out of there again.

How did Larry do it so often with his clients?

How did loved ones visit their incarcerated family and not have panic attacks while trudging the hallways to see them?

David had followed in the Range Rover, even though I'd traveled with Larry in his Town Car. I'd refused to let David come in with us, and the last I'd seen of him, before entering this awful building, was his pissed off and frustrated expression where he sat in the parking lot.

"Why did it take so long to grant visitors?" I asked, handing over my gray cashmere jacket to go through the x-ray machine.

"Long?" Larry chuckled. "My dear, this is quick. I'll admit I leaned heavily on a few people to make this happen. But consider this super-sonic."

"It's been two weeks."

"Two weeks is nothing for a remand prisoner."

"Remand?"

Larry slowed his step, educating me on this terrifying new world. "Being held in remand is what Penn is currently facing. He hasn't been convicted or even given a trial date. He wasn't granted bail based on his prior record and could technically endure a long stint before we can show them the truth and get him freed."

I swallowed hard.

Two weeks had been awful. I didn't think I could wait much longer. It wasn't the fact I needed him with me or that I desperately needed to just *talk* to him to smooth out our crinkled edges—I just hated to think of him in here, locked up like a beast. "How long?"

Larry cleared his throat; his unwillingness to answer made

his cheeks flush. "Well, I've already invoked the right for a speedy trial which technically means it should go before a judge within forty-five days. However, Penn is special. I wouldn't be surprised if paperwork goes missing or 'inevitable delays' occur."

My shoulders sunk as if he'd piled sand on top of me, burying me alive.

His voice shifted into caring. "We'll get him out, Elle, but I've had some cases that can take anywhere from one to three years for a verdict to be reached."

The floor wobbled as if it suddenly became a surfboard in high seas. *"What?"*

His hand landed on my forearm, features filling with pity. "That's why so many people take a plea bargain because it means they can skip the long wait time. But in Penn's case—he can't."

My brain throbbed. "Why?"

"Because any plea bargain would bury him—thanks to enemies in high places. His only chance now is to plead not-guilty and accept however long it takes to get that hearing and have evidence speak for itself."

I wedged a fist into my stomach, trying to hold in the acid threatening to wash away my heart. "Greg will testify against him."

Larry's face darkened, but he shrugged as if it wasn't a big deal.

He couldn't hide the fact that it was a *very* big deal.

"Well, I have a few game plans up my sleeve so that shouldn't matter too much."

I didn't want to ask but my lips formed words, and they traveled to Larry's ears. "What if they don't work? What if they—"

He shook his head, squeezing my arm kindly. "One thing this business has taught me is not to play the 'what-if' game. If there are any monsters in this word, Elle, it's those two inconsequential words. 'What-if'...well, if you invite that question into your life, you'll go insane, and nothing else will matter but the ever revolving answers and terrors that 'what-if' can provide."

I shivered. It wasn't the first time Larry had been so wise nor would it be the last I was sure.

"In here." The officer acting as our escort guided us down stark gray hallways where harsh lighting offered no comfort. My heels clacked as we passed through another locked door with bars on the glass window. "You have thirty minutes. No touching. No tampering with prison property. No giving the prisoner gifts or contraband. Break the rules, and you'll be asked to leave with a three week non-admittance. Got it?"

Larry rolled his eyes. "Frank, you know me. I'm here all the time. When have I ever broken the rules?"

Frank coughed, rubbing his prison guard uniform importantly. "It only takes one, Mr. Barns." He narrowed his eyes at me pointedly.

Larry rubbed his mouth. "You know, I had asked for a private room. Important lawyer stuff to talk over. You understand."

Frank scowled. "Not today. Fully booked. Take what you get. Next time, maybe."

Larry tapped his temple in farewell. "Next time, it is." Taking my elbow, he added, "Come along, Elle. Let's not keep Penn waiting."

We pushed into the room, and instantly, my eyes leaped over the couples and families gathered with their heads close over metal tables. The gray day outside offered no warmth to the gray misery inside. The only window showed gunmetal clouds with the odd speckle of rain on the barred glass.

Larry muttered under his breath. "He'd better not have refused his visitation rights again." He searched the room, looking for a handsome, arrogant prisoner and finding nothing.

"He can refuse?" My heart lurched. "Why would he refuse?"

"Because he has this stupid thing called pride." He lit up.

"But it seems today, he's decided to join us, after all." Pressing my elbow again, he guided me toward the back of the room where a man in dark green overalls—same as all the other men in this place—appeared by the door escorted by a guard.

The instant his eyes met mine, the prison faded.

It was only him and me.

Me and him.

Larry didn't even factor.

My arms ached to hug him. To tell him I was here even if I wasn't there the first time he'd been arrested. I muttered under my breath, "I hate that stupid rule."

Larry raised an eyebrow. "What?"

"The no touching one."

He chuckled. "Ah, yes, I didn't factor in how hard that would be for you two. For me, touching clients isn't exactly normal procedure."

Penn was in hearing distance, striding forward to join us. "I stopped being your client the moment you gave me a bed for the night."

Larry grinned, relief coming off him in waves. "That's true. And you became the son I never had when you agreed to come back to New York with me for my treatment. I know how hard that was for you."

Penn flicked a quick glance at me. Hiding yet more things. Where had he been before Larry got sick? Did he hate New York because of the imprisonment or were there other factors, too?

Factors like me?

"Hello, Penn." I tucked my hands behind my back, mainly to stop myself from reaching for him but also to hide the shakes at seeing him again. It was the strangest date I'd ever been on with a lawyer as our chaperone and the state prison as our restaurant of choice.

"Elle." He crossed his arms, his biceps tight and arms ropy. Did he cross them for the same reason I kept mine behind my back? So he didn't reach for me?

"Are you—are you okay?" I glanced around the room as Larry took a seat at a free table.

"Fine." Penn motioned for me to sit too, pulling up a chair to face us. "You?"

"Good." I grabbed my hair, twisting it into a rope over my shoulder like I always did when I was nervous. Penn's gaze followed my hands, black hunger flashed with desire. His eyes stopped on the fading bruise on my face, his jaw clenching. "If he wasn't already in lock-up, I'd punch him all over again for what he did to you."

I had no reply.

Should I tell him I'd paid Greg a visit? That I'd been idiotic on his behalf? That I would never stop fighting for him?

The awkwardness between us reached an epic ten. My hands itched to grasp his. My lips ached to kiss away the pain of our last meeting and start anew.

Why couldn't we touch? How would we delete this strange tension?

I couldn't stop looking at him. His tussled hair, the thicker growth on his face. He hadn't shaved, and for the first time, he looked like Nameless from three years ago. His lips were the full kissable ones framed by a dark beard. Half of his prettiness masked by stubble.

My heart growled with possession and apologies. I couldn't stop reliving the awfulness of him walking down the stairs in police custody telling me he had no way to convince me he was who he said because he'd never told me his name.

How I could be so *blind?*

Tears tickled, welling from the constant pit I tried my best not to swim in. "Penn, I'm so sorry."

He stiffened. His jaw worked as his eyes filled with emotion so deep and tangled, I'd need a century to learn everything there was to know about him.

"I know." He lowered his face, his gaze hooded and dark. "Me, too. It's me who should apologize for—"

"No." I shook my head fiercely. "You have nothing to be

sorry for. It's all my fault." A lonely tear escaped. "It's my fault you were taken the first time and now history has repeated itself. It seems whenever you're around me, I get you locked up."

He chuckled, his chest rising and falling, begging me to touch it. To smooth away the remaining faded yellow and green of his bruises. To reassure myself that he was still eating and drinking and staying alive even while caged up.

How did I ever believe I could walk away from him? How did one truth delete so many lies and make everything seem inconsequential now he was back in my life?

Technically, Penn was a stranger.

Realistically, we had two lifetimes to reveal and compatibility to test.

But something intrinsic and basic linked us together, ignoring timelines and date-numbers. I'd wanted him from the first moment I met him. I wanted him now I knew the truth.

There was so much to say but how could we with so many people watching and listening?

I wanted to spill how many sleepless nights I'd had while searching for him. How my need to find him wedged a small splinter between my father and me. How I'd never looked at another man because a part of me still believed he was the one.

You can *say all those things.*

The other prisoners are here with their own families.

They wouldn't listen to us when they had such a finite amount of time to listen to the people they loved.

I opened my mouth to blurt a billion things at once. To tell him just how desperate I was to fix everything I'd done wrong.

However, Larry saved me from tripping over myself with inappropriate nonsense. "I'm in the process of finding out when your hearing will be. I'll get it fast tracked as quickly as I can."

Penn nodded, keeping his thoughts about that hidden. "Thank you."

"Anything you need? Anything you think will benefit me in overthrowing this?" Larry pulled out a legal pad, ready to take notes.

Penn snorted. "Apart from getting Arnold Twig on the stand and interrogating him with hard evidence of his tampering with my life? Nope." He leaned back in the chair. "Talk to Gio. See if he's had enough and is ready to throw Sean under the bus. He was coming around to the idea the last time I visited him. He agrees it's fucking stupid to serve time for a crime that he only did on Sean's encouragement."

That reminds me.

Talking about Gio poked awake all my questions, making them buzz like angry bees. "Why do you have Gio's license in your safety deposit box?" The sentence splattered against the table with an offending command.

I hadn't meant to say it with no lead in or kind words.

Whoops.

Penn stilled, his eyes narrowing on mine. "You went through the box?"

I jumped, lies sprang to spill.

No, of course not.

I would never.

But I was sick of lies.

Truth only from now on. "Yes." I took ownership. "Every piece."

His lips ghosted a smile. "And?"

"And?"

"You want to know why I have Gio's license."

I nodded. "Yes."

"Anything else?"

I frowned.

Penn leaned forward, toying with me in his sexy, cocky way. Even trapped in here, he still captured me with every look and word. "You must have other questions, apart from Gio."

My heart turned into a hot piece of coal, desperate for the prison to vanish and a bed to miraculously appear so I could torture Penn with kisses to tell me the truth. Or let him torture me with them while telling me anything he wanted.

I licked my lips, my body heavy and wanting. "I have so many questions. We'd be here until next year if I asked them all."

His nostrils flared, hearing the sex in my voice. "I don't care if it took ten years." He switched to an intoxicating whisper. "But not in here. It fucking kills me to see you in here." Pain cloaked him as if remembering to cover his emotions from the harsh elements of incarceration. "If I'm being honest, I didn't want to see you today."

I flinched as if he'd slapped me. "What? Why?"

Larry sighed, understanding when I didn't, allowing Penn to enlighten me.

The intensity between us hummed as his gaze dropped to my lips then back to my eyes. He throbbed with frustration but most of all embarrassment.

His voice snapped, "Because I don't want you seeing me like this..." His sudden temper couldn't hide his anger. "It isn't a good place, Elle. Having you here? It fucks me off all while making me so damn grateful that you're willing to step foot inside just for me."

He scrubbed his forehead with both hands, hiding behind his palms for a second. Inhaling hard, he murmured, "I fucking hate all of this and most of me wants to tell you to leave and never come back, while the other part wants to beg you to stay so I don't have to be so goddamn alone. It fucking hurts that in a few minutes, I have to watch you walk away and I'm not allowed to go with you."

He shook his head, a slave to his own crippling rage. "Goddammit, I feel like I'm going to explode."

Larry looked around stealthily, vibrating calm. "Just keep it together for a little longer. You know the deal. Don't do anything to warrant longer sentencing." His face turned full of encouragement rather than pity. "Don't worry about Elle. She's here because she wants to be. Don't deny her the right to see you."

My throat swelled with so many things. I barely managed to breathe with the paralyzing need to touch him. To take away his pain, his loneliness, his entrapment. I would give anything to stay with him—regardless of where we were.

To realize that I would willingly trade my rich little life for a world of threadbare sheets and plastic furniture made me understand just how far I'd fallen with no comprehension of what I'd done.

He was hurting because of me. And I couldn't do a damn thing to help.

My hands balled as I said, "I don't care where you are, what you're dressed in, or what you say. I want to be here because *you're* here. Don't make it sound like I'm not strong enough to be here for you."

Temper I kept wound tight unspooled. "This isn't about you anymore, Penn. This is about you, me, Larry. *Us.*"

His back turned ramrod straight. "Us?"

"Us."

"Even after everything I've done?"

"What about everything I *haven't* done?"

We sat staring, breathing, understanding the weight of our own admissions. He'd made me pay. I'd given him a reason to. We both suffered for it.

Penn leaned forward, placing his hands on the table. His voice was dark and raspy, filled with fervor. "I like that word."

Almost unconsciously, I mimicked his position, placing my hands so close but not close enough to his. "What word?"

He glanced subtly left and right, checking where the guards were. Then, with his eyes capturing mine, he ran his pinky over my thumb, sending an electric fire bolt down my finger up my arm and directly into my heart. "Us. It gives me something to fight for."

That one simple touch made me wet in an instant.

I trembled, eyes hooding. "Please…"

Us was a word connected to love, companionship, and

family. Please was a word belonging to a request, a plea—a blatant demand for connection.

I hadn't meant to moan it.

I didn't mean to press against his fingers as if he could take away the unbearable desire in my blood with a simple touch.

But he felt too good.

Too real.

Too warm.

Too Penn.

All my remaining questions evaporated as he stroked me again, breathing, "Fuck, I want to kiss you."

Larry cleared his throat in warning as a guard looked over at us. He didn't care how passionate or reckless this conversation had become. He allowed Penn to sweep me away and believe for just as second we weren't in a prison, we weren't facing separation, we had all the time in the world to talk and build a bridge over the whitewater of our past.

Penn licked his lips as I ran my finger along his.

I completely forgot Larry sat beside me as I moaned, "I'd give anything to kiss you."

That one piece of honesty allowed the rest to flow unhindered.

We tumbled over each other as I said, "I'm so sorry for not believing in you, Penn. There's no way you could've been anyone else. I hope you can forgive me."

While he said, "You hurt me, Elle, but fuck if I don't care anymore. The past few weeks with you…I want more. I want to tell you who I am. All of it."

Tears sprang to my eyes. "You go."

"No, you."

We laughed, our hands inching tighter, brushing pinky to thumb.

"Hey!" A guard pointed at us. "No touching."

I yanked my fingers back but couldn't swallow my smile. "We're going to get you out of here. And then we'll talk."

"Then we'll do a shitload more than just talk." He smirked a little; moving from intense connection to lighthearted joking, a genuine smile breaking his lips. "Going back to my safety deposit box. I always knew you were nosy."

I laughed softly. "Only where you're concerned. And only because you never tell me anything."

"He'll tell you now, though, won't you, Penn?" Larry asked, deadly serious, reinserting himself into the conversation. "Just like you'll tell her the reason why you have Gio's license is because you're listed as his next of kin and agreed to keep his possessions safe."

Larry turned his black-rimmed glasses onto me. "Gio and Penn have become friends thanks to me taking custody of Stewie. It was complicated for a while, but we're all on the same side now."

I liked how he barely knew me, but he was on *my* side as much as he was on Penn's. I'd never met anyone so unbiased and willing to trust than him.

Penn's forehead furrowed. "I know that must sound idiotic seeing as Gio hurt you that night and I roughed him up pretty good. But we've shared the same upbringing too long to turn away when the other needs help."

I blinked away the memories of my clothes being torn in the alley. "I agree. Enemies can become friends. Sometimes, they make better friends as you know the worst."

Penn shrugged. "I suppose." His features shadowed, thinking of things that left a strain around his eyes. "A couple of years ago, I was your enemy."

My heart skipped unhappily. I had no idea what he meant. "You were?"

His desire to talk faded. He reclined in his chair, hiding everything I needed to know. "Shit, I have so much to tell you but I can't do it here." He kicked the table leg, making it rattle.

A guard pointed at him in warning. "Quit it or you're back in your cell."

Larry rolled his eyes. "Plenty of time to talk later. Don't

get yourself riled up."

Penn raked both hands through his hair. "This place makes me insane." Stark panic filled his brown gaze. "How long, Larry? How fucking long do I have to keep everything bottled up so I don't screw myself over even more?"

Larry consulted his notepad, void of scribbles but filled with whatever processes he'd already put in place. "You know I can't give you a time. I don't like dangling promises because they hurt like hell when they don't come true."

"I know." Penn sighed. "Fuck." His shoulders tightened, masking the truth that he was nervous and had no one else to trust but us. Trusting someone and then *trusting* someone were different things. He had no power over what we did on his behalf. He merely had to let Larry arrange dates and file paperwork while I went after Greg and fought for his assurances that he'd retract his statement and redeem himself by doing the right thing.

It was heartbreaking as well as chilling to play God with another's life.

Penn gave me a sad smile, wordlessly apologizing for ruining the remaining time we had left.

Larry took over, murmuring about strategy and evidence.

Penn and I never took our eyes off each other. Desperately aching, constantly seeking for a way to erase this mess and be together.

The thirty minutes went far too fast, and it physically killed me when a bell rang and the inmates said farewell.

No hug.

No kiss.

Nothing but a tear-filled grimace as Penn disappeared all over again.

* * * * *

"Ms. Charlston! Over here!"

Stepping out of the correctional facility, I found a sea of reporters, cameras, and microphones angled toward me instead of a clear path leading toward the black Range Rover and my trusty bodyguard.

What the hell?

Larry instantly covered my face with his briefcase, wrapping his arm around me as he guided me toward David who leaped out of the Range Rover, barreling through the reporters to get to me.

Wrapping me in his protective embrace, David glowered at the churning body parts in our way. "Leave!" he boomed, protecting my other side, marching with Larry as we bulldozed through the paparazzi.

They side-stepped to avoid being run over but it didn't stop their probing questions.

"Ms. Charlston. Are you in a romantic relationship with Penn Everett?" a young man shouted.

"Are you having an affair with Greg Hobson?" a middle-aged woman with blue-rinsed curls yelled.

"Do you think it's appropriate for the owner of such a prominent retail store to be dating two men at once? Both who are in jail, no less?" a male reporter with a squeaky voice asked.

Each question I cowered a little more.

Oh, my God, how did they hear?

Who leaked? Who tattled?

"No comment," Larry snapped, keeping his briefcase obscuring my face. "Go away."

I kept my head down as David opened the back door to the Range Rover, giving me shelter to hop into.

Larry jumped in too, not bothering to call his Town Car.

The questions kept plowing through the windows. Questions I had no answers to. Questions I should've been prepared for thanks to my high-society position, and how juicy my tale would be the moment the smell of controversy arose.

Right now, I was considered top news.

Penn's background would be dug up. Mine would be plastered beside his. Greg's actions would be known nationwide.

Oh God, Dad is going to flip.

The pandemonium of journalists brought everything home.

How deadly serious all of this had become.

How far we still had to go before it would be all over.

Exhaustion pressed me into the soft leather seats as David honked the horn and took off, barely giving the reporters time to jump out of the way.

CHAPTER TWENTY-FOUR

PENN

DINNER WAS YET another sad affair of under-cooked potatoes and over-cooked beef.

At least this time, no one tried to talk to me. I'd earned a reputation over the past couple of weeks that I was a loner with history. I had respect because some old timers remembered me from my previous stints, but I had a mystery that newbies wanted to ruffle up and put me in my place.

I'd avoid all confrontation as long as I could, but eventually, something would snap, and I'd be in the middle of a war I didn't want.

Yard time after Elle and Larry left ensured I could run off some of the stress of seeing them. I'd fucking promised myself I'd deny visitation if they came. But that was before the temptation and overwhelming desire to see Elle overrode my common sense.

I'd braced myself for pity or loathing in her gaze, looking at me in my prison uniform. I waited for hesitation about her feelings for me, or the awful condemning admittance that she couldn't handle this.

But she hadn't done either of those things.

She'd watched me as she always did—as if she wanted me to jump on top of her and fuck her in terribly dirty ways. She listened to me as if I *meant* something. She spoke as if this was personal, and she'd have my back all the way. She touched me as if she cared for me despite everything I'd done.

It didn't escape me the way Larry looked at her. He was proud of her. Shit, *I* was proud of her. It made me wade through guilt that I could ever think she was a spoiled brat. Sure, I knew how hard she worked now. I understood that Belle Elle wasn't given to her or that she coasted through life on a trust fund. She worked her fingers to the bone. And she was strong—so fucking strong.

Why did I ever doubt she would fight for me if I'd given her the chance?

I'd had everything so wrong.

Assumptions had sure made an ass out of me and look how fucked I was. If I'd just knocked on her door that night, we might've avoided this whole disaster. Greg would never have thought he stood a chance with her because I would've claimed her.

I would've ensured she was mine just like the necklace I'd given back to Stewie was hers.

I was a moron back then, but I wouldn't be a moron now.

She wanted me? She had me. Because, Christ, I wanted her.

Tonight was TV night for the guys in my block. A lot mingled, not really listening, playing cards or placing bets on events they'd never be able to pay regardless of winning or losing—unless it was with things gained from inside.

Rubbing my face, I forced my body to let go of the lust Elle had created. Unsuccessfully reminding myself that Elle and I wouldn't be fucking for a long time to come. Celibacy was the new rule in our relationship. Which made it so goddamn hard as I wanted her so bad.

I needed her even worse.

I needed her to lie to me for a change and tell me this would all go away and I'd be free again. I needed her to touch me and tell me she'd wait for me no matter how long it took, even while I pushed her away so she didn't waste her life alone.

I scoffed at the thoughts, hearing the truth behind them.

She didn't need to touch me to assure me she'd wait for me—I saw her loyalty in every blink and heard it in every vowel.

And she didn't need to lie about my freedom.

I would get it back.

Eventually.

Larry was fighting for me. He'd win.

He has to.

There was no other scenario I could accept.

Stretching out my legs with ankles crossed, I did my best to unwind and watch the men around me—taking note of their weakness and strategies, cataloguing who to chat with versus those to stay away from.

I had to be smart and play a long game even if I hoped I'd only endure a short inning.

The sound of a car horn wrenched my head to the TV where local news was playing.

My chair legs screeched on the linoleum as I sat up and scooted forward.

Elle filled the screen.

A blurred photo of her climbing into the Range Rover with David and Larry doing their best to obscure her. They couldn't hide the tangle of pretty blonde hair or her sexy body, though.

I'd recognize her anywhere.

The news anchor in her bright red suit droned, "Today, a name that is normally reserved for retail news has been dragged into controversy with the recent love triangle. According to sources, Noelle Charlston, who is the head of the family's empire Belle Elle retail chain, has been dealing with a few unusual matters of late. Things haven't been smooth sailing for the young CEO ever since rumors began of her engagement to Penn Everett.

"After a string of unsuccessful romantic set-ups over the past few years, Ms. Charlston has somehow wound up dating two men—both who have ended up in jail for reasons not entirely known. What we do know is Greg Hobson, the son of Steve Hobson, who has worked for the Charlston family for four decades, is being held for kidnapping and attempted rape while Penn Everett, a well-known offender who struck it big with a penny stock a year ago, is being held for aggravated assault including attempted murder.

"We tried to get more facts from Ms. Charlston as she was leaving the correctional facility, but she declined to comment."

A prisoner turned to face me, his eyes glowing with violence. "Hey, you're Everett, aren't cha?"

Shit.

Another guy with tattoos all over his arms and a shaved head stood up, his posture screaming *'oh, it's on, buddy.'* He cocked his head. "Seems we have a celebrity in our midst, boys."

Christ, I didn't want to fight.

I smirked condescendingly, slipping back into the armor I'd perfected from the streets. "Nothing to get excited about. Typical news junkies don't know what they're saying."

The tatted inmate chuckled. "Oh yeah? Guess, we'll just have to find out for ourselves, won't we?" He cracked his knuckles. "Be prepared to spill, Everett. We'll plan a nice chat, you and me."

Goddammit.

I'd done my best to avoid this.

But the games had begun, all thanks to the fucking news.

A prisoner, who wasn't aware of the showdown about to start, bellowed at one of the guards. "Turn the news off, man. Who fucking cares about that shit."

No one cares.

Apart from me.

Never taking my eyes off the two men squaring me up, I stood and left the room. They'd let me go—they'd have no choice.

But tomorrow, they'd ambush.

I had to be ready.

I had to attack them before they attacked me.

I had tonight to prepare.

After that...*it's war.*

Chapter Twenty-Five

Elle

"YOU CAN'T GET mixed up in this, Elle."

I looked up as Dad appeared in my office, his fingers wrapped around the daily newspaper. He still wore his three-piece suits as fashion statements. The one of choice today demanded obedience in sharp midnight blue. His cheeks glowed warm; his eyes bright but disapproving. He'd lost the stress of my disappearance and bounced back healthier than ever.

I no longer leapt to my feet to hold his elbow in fear of his heart playing tricks. He was robust and old-fashioned, and my hackles rose as he marched to my desk, then perched on the side as he always did, looking down at me in my chair.

I'd expected this.

Ever since I'd turned the news on last night and seen myself being shuttled like a convict to the awaiting Range Rover, I'd waited for my father to railroad me.

To be told I couldn't be seen in such unflattering situations.

That all news was bad news, and it was up to me to keep

controversy as far away from Belle Elle's shop shelves as possible.

"This will slander Belle Elle's name," Dad said.

Didn't he see it would slander me for the rest of my life if I did nothing? Belle Elle was decades old. It was more than just a company—it was a lifestyle: a part of so many people's lives. Our quality merchandise was in every adult's and child's wardrobe across the States and Canada.

Belle Elle didn't need me.

Penn does.

Meeting his eyes with confidence I didn't necessarily feel, I said, "Hello to you, too. Please, I'm not busy or anything."

"The passive-aggressive comments won't fly with me, Elle." He scowled, his elderly face becoming even more wrinkled than normal. "We need to talk about this." He waved the rolled up newspaper, no doubt filled with more tabloids and finger pointing.

"There's nothing to talk about."

Penn is mine and I'll stand by him.

I don't care what you say.

I cleared my throat with impatience as Fleur came in. She paused on the threshold, her arms full of paperwork that I'd neglected. "Ah, just in time." I stood, waving her over eagerly. I would use anything I could to postpone the inevitable fight with my father.

I didn't want to have to yell at him. I didn't want to be disrespectful, but I knew what he was about to say, and I wouldn't let him stop me anymore.

"You sure it's a good time?" Fleur rocked back on her heels, making her escape—knowing as well as I did what sort of argument was about to explode.

"No, don't be silly." I patted my desk. "Just put those here."

"Okay…" Fleur clipped forward, smiling politely at Dad, not giving me the usual broad grin of friendship. "Hello, Mr. Charlston." Placing the folders on my desk, she gave me a quick arched eyebrow. That eyebrow said: *are you okay? Want me to do anything? Should I get the tranquilizer gun?* Her voice said, "Anything else?"

I had no doubt she would do something crazy if I asked, but this conversation was all on me.

I shook my head. "Thank you. That's all. It's getting late; you should head home."

"Only if you're sure?"

"I'm sure."

"Thanks for your help." Dad smiled kindly at her. "You've been a very loyal staff member to Belle Elle and my daughter."

Fleur wasn't the blushing sort, but her cheeks pinked. "You're welcome." Turning for the door, she glanced back before disappearing into the hallway.

Her interruption had been too short, but to Dad, it had been too long.

His eyes glowed with irritation. "Elle, what the hell were you doing at the prison yesterday?"

And so it begins.

I held my head high. "I went to see Penn. Or did you forget we're engaged?"

It seemed like years ago since Penn had pulled that particular lie over my father and everyone at the office, but for the first time, I found it convenient rather than a nuisance.

He scrubbed his face. "Are you sure about that? I've been having doubts about you two. It happened too fast, Elle. After what just occurred with Greg and now court dates and testimonies—I don't want you getting stressed out."

"Me?" My voice rose with a perfectly curled question mark. "*Me* get stressed? What about you? Are you taking the meds your doctor prescribed? I don't think you should even be at the office. I have things under control."

All right, that lie was obvious and entirely hollow.

I wasn't coping. I didn't have things under control. Mainly because I couldn't stop my mind from drifting to Penn and Nameless and Penn and prison.

Penn, Penn, Penn.

It was a vicious circle and not one I could stop.

"Don't you worry about me." He took my hand, pulling me forward to pat it dotingly. "You were kidnapped by a man who's been a part of our family for years. You won't tell me what happened in the cabin. All you'll say on the matter is that Penn saved you, but then Greg filed charges." He scowled. "There's more to that story, Elle, and I don't like you keeping things from me. Why did you go see Greg in the hospital if he hurt you?"

I sighed heavily. "I'm not keeping things from you, but I am going to keep fighting for Penn. He didn't do anything wrong."

"Ah, yes, about that." His face fell even further, resembling an unhappy hound. "You can't be seen visiting inmates, Elle. You have a reputation to maintain. Our company as a whole has to do what it can to stay on the right side of the law with no controversy."

I laughed a little. "Don't you think Greg already caused controversy? No matter how we keep that under wraps, details will get elaborated and the story will snowball on its own. The best way to deal with the media is to grant an interview asking for understanding and give them the hard truth, so false rumors don't destroy everything we've created."

Dad blanched. "You can't be serious. The right thing to do is stay away from those vultures and just let it die a natural death." He paused before saying with fatherly authority. "Just like I don't want you seeing Penn again."

I gasped. "How can you say that? You liked him. You gave him your blessing to *marry* me even when I was telling you it was fake."

"So your engagement *is* fake?" His features lit up. "Well, in that case, I believe you now. That means you don't have to do anything reckless when it comes to—"

"Dad…" I shook my head with disappointment. "You don't get it. It started off fake, but it turns out he's—"

The man from Central Park.

The words dangled on my tongue, clinging with little claws to stay unsaid. I swayed between delivering them and swallowing them back.

For three years, Dad did everything he could to stop me from looking for Nameless (after he'd been cooperative at the start). When my hunt for him started to interfere with my work, Dad swiftly put a stop to it.

This time, I wouldn't give him any more reason to block my helping Penn.

Dad had an obsessive desire to keep Belle Elle and me away from less than satisfactory circumstances—including people.

Only, he didn't understand that no one was perfect. He wasn't. I wasn't. The world wasn't. Penn was no different, and he deserved every chance to prove he was more than just a liar and reveal the truth.

He's special.

To me. To my life. To my future.

I wouldn't jeopardize that for anyone.

Including my father.

"He's what?" He cocked an eyebrow. "Finish that sentence."

"He's on his own, Dad. Sure, he has Larry fighting for him, but I want to be there, too. I'm sorry if it upsets you, but I'm not going to stop."

He slid off my desk, crossing his arms. "It's not that I don't want you to be there for him, Elle. I'm not trying to be cruel by cutting him off from emotional support. But sometimes, other things take paramount. I'm thinking of the company. It's not good PR."

"Well, we'll hire a team to reinvent our image after it's over."

"Over?"

I nodded. "Yes, Penn will be given a court date soon, and we can finally get the truth out. Then he'll be released, and it will be over."

"How long do you think that will take?"

I shrugged. "It depends on the justice system."

I sounded so much more knowledgeable than I was.

The way he gnawed his bottom lip gave me an idea. "You know...you could help speed this process along, if you wanted."

"I can? How?" He narrowed his eyes warily.

"By calling your judge friend. Put in a good word. Get a court date, sooner rather than later, so we can all move on with our lives."

"You want me to tamper with courts and trials now, Elle?" He looked at the ceiling. "What's become of you?"

"The need to fix everything I did wrong."

His look was quizzical, but he didn't ask for a structured explanation of my cryptic reply.

Instead, he kissed the top of my head. "Oh, very well. If it means this will all blow over faster, I'll see what I can do."

CHAPTER TWENTY-SIX

PENN

THE AMBUSH HAPPENED four days later in the recreational yard.

Three men stopped me mid-jog.

After doing my best to come up with a counter attack, I gave up. I had no weapons, no friends to back me up.

I was on my own. And unless I wanted to die in retaliation, I had to let it happen.

So I did.

No matter how much it fucked me off.

Their fists gave me an unwanted 'welcome to the neighborhood' rough up. Their feet delivered a well-heard 'this is our turf, so don't get any fucking ideas' kick. Their growls told me exactly how to toe the line and behave.

They seemed to know where a dead zone existed in the security cameras on the jogging track. They didn't hesitate to gift a beating that activated old injuries, memories, and wounds from my past.

The punch-up only lasted a few seconds, but they knew how to deliver pain.

And I knew how to listen to their message.

I let them get in a few good strikes then exploded and delivered a few myself. I'd let them put me in my place because it meant I wouldn't be harassed further. But I wouldn't be a fucking pussy because that was just the start of a worse war.

The tightrope to walk was so damn narrow, but I'd walked it before. I could walk it now.

They were the shit in here. Not me. They thought they'd disciplined me. They hadn't. Everyone went away slightly happier and settled.

Even if I limped rather than stalked and their punches activated old injuries from Greg's morning wake-up call the day he took Elle.

I gave up running for the rest of the afternoon and sat on the bleachers tending to a busted lip and bloody nose.

No one commented on my state, and I nodded curtly at the assholes who'd given me the lesson when they walked back to their cells after the bell rang.

Just like school had bullies, prison had thugs. It was all a chessboard in the end. No one was king for long. And no one stayed a rook forever. We were all jumping over each other trying to win the queen.

Trudging back to my cell, I spat out a glob of blood. I'd never been soft or naïve in my life—I couldn't after seeing death and never having a home—but the awful fact was, I *had* begun to relax a little. I'd relaxed knowing Larry had my back, and Elle was mine after so many mistakes.

I'd relished in playing games with her because it soothed some of the pain. I'd become the bully, and with my belly bruised and face forming a nice black eye, I was reminded how much it fucking sucked to be the victim.

Yet here I was, held in remand with no way out on an attempted murder charge, buried up to my balls in shit.

At least, now I was in jail, Arnold wouldn't be able to fuck up my life as bad. Unless he was in the habit of bribing the warden or commissioner of corrections, I was out of his control.

For now.

I needed to see Larry.

And Elle.

Fuck, I needed to see Elle.

* * * * *

Another two weeks.

Fourteen measly days on top of all the rest.

A fucking lifetime.

I lived in sameness every day, tormenting myself with thoughts of a happier memory, spending whatever freedom I was given between working, eating, and yard work in the library.

The books hadn't changed.

The reading material was no better.

But at least the notepad and pen gave me an outlet to scribble my thoughts and see if there was any way around my mess.

I kept those notes with me safe, posting pages to Larry on mail days so he could have some idea of what I knew and suspected between our meetings.

Today was Wednesday, which meant the only thing to look forward to were spaghetti and meatballs for dinner and our turn in the media room for the allotted ninety minutes.

My life is fucking riveting.

As I made my bed, preparing for a new day in this walled city, a guard appeared. He had to be just out of his teens, filled with the need to be the best and most liked officer on staff. It made me hate him immediately.

"Everett, visitor."

I dropped my pillow onto the bed. "You sure?"

The guard rolled his eyes as if I was a simpleton. "Of course, I'm sure."

I had no response to that cocky attitude. I didn't feel like getting into a fight with a newbie. I'd been told that other personal visits would be strictly monitored and most likely denied because of the upcoming trial. Turned out, Larry got around it.

Then again, what trial?

I had no correspondence on when my case would be heard. If it was anything like last time, I'd end up serving more time waiting for the trial than I did after being convicted. The fact that the time served was subtracted from my sentence wasn't a relief. It was hollow—especially if you'd served six months and the offense only deserved a three-month term.

This entire process was screwed the fuck up.

Innocent until proven guilty my ass.

"Fine." I dragged my fingers through my hair. "Let's go then."

Following the officer through the usual riff-raff of prisoners, I kept my eyes forward, not lingering on anyone in particular. My prison-issued sneakers squeaked on the linoleum as the guard swiped his I.D and ushered me through to the small processing room then through another security point to the visitation areas.

I swayed to the left, following the hallway I knew led to the meeting hall where I'd last seen Elle and Larry.

"Not that way." The guard rubbed his nose, his dark hair dull and needing a haircut. "This one." He pointed at the right hallway.

I probably shouldn't but I asked, "Private?"

He nodded.

My heart did a strange skip cough. Private meant Larry had come to talk—away from prying ears. Private meant Elle wouldn't be with him because only client-attorney relationships were deemed sacred enough to have privacy.

Conjugal visits in this place were like fucking gold nuggets—rare and hard to earn. There was no way to hug your lover or even touch to reassure both of you that this fucked-up place couldn't tear you apart forever.

Goddammit, I hate it here.

Swallowing back my frustrated anger, I followed silently.

Passing a few meeting rooms with matching metal doors, bars on viewing windows, and large locks, we stopped outside private room number six. The officer rapped on the door with his knuckles, giving me a quick glance.

I linked my fingers together in front of me. Remaining the perfect prisoner when all I wanted to do was handcuff the fresh-out-of-the-academy idiot and teach him what it was like to have your freedom stolen.

Larry opened the door, beaming. "Ah, great. Thanks for bringing my client."

The officer nodded. "Welcome. You have thirty minutes. Press the button if you require assistance before that. For your safety, we'll record visual but not audio."

Larry nodded, ever the professional. "Great. See you in thirty." Pulling my arm, he tugged me into the room and closed the door in the guard's face.

We couldn't lock it from the inside, but the illusion of having a door between them and us…fuck, it was the best goddamn thing in weeks.

"Hey." Larry slapped me on the back. "How you holding up?"

I shrugged. "Can't complain."

I could fucking complain, but Larry was already doing so much for me. I wouldn't turn him into my agony aunt, too.

"I'm glad." Pointing behind me, he added, "By the way, I brought you a gift."

"Better be a burger and fries." I smirked, turning on the spot.

Something light and sexy and so fucking addicting leaped into my arms. "Penn."

Instantly, my embrace wrapped around her, squeezing so tight I had to remind myself not to kill the girl I wanted more than anything.

I forgot about Larry.

I forgot about cameras and guards and court dates.

My body took over.

I did the only thing I could.

Her face tipped up.

Mine tipped down.

I groaned long and low as our lips connected, and she deepened the kiss the moment we met. I switched from expecting a friendly but purely platonic meeting with my benefactor to slamming Elle against the wall and kissing her until I couldn't goddamn breathe.

My hands no longer obeyed my brain; they tracked over her, my thumbs rubbing the beads of her nipples, barely hidden beneath whatever clothes she wore.

I was so drunk on her, I couldn't look away to see if she wore a convenient skirt to hoist up and delete the remaining space between us.

Larry cleared his throat.

It didn't register or stop me in the slightest.

But it did stop Elle.

She withdrew from the kiss, pushing my chest a little to give her some space.

I blinked, coming back to earth with a smash.

Fuck, what was I thinking? Touching wasn't permitted. I didn't want to layer yet more crimes to my long tally.

I'll never fucking get out of here.

And that was suddenly so important now I'd had a tiny taste of what I was missing.

Holding up my hands, I backed away from Elle, looking at the ceiling where a camera had recorded every passionate indiscretion.

"Shit." My cock throbbed, heavy and noticeable in my prison scrubs.

Elle rubbed her mouth. Her lips puffy and red from my overgrown stubble. Had it really been over a month since I'd kissed her? Fucked her in my limo? It felt like decades.

She smiled. "That was quite the hello."

I smirked. "You started it. You launched at me, not the other way around." And Christ that made me happy. To know she'd moved past the issues I'd caused, the lies I'd told. That she was willing to accept me as *me*, not as Penn or that phantom she called Nameless. Me. With no more bullshit between us.

I opened my arms, encompassing the room and jail behind. "You're here."

"I am." Her gaze skated to Larry then back to me. Her fingers pulled the hem of her black blazer; smoothing it over the hip-hugging skirt that kissed her knees.

Black suit, white shirt, and silver heels. Her hair was twisted up on top of her head—showing off the expanse of her long neck where my canines watered to bite. A pair of black framed glasses stuck out of her blazer breast pocket.

She looked like a sexy librarian...or—

"Elle is my assistant for the day," Larry explained as he pulled out a chair and sat at the single table. "It was the only way she was allowed in."

My lips tilted, remembering other times when I'd been his assistant. He'd gotten me into Fishkill countless of times to see Gio—partly to be his helper and note taker but also to nurture the slowly developing friendship between the man I'd fought with on the streets and the man now begging for scraps of news about his brother.

We put aside our petty grievances and discussed Stewie's progress and intelligence at school.

We bonded over caring for his younger sibling.

We grew up.

Leaving Elle—even though it killed me—I marched to the table and sat. My skin tingled to touch hers. My mouth watered to kiss her again. But I'd already risked Larry's generosity by slamming her into the wall the second they arrived.

I twisted to look at the camera again. "They'll have that on tape." I licked my lips, tasting blueberry lip-gloss. "I shouldn't have done that."

Larry opened a folder holding the scribbled notes I'd sent him, along with a few computer typed ones from his own homework. "It'll be on record. There's no way for someone to alter the footage—not the lowly guy I have an understanding with anyway. But rest assured, they won't use it." He pulled his pen from his pocket, chuckling. "However, don't go thinking you can get away with sex. I'm not leaving and I can't go without my lovely assistant. Besides, screwing my staff would most likely end up on some dodgy prison porn site that would go viral and screw you over even more."

Dropping my hands below the table, I did some subtle rearranging of my hard-on. "I know you have a point but being in this room with Elle. Shit, you're asking a starving man not to eat the banquet."

Elle blushed, pulling out the last seat next to Larry. Her hand snuck across the table.

I snatched it, holding it sweetly as if we were first-time boyfriend and girlfriend rather than the reality that if I didn't hold on, I'd drown in this motherfucking place.

It took a lot to keep my cool and pretend nothing bothered me here. That I could handle whatever they threw at me. That I didn't give a shit about Arnold Twig and his lying sack of shit son, Sean.

But with Elle here…it made me softer somehow. Showed me how much I bottled up and how much I wished I could just run and be free.

Elle's gaze narrowed on my lower jaw where the fading bruise of the beating two weeks ago remained. "You're hurt."

I shrugged, down playing it as Larry narrowed his gaze. He knew full well what went on in places like this. Elle had no idea. I squeezed her fingers. "I'm fine."

Her blue eyes glossed with tears. "But someone hurt you."

"I'm okay, Elle. Don't. Don't torture yourself." My voice echoed with need for her to listen to me, obey me. She'd go mad if she didn't. "It's nothing that I can't handle."

And it was true.

Ever since the beating, I hadn't been touched. Sure, I'd endured a few curse words and stolen lunches, but overall, my strategy of staying low and alone was working. Half of the inmates couldn't be assed with me and the rest were slightly afraid, wondering why I was so quiet.

"Why did they hit you?" Her gaze danced over my face, latching onto a healing scratch on my neck. "Can we do something?"

My heart raced in fear of her making things worse. "Don't do a thing. It's my fight. Not yours."

Larry backed me up. "He's fine, Elle. Leave him be."

She sniffed, anger replacing her sadness. "I hate all of this."

"Me, too." My joints splintered to drag her over the table and into my lap. To kiss her and delete the awful cluttered space between us.

Larry caught my wistful expression. I wished he hadn't.

"It's going to be okay, Penn." He patted my arm, smiling at mine and Elle's joined hands. "You're doing great."

Once upon a time, I hadn't trusted him when he'd said the exact same thing. I'd laughed in his face. This time, I merely accepted his assurance with a grateful nod.

Elle brought my hand to her lips, kissing me quick. "I positively hate seeing you in here."

Her passion and affection electrocuted my heart.

She gave me the power to keep fighting.

Returning the favor, I ran my lips over her knuckles. "Same. Prison doesn't suit you."

She shuddered, sucking in a breath similar to what she did when I first entered her.

My body hardened, my voice softened, my promise beckoned to be believed. "Don't worry, I'll be out soon. And when I am, I'm never letting you go again."

CHAPTER TWENTY-SEVEN

ELLE

THE LOCUSTS FOUND me the moment I stepped out of jail.

"Ms. Charlston, can you confirm you're engaged to Penn Everett? Do you know he's served time for three other incidents?"

Larry gathered me in a hug as we walked swiftly to David and the Range Rover. David once again barreled through the journalists, his large mass shoving people out of the way with no apology. Once in front of us, he cleaved the crowd like a giant snow plow, giving us a clear path.

He couldn't stop the photos or recording devices from being shoved in my face, but he could at least get me to the vehicle a lot faster than before.

Penn's words echoed in my head. *"I'll be out soon."*

Would he?

The more time I spent with Larry, the more I understood his mannerisms. Just like Penn favored shoving his hands in his pockets, Larry favored scratching his jaw where salt and pepper stubble appeared at the end of a long day when he was either unsure or telling a white lie.

I said white because I doubted he'd ever truly lie. But he definitely wasn't showing his own nervousness about Penn's particular case.

He'd already been locked up for four weeks, four days. The fear that he could be held so long before a resolution or verdict was reached petrified me.

It couldn't be much longer.

I can't leave him there.

I have to do something.

If Greg wouldn't retract his statement and admit he lied under oath about the attempted murder, then I'd have to find other ways to free Penn.

I slammed to a stop in the midst of our rush from the paparazzi.

Larry glanced at me. "Are you okay? Did you trip?"

David looked back, his eyes darting to my feet. "Do you need me to carry you, ma'am?"

I scoffed. "No, I do not need to be carried." Peering at the reporters, losing count after seven of their eager faces and blinking cameras, I said, "I wish to make a statement."

"Of course, Ms. Charlston. We would be honored!" A female shoved her mic close.

Another said, "We offer great packages for exclusives if you'd like to come with me to the office!"

I ignored both, pushing Larry away to stand firm and on my own. I shouldn't do this. I shouldn't feed the vultures when they circled over carrion. But if I could start the campaign on Penn's innocence, perhaps it would help us get him home faster.

David's shoulders tensed, but he didn't try to grab me or interrupt what I was about to do. Thank God because the picture of a silly little CEO being bundled up by her security guard and driven away was not the look I wanted to portray.

Dad will kill me.

But I was past caring.

Inhaling hard, I said, "Penn Everett is innocent."

Questions landed around me like slingshot pebbles. I tuned them out, focusing on the short statement I wanted to make on his behalf. "Penn is innocent, and we will prove that."

"What do you mean by that, Ms. Charlston?" another reported asked.

I held my head higher. "I mean that Mr. Everett has been incarcerated unjustly and when he's freed, I won't stop from persecuting those who stole weeks of his life with lies."

The irony that lies had come back to bite the liar wasn't lost on me.

Penn wasn't innocent on that account. But I'd claimed him, and I wasn't an enemy people wanted.

I had funds.

I had power.

I had a grudge.

I'll make those people pay.

Smiling at the flashing cameras, I hoped my stand had finally shown New York (and my father) that I wouldn't run away from this; I strode confidently to the getaway vehicle and climbed inside.

"Let's go home, David. I have work to do."

CHAPTER TWENTY-EIGHT

PENN

ANOTHER THREE WEEKS passed like soldiers marching me closer to battle.

Two months in this shitty place.

Two months of slop for breakfast, lunch, and dinner.

Two months of bad sleep, aching misery, and unbearable loneliness.

Two months that Elle and Larry went above and beyond for me.

Twice a week—which was my total allotted amount—regardless if I argued or begged for more—she and Larry would call. His conversations were upbeat and positive. Her chats were sex-loaded and frustrated. Talking to Elle made my cock ache and heart squeeze with need.

We never stepped over that line of turning a call into a pleasure fest, but it was hard. So fucking hard.

Especially when her innocent questions like if I was comfy in bed at night were answered by my libido admitting how hard and uncomfortable it was—just like every inch of me dying to sink inside her.

When visitations were permitted, she and Larry came as a pair. A new duo with a bond building by the day. They were no longer acquaintances brought together because of mutual affection for me. They were friends fighting the same battle.

Elle came with gifts such as freshly baked lemon squares from her kitchen. Prisoners weren't allowed to take such presents back to our cells, but we were allowed to eat as much as we could while in the common room, listening to tales of the outside world.

The world I should be a part of but had been stolen from.

Would I have gone after her if I'd known this would happen? Would I have beaten Greg up or merely waited until David arrived to do the dirty work?

I liked to think my answers would switch on those questions. But they never did.

I wouldn't change a thing. I wouldn't have waited for her father or bodyguard to do my job as her lover and protector. I wouldn't have been able to keep my hands to myself, knowing Greg had touched her.

He got what he deserved. And who knew? Maybe I got what I deserved, too.

I'd been an asshole to her. I'd lied and manipulated and cheated her feelings for me three years ago with the feelings she had for me now.

If this was my karma, I'd learned my fucking lesson.

I just wanted to go home with her and never let her out of my sight again.

I would never tell her, but her visits kept me breathing, yet they also stole my courage to keep going. She was so vibrant— so passionate in her fight to free me. So full of trust when before she'd been so riddled with doubt.

Two weeks ago, she broke the rules and hugged me in the common hall just because she couldn't be close and not touch. She risked a visitation ban when she kissed me last week to catcalls of other inmates. Promising me that we would find a way to get me free while being so goddamn sexy, I struggled not to come just from inhaling her perfume.

She gave me life, and she took my life. I hated that she was out there, working so fucking hard on my behalf when all I could do was sit on my ass and count the seconds as they evolved into minutes.

She didn't notice my slowly dwindling enthusiasm or my wavering belief that I'd be acquitted soon.

I smiled, I teased, I lusted.

But behind that, I slowly became lost. I reverted to the homeless kid who had nothing but a pillow and a blanket surrounded by thieves. I struggled to maintain my humanity when all I wanted to do was *kill* the motherfucker who put me here.

Arnold Twig shared my mind almost as much as Elle did.

My hate festered, making me snap at those I cared about when really I should grovel on my knees for all they'd done.

Larry kept pushing for a trial date and kept being told everything was going as fast as it could. No matter who he called or threatened, nothing progressed.

And through it all, I slowly shut down. I packed away my need for Elle, my love for Stewie, my friendship with Gio, and my gratitude to Larry. Piece by piece, I systematically placed each person I cared about into boxes and sealed them tight.

I placed them in the basement below my heart and locked the door.

Because part of me believed the worst.

I was in here now.

And no matter what we tried, I wasn't getting out.

Chapter Twenty-Nine

Elle

"SOMETHING'S WRONG, LARRY. I can feel it."

I pressed my cell-phone hard against my ear as I paced my office. Sage trotted after me with every beeline from my desk to the door. The same door where Penn made me drop to my knees for him. Where he made me come just by pressing against me. Where he'd come the first time and showed me there wouldn't be any bullshit between us when it came to how much we wanted each other.

Those first weeks of our relationship seemed shallow now—all based on sex and no emotion. I'd allowed him to entrap me in orgasms and pleasure, keeping his truth hidden because I didn't have the courage to poke behind his lies.

But that was all over now.

Now, I only needed to look at Penn to know how he was feeling. His dark coffee eyes were so expressive; I doubted how I ever listened to his fibs in the first place. The way he held his stress like a boulder across his shoulders, how his jaw never fully relaxed, how his nostrils flared when he answered questions he didn't like, how his voice pitched into gravel whenever he told me how much he missed me.

His face was an encyclopedia into his heart. It had dictionary references and thesaurus connotations, revealing what an arched eyebrow meant compared to a tongue flicking over his bottom lip.

He'd never come out and said it, but I knew he loved me. I knew it in the way he whispered his thumb over my pinky when the guards weren't looking. I trusted it in the way he looked into my eyes, so deep, so pure. Whatever words he'd spoken were irrelevant because ultimately, all he'd been saying was *I love you*.

His face could even swear eloquently. A tip of his chin or scowl of his forehead was the perfect *fuck you* to the guards who broke us apart.

All this I knew now.

There was nothing shallow about falling head over heels for a man incarcerated where privacy was a none-given luxury, and physical intimacy was denied at all times.

Penn loved me. I loved him.

And that was why I knew something was terribly, terribly wrong.

Larry yawned, causing me to look at my watch. "What's up, Elle? What's wrong?"

It was almost midnight, and I still hadn't left the office. I couldn't. I was too wired, researching bits and pieces Larry had tasked me with, putting together a well-thought-out and correctly edited document to read in court if and when Penn was given a date.

I quit my pacing, forcing my heart rate to return to sane rather than crazy. "Penn isn't doing so well."

That was an understatement.

How could I expect him to be happy and thrive in a place where violence and misdemeanors were the only forms of conversation and habit?

He pretended otherwise, but each time I saw him, he seemed a little more…empty. As if he'd stuffed every feeling he'd had, every love and goodness, and buried it so deep, he was vacant inside.

"You noticed too, huh?" Larry cleared his throat, giving me his full attention. "He's losing hope."

"But he can't lose hope. He has to stay strong." Tears sprang to my eyes. My emotions these days were haywire—completely uncontrollable. Most likely from lack of sleep, too many things to juggle, the stress of Dad's frustration and Penn's distancing, and my own belief that I should be able to fix this and couldn't.

I'd tried calling the penitentiary where Greg was being held to ask again if he would revoke his statement—but he refused to take my calls. I requested visitation—he denied my name on his list of approved visitors. He blocked me from finding any relief or answers to 'will he or won't he' try to bury Penn alive?

"He's strong. He's been strong on his own for a long time before we came along, Elle. Don't take it to heart. He's only doing what's natural."

"Natural? Shutting down is natural?"

"It is to him." Larry sighed. "Think about it from his point of view. For years, he only had himself to rely on. He was hungry? He had to go steal or beg. He was cold? He had to find shelter or come up with a blanket. He was sick? He had to search for medicine or seek a place he could rest unmolested. He couldn't feel down and let another carry his troubles for a while. He couldn't hurt himself and expect someone else to feed and clothe him while he got better. It's a coping mechanism."

"I understand how it would've been imperative to keep his emotions in check when he was homeless, but he has us now. We'll get him medicine, we'll find him food, we'll give him shelter—"

"You don't get it, Elle," Larry said softly. "Even though he's placed his entire trust into our hands—his life and future, and he does believe we're doing everything we can—he can't help but expect to spend the rest of his life in there. Twig will try his hardest to make that come true. Greg will testify against him. His own past will throw away the key."

"But...he can't shut us out."

He can't shut me out. Not now...

"He can, Elle. If that's what he needs to do to keep himself alive and stay above the severe depression that prisoners succumb to, he can do whatever it takes. We'll stand by regardless if he's the confident, slightly egotistical man we've come to love or a cold-hearted, standoffish son-of-a-bitch. You can't give up on him."

I marched to my desk and threw myself on the chair. "I'm not giving up on him." My eyes fell onto the screen currently open on my laptop. A web browser I'd brought up this afternoon on a stupid whim.

I hadn't expected any results...only...

"Wait a minute..." I pulled myself forward, clicking on the link. Information spewed forth, giving me a different kind of hope. If Penn was shutting down, he needed reminding of why he needed to stay very much alive. He needed to be touched, kissed, given the age old cure of a hug.

Guards wouldn't allow that.

Visitation would only make it worse.

But there was one way.

A smile spread my lips. A sexy, sultry, entirely seductive smile, already imagining how incredible it would be if I could make it happen. "Larry, I have an idea."

* * * * *

"I can't believe you talked me into arranging this." Larry rolled his eyes, but beneath his over-puffed drama, excitement and relief glowed.

He knew as well as I did something had to happen to get Penn back. We needed him with us to continue fighting, and hopefully...I could be the one to remind him of that.

"Sign here." The prison guard pushed a form toward me. The fine print and pages of disclaimers were enough to put anyone off from signing.

But not me.

I grabbed his crappy pen and scrawled my name.

Honestly? I couldn't believe this had happened. I hadn't told Dad, Steve, or even Fleur. The only person who knew about my little quest and tonight's accommodation was Larry, and even discussing it with him had been nerve wracking.

It had taken two weeks.

Two very long weeks since Larry had given me the contact details of the person I needed to hound and then together, we didn't stop. Morning, afternoon, evening. Email, call, text, messenger, even tweet.

Over and over, we hounded and hounded until *finally*, we got an email giving us access with the firm instruction never to contact them again.

Never was a long time—especially if Penn's court date remained forever locked in the future. But I wouldn't worry about that now.

We'd won.

We were here.

At eight p.m. on a Wednesday, signing into the jail after visiting hours.

According to the prison roster, all inmates would've eaten, enjoyed rec time, and now be in their respective cells ready for lights out. Bedtime was early in this place. Morning alarm was even earlier.

Every man would be most likely stretched out on his cot, reading or passing the time in his imagination.

But not Penn.

Penn would be taken somewhere different. Somewhere he'd probably argue about and wonder why the hell he'd been separated and locked up in an unfamiliar place.

"Do you have all the necessary belongings?" The guard looked at my plastic see-through Hermes that held a change of clothes, my toothbrush, and other nighttime required accessories. The security processing had already x-rayed my things and cleared me.

"Yes, I'm all ready to go." My voice pitched slightly higher with nerves.

"You'll collect her first thing tomorrow?" The guard looked at Larry.

Larry gave my shoulder a squeeze as if I was about to go into a cage with a lion to tame it, instead of entering a cage with Penn to seduce him. "Yes, I will. Eight a.m. On the dot."

Knowing he knew what I'd be doing tonight made me blush, but the experience at having a night alone with Penn made me bounce on the spot.

Thanks to my online research, I'd learned that only four states allowed conjugal visits and one of those states was New York. I also learned that only medium and lesser security prisons permitted them, and were entirely dependent on prisoner behavior. The lesser infractions the inmate had, the better chance of being granted one of three conjugal options: six, twelve, or twenty-four hours.

I'd pushed for twenty-four. I'd been granted twelve.

I wouldn't argue because technically, in some states, you had to be legally married, and I didn't want that nuisance to stop me.

We were engaged. I had witnesses from the office stating as much. If it came down to that…I would no longer fight against it or call it fake. Technically, I wasn't even in a relationship with Penn. We'd never discussed exclusivity or rules. But just like I could tell he loved me, our hearts had decided that whatever this was—it was too deep to be labeled and too real to require laws to keep it alive.

Taking the form back, the guard checked I'd initialed each page and signed. I supposed the waiver was so in-depth because of prior incidents. The same website said an inmate murdered his girlfriend and committed suicide during one such visit in 2010.

The screening had tightened a lot since then.

"All right then, if you'll follow me, Ms. Charlston." The guard buzzed open a door, waiting for me to step through.

Larry gave me a wave, a chuckle escaping. "Well, Elle. Go give our boy one of the best nights of his life."

My cheeks burned, but I smiled. "That's my plan. See you in the morning." As the door closed, absorbing me into the prison to have sex with my incarcerated fake fiancé, Larry blew me a kiss.

For a moment, my heart fluttered like any exciting date.

For a second…things were normal.

And then the door clanged shut, and my twelve short hours began.

CHAPTER THIRTY

PENN

WHEN THE BELL rang to return to lock-up, a guard came for me.

All I earned was a barked command to grab my toothbrush and prison-issued pajamas and follow him.

To be honest, it freaked me the fuck out.

Why was I being picked on? Why had no one else been told to grab their shit and march to unknown territory?

He didn't give me any other instruction, and I didn't make small talk as I followed him out of general and through security. I was patted down as if I had an arsenal made from soap bars and candy wrappers stuffed in my pants, then directed down a series of hallways to a more modern, renovated side of the prison.

"In here." The guard pointed at an open door. Inside was a king-sized bed with black linen, tables, lamps, a dark red rug, two towels rolled on a chair, and a plastic basket with lube and condoms. A door ajar hinted at a private bathroom complete with shower.

What the fuck is this place?

Was I about to get ass raped by some dude I'd somehow pissed off? Had the warden suddenly taken a liking to me?

Shit.

When I didn't move, the guard pointed with a scowl. "Get in."

"I, eh—what's going on?"

"You'll see if you get in." He pointed again. "Now, Everett."

Not given a choice, I stepped into the love dungeon and spun around just as my roommate for the night appeared.

A fucking angel with debauchery on her mind and sex in her smile.

Elle.

CHAPTER THIRTY-ONE

ELLE

I'D SURVIVED TWO and a half months without Penn in my day-to-day life.

I'd slept alone, I'd worked alone, I'd plotted his freedom every second I was awake.

Yet standing in that doorway, drinking him in while the guard reeled off the rules—

    1. No BDSM
    2. No anal
    3. No toys
    4. No role-play
    5. No restraining
    6. No airplay

—the minutes multiplied into years.

I wanted the officer gone. I'd never despised someone purely for talking before. Couldn't he see how unwanted he was? How Penn undressed me with his eyes and I made love to him with mine?

God, I'd missed him.

To be so close but then have to listen to this idiot

pompously announce the rules as if we were about to be introduced to the president was too much.

Penn locked in place—a mirror image of me. His hands curled into fists, the dark green of his uniform bunched with power from his muscles. He looked ready to explode, like a track runner waiting for the starting gun.

I trembled with the desire to kiss him. I melted with the need to have *him* kiss *me*. And still, the guard stood in our rapidly growing sexual tension, utterly oblivious.

"At seven a.m., you'll be given breakfast and an hour to shower. Then at eight, you'll be escorted back to your cell while your guest returns home." The guard tapped his chin. "I think that's it...oh, almost forgot—"

Penn snapped. "Goddammit."

With bared teeth, he grabbed me by the hand, jerked me inside, and slammed the door in his face. "Fuck, we get it."

A giggle erupted from my lips—partly from lust, mostly from giddiness at how vicious he looked. How wild and untamed and already delirious with the temptation of me...alone.

I doubted an inmate had willingly locked himself up before. I opened my mouth to joke, to break the unbearable awareness between us, but Penn marched me backward, his eyes sharp with need, and his face black with lust.

"Fuck, Elle." His nose skimmed my throat, inhaling me, imprinting me, drowning in me. "What the fuck did you do?"

My spine slammed against the wall. His hands grabbed my wrists, pinning them brutally above my head; his body landed on mine, his hips drove forward, and his mouth...

God, his mouth sought mine with raunchy speed.

He didn't speak again. He didn't question or tease or ease into our physical reunion with soft licks or sweet caresses.

He exploded as if he'd ultimately die if he didn't have me that very moment.

We kissed until we were breathless. Until his voice returned and he mumbled incoherent thanks. Nuzzling my hair, he whispered, "Christ, Elle. Did you arrange this? Arrange a night to be together? *How?*"

Kissing my cheek, my chin, my jaw in his race to capture my lips, his groan unraveled the rest of my decorum. I'd come here to seduce him. I'd expected a moment or two of uncertainty before we attacked each other.

I hadn't expected him to turn rogue on me.

His lips found mine again.

He came utterly undone. His groan turned to a grunt, switching to a growl. He hummed, he purred, he sighed in utmost need.

His hips rocked forward, robbing me of breath as he pressed into me as hard as he could. His body tried to either consume mine or become one; regardless, we were still fully clothed.

I gasped, giving him access to my mouth as his hands formed tight cuffs around my wrists, his tongue diving deep, licking mine with impatience to join him in the frenzy.

He kissed and thrust as if he had twelve seconds to climb inside me not twelve hours.

There was no reprimand for touching. No bullhorns to separate. No knocks to keep our distance.

Just Penn and me.

Together.

Alone.

It didn't matter we were guests of the state or the bed wasn't our own.

All that mattered was our body heat as it exploded into sinful, the sweat slicking our skin in anticipation of joining, and the clenching in our bellies at just how good it would be to finally devour one another after so, so long.

Capturing both my wrists with one hand, he dropped his other to my neck. His fingers wrapped around my throat as he angled my head, taking me past the realms of sanity and into chaos with his kiss.

It hurt. It broke. It freed. It destroyed.

Teeth and tongue and wet and heat.

Our heads tilted and fought. Our breathing ragged and short. My lips burned from his as if we'd burst into flames.

His hand dropped from my throat, reacquainting itself with my breast. He pulled my nipple, rolled my weight, and squeezed the flesh until I cried out for more.

His touch moved again, this time dropping down my side to jerk my leg over his hip and angle my core, so his pants-clad erection pressed as perfect as ever, driving me crazy.

I'd deliberately worn a floaty daisy print skirt. Something he could gather and hoist up—which he did.

I'd purposely gone without underwear. So he could reach between my legs and find—which he did.

His mouth tore away from mine as his fingers found the slick heat that'd burned in me for months. Nothing could damper my need for him. No personal late-night ministrations. No celibacy. No tricks. Only he could help me because he was the one who ruined me.

"Fucking hell…" Pulling his fingers away, he brought them to his lips and licked. His eyes rolled back, his knees buckled. He stumbled away to slam onto the bed. "Christ, I missed you."

I expected him to command me to join him. To reach out and tug my wrist to strip me of everything and command me to my hands and knees. I didn't care what position he wanted. I just *wanted*.

But he leaned forward with his hands clutching his head, the slickness of my desire still coating his fingers. "As much as I want you. Shit, I can't—"

Ice water replaced the fire inside. I brushed my skirt down, wishing I had scaffolding for my knees to hold up the wreck he'd made of them. "Wh—what?"

He shook his head, bending over his legs. "I can't. We're in fucking prison. You came here for me. You're ruining your life for me just so I can get laid."

"Hey!" My temper burst. "You have it all wrong." Moving

to stand in front of him, I snapped, "I'm here because I want to be here. I want you to do this." I stroked his hair, running my fingers through the overgrown strands. "I *need* you to do this."

He looked up, swatting my hand away with rage. "I'm not going to fuck you in jail, Elle." His eyes turned tortured as they skimmed over the beads of my nipples visible in the tight singlet I wore. "Even though I'm dying to be inside you."

I stepped back, searching his face.

In all my planning and hounding for this night to happen, I never envisioned him *refusing* me.

God, it hurt.

My chest squeezed as if my ribs had become an overzealous corset. My heart slunk away, reprehended with its tail between its legs. My breath caught when he looked up, glowering with unflinching morality. "You should go, Elle."

"Go?"

He nodded. "I can't do this with you."

I hated he was firm with commitment and convicted with certainty. The decision to deny what we desperately needed from each other all because of some stupid ideal.

He'd made that decision without me. He'd reached that conclusion without discussing it.

As we stared, I fought for calmness. An assurance that he couldn't just kick me out. That we had twelve hours. I'd paid ten dollars for this room. I'd signed the forms that promised no cameras would record our time, no recording devices, or guard supervision.

We were on prison property, but this room was neutral ground.

I crossed my arms. "Nope."

"Nope?"

"Just nope."

He frowned. "What?"

"I'm not going to let you ruin this."

Anger etched his face. "Let *me* ruin this?" He pointed at me. "*You're* the one ruining it."

I threw my hands up. "How exactly am I ruining this? We have an entire night together. We should be tangled almost at an orgasm by now, but you're the one who pulled away and complicated things."

He stood, raking fingers through his hair with a rage that sent my heart grabbing a white flag of surrender. "Don't, Elle. Don't start a fight you can't win."

"Oh, it's a fight now?"

How had this veered off course so badly?

But maybe…maybe that was what we needed?

We'd never had a fight. We'd started under false pretenses and then been torn apart before we could reconcile them. I still had unresolved frustration at being lied to. He still had issues from the past. Everything I knew about Penn was obscure and given to me by third parties.

The more I searched inside—past the guilt at being the reason why he was locked up, beyond the drive to get him free, was anger.

I thought I'd let it go. That I'd forgiven him for treating me as if I was nothing. That I understood why he'd been a jerk.

But…I haven't.

The anger still burned, bright and red and throbbing with explosives ready to spread shrapnel far and wide.

"It's not a fight if you just leave. Go home where I know you're safe." He sighed, pinching the bridge of his nose. "I don't want you here, Elle."

I understood his pride. His desire for me not to see him caged like an animal. But at the same time, he had to get over that. This was our life—for however long the gods in power wanted to play with us mere mortals.

He couldn't take the brief moments of happiness we might find and throw them in the gutter.

"What about what *I* want?"

His head whipped up. "What about it?"

My eyes burned with tears, but they were rage-filled tears. Tears I could hold back and swallow while I spoke the words clambering over one another to be spoken. "Don't I get a say in any of this?"

"Any of what?" His jaw clenched. "You're not the one locked up, so don't—"

"You're right. I'm not. But I *am* the one paying for what I failed to do three years ago."

All the oxygen evaporated.

I couldn't breathe.

Penn didn't breathe.

We stood in solid gravity, waiting for life to return.

When it did, it smashed into us, and everything we'd held back—all the truths we daren't speak and accusations we daren't think ricocheted like bullets.

Penn shouted, "You want to go there, Elle? Fine, we'll fucking go there."

I shouted, "You still blame me for not finding you. That I wasn't there when Larry helped earn your freedom."

Penn snarled. "You pretended to be poor. You broke into Central Park with me, you fucking kissed me—you lied to me the entire time I fell for you."

I snarled. "Larry told me you came to visit me the night you were released. That you left with my necklace and returned with my necklace. I never saw you that night. Where were you? What made you refuse to see me?"

Penn growled, "I did come find you, I admit. I wanted to return that damn sapphire you'd mentioned. I'd thought about you every day for nine months. You were my happy place, the reason I didn't let Twig get to me. I let myself fall in love with a lie, and when I went to your house, and you were there with Greg and your father and a maid providing everything your hearts desired, I saw everything I thought I knew about you was false."

I growled, "So you created my backstory on one voyeur through a window? You hated that I had money—"

"I hated that you were fucking rich and hadn't used that power to find me. I didn't expect you to. I never thought it would truly happen. But dreams are brutal friends, Elle. I lost count how many fucking times I dreamed of you in a tiny studio, cooking meals for one, pining for me like I was pining for you. Only to find out you were fucking loaded. A spoiled little brat."

Oh, my God, he called me a brat!

After years of toiling and sweat equity for that company.

I yelled, "Is that why you were a jerk to me? You thought I was a spoiled rich bitch who deserved to be lied to? Deserved to have her virginity stolen by an egotistical, unfeeling bastard...to what? Teach me a lesson?"

He yelled, "Yes, all right? I wanted to hurt you. I wanted to take that privileged little ass and make it mine. I wanted to control you just like you'd controlled me for years without knowing."

My heart literally broke in two, blood rivered in despair.

I shook my head. "So from the very beginning, you chased me, not because of attraction or because you felt something for me, but because of hate? A damn vendetta?"

He shook his head. "It started that way, but the entire time I was lying to you, I was lying to myself more."

My anger spluttered; my heart grabbed a bandage. "What do you mean?"

He sighed. "I mean that I *wanted* to hurt you. I wanted to make you pay for things you didn't have any reason to pay for. I was angry. I was an idiot. I thought I could fuck you and then walk away." Coming toward me, he held out his hand. He knew better than to touch me, allowing me to make that choice to build a link.

I did so. Hesitantly.

The moment our fingers knotted together, he exhaled in a rush. "Dammit. I ruined this, didn't I?" He rubbed his forehead as if all the tension of our fight appeared as a headache. "I'm...confused, Elle. I'm so fucking strung up over you, but at the same time, I'm just waiting for you to end it. You *should* end it. You should walk away, and a part of me *wants* you to walk away. I've been nothing but a bastard, and now, I'm locked in here. You can do so much better."

His stoic frame shook violently. "You don't see what I do, Elle. What I'm turning you into. You used to be so pure, and I'm…ruining you. I've trapped you in this life when really I should be cruel to you, so you'll leave me to my own fuck ups."

His honesty about hating me came full circle with his admission about why.

He was confused. I was confused. Just like every couple who ever had to climb over a few stumbling blocks was confused.

That was romance.

It wasn't paint-by-numbers or color within the lines. It was messy and scribbly and up to us to draw it how we wanted.

I'd forgiven him the moment he admitted he was hurting.

Taking the argument and turning it into confession, I said, "Despite what you think, I *did* try to find you. Every day for months, I called police stations. I asked David to hire private investigators to learn your name. I even hired a sketch artist to draw a likeness of you, so people didn't laugh me out of offices when I mentioned I had no idea who you were but had to help you."

Penn's face shattered. "You did?"

"Not a single day went by that I didn't have guilt on my thoughts. I fell for you, too. I think that's why I fought you so much when you came back. I couldn't stomach the thought that I could be attracted to another when I was still hung up on Nameless."

He swallowed, shaking his head slightly as if he wanted to take every nasty thing he'd done and destroy it.

I wished he could.

I wished we could go back to the night we'd met again at the Weeping Willow, and he'd pulled me into his arms to whisper about Central Park and chocolate kisses.

"You called me Nameless?"

I laughed under my breath. The angry tension snapped,

leaving a calm rain-battered landscape in its wake. "What else could I call you?"

"I had no idea you tried to find me."

"Because you didn't ask."

He closed his eyes, tormented and full of regret. "Christ, I ruined everything."

"No, you didn't," I murmured, staring into his haunted gaze. "You just complicated it a little." Brushing my skirt with suddenly nerve-damp fingers, I added, "But you can't tell me what to do, Penn. Just like you couldn't pretend you were something you weren't."

I closed the distance between us. "I agree you screwed up. You should've given me a chance when you first came to find me. You should've trusted in what you felt that night and let me explain."

His throat worked as he swallowed. "I'm an idiot."

"You're not. You're just not used to trusting people."

"If I trust you, Elle, I give you everything I have. I don't— I don't know if I can."

I squeezed my fingers with his. He reluctantly squeezed me back, then almost crippled me with pressure-filled apology.

I brought our joined hands to my mouth and kissed his knuckles. "You have to. Because I've already given you everything I have. Even if we end up killing each other, you have every piece of me."

Penn smiled sadly, utterly solitary and unreachable. "I don't deserve that."

He said it as if rejecting my gift.

I'd come here to be connected, yet at that moment, all I felt was loneliness. It wasn't just physical distance this time but emotional. Penn successfully tugged on all my self-doubt and made me wish things could've been different.

That we'd clung to each other that first night.

That I'd been honest and he'd been honest, and we'd fought for each other.

But things weren't different and could never be.

We had to fight for our future, not what went wrong in our past.

"I can't have that responsibility," he whispered. "I can't let you give me what I've always wanted when I don't fucking deserve it."

"But you do—"

His lips twisted into a snarl. "I don't. I was wrong, okay? You were never spoiled. I know how hard you work for your company. I see how much you dote on your father. I understand how Belle Elle and its staff wouldn't exist without you. You're so much better than any dream version I could've created of you, and that…well, it fucking terrifies me."

He looked at the floor, severing our connection. "That night in the limo…I was going to break it off. Hell, I was supposed to break it off with you the first time I let you walk out of my apartment without me and almost got hurt by that asshole on the street. I told myself I didn't care what happened to you. I'd got what I wanted. You'd gotten what you wanted. We were through. But that fucking night three years ago."

He squeezed my fingers. "I can't explain it. Maybe I was so lonely I would've fallen for anyone who treated me with kindness. Perhaps, I would've handed over my soul to the first girl who saw past my rags and lack of riches and kissed me. But I don't think that's true. It was you, Elle." His eyes shone with dark passion. "I fell for you the second I met you. I don't care if that's idiotic or improbable; it's true. The one piece of truth I could never hide with the countless lies I told. I just—"

His head hung. His fingers spasmed. "I'm sorry."

All my fight trickled away.

I walked into his embrace, slotting myself neatly into him as he rested his chin on my scalp. "I'm sorry, too. I'm sorry I didn't find you. I'm sorry I left you."

"You have nothing to apologize for."

"I do." I kissed his t-shirt over his heart, doing my best not to inhale the scent of imprisonment and cheap detergent. "And I might as well apologize for this, too."

He pulled away, searching my eyes. "For what?"

"For this." Standing on my tiptoes, I pulled his head down to mine.

My lips slotted over his, and I held on, linking my fingers tight around his nape as he tried to yank away. "Kiss me." I fed into his mouth. "Trust me." I poured down his throat.

We needed this now more than ever.

We'd ripped off scabs over old wounds. We needed to heal them rather than let them scar.

"Elle—" His hands landed on my hips, holding me firm. "Stop…" His voice said one thing, but his mouth said another. Slowly, he turned from stiff to pliant, unyielding to full participant.

His head tilted, angling me closer, kissing me deeper.

My anxiety quickened then lessened. My need thickened then loosened.

This was our night.

I wouldn't let him steal it.

"If we do this, there's no turning back…you understand?" He broke the kiss, whispering so soft my ears strained to catch it. "You let me have you, then you accept that I might never get out of here. That you'll forever be restricted to a lover who can't touch you, hug you, hang out and watch movies with you. If you stay, that's it…the sum future I can offer you."

He brushed his lips over mine. "I'm giving you a way out, Elle. Say the word, and I'll let you go. It will fucking kill me. You'll rip my heart out, and I'll die in here, but at least I'll be happy knowing you were free. Leave me, Elle. Don't let me get away with stealing yet more from you."

He was so open, so ardent.

He didn't have a clue he just glued me to him for the rest of my life.

My lips twitched. I hid my smile for as long as I could before it crept over me. "Tell me one thing. Then I'll make my choice."

He swallowed hard as if bracing himself for me to walk

out of this room and take him up on his offer. But even in his terror, he nodded with shoulders braced. There stood Nameless, not Penn. The man in the hoodie who drove off two men to protect me. He'd drive himself off, too, if it meant protecting me from him.

That's what he's trying to do by refusing to sleep with me tonight.

Well, it wouldn't work.

He was mine. Simple.

"Tell me you don't love me." I placed both palms on his chest. His muscles beneath my fingertips rose and fell with rapid breath. "Look me in the eyes and tell me you don't love me and I'll go. I'll leave you alone."

He crumpled. The answer blared so loud and bright it filled the entire room. It didn't matter he'd said it already with admitting he'd fallen for me three years ago. I let him verbalize, so we both knew he could never take it back. That he willingly admitted that despite wanting to live in an ideal world with picnics and vacations and lazy Sundays in bed, we might never have that. This might be our world with precious conjugal visits and achingly hard visitation.

But love would overcome that.

It had to.

Because I didn't want, *couldn't* stomach the thought of loving anyone else.

Finally, his shoulders realigned into confident, not angry. His spine unlocked. His face shed its mask, and his voice said what his eyes had all along.

"I can't tell you that." His hand cupped my cheek, his thumb running along my bottom lip. "I can't tell you I don't love you because that's not true. It's never been true." He tipped forward, kissing me so, so soft. "I love you, Elle. I'm obsessed with you, consumed by you. You make me crazy and not necessarily in good ways. But I can't lie to you anymore. I love you. So fucking much it kills me."

My smile was sunshine and hot days as I kissed him back. "Then trust that. Trust that I love you, too. Trust that whatever happens, we'll fight it together. Turn off that voice inside you that's trying to screw everything up. Just trust like you've told me to do so many times before."

He nuzzled into my neck. "You're bossy as well as nosy."

I laughed softly. "You bring out the worst in me."

His eyes filled with intensity. "Yet you bring out the best in me."

"Guess that means we're perfect for each other." My lip trembled, happiness overflowing.

Penn frowned, kissing me gently. "Suddenly, you don't look convinced."

"I am convinced. Completely. I'm just—" More truth bubbled, and I blurted, "I'm so afraid of losing you. That I'm the reason why you're in here, and I don't know if I have the power to get you out."

"Hey…" He captured my cheeks with both hands, holding me tight. "You have power over me. That's all you ever need."

"Does that mean I can command you to spend the night with me, and you have to obey?"

A sly grin transformed him from serious to player. "Are you asking me to fuck you, Ms. Charlston?"

I nodded. "Again and again, Mr. Everett. Multiple times. Will you?"

Chapter Thirty-Two

Penn

I'D TRIED TO do the right thing.

I really fucking had.

The thought of having Elle in this place turned me right off, but kissing her blueberry-glossed lips and knowing she had nothing on underneath her skirt scrambled with my right and wrong.

My brain had had its chance at ending this.

Our fight had had its opportunity to push her away.

Our connection hadn't ended, and she hadn't gone.

That left only one thing to do.

"When it comes to you, Elle, I'll do whatever you damn well want." I kissed her softly, keeping my desires in check this time.

I couldn't believe how quickly I'd pounced on her before. I'd been a fucking animal. She'd arranged this for us. The least I could do was make it good for her rather than a three-second humping against the wall.

"How long do we have?" I murmured as her hands slid around my waist, gripping me close.

My tongue massaged hers. My heart thundered as she moaned. "Twelve hours."

"Really?" I could do so much to her in that amount of time. It would be the longest we'd ever spent together consecutively. Which, in the scheme of how many months we'd been 'dating,' was an embarrassment.

She pulled away, looking up. Eyes shining, lips bruised, skin flushed. The tank she wore showed the lacy indentations of her bra, revealing the pinpricks of her nipples, encasing her tiny waist in cotton just begging me to rip it off her.

My throat burned. "Christ, you're so beautiful."

She shook her head. "You're the beautiful one. Do you know that's what made me say yes that night? I thought you were so pretty. I couldn't say no."

"So you only agreed to sleep with me because of how *pretty* I am?" I kissed my way down her throat, adoring the way she shivered.

"I said yes because even then I think my heart knew. You reminded me of him. You put your hands in your pockets like him. You had demons like him."

I didn't doubt her. She could've cut off her long blonde hair, got piercings, indulged in tattoos, and put on weight, and I would still have recognized her.

It was one of those serendipitous things that couldn't be explained.

Our kiss turned into a conversation on its own, rolling like waves on a beach, sometimes deep, sometimes shallow, always rippling with power.

Pushing my fingers through her hair, I breathed, "Know what I want to do more than anything?"

"What?" Her head tipped back as I tugged the yellow-gold strands.

"For the next twelve hours, I want to be inside you for as long as possible. I really, really need to fuck you, Elle. Who knows? Perhaps for the entire twelve hours, I'll take you every way I can."

She shuddered, her arms tightening around my waist. "Do it. I miss having you inside me."

Electricity flowed from her to me, dragging me closer to the edge I'd almost fallen off before.

"If I let go…I don't know how controlled I'll be." My confession floated in the subspace we'd created, the soft protective bubble where no one could find us.

She smiled beneath my kiss. "I love the sound of that."

I clung tight to the rest of my self-control, desperate to ask a few more questions. Learn a bit more about her. Imprint her further on my soul. But all I could think about was sex. I'd study her body tonight…but it wouldn't be intellectual it would be entirely sexual.

"I'm going to take away all your control. I'll fuck you the way *I* want to fuck you. I'll look after you while I ruin you. I'll protect you while I hurt you—just like I promised that first night. I'll take everything you have to give. We play rough. We love hard. We live every fucking fantasy." I traced my hands up and down her spine, caressing her while forcing myself to stay gentle. "You came here tonight to sleep with me. Well, you're at my mercy. Locked in a room with a convict. Completely helpless."

Fuck, I was turning myself on. My balls drew upward, hard as marble. My cock twitched, dying to put what I'd said into practice.

"You're mine, Elle. No more secrets. No more lies. You fuck me knowing entirely what you're getting into."

She squirmed as if both aroused and scared, but her eyes glittered with lust so bright she incinerated me. "Penn…"

Cupping her breast, I squeezing her softness. Memories that she'd been a virgin before I'd taken her almost made me snap. Knowing she'd only had me inside her and only ever would turned me on so much I almost climaxed as her hand cupped my cock.

She moaned again as I pinched her nipple. "Do you want that?"

Her head rolled back. "Yes. Very much."

"Yes to me possessing you?"

"Yes."

"What do you say?" The precipice was there. I was about to fall. "Answer me."

"Please, Penn. Possess me. Do whatever you want. I'm yours."

"Fuck." My mouth sealed over hers, preventing any more talking and setting fire to the rocket fuel that'd replaced our blood.

She leaped into my arms. Her teeth nipped my lower lip; her tongue fought mine for dominance.

She tried to win. But she never would.

She was mine, and I'd spend all night teaching her that with fucking pleasure.

Fisting her hair, I yanked her head back. My message about who was in charge was undeniable as her throat arched.

She groaned long and low as I bit her neck, tossing her onto the bed. She bounced on the mattress, her legs parting and skirt hoisting up her thighs.

A flash of nakedness bewitched me. I couldn't control myself anymore.

Hunger surged.

I climbed over her, yanking at the tight tank. In one rip, I tore it over her head. Her pretty white bra stopped me from seeing what I wanted.

It has to come off.

Rolling her over, I undid the clasp and threw it across the room.

It landed on the basket full of lube and condoms.

Elle looked up as it crashed to the floor, spilling sex aids everywhere. She bit her bottom lip, hiding a smile. Slowly, like a sexy vixen, she opened her legs, pulling her skirt high.

I told her I'd be in charge but, goddammit, that one motion made me her slave for life.

I panted as she revealed her pussy, glistening with need. I

became hypnotized with lust, barely able to register words as she said, "I don't think we'll need the lube."

"Christ." I slid off the bed, dragging her hips with me. The moment she was in licking distance, my mouth connected and my tongue speared inside her.

Hot. Wet. Elle.

She writhed on the bed, her fists grabbing at the sheets, her teeth biting at comforters. She whimpered as I inserted a finger then two, profanities hissing through clenched teeth.

I loved that I could make her come undone so easily. How ready she was for me. How greedy.

I could spend all night making her unravel, but there were other places to taste, touch, worship.

Crawling up her body, I locked my teeth around her nipple followed by the heat of my mouth. She bowed upward, her hands sinking in my hair, her fingernails unsheathed as she threw her head back. "Oh, my God."

While I sucked on her breasts, my hands shoved down her skirt, tossing it over my shoulder.

Naked.

Beautiful fucking Elle was naked.

And I'm not.

Moving to her other breast, I bit gently as I pushed at the elastic green pants and disengaged her hold on my hair to tear the t-shirt over my head.

The white boxer-briefs vanished next, leaving my cock bouncing with need and shining with pre-cum.

Elle scrambled to her knees, pushing me hard.

I fell backward in surprise, shocked at her aggression. She made a low sound of appreciation and hunger as her fingers latched around my cock, pumping me once.

I bowed upward, almost coming from how good her tiny fingers were.

But it was nothing compared to her mouth.

I'd teased her in her office. I'd made her believe I'd force her to do something as intimate as blowing me. I would never have forced her to do something she didn't want.

But now...fuck, she wanted it.

She wanted me.

She had natural talent, sliding her tongue flat and long along my shaft, sucking hard until blood pressure throbbed in the tip. Her hands drifted low to cup my balls, rolling them gently—pressing at just the right spot to make stars twinkle in my eyes and my belly tighten, ready to explode.

"No. Fuck, I don't want to come in your mouth." I pushed her gently. "Not yet anyway."

Hooking my hands under her arms, I pulled her upward. We both groaned as our nakedness slid over one another. She spread her legs, straddling me, rubbing her wetness over my saliva-damp cock.

Having her so fucking close. Having the heat of her, the knowledge I could be inside her in one quick move made me lose all sense of what creature I was and turned wild.

I wanted to be inside her.

I would make it happen.

Now.

Palming her back, I pushed her forward as my hips rocked backward. The tip of me nudged inside her.

Elle sat up, pushing down, making my eyes snap shut, and my body turn into a weapon ready to fire.

"Fuck, fuck, fuck," I chanted at the moon, at chocolate, at kisses in the park. My fingers dug into her hips, holding her half way down me. "Wait...condom."

She arched again, hollowing her back until her breasts stood proudly and in grabbing distance. "I'm on the pill. I brought some condoms with me...just in case you wanted to use—"

I didn't let her finish. Sitting up, I clutched her nape, dragged her mouth to mine and thrust up.

I thrust so fucking hard, she cried inside my mouth. I embraced her with one arm while my other dropped to fist her breasts.

I impaled her on me, and it was the best thing in the world. My brain short-circuited. I forgot about breathing and prison and court dates. She made me go to battle, putting me under siege as our bodies strained to dominate and claim.

The bed rocked as I speared upward.

I groaned as she sank downward.

Our rhythm perfectly synced right from the start.

Her hips moved forward and back.

Mine shot upward and down.

The combined motion made this the best sexual experience of my entire goddamn life.

Flesh on flesh.

Body on body.

It was physical, but this time, it touched something spiritual, too. Opening my eyes, I latched onto hers. The blue turned black, full of rock pools and tidal waves, making me drown in her.

I hadn't been a monk while I'd been locked up. I'd serviced myself on regular occasions thanks to memories of that night at my place and the limo ride. But I was about to seriously embarrass myself.

After three months apart, the tremors rippling through me couldn't be denied any longer. Sexual deprivation only made my senses extra sharp. The scent of her lust. The taste of her kisses. The heat of her pussy.

Fuck me...

I'm gonna come.

Reaching between us, I stroked Elle's clit.

"Oh, God." Her entire body rippled with building pressure. Violent shivers hijacked her muscles. She tried to push my hand away, but I pressed harder.

"Oh, oh..." Her face pinched into a grimace, chasing her orgasm just like I fought against mine.

My legs burned with pleasure just waiting to shoot through me. My belly locked. My spine full of electricity.

Her legs wrapped tight around my hips as I continued

thrusting faster, harder, deeper.

"Come, Elle. I need you to come."

A tortured moan trickled from her lips. Her hands landed on my shoulders, locking onto an anchor so I could take her deep into pleasure and know she could find her way back.

I felt her release in her back first.

She gasped as the first surge worked from her shoulder blades and down her spine. Her stomach tightened, her muscles trembling as the breaking orgasm fisted and milked me inside her. Her legs scissored, fighting the onslaught, but it was too late.

One wave, two waves, three, four, five. On and fucking on, she came, giving me no choice but to join her.

"Holy shit." My climax made my eyes water. It squeezed my balls until I groaned in pain mixed with pleasure. My quads cramped. My cock spurted everything it could into the girl I would never let go.

We jolted in each other's arms as the last dregs of our orgasms left us boneless and breathing hard.

With the softest smile, Elle curled into me, pressing kisses to my chest, wrapping her arms around my neck.

I thought I'd loved her before that. Before she showed such vulnerability, such trust, such affection.

I was wrong.

My heart swelled until it no longer fit inside me. All the mess, the lies, the uncertainty in our future couldn't steal how fucking happy I was with my body inside hers and her kisses forever imprinted on my soul.

Brushing my fingertips over her temples, cheeks, to her jaw, I tipped her head up so I could look at her. "I hate this. Being in here. Forced to stay away from you when I need you so damn much."

"I know. But you're innocent. They'll see that soon. And then you're coming home with me."

I kissed her puffy sex-swollen lips not agreeing or disagreeing because as much as I hoped she was right...

I had no idea if it would come true.

CHAPTER THIRTY-THREE

ELLE

THREE TIMES FOR almost three months.

The second was in the shower with tepid water and threadbare towels, but my two toe-curling orgasms shattered the record for all other showers, making it the best I'd ever had.

The third was lazy and sleepy, under the covers half-awake, half-dreaming, my back wedged to Penn's front, his cock slipping between my legs and filling me effortlessly.

We'd fallen asleep with him still inside me.

And for the first time in years, I slept soundly in his arms. We didn't have time to talk or share things we needed to know. We'd depleted ourselves by showing our love in physical form before the beauty of touch could be stolen from us.

Our bodies reacquainted, our hearts pattered to the same rhythm, our minds synced into one frequency.

At seven a.m., our wake-up call came in the form of a prison guard carrying a tray of scrambled eggs and over-cooked bacon with a cup of chocolate-covered strawberries.

To have breakfast served in bed in jail would forever remain one of the most random experiences of my life.

We stayed where we were. Unapologetic and tangled together beneath black sheets.

The utensils were plastic, the crockery had seen better days, and the strawberries were slightly over-ripe, but it was the best breakfast we'd ever had.

Who knew the Department of Corrections would forever hold a fond place in my heart as well as the most hated?

We didn't dally over eating, our anxiety levels steadily increasing with every tick of the clock. Our twelve hours were almost over. I would be forced to leave. Penn would be forced to say goodbye.

Tears filled my eyes at the thought.

I couldn't do it.

I didn't have the capacity to walk away from him not knowing when we'd next be together.

"Elle, don't." His finger caught a tear, rubbing it into my cheeks as if it'd never existed. His fingers smelled of chocolate and berry, adding a flavor to the already familiar one associated with him. It reminded me of the night he brought chocolate mousse to my apartment and took me on the couch. It granted so many memories eternally tangled with him.

"You can't." His handsome face with soulful eyes and sharp jawline fractured with truth. "I won't be able to say goodbye if you cry."

Another tear escaped.

Tilting my chin, he licked it away then brought his mouth to mine.

We kissed long. We kissed slow. We kissed to last us however many months until the next time we could.

Pulling away, a mischievous smile spread his lips. "You know...we have time for one more."

"Lucky number four, huh?"

I was sore. I was achy. I didn't care in the slightest. I'd keep going forever if it meant I could keep him with me and not hand him back to the guards.

He nodded, springing from the bed and yanking me into a

kneeling position. "I think four is a good number, don't you?" Grabbing me around the waist, he hoisted me from the mattress and planted me against the wall.

The cold concrete bit into my bare ass, but I didn't care at all as his lips found mine again and kissed me hungrily, violently—as if he could eat me for breakfast, lunch, and dinner, and I'd never have to leave him.

His cock pressed against my belly, grinding into me with unashamed sensual insanity. His hands slid down my body, cupping my ass as he lifted me up and I automatically wrapped my legs around his hips.

Any second, a guard would come to remove me. Any moment, this would all be a dream. But I couldn't think about that as Penn angled himself and sank inside me, inch by devouring, delightful inch.

One hand remained on my hip as he sank all the way inside, rocking harder when he filled me as if he could climb deeper. His other hand crept to my breast, tweaking my sore nipple from a nighttime of pleasure, then fisted my hair to hold my head exactly the way he wanted. He consumed my mouth with his. His hunger palatable—washing off him with droplets of needs.

The unabashed way he desired me made the upcoming separation so *incredibly* painful.

We'd wasted so much time when we could've been together. We'd lied and ruined, and who knew what the future held.

Now, we were together and committed, but we weren't permitted the freedom to consummate, grow, and find a home in this new relationship.

How cruel. How unfair. How unjust.

His thoughts must've been where mine were because he kissed me desperately. He kissed me savagely. We kissed as if we were starving. Our tongues fought, our teeth nipped, we became drunk on fucking with our bodies and our lips.

He pounded into me, slamming me repeatedly against the

wall. There was nothing gentle. Nothing kind about the slapping of our skin against skin.

But my body ached and slicked, welcoming him to take me harder, faster.

His teeth captured my ear, breathing hard. "Fuck, I love you. I love fucking you. I'll never stop."

I trembled, undone by the circle of his hips and the frantic way we clawed at each other.

The ferocity unbound me. The fury at not being allowed to be together made us rebels in our desire to consume each other.

Perhaps, we *did* want to hurt each other. Perhaps, that was what our love was—forever tangled up with hate from past misconceptions. But *God*, it made for hot sex.

"You're going to make me come." He sucked on my throat, deliberately marking me, branding me for the entire world to see when he couldn't be there.

I sank deeper onto him, trusting him entirely to support my weight while he drove me off the cliff. "Good because I'm going to come. *God*, I'm going to come."

The tingles were back. The stars, the streamers, the candy floss and fairy wings. They all vortexed in my belly, spiraling outward, clenching my core as bliss I'd forever associate with Penn wiped me out completely.

I shuddered in his arms as I gave into the bands of pleasure.

"Christ, you'll be the death of me." He gripped my thigh, sinking fingernails into flesh. "Don't wash me away."

I wanted to ask what he meant, but his head fell back as his entire stomach sculpted into granite. His muscles seized as the pulsing of his orgasm deep inside me echoed with his groan of release.

His knees buckled as endorphins drenched his body, making him lethargic and sated.

Dropping my legs from around his hips, he gently placed me on my feet, withdrawing from me, watching the vision of his cock sliding free for the last time.

Tears wobbled over my retinas, but I sniffed them back.

He tipped my head up, kissing me. "Promise me you won't shower for the rest of the day. I need to know a part of me is still with you, even though I'll be locked up in here."

"Of course." I threw my arms around him, hugging him so damn hard. "God, I hate this so, so much."

He hugged me back, squeezing me until I couldn't breathe. "I love you."

And then the guard knocked on the door. "Ten minutes. Get ready to go."

Penn let me go.

We dressed in silence.

We kissed goodbye in pain.

We separated in agony.

LETTER FROM PENN

I DON'T KNOW how you knew, but you did.

You knew I needed a reminder on how to fight. You knew I needed to taste and touch you, not just talk to you across a fucking table.

The fact you knew that—that you managed to find a way for us to be together—proved I was right to fall for you.

You're everything I want and everything I need.

Because of you, I feel strong again.

I won't give up.

I won't let those bastards win.

Tell Larry I'm ready to take him down. I'll testify if he gathers the evidence. I'll do whatever it damn well takes to get out of here and be with you.

Because one thing's for sure, Elle—that night in the alley, I wanted to keep you.

After last night, I want to fucking marry you.

LETTER FROM ELLE

FROM FAKE ENGAGEMENT *to prison letter proposal, your romance never fails to astound me.*

I think you know I won't argue this time. In fact, if you tried to walk away, I'd use everything at my disposal to convince you otherwise.

Your letter took a week to be delivered.

A week where I couldn't stop thinking about you and how good it felt being together.

All my life, I've had privilege. I thought I never took it for granted, but I know now that I did. I'm grateful for the staff who do what I tell them. I'm thankful for the company that gives me power.

But none of that experience helps me help you.

I'm going out of my mind, needing to do something.

I spoke to Greg when I probably shouldn't have. I told the press you were innocent when I should probably have kept my mouth shut.

You're in there because of me, and I can't help.

Do you know how helpless that makes me feel? So pointless. So useless.

Knowing I was able to remind you to keep fighting helps me keep fighting because missing you is the most exhausting thing I've ever done.

But it's worth it.

Because that night in the alley, I needed you.

But after last week, I can't imagine life without you.

CHAPTER THIRTY-FOUR

ELLE

I TOLD LARRY about Penn's readiness to go after Arnold Twig.

I'd never seen someone go from already working manically hard to increasing his energy until it reached chaotic proportions. He was a salt and pepper whirlwind with vengeance on his mind.

It didn't matter that he muttered about not being able to combine one trial with another—unless he could prove Arnold Twig's corruption affected this arrest and not just prior ones. It didn't matter that he mumbled about how tricky it would be to prove Penn's innocence on all accounts and expunge his prior convictions.

He threw himself into the task as if he'd been waiting for Penn to give the go-ahead for years. Which, according to another distracted reply, he had.

I asked why he hadn't gathered this evidence before so he'd be prepared for when Penn finally chose the right moment. He'd said evidence like this would poke the hornet's nest. He wouldn't be able to gather it without someone noticing, and when someone did, Arnold Twig would know.

It was risky to hunt for answers and prove Penn was innocent all while still in jail where Twig would bury him. But according to Larry, Twig had friends on the police force and a few corrupt district attorneys, but he hadn't been able to bribe the head warden yet, so technically, Penn was as safe as he could be.

We just had to hope that the judge who would preside over the case wasn't bought and paid for.

Life—as much as I hated it—had to continue without Penn.

Ever since our night together, it had become harder and easier in equal measure. Harder because I missed him so much my bones ached with it. He'd injected himself into my veins with no promise of another hit. And easier because by giving him strength, it gave *me* strength. I didn't do anything reckless like try to have Greg murdered or go on some silly TV program with conspiracy theories.

I kept my eyes locked on the future—on a trial that would eventually have to move forward, despite lost paperwork, internal delays, and every other excuse they'd given us up until now about why Penn hadn't been granted a trial date.

Despite having no date to fight toward, Penn and I wrote often. We got to know each through ink and paper rather than voice and language. I found out he had a sense of humor hidden beneath his suspicious outlook on the world. That he could be self-deprecating behind his surly attitude.

That sickly feeling I'd had after his lies unraveled was gone now. With every note, every phone call, every snatched meeting with prison guards and escorts, my heart increased with shots of helium, slowly floating, becoming weightless until it bounced on a string tied to my ribs.

The three-year-old lust I had for him as Nameless and the four-month-old attraction I had for Penn finally merged. The infatuation I had with him irrevocably switched to love. That love (although new and fresh) morphed into a solid protector that would accept anything, tolerate everything, and care for him unconditionally. It made me grow up.

I was no longer a girl masquerading as a woman.

I was all woman, and if Penn was ready to take on the chief of police, I was ready to stand behind him and give him all my power, wealth, and notoriety to make that happen.

Four months to the day of my abduction and Penn's arrest, Larry called me—like he did most days with requests for help, updates on Penn from my point of view, or just catching up to see how I was. However, this phone call smashed through our limbo of waiting. Making everything we'd worked for become real.

"One month from now," Larry said, breathless with adrenaline. "Best I could do. Finally heard back."

Tears welled in my eyes. One month? Four more long weeks?

But what was four weeks compared to three years?

"That's wonderful."

It's too far away.

"I'm so happy."

I'm gutted.

"He'll be home soon."

Just focus on that.

"Your father really came through, Elle," Larry added gently, knowing I struggled with how my loving Dad could suddenly become so judgmental. "It's his friend who rearranged his time. Patrick Blake. I don't know if another case fell through or if he's taken on some extra hours, but he's granted us the hearing. God knows how he arranged for a twelve-seat jury to be ready in time, but he has."

Shaking travelled down my arm, making the phone thwack against my ear. "That's—I don't know what to say."

I wanted to run back to the brownstone and kiss my father stupid. I'd make him blueberry pancakes and apologize for being distant. I'd forgive the grudge I'd held for him for accepting Penn when he was an upstanding businessman and then shoving him into the shadows the moment he was arrested.

The fact that we hadn't been as close these past few weeks hurt.

"What happens now?" My voice wobbled. "What do you need me to do?"

Larry sighed heavily, sounding as exhausted as I was. "Well, I'll work extra hours on gathering the last few bits of evidence against Arnold Twig and his delightful son. In the trial, I'll use that to point direction at the true criminal and show the jury that Penn was innocent of those crimes, just as he's innocent of this one. With any luck, we'll be able to link it all into one, expunge Penn's prior convictions, and get the charges dropped."

"And if that's not entirely true?"

"What's not true?"

"Well, technically, he did hurt Greg. The hospital took photos, and Greg's moaning ensured a lot of people heard what happened. It's his word against Penn's."

"That only shows there was a fight." His tone turned sharp. "Penn didn't go to that cabin to kill Greg. The attempted murder charge will be easy to overthrow."

"How so?"

"There's no evidence whatsoever of intent or premeditation. No paper trail to link Penn to any prior thoughts of violence toward your employee."

There wasn't, but I didn't trust the law not to look into hearsay and find hard truth where there was none.

"They had a fight." Larry sniffed. "Two men in a fight over a woman. Shit, if the state locked up everyone for that misdemeanor, most of the male population would be behind bars."

Larry chuckled in frustration. "Greg was in the wrong for indecently assaulting you and holding you against your will. If he continues to say Penn went there to kill him, I'll personally go after him so hard, he'll be laughed out of court and be done for defamation and lying under oath. If there's anyone with premeditation and a paper trail, it's Greg. The packed supplies, the second vehicle—it all paints a picture of dishonorable intentions."

An icy gale blew down my spine like it always did when I thought about Greg.

I hated that he hadn't gotten in touch. The fact he'd gone from a patronizing presence—constantly popping into my office uninvited—to suddenly being completely elusive and silent…

It petrified me.

I'd told Larry what I'd done at the hospital—trying to bribe then blackmail him. He'd scolded me. Said how reckless I'd been. But after grilling me if there'd been anyone else in the room or any recording devices, he'd patted me on the back with pride.

The fact I'd put my neck on the line for Penn made his fondness for me triple. This entire stressful situation surrounding the man we both loved had brought us closer together than any normal situation.

Larry was the uncle I'd never had. My father-in-law, for all intents, if Penn ever did anything about our fake engagement.

"Okay." The word was woefully underwhelming, but I had nothing else. I thought I'd be able to save Penn months of lock-up when we'd first begun this journey. The fact he was still imprisoned irritated me to angry tears.

Being part of the family dealing with freeing innocence was the hardest thing I'd ever had to do. Turned out, I sucked at this hero stuff while Penn was such a natural.

"Tell me what I should do, Larry."

"I hoped you'd say that," he replied. "What are you doing tonight?"

"Nothing, why?" I looked up as Fleur came into my office. She carried a bottle of wine with two glasses. Ever since the afternoon I'd spoken to the reporters, she appeared at the end of our workday with alcohol of some description—ready-mixed watermelon vodka, Midori shots, even champagne.

I'd told her I didn't drink.

She'd told me I would have to start to survive the next few months.

I hadn't argued.

We'd gotten drunk that night, and for the first time in forever, I was able to laugh even though guilt slithered inside me. I despised that I had a good time with Fleur, that my job kept me busy, my cat kept me sane, and my self-control kept me rational enough not to become a serial killer and hunt Arnold Twig or his son.

It was wrong that I lived while Penn was caged.

She cocked an eyebrow as Larry spoke into my ear. "Come over. I'll be pulling an all-nighter. Need an assistant if you're interested."

The wine bottle in Fleur's hand would remain untouched. "Consider me there already."

A smile existed in his tone. "Excellent. Stewie will be relieved to see you. He wants to apologize."

"Apologize? Why?"

"He finally told me what happened with the necklace at the charity event after he acted so weird around you the last time you popped over. He's not coping well. Thinks he's the reason why Penn is in jail like his brother, Gio."

I rubbed at my heart. "Oh no, it's not his fault."

"Yep, all the more reason to come around. You can talk to him. I'll brew a pot of coffee. See you soon, Elle."

"Sure." I hung up, looking reluctantly at the alcohol in Fleur's grasp. "Can't. Have to go do lawyer stuff to break Penn out of jail."

"Oh, sounds fun." She waggled the bottle. "Any room for this bad boy and me to tag along?"

I stroked Sage as she padded over my desk and hooked her claws around the stem of one of the wine glasses. She tipped it over before I could catch it. Luckily, the glass bounced on the carpet and didn't shatter.

"Why would you want to come? It's just more work. More computer time. More fine print." I stood, slinging my black with pink-lace jacket on over the dark pink dress I wore. Pink didn't spring to mind as corporate, but once again, Fleur picked it out and was right.

"Well, my hubby-to-be is out on a bachelor night with friends. I don't want to sit at home wondering if he's motor boating some stripper's boobs." She pulled a face. "I'd much rather be sitting with you doing exciting things like researching how to break your lover out of jail. It's all very cloak and dagger." Her eyes twinkled as if spending a night bent over paperwork was as raunchy as watching the Chippendales.

"Well, if you're sure." I smiled. "You're more than welcome, and I'd love the company. I'm sure Larry would say we need all the eyes we can get." I took the wine from her and placed it in my large tote. "And for the record, your hubby won't have his face in some stripper's boobs."

"That's what everyone says." She rolled her eyes. "But bachelor parties are the Bermuda triangle of good decisions and decent men. They all get lost along the way, only to be spat back out the next day with no memory of it."

Looping my arm with hers, I patted my thigh for Sage to follow and prepared to work my ass off for Penn. "In that case, consider tonight as reckless as a motorcycle crack party."

"Oh, yay. I've always wanted to see what those two-wheeled outlaws do for fun."

LETTER FROM ELLE

TWO WEEKS, PENN.

Two weeks until this is all over and you walk free.

Larry has everything arranged.

I have duplicates of his research and evidence locked safe.

We're not backing down this time.

You're no longer on your own, and when you're free, I'm going to show you exactly how much I missed you.

With every part of me.

Lips.

Tongue.

Hands.

You get the idea.

I'll stop before this letter gets censored and not delivered.

Fourteen days.

I can't wait.

LETTER FROM PENN

ONE WEEK, ELLE.

I'd be lying if I said I wasn't freaking out. That the thought of facing everyone, of hearing that bastard testify against me in court when he was the one who stole you...fuck, just thinking about it makes me livid.

Seven days until I get to see you, smell you, feel you behind me in the gallery and know how much you mean to me.

Seven days until I'm hopefully free and I'm going to do so many dirty bad things to you I'll probably get locked up again.

And I'm fully aware that has probably just flagged me, and a guard is watching me extra close from now on. But I don't fucking care.

So close yet so far.

So easy yet so hard.

I've shared pieces of myself in these letters, but writing it down is different to pillow talk. I want to stroke your skin while I answer any question you wish to know. I want to hug you close while you tell me about your childhood.

We have a lifetime to get to know each other, Elle.

And soon, we can start living it.

CHAPTER THIRTY-FIVE

PENN

THE CALENDAR HAD crawled by.

Yet, as I was given a black suit rather than freshly laundered prison scrubs after an earlier than normal wake-up call, five months seemed like it'd been five minutes.

I was ready.

I wasn't ready.

I was prepared to fight.

I was terrified to fight.

I hated that half of me was unstoppable while the other was a fucking pussy.

I almost wished I didn't have Elle and Larry fighting for me, supporting me. Because if we lost today, losing them would rip out my heart and I wouldn't have the energy to keep going. If I was alone with only empty streets and long nights to look forward to, I might be more willing to play hard ass and point fingers at those who could destroy me.

I'd say goodbye to everything I ever wanted if this backfired.

But I'd told Larry I was done keeping Twig's secrets.

He'd spent months gathering what was needed.

I wouldn't let him down.

With my heart jumping like a heroin-cranked addict, I showered and shaved, hacking off the beard I'd grown, revealing some of the scars I'd earned thanks to my days on the streets.

Slipping into cotton instead of polyester somehow gave me a sense of power I'd been lacking while locked up like a dog. The too-big-for-me suit gave me courage that everything would go to plan and I wouldn't end up trapped in here for the rest of my life.

Once I was dressed, I hopped into a barred minivan and was driven to court where I ended up sitting in a holding cell for two hours. A kind-faced elderly guard took pity on my growling stomach—brought on by hunger but mostly stress—and delivered a sandwich complete with mayo, mustard, and roasted chicken.

Nothing had ever tasted so good.

I didn't have access to a clock, but noise slowly gathered as more prisoners arrived for their court time. I eavesdropped on the guard's discussions about who was next on the roll call.

The drone of conversation and the scuffing of feet above in the courtroom gave a perfect backdrop for my mind to drift and contemplate.

This was the first break from the monotony of jail in four weeks.

I hadn't been allowed visitors, and Larry and Elle hadn't been permitted to call.

Some stupid rule about preventing tampering of evidence now I'd been granted a court date. I hadn't had any other visitors, but I had enjoyed one phone call from a very pissed off chief of police. Not that the prison would ever know it was him. He'd called from an unknown number and given a fake name on a cell-phone handed to me by a guard on his payroll.

He'd pulled strings to talk to me, despite the risks.

He'd heard about Patrick Blake agreeing to preside over my case as the judge. He'd also noticed Larry digging for dirt—just like we expected.

The conversation hadn't lasted long and had been layered with cryptic connotations to get around anyone listening.

Those few sentences echoed in my head as a prisoner in a baby blue tuxedo was escorted from a cell for his turn at professing his innocence and begging for a second chance amongst the rest of corrupted civilization.

"Everett. I hear you're about to head to the slaughter pen."

I gripped the phone tighter. "If you mean finally revealing the truth then yes, you heard right."

"Enjoy your last words before they throw away the key." He chuckled, but it layered with blackness. "Who knows? Perhaps, they'll put you out of your misery and grant the death penalty."

"Funny." I laughed back, matching his tone. "If I were you, I'd stay away from that party. I have no intention of keeping my mouth shut this time."

"You fucking—"

"Ah ah, language, Arnie." I grinned so hard it almost broke my face. Tormenting him like he'd tormented me for years felt so fucking good. "Thanks for calling to wish me luck, but the next time we talk, I'll be free, and you'll be ruined."

The shot of pure energy at hanging up on him raced through me now.

I pictured him spitting red and throwing furniture around like a demented gorilla. Hopefully, the stress of what I might say in court and the anger at not being able to control me anymore would give him an aneurysm or heart attack.

"Everett?" A guard appeared in the hallway. Holding cages decorated either side—some filled, some empty with awaiting inmates.

I stood, moving toward the bars, waiting for him to let me out of this damn zoo. "That's me."

"You're up." Striding forward, he pulled out a keychain, inserted a key, and hollered to another guard to press unlock at the same time as he twisted the deadbolt. Everything was so minutely controlled, as if I'd commit murder right here beneath the courtroom surrounded by police.

The moment it was open, he held up silver handcuffs and waited until I pushed my arms forward for him to shackle me.

I cringed against the cold metal but kept my head fucking high.

Once pinioned, I stalked forward in my second-hand suit, walking beside the guard instead of behind him. Filled with conviction of truth, drowning in worry of failure, I told myself to stand tall and be ready to accept whatever happened.

I was innocent, not guilty.

And after today, I would be free for the rest of my goddamn life.

CHAPTER THIRTY-SIX

ELLE

I WASN'T ON trial, but I'd never been so terribly nervous.

The jurors sat in their little tiered stands glowering at Larry as he sat proudly beside Penn. Dad had argued with me not to be seen at the trial. That it would be bad PR for Belle Elle.

I'd hugged him and told him I loved him then told him— in the nicest possible way—that he couldn't stop me from being there for Penn, and he might as well get over it.

I loved Penn.

I was here for Penn.

I loved my company too, but if he forced me to choose…well, it was probably best not to make me.

I stared at the back of Penn's head from where I sat in the rows designated for family. The courtroom was basic in its build with harsh wooden barricades and pews. The bench I sat on had already flattened my ass, and we hadn't even started yet.

Fleur crossed her legs beside me, reaching for my hand as a door banged loudly and hate filled my heart instead of love.

Greg.

He marched with playboy grace, dressed in a similar looking suit to Penn. He didn't make eye contact with anyone, keeping his nose high and arrogance wrapped tight around him.

He followed the guard escorting him until they stopped at an identical table next to Penn and Larry, holding out his hands to be uncuffed.

While the officer freed him, tucking the silver handcuffs back onto his belt, Greg's lawyer placed her satchel on the desk and pulled out documents relating to today.

I disliked her immediately.

Not because she represented my nemesis but because she was a hardnosed woman with hair tied so tight, her eyes turned cat-like with red lipstick smeared like blood across her mouth.

She looked like a weasel who wasn't afraid to fight dirty and tear off a few body parts to win.

Sharing a few whispered words with his lawyer, Greg took his seat, his gaze catching mine.

He flinched before straightening his shoulders and giving me a smirk. He waved a little, mouthing, "Hi, Elle," before his lawyer grabbed his shoulder and spun him to face the front.

I wanted to leap over the small wooden wall separating witnesses from accused and wring his damn neck. Not for what he'd done to me but for what he'd done to Penn.

Another door banged, and a judge arrived, climbing up to his podium in a regal robe. His black attire made my heart hammer.

"All rise for honorable Patrick Blake."

The court rose as one.

There weren't many people here—mainly court appointed reporters and the odd colleague from Belle Elle being nosy rather than supportive. I was glad and disappointed that the pews weren't full of people waiting to hear the truth. Glad because what if we all failed? What if the long nights of research and evidence gathering wouldn't be enough to save Penn from this bullshit charge? And disappointed because what if we did and he walked out of here a free man? No one would see honesty win over corruption or know how hard the battle had been.

The victory of winning over men who believed they were better than everyone would be so, so sweet but the failure would be so, so bitter.

"You may be seated."

The court sat in perfect synchronicity.

I stroked my somber suit, hoping the all black affair would grant me strength. I wished I had something of Penn's—a trinket or keepsake to clutch and give me hope.

Not for the first time, I thought about my sapphire star and how much was now tied to that silly piece of jewelry. It had my dad's love imbedded in it. It had Penn's rescue and then subsequently his lies swimming in the blue gemstone.

And now, even though it wasn't mine anymore, and Stewie had refused to part with it, it bore witness to this thanks to the kid himself sitting beside me, his tiny fists tight in his lap; a look of utmost concentration on his face.

He was my keepsake.

Over the past few months, I'd learned to truly like Stewie. He was rough around the edges thanks to his prior years of running wild with his reckless older brother, but there was a sweetness too. He adored Sage and couldn't stop petting her when I took her with me to help Larry research.

Unraveling my fear-sweaty locked-together fingers, I wiped them on my black skirt then took Stewie's small hand in mine.

He jumped, so focused on watching Penn and Larry as they bent to talk in hushed whispers in front of us.

I smiled, hiding my nerves, granting him some courage at the expense of my own. "It will be fine. You'll see."

His throat worked as he swallowed. He didn't nod, merely turned his gaze back to the two men who'd saved him from a life of homelessness and settled in for the longest day of our lives.

"Truth will prevail, Elle." Fleur leaned close. "That creep

Greg can't get away with this—"

"Today, we have Penn Everett versus Greg Hobson," the court officer said loudly, narrowing his eyes at us lowly supporters. "Please remain silent. No outbursts will be permitted. No interruptions of any kind or you will be asked to leave."

When everyone hushed, the officer nodded at the judge. "Ready to begin."

The twelve jurors sat tall with importance with a rustle of clothing and murmurs of voices.

The rest of the court settled to watch, wound with tension, stiff with hope, wishing for a quick and fair verdict.

* * * * *

Recess.

How could there be such a thing?

I didn't want coffee and cake when the life of the man I loved hung in an uncertain balance.

For the past hour, opening statements had been delivered. Greg's lawyer went first, prancing around in knife-sharp stilettos, speaking to the jury as if they were dimwitted barn animals.

According to her, Greg had been mentally abused in his childhood. He'd been brainwashed by his father to believe he would end up marrying me and inheriting it all. When he wanted to travel the world after he finished college, he claimed his dad told him not to go. Otherwise, another man might steal our arrangement and my heart.

I burned through so many calories sitting through such filth.

Steve was a good man, and if he'd lied to his son about winning my hand, then I didn't know him as well as I thought I did. But I had a sneaking suspicion if he was here, he'd be as mortified as I was about the lies Greg spread.

Greg painted a picture of a tireless worker who would do anything for Belle Elle, but in the same breath, he came across as a brokenhearted lover who only wanted a second chance with me away from the influences of the company.

He claimed I went with him willingly.

That I wore chains and let him hit me all because I wanted what he had to offer. I wanted to be with him because that sort of thing turned me on.

Please.

Not for the first time, I wished Steve and Dad had come to bear witness—to finally see the games Greg loved to play, and they'd been so oblivious of. I understood why Steve wasn't here—he loved his son, but he couldn't stand by and watch two children he'd help raise battle in court. And I appreciated why Dad wouldn't step foot in the court because he fussed over Belle Elle as if it was his wife and needed mollycoddling while this nightmare carried on.

Greg pouted for the jury, saying how happy we'd been, only for our romance to be destroyed when Penn swooped in and claimed me for himself. He came across far too convincing.

I was glad I hadn't had anything to eat because I would've thrown up.

Bastard.

Larry's opening statement had been short and to the point. That the accusations were false. That Greg had kidnapped me and Penn had rescued me. The end.

The jury fazed out a little, hearing the same rebuttal most of us had heard on the news or TV once upon a time.

I squirmed in my seat, wanting to leap to my feet and beg the jury to listen to the girl who'd been there, lived it. Prove to them that I loved Penn, not Greg. It had *never* been Greg. Penn had ruined me for all other men even when I didn't know his name.

But Larry had sucked up their attention the moment he'd said, "What is on trial today isn't if Penn went to that cabin with the intention of murder but whether or not the chief of police, Arnold Twig, has been using Mr. Everett for his own son's misdemeanors for years."

The judge had come alive, rapping with his little hammer. "Stick to the case at hand, Mr. Barns. We're here to discuss the aggravated assault and attempted murder charges—not some fictitious witch-hunt on a respected police officer."

Even though Dad was friends with Patrick Blake, we wouldn't earn any special treatment. Which was a good thing and a bad thing. I was glad it would be fair for both parties but was sick of evil managing to hoodwink good far too often.

Greg had snickered, pleased Larry had been told off.

Penn stiffened, his shoulders high, begging me to massage away his stress if only I was allowed to lean forward and put my hands on him.

I'd probably be arrested for touching the defendant.

I'd sat on my fingers, turning my attention from the man who turned my heart molten to Larry.

He'd merely smiled at the judge with his hands crossed politely. "It's all linked, sir. And I can prove it."

Goosebumps darted down my spine for the fiftieth time since he'd said that. My mind snapped out of the last few hours in court, slapping me back into the present.

Sitting on plastic seats outside the courtroom, holding a flimsy cup of coffee thanks to Fleur shoving it in my hands, I hoped and prayed that Greg would do the right thing.

I would've given anything to speak with him. To find out what his decision was and if Penn would be free or convicted.

There must be a way.

"Court resumes in five minutes." An employee stuck his head into the hallway where we gathered beneath monolithic arches and portraits of dead judges.

Minglers stood, gathering handbags and finishing coffee dregs.

"Ready?" I smiled bright as Stewie climbed to his feet, shuffling toward the double doors where we'd endure yet more torture while waiting for Penn to be freed.

He shrugged, his eyes large and worried. "I guess so."

Fleur and I exchanged looks.

My arm found its way over Stewie's shoulders, hugging him close. "It will all work out. You'll see."

He wriggled under my embrace but didn't push me away. He wore the suit Penn had bought from Belle Elle—a smart little man ready to battle for his friend. "I dunno. Shit happens."

I didn't reprimand him for his language.

Because he was right.

We might have every truth and honesty on our side, but at the end of the day…shit happened.

And there was nothing we could do about it.

CHAPTER THIRTY-SEVEN

PENN

SMUG FUCKING BASTARD.

Greg sat next to his zombie of a lawyer, not even bothering to hide his arrogance.

Larry prowled in front, speaking to the court, blocking me from trying to kill Greg with my eyes.

My gaze met Larry's from the witness stand, remembering this was my time to be cordial and well-spoken, not fuming with fury at the bastard who'd stolen another five months of my life. Five months away from Elle. Five months away from happiness.

Larry interrupted my hate. "In your own words, can you describe that night in question?"

That night.

What night?

Oh yeah, he'd been talking about the charity gala. I sat up straight, glancing at the jury with a soft smile. "Ever since my success, I've given what I now have to those who don't have anything. I know what it's like to have nothing, and it's a driving force of mine to give them a chance like another gave one to me."

I gave Larry a look crammed full of gratitude. It might be years since he'd taken me in, but when I thought about what he'd given me, motherfucking tears almost came to my eyes.

"So the event was your charity?" Larry asked.

"Yes."

"What is it called?"

Shit.

I glanced at Elle. I hadn't told her this part. Would she think I was an idiot? I'd gone through so many names for many months. After the penny stock I'd invested in hit an all-time high—going from five cents a share to seventy-five dollars in a matter of months—a majority of the profits were reinvested into the stock, gradually buying more and more until I became the main shareholder of a company that recently got bought out by the CIA for an undisclosed, obscene figure.

After that success, I couldn't just let the money sit there.

I was set for life.

I might as well help others as well as myself.

I knew I wanted to help people but didn't have a clue what to call the charity.

I'd discounted the more generic names like *Homeless No More*. Or *Roof Over Your Head*. Things that would say what the charity entailed. But the charity wouldn't have existed without Larry's faith in me and Elle's ability to reach into my chest that night and start my heart beating for other things.

Things like her.

Things I could never deserve unless I got my shit together.

I cleared my throat. "It's called Chocolate Runaway."

Chocolate for that kiss.

Runaway because if she hadn't, we would never have met and my life would be so fucking different.

I might not be sitting here on trial, but then again, I might never have gotten free from the last arrest because I wouldn't have had the gumption to take Larry up on his offer.

I wouldn't have been ready to fight because I didn't have

anything to fight for. And I definitely wouldn't have taken him up on his offer to stay in his house and obey his rules. I would've run back to the life I knew, not thinking I deserved anything better.

Larry hid his smile. He'd given me such a ribbing when I came home that day with the name registered and proud as fucking punch. I noticed some of the jurors smiling while others rolled their eyes.

My hands curled. "It's personal. I stand by the name just like I stand by the millions of donations the charity has been able to provide."

Larry nodded. "It's an honorable achievement."

"No, it's an ongoing dream. Even while I've been incorrectly imprisoned, the charity has still run and provided for countless of homeless kids."

A few jurors looked at each then glared at Greg.

Score one for me.

Larry marched in front of the witness box where I sat. "So that night, you and Elle were happy?"

Goddammit, I wanted to skip over this part.

It wouldn't exactly paint me in a good light, but Larry had told me to trust him, so I did. "Not exactly." Inhaling, I said loudly, "I'd lied to her. I'd entered into a relationship with her all while letting her believe I was a businessman with no ties to her past. She didn't know I was the homeless man who'd rescued her from two attackers three years ago. I lied because I was hurt that she hadn't come for me. I was pissed off because I'd developed feelings for her and thought she didn't feel the same way."

"What way is that?"

"In love."

The jury shuffled.

I kept my eyes averted. Right now, I sounded like a fucking pussy. Greg chuckled while the judge hammered his gavel. "What link does this questioning have to the case in point, Mr. Barns?"

Larry stormed to the judge, craning his neck. "It's introducing the accused, so the jury can make a better informed decision, your honor."

For a second, I thought he'd overrule, but he reluctantly nodded. "Get on with it."

"Thank you." Larry returned to me. "So that night in question, Ms. Charlston thought she'd figured out who you were and left before you could explain she'd concluded wrong?"

"Yes."

"And you chased after her?"

"I did."

"Only she didn't answer her door or phone, correct?"

"That's correct."

"And you gave her some space as you believed she was upset with you?"

"It wasn't easy, but yes, that was my reasoning."

Larry nodded importantly. "However, you changed your opinions a little later that night, didn't you?"

"Yes." I glowered at Greg. "I woke to being beaten by two men Mr. Hobson had paid off to scare me away from Elle. They said she was with him now and to back off."

"And *was* she with him?" Larry asked.

"No. She'd confided in me that she didn't want anything to do with him."

Larry headed to his desk and collected photos of the day I was placed in custody. Sharing them with the jury, he said, "These are photos of Penn's condition received by Greg's courtesy."

"Incorrect evidence." Greg's lawyer stood up, planting her hands on the table. "Those injuries were given by Greg as he fought for his life while Penn tried to murder him."

The judge looked between the two lawyers. "Is that true?"

Larry shook his head. "No, your honor. I'm sure a few scratches were from the fight, but the majority were from being beaten awake hours earlier. I have doctors reports stating how long the contusions and bruises needed to form and discolor."

He picked up another piece of paper and handed it to the judge. "In his opinion, the discoloration on Penn's ribs, face, and other limbs were six to ten hours old before he had a chance to detain Mr. Hobson."

The judge accepted the evidence with a nod.

Larry turned to me. "In your own words, Mr. Everett, can you describe what happened when you found Mr. Hobson?"

"With pleasure." I bared my teeth. "Ms. Charlston was in chains. He had her bent over a couch about to rape her."

"Not true!" Greg blurted. "She'd just agreed to go to the bedroom with me."

"She knew I was sneaking up behind you, you fool!" I replied before the judge could yell for us to shut the hell up. "She used misdirection so I could incapacitate you."

"Silence!" Patrick Blake commanded. "Another outburst and you'll both be thrown back in the cells."

Greg crossed his arms, slouching like a pissed off child.

I sat taller, embracing fearlessness because I'd done the right thing. I wasn't the one lying.

For a change.

"So you don't deny you touched Mr. Hobson?" Larry waited patiently, his eyebrow rose.

I knew the answer he wanted. What we'd schooled over. *'Yes, I did. But only what was necessary to release Ms. Charlston and put Greg under citizen's arrest.'*

But I was done being polite. I wouldn't waste any more time. I'd tell the truth but in my own words, not his. "I didn't just touch him. I punched him. Multiple times."

The court gasped as one.

I turned my vision to the jury. "He hurt my girl. He was about to *rape* my girl. I wasn't going to have a conversation with him and ask politely if he'd stop abusing her. How many of you would have done that, instead of attacking the asshole who hurt your loved one?"

The jurors broke silence, muttering loudly amongst

themselves. The reporters in the back pews started asking questions, adding to the mayhem.

Court propriety broke down.

The judge hammered his gavel. "Enough! Quiet down. All of you!"

Greg stood up, adding to the mix. "He's lying. She was mine. She loves me. Don't listen—"

"Enough!" the court officer bellowed.

A fight broke out between two jurors for reasons unknown but most likely had something to do with my question about what they would do and their mixed opinions on the matter.

"Quiet!" Judge Blake boomed.

The chaos only grew worse.

Desperate for order, he yelled, "Right, court adjourned. Reconvene tomorrow. Go home. All of you!"

And just like that, my time in the limelight was over.

Back to prison I go.

CHAPTER THIRTY-EIGHT

ELLE

LARRY AND I stood on the steps of the courthouse.

Fleur waited ahead with Stewie, bribing his attention with a stick of chewing gum.

I'd asked her to. I needed Larry on his own because I had a plan.

After the disaster in the courtroom, I couldn't leave things to chance anymore. I couldn't let my heart gallop and my stomach sizzle with fear that Greg would be utterly vindictive and testify against Penn with every viciousness he had in him.

I couldn't watch Penn be handcuffed and marched back to prison like this afternoon. I couldn't survive with one conjugal visit a year and weekly phone calls.

Penn was innocent.

Greg was wrong.

He had to be stopped.

Threats wouldn't work.

But I knew something that would.

"You have to get me a meeting with him, Larry. Tonight."

Larry slammed to a stop. "Penn? No can do. He'll be

under lock-down now."

"No, not him. Greg."

His eyebrows disappeared into his salt and pepper hair. "What?"

"I want to speak to Greg."

"I don't—" He pursed his lips. "Why?"

"I need to try something. Before his turn to testify tomorrow."

Soon, it would be my turn to testify against Greg. I still had that trump card over him, but I doubted that would make him change. He was too naïve to understand what life in prison would do to him. He was too used to being the spoiled little rich boy and given everything he wanted.

He believed he was untouchable.

I didn't have the time or power to show him otherwise, but I could dangle a carrot he valued more than his own life to change his mind about Penn.

"What are you thinking?" Larry's eyes narrowed. "Don't tamper with things you don't understand, Elle."

In the past few months of working late and getting to know Larry, I had great affection for this man who had saved Penn. Who had given him money, a home, kindness, a family. A true benefactor in every sense of the word—offering security after a lifetime of none.

But he was also nosy, and I didn't have time to satisfy that curiosity.

"Can you do it or not?"

He shrugged. "I can't promise anything. He's probably been transferred back to corrections."

"Can you try?"

He frowned but nodded. "I'll do my best." Gripping my hand, he squeezed kindly then marched back into the courthouse.

* * * * *

"Greg?"

I clutched the phone tight.

Larry hadn't been able to work his magic and get me a face-to-face meeting, but he had managed a two-minute phone call.

No more.

No less.

I had one hundred and twenty seconds to make Greg an offer he couldn't refuse. And do it in a way that didn't sound like bribery, blackmail, or any other illegal action that could end up with me taking his place in lock-up.

I didn't care it would be recorded.

I didn't care it could backfire if they decided to pull the records and use it against me.

Penn's life was on me. I would do anything I could to save it. Did that make me stupid? Most likely. Did that make me reckless? Most definitely.

But I was done playing nice, and Greg endangered everything I held as priceless.

"Elle?" Greg snapped. "What the hell do you want?"

I didn't waste time. "Tell the truth."

I wanted to barter with him. To say if he dropped his statement, I'd drop mine. That I wouldn't press charges because I didn't care about justice for me, just freedom for Penn.

But I couldn't—not on the phone.

Every word was a damn minefield. "Tell the truth, Greg, and I'll change your life."

A long pause then he finally bit. "How? How can you change my life?"

"I'll give you fifteen million. I'll put it into an account that will earn interest until you're released. You'll never have to work again."

"Is this some sort of joke?"

"No joke." My fingers turned white around the phone. "All you have to do is tell the truth."

Retract that Penn was trying to kill you. Stop saying I loved you. Be a man for once in your damn life.

"Be honest, Greg. And I'll send you the bank account number the moment court is adjourned."

My heart raced, bucking for his reply.

Finally, the words I feared I'd never hear came back.

"Twenty and you've got yourself a deal."

I didn't even hesitate. "Deal."

CHAPTER THIRTY-NINE

PENN

GREG TOOK THE stand the next day, his gaze glaring into mine.

Freedom practically slapped me on the back and said *'see ya later, buddy.'*

The way he licked his lips—rubbing his jaw with deliberate poise as if he couldn't wait to get my ass thrown into jail where I'd never see Elle again.

His lawyer stalked in front of him like a rickety stick insect, her red lips barely moving as she asked him clipped questions.

"Did you love Ms. Charlston?"

"Did you have a happy childhood growing up together?"

"Did you get along with her father?"

"Did you kidnap and rape with the intention of forced marriage and company takeover?"

Such generic, everyday questions…apart from the last one.

Greg delivered his answers in fluid, concise ways.

I had to hand it to him. He sounded sane and came across as any hard working individual and not a greed-hungry psychopath.

"Yes, I did. Still do."

"Yes, we did many things together. Picnics, bike rides, you name it."

"Of course, Joe Charlston and I go way back."

"No, I did not. That wasn't my intention at all."

Time ticked onward. Jurors yawned a little.

Elle's eyes seared me from behind, and Larry didn't move in his chair.

The courtroom had turned from an explosive kettle yesterday to a stagnant pressure cooker today.

Tension gathered the longer Greg blah-blahed on the stand. I felt sick just waiting for that one question. That simple phrase guaranteed to launch him into a tirade destined to send me to hell. *'Did Penn Everett try to kill you?'*

I thought I wanted to get this farce over with. But being this close to a guilty verdict—again for something I didn't do— turned my heart to icy stone, trying to protect itself before the inevitable happened.

Already my ears rang with the jurors' conclusions.

Guilty.

Guilty.

Guilty.

I froze with visions of the judge bringing his fist down with a life sentence without parole.

Sweat trickled down my back the longer Greg and his lawyer enjoyed their question-answer dance.

And then, the question arrived, blaring like a freight train, smoking with authority ready to steal any happiness I might've earned.

His red-lipped lawyer muttered, "And do you, Greg Hobson, stand by your statement that Penn Everett went to that cabin to kill you? That you had reason to believe he'd plotted your murder and intended to carry it out?"

Greg glanced at me then Larry. His eyes flew behind me, no doubt looking at Elle.

The sound of fabric shifting on seats itched my ears. The entire courtroom didn't breathe.

I desperately wanted to turn around, to grab Elle's hand and thank her for everything she did and apologize that it wasn't enough. That my past had ruined everything anyway.

But I couldn't tear my eyes off Greg. Some masochist part of me needed to sear this moment into my brain forever. I'd use it as fuel in any prison brawls I had to win. I'd punch and punch and *punch* some asshole and pretend it was Greg.

I almost stood up and held my hands out for the cuffs, tasting the inevitable.

But something fucking miraculous happened.

Greg leaned back, shrugging like a toddler caught with his hand in the cookie jar. "You know what? I've had time to reflect on what happened that night, and I *think* I might have got it wrong."

Fucking what?

My chair legs screeched as I scooted forward. Did that really just happen? I needed a replay. To press rewind and see if my brain had fritzed or if this was real life.

Greg relaxed into his tale, bringing his leg up to cock over his knee as if he spoke to his brethren at a bar not a jury in court. "I didn't lie—I honestly thought he did want to kill me—but I'm a reformed man and recently been using the downtime to truly assess what I thought and what was real."

Christ, he had the jury eating out of his goddamn hand.

Everyone sat up, the jaded glaze fading from their eyes as if grateful he was about to tell them exactly what they should believe in so this sham could be over, and they could go back to their families.

Greg sighed heavily, acting the perfect grieving witness. "I won't deny that Penn Everett hurt me. Shit, I still have the bruises to prove it, and he did put me in the hospital—those are facts." He smiled at the jury. "My ribs were cracked and larynx bruised. The doctors said I was lucky to still have a voice box."

I rolled my eyes.

Fucking, please.

"But Everett had a point yesterday. I would've gone crazy over any dude touching my girl and thrown a few punches, too."

My mouth hung open.

Did I just hear that correctly?

Wait, that can't have just happened?

I'm in an alternative universe.

I've stepped into the Twilight Zone.

Elle's softest gasp sounded behind me, dotting my skin with goosebumps.

Larry sat ramrod straight, his fingernails scratching into the table.

I was glad I wasn't the only one fucking stupefied by this change of events.

What the hell is going on here?

"He got it wrong that I was raping her." Greg's face turned black with familiar greed then lightened to innocent once again. "We were role playing." He leaned into the jury as if it was a secret between them. "Ms. Charlston likes a bit of bondage, if you know what—"

"Stay on topic, Mr. Hobson," the judge muttered.

Greg held up his hands. "Hey, kink isn't on trial here, is it?"

A juror or two snickered.

Judge Blake scowled. "Continue without the sexual references that may or may not be true."

Greg nodded. "Yes, your honor." Sitting tall, he added, "Penn was jealous of Elle and me. Elle was going to break it off with him to be with me—"

Another noise came from behind me. A small keen like a broken kitten. The chemistry between Elle and I exploded as I felt her tension, endured her panic.

"Overruled." Larry stood. "We have multiple witness statements from Ms. Charlston's bodyguard, father, and other staff that state that is incorrect. Ms. Charlston and Mr. Everett were engaged to be married." Larry shot me a quick smile. "They still are."

"Sustained. Strike from the record," the judge commanded. Looming over Greg from his podium, Patrick Blake swiped his forehead as if this entire trial caused him a migraine. "I suggest you stick to the facts and not make-believe, Mr. Hobson."

Greg chuckled. "Fine. All I have to say then is Mr. Everett didn't try to kill me. I revoke my statement."

The judge's mouth fell open. "Are you sure?"

Greg looked at Elle again. Something passed over his face—half with loathing and half with utmost satisfaction. "I'm sure."

Larry stood up just as Greg's lawyer spluttered, "But—"

Larry clapped his hands. "In that case, I motion for my client to be freed from the incorrect charges immediately. As for the other evidence about corruption and unlawful imprisonment by Arnold Twig, I'd like to progress with pressing charges at a later date with intentions to expunge my client's record."

My head swam.

I felt fucking faint.

Christ, don't faint like an idiot.

I couldn't follow what had just happened.

I stood up on shaky legs only for the judge to bark at me to sit down.

I did, swiveling in my chair to face Elle.

She beamed with a happy smile.

"Did you do this?" I whispered.

She shook her head, tears glittering in her blue eyes.

She's lying.

All I wanted to do was kiss her stupid. She'd done something—regardless of her denial.

There was no way Greg would've retracted his desire to see me rot unless he'd been given something he valued more than making me suffer.

Understanding suddenly filled me.

Money.

I pursed my lips, tilting my head for her to enlighten me.

She merely bit her bottom lip to prevent glowing like the damn sun.

The glint in her gaze told me all I needed to know.

I'm right.

She'd bribed him.

Fuck knew how much she'd promised to save my stupid ass, but she'd done it.

I was…free.

I spun around, facing the court.

Wait, *was* I free?

Nothing had been said.

Only scrambles of papers and impatient reporters to deliver a story to their editors. The jurors mumbled amongst themselves as if pissed that not only would they not get to contemplate a verdict but they'd also been robbed of delivering it.

With no accuser or statement and a thousand pieces of evidence about Arnold Twig, Sean Twig, and my past riddled with bad luck, nothing else could happen.

I was a good person—contrary to what most believed.

"Quiet!" The judge brought down his gavel. "In the case between Greg Hobson versus Penn Everett, I hereby dismiss all claims. The case is closed. Mr. Everett is innocent. You are free to go." In the same breath, he looked at Greg. "Mr. Hobson, you shall return and continue with the state as your host while awaiting trial for your own court case against Ms. Charlston. Until then, I hope everyone obeys the law and stops wasting public time and money." He stood in his robe then stomped down the podium.

There was no fanfare or clapping.

Only the surreal silence that it was over.

Greg threw me a sizzling stare full of contempt even while

297

his fingers counted imaginary dollars. His lawyer stomped off with her satchel thrown over her shoulder. Larry grabbed me in a bear hug. Stewie wrapped himself around my legs. And Elle grabbed my face and kissed me.

She broke the spell.

She popped the bubble and proved it hadn't been a dream.

It was real.

It had happened.

I was *free*.

CHAPTER FORTY

ELLE

THE PRACTICAL THING after being released from jail would be to go for dinner with those who fought by your side. To answer the flocks of seagulls as news reporters begged for scraps of how I entered the court this morning with only Fleur and Stewie by my side and left in the afternoon wrapped in Penn's arms.

And we did do those things.

We stopped and kissed for the papers. We waved away questions and grabbed a quick celebratory drink with Stewie, Larry, and Fleur. We didn't think about the upcoming fight with Arnold Twig, and we didn't worry about my turn to testify at court against Greg.

He was back in prison, rolling in promised cash, waiting for his hearing.

I had no doubt he wouldn't care at all.

He wouldn't care because he had twenty million reasons to be happy.

And I didn't care because I had twenty million reasons to

be grateful Penn was free. That he could stand beside me without shackles. That we could kiss whenever we wanted and whisper about a life we could claim rather than lament about the one we'd had stolen.

We allowed ourselves to celebrate the present without the future robbing us of our hard-earned joy.

My father called Penn to congratulate him, but he didn't join us for food due to indigestion brought on by stress of the trial.

I ordered him to bed, comforted to know Marnie, our housekeeper, would be there to keep him happy.

Steve didn't join us for dinner either. Technically, today was not a happy day for him, as Greg would remain in prison without bail until his court date—and then who knew how long he'd serve.

But sitting at a table at a local bar with generic coasters, beer-soaked carpet, and red-leather booths in dim lighting, we toasted to Penn and grew drunk on the relief at having him back.

The celebration started off as a group endeavor. Penn accepted hugs from everyone. He chatted and joked, but he always had one hand touching me—my wrist, my hand, my hip.

After an hour, electricity laced those touches, zapping my belly, liquefying my insides. I couldn't prevent the way my heart imitated a bowling ball, knocking down my ribs as if they were skittle pins.

No one else noticed but my cheeks slowly glowed—and not from alcohol. Desire for him bubbled inside until the barest brush sent a lustful convulsion through me.

Need built and built until it was unbearable.

Half an hour later, Fleur whispered in my ear that she was taking off because she had a feeling Penn and I weren't going to be around much longer.

I playfully scolded her then kissed her goodbye.

I needed to be alone with Penn, but I wouldn't be rude and rob the others from sharing in this hard-earned party.

So, despite fireworks fizzing in my blood, we ordered French fries and prawn twisters. We downed more drinks. And when I excused myself to go to the bathroom, Penn found me like he had the night at the Palm Politics.

He didn't say a word.

He slammed me hard against a wall and kissed me so deep, I almost combusted. His tongue was totally sinful. His hands absolutely sexual. His cock throbbing as he wedged it firm against me with a glitter in his gaze. "I need to be alone with you. Now."

Words were hard to come by. He'd incinerated my insides. Burned my synapses. I merely nodded and allowed him to take my hand.

He dragged me back to the table of partiers where we said a guilty goodbye.

Then we caught the first taxi we saw back to his place.

* * * * *

"The blood's gone."

A random thing to notice the moment I stepped into Penn's apartment, but my nerves jangled. I hadn't been in his place since the day he'd rescued me and started to tell me the truth, only for the police to rip him away for the second time.

"You're right." His calculating eyes, which once made me nervous, but now only revealed his keen intelligence, flickered from spotless kitchen to tidy living room. No bed sheets strewn across the floor, no blood, no signs of a fight. "Larry must've arranged a cleaning crew."

I hid a grin, kicking off my black heels and placing my handbag on the kitchen counter. "I'm glad. I don't exactly feel like doing housework." I hadn't meant it to come out so sexual, but it did. My voice was scratchy with desire, the need to touch him with no more rules or cages unbearable.

Only, he didn't attack me like he had on the night of our conjugal visit. He didn't pad barefoot toward me sensually. He merely stood in the center of his home and jammed his hands into his pockets the same way he did the very first time we met.

Knowing what I knew now, I understood why.

It was his form of protection against others and himself.

His arms bunched beneath the white shirt he'd rolled up to his elbows; black slacks hung off his hips too big, and his fists balled in pockets that made my heart sob with familiarity.

Despite the events keeping us apart, we'd grown to know each other. I knew enough to predict how he would react. And he knew enough to preempt my answer.

We stood staring at each other as if we couldn't believe this was real. That we were back here, alone, and unsupervised. Free to do whatever we damn well wanted.

I smiled, suddenly shy and overwhelmed by how simple but heavily charged the moment had become.

Penn's lips matched mine in a sweet smirk, the stress, worry, and panic of the trial finally slipping off his shoulders, down his arms, and into his pockets. Instead of loose change and old receipts, those slacks held five months of jail time, so Penn no longer had to.

It was me who moved first.

Undoing the buttons on my dark gray blazer, I stepped toward him. My pantyhosed feet slicked over the hardwood floor, making me shiver. Penn didn't move as I released the final button and allowed the jacket to puddle down my arms to the floor.

Never breaking eye contact, I reached behind me and undid the zipper on my skirt. Running my hands over my hips, I pushed the slinky lining down my body, wriggling slowly to ease the fabric off.

Penn clenched his jaw, his chest flexing as he forced himself to keep his hands in his pockets. "Elle…" He bit his bottom lip as his eyes glued to my fingers gliding up my body to undo the tiny buttons of my pale cream shirt.

I had no plan of seduction. I hadn't come here with the idea of stripping for him. But the way he watched me, drank me, breathed me.

God, it was the best aphrodisiac.

My stomach fluttered beneath the buttons as I undid them one by one. My core clenched as he let out a long ragged groan of pure male appreciation.

Yet he didn't touch me.

His lips parted to breathe heavier. His body swayed as if summoned by some invisible force to link with mine, but he permitted me to finish whatever striptease I wanted.

I had no urge to speak as I undid the last button and slid the shirt down my arms, letting it cascade on top of my jacket and skirt. Words were cheap when our stares said everything we ever needed to hear.

I want you.
You're mine.
I need you.
I'm yours.
We're free.
We're together.

Standing before him in my cream bra and panties decorated with black lace stars with garters and stockings, I felt stronger than I ever had before.

I'd worn a suit to court to borrow authority from cotton and silk but stripped of them now, left only in lace and pantyhose, I was more powerful, more invincible, more desirable than any outfit in the world.

Penn sucked in a gasp. His voice teasing a whisper. "You're so beautiful."

His words touched me, but his hands didn't. They remained in his pockets as if the moment he pulled them free, he'd reach for me, and this precious memory would shatter into passion.

I needed to see him. I wanted to run my fingers along his chest and assure myself he was here. That this wasn't some incredible fantasy.

Deleting the final step between us, I pressed my fingertips to his belly, relishing his sharp inhale.

Beneath my touch lived muscle and sinew—bone of the

man I'd given my heart to and hoped he'd keep forever.

Tugging on his shirt, I slowly pulled it from his waistband, letting it hang roguishly undone and handsome, curling around his hands still wedged deep in his slacks.

He stopped breathing as I undid the bottom button then another, slowly working my way up his body, allowing the cotton to stay close together until I reached the top.

The courts didn't give him a tie, and the second the last button was undone, I invaded his warmth. Inserting my hands, I washed them over his smooth chest, his pecs, up his shoulders, and down his back until the shirt rippled down his arms to hang where his hands still remained wedged at his thighs.

The white against black looked as if I'd cut off angel wings. As if I'd corrupted a god and made him trade a celestial existent for lowly all because I wanted him.

My mouth watered to suck his skin.

So I did.

Leaning forward, I pressed the softest kisses over his breastbone, working my way to his nipple. As my mouth latched over him, he grunted, bowing backward, sacrificing himself to whatever pleasure I wanted to give him.

He trembled, his toes gripping the floor until they turned white as my tongue circled his nipple and my hands trailed down his belly.

His erection tented his slacks, but I didn't reach for it. Not yet.

Undoing the cheap synthetic belt, a ball of lust replaced my heart as he shuddered so hard—part from keeping himself in check and not reaching for me, but mostly, from what I did to him.

From my touch. My lips. My methodical way of stripping him of everything that'd happened.

I didn't just remove his clothes.

I removed his past.

I tore off the months of imprisonment.

I slipped off his lies and half-truths.

Piece by piece, I revealed the man I'd always known existed.

Someone kind but ruthless. Supportive but possessive. Intelligent but quick tempered.

He was an angel and monster in one.

Just human with perfections and imperfections.

"Elle…" he breathed as I undid the button of his slacks then slowly pulled his zipper down. With my bare feet, I moved my skirt and jacket to wedge in front of me then kneeled on the soft padding before him.

"Christ…" He sucked in a gasp as I left his slacks open, circling my fingers around his wrists. His hands remained locked tight in his pockets, but with a soft tug, he allowed me to lift his right one, giving me utmost control.

Never saying a word, I undid the cuff button so his shirt could fall then pressed a kiss onto his palm.

He shivered as I let go, moving toward his left hand.

Once again, he willingly gave me control as I pulled it gently from his pocket. His slacks fell around his ankles, leaving him in tight white boxer-briefs that only highlighted how hard and thick he was.

My mouth went dry as I undid his final button, undoing the cuff around his left hand. The moment it was free, the shirt fell, joining the rest of discarded clothing.

Only one piece left on him. It was a piece I savored as I pressed a kiss, blowing hot air on his shaft through the soft cotton.

He jerked, his hands (now with nothing to use as imprisonment) landed in my hair. "Shit, Elle…what are you doing to me?" His voice was faraway, in a land where nothing bad—no nights alone, no days unsafe, no cold or fear or hunger could find him.

He was mine now.

Tomorrow, I could cook him breakfast like I'd always wanted. I could keep him close, protect him for protecting me.

My hands wrapped around his hipbones, skating fingers over the tight elastic of his boxer-briefs. With my heart lodged in my throat at how turned on I was—how wet, how hot, how heavy and ready—I pulled his underwear down.

His quads clenched until delicious muscle rippled beneath perfect hair-sparse skin. His head fell back with a tattered groan as my hands stayed with his boxers, landing around his ankles but my mouth…that went on its own quest.

I opened and found his crown. I moaned at the taste, at how warm he was, how hard, how satin sheathed steel.

His legs buckled, his fingers digging harder onto my head—not to take control but to support himself, so he didn't collapse.

"Holy Christ," he groaned as I sat taller on my knees and swallowed him deep. My fingers came up, left hand cupping his balls, right hand gripping his girth.

I lapped over the thick veins coursing down his length. I sucked with long pulls, wanting to drive him to the pinnacle within seconds.

Penn turned mute, soundless. His fingernails scraped my scalp as he held himself back, his self-control fraying with every second.

Pumping his base, I licked with a feathering tongue. My tummy coiled tight, taking pleasure from giving pleasure.

His spine locked as a ripple of bliss worked up his shaft, coating my mouth with pre-cum. I wanted him to come. I wanted him to let go and relax.

But he captured my chin, bringing my eyes to his. His heartbreakingly gorgeous face was savage with self-control. "I'm not coming in your mouth, Elle."

I unsheathed my teeth and bit softly.

His hips jerked forward as I sucked him off.

I did what I'd been dreaming off since he made me get on my knees in my office then told me my two minutes were up.

It wasn't a competition to show him how well I'd learned my lesson, but if I could make him come undone in two minutes like this, I would gloat for life.

His eyes shadowed to coal black. "Fuck." He shuddered as I sucked him again, his throat working as he swallowed. "Answer me one question."

I flicked my tongue over his crown, nodding permission.

He swallowed again, croaking, "Are you wet?"

Was I wet? I was drenched. I was so turned on; I could come with the slightest whisper over my clit.

I nodded.

My tongue licked him, adored him, and that was the breaking point for Penn.

One second, I was in control on my knees. I had him by the balls—literally. The next, I was tossed over his shoulder with his hand spanking my ass and the floor moving fast beneath my eyes.

"You'll pay for that, Elle." Swatting me again, he stalked into his bedroom.

From my vantage point, I noticed the black bag still holding the dildo samples sitting on his dresser along with a freshly made bed full of white sheets and pillows.

Pristine, virginal, until he threw me onto the mattress and cupped my jaw in his hands. I sat on the edge while Penn slammed to his knees. The reversal of our roles sent my heart spinning wild like an out of control ballerina.

His dark, delicious eyes speared mine. "I've wanted you since the first moment I saw you. I want you so damn much it interferes with my head, my heart, my very fucking existence. Yet you fight for me, you bribe my enemies for me, you deliver my freedom, and then you get on your knees and pleasure me so fucking selflessly?"

He shook his head, anger dragging his brow over his eyes. "No. You deserve to be worshipped, Elle. You deserve pleasure and protection and everything your heart deserves."

His features flickered with nervousness. "I hope to God you want me as much as I want you. My shitty life has taught me that the things I want the most are the first to be taken away. I can't let that happen with you."

He kissed my lips, inhaling hard, his fingers shaking. "I've done things I wish I could undo. I'm not proud of who I've been, but, Elle, fuck, if you can stand by me in prison, if you can stand with me in court, then I will stand by you for the rest of your life."

I swayed forward, slinging my arms over his shoulders and grabbing a fistful of his hair. His obvious need to show me how he felt, his insatiable desire tainting the room—it all matched the depth of emotion I held for him.

It was endless. It was new. It was our future.

"Kiss me."

He froze as if to argue. But then his mouth smashed against mine. His teeth caught my bottom lip, his tongue plunging as if to bypass any more conversation and make me drink his vows.

I crab-walked backward on my elbows until I had enough mattress to lie down. Penn followed, stalking over me on his hands and knees, his mouth never ceasing in its dominance of mine.

His fingers traced my bra, then my naked belly, before teasing the topline of my panties.

His palm crept between my legs, grabbing me firm. "I'm going to fuck you for days, Elle. We're not leaving this bed until we're boneless and on death's door from orgasms."

I moaned as he ripped my panties down my legs then unhooked the garter belts to unroll my pantyhose.

I arched my back for him to undo my bra, and when I lay naked, same as him, his fingers found me again.

This time, there was no lace, no boundary.

Grinding his erection onto my hip, he sank a finger unapologetically deep.

My mouth popped wide. My body bucked in his control.

"Let go, Elle. Forget about rules and society. Ignore what civilization says we should be and how we should act." A second finger joined the first, filling me, stretching me as his cock throbbed hot and hard against my hip. "Let go and let me see you. Cry for me. Scream for me." His voice slipped into volcanic ash. "Beg for me."

My body rose to meet his thumb as he pressed my clit. "Penn…"

"Penn what?" he growled in my ear, his fingers fucking me, punishing me with pleasure.

My body surged to meet then bowed away. He pressed harder on the tiny bundle of nerves, making my eyes water, and a climax twist into a ravaging storm.

"I'm—I'm—"

I was so close to coming already. The sparkling transformation of my womb and spine warned me that it would happen.

I couldn't stop it.

Because that was what Penn did to me. The magic he held over me—the same magic he'd had from the start.

"You're?" He nipped my throat, his fingers driving faster. "Finish your sentence. Tell me." His thumb gave me no escape. I gave up trying to move away from pleasure and threw myself head first into it.

"I'm coming." I thought it would come out as a whisper.

It came out as a scream as I did exactly what he'd told me to do and let loose.

My body took control with the speed and power of a runaway train. The orgasm grabbed me, squeezed me, obliterated me.

Clenches and waves, I milked Penn's fingers until I moaned unintelligently.

He kissed me deep, soft, languid as I came down from the most piercing high.

"I knew you could come fast." His lips caressed my cheek, moving to my jaw. "That first night when you said yes—in the alley before I gave you back to David to take you home. Remember?"

I blinked, dragging myself back to human rather than

liquid bliss. "When you made me come against the wall?"

A smug glint filled his gaze. "Yes."

I shared a piece of me, giving him access to who I was. "I worried you'd take me that night. That I'd lose my virginity against a brick wall."

"Did you prefer losing it in this very bed?"

"I did." I smiled.

"You came that night too with my cock inside you." His eyes rolled as if reliving heaven. "Fuck, you were so receptive. Have you always been that way? That sensitive?"

I nodded. "It comes in handy when I'm on my own and need a quickie."

"You'll never be on your own again."

I arched up, seeking his lips. "You too."

I wasn't prepared for the way his arms latched around me with a vicious hold. He hugged me as if thanking me for becoming his. Telling me with actions that loneliness had been his cross to bear for so long, and now he no longer had to carry it.

His lips sought mine again.

And our conversation ended.

Just like that.

CHAPTER FORTY-ONE

PENN

I'D WANTED TO make this last.

I wanted to memorize every inch of Elle so she wasn't just a girl in my past who I'd mistakenly despised or a woman in my present I was fucking.

She was my future.

She was my home, and I wanted to know every freckle and birthmark, every ticklish spot and turn-on zone.

But that was before she sucked me off then came in two seconds flat as if she couldn't stand having my hands on her and not reward me with every drop of her pleasure.

Slow would have to come later. Along with fun and toys and games and all the other exciting stuff we had to look forward to.

This was a hello after months of painful separation.

I wanted her heart thundering against mine, body to body, soul to motherfucking soul.

Without a word, I wedged my hips between her spread legs. My cock throbbed to come. My back locked as Elle grabbed the base of me, guiding me to her entrance.

Her eyes blazed blue as she rubbed my crown through her wetness, torturing both of us, coating me in her orgasm, begging me to do whatever I damn well wanted.

And I wanted.

So fucking much.

She was passionate, free, a lover and friend and partner. She was no longer a stranger or a spoiled brat I'd hated.

She's mine.

My lips locked together as I pressed the first inch inside her.

A low, feminine moan echoed in her chest. Her legs opened wider, showing me everything, making me drunk and embarrassingly close to losing control.

Our gazes never unlocked; I looked at her with utmost awe. She bit her bottom lip, reading me better than I could read myself. Knowing I'd reached my limit on gentle and needed to be a beast.

She clenched around me, giving me permission to let go.

Slamming forward, I slid straight inside her. She spread wide and wet. A cry tumbled from her mouth and into mine as I kissed her fast and messy.

My arms went around her shoulders and nape, cuddling her close even while my hips attacked her.

The bed rocked, our breathing tore, her legs looped over my back, her ankles digging into my spine.

"Jesus," I bit out.

"Yes…God, yes…" Her fingers landed in my hair, twisting almost cruelly, adding fine-edged pain.

Christ, she shouldn't have done that.

I lost it.

Utterly fucking lost it.

My body was hard as stone, my stomach slapping against hers, my balls drawn up in preparation of shooting everything I had into this woman.

Her pussy clung to me every time I withdrew to slam inside her again. Her back arched until her breasts stuck to my chest, and I held her so close, gluing us together, slick with sweat and need.

The friction was too much. Every wet ridge of her, every hard inch of me. I pushed up, she pushed down; I thrust in, she welcomed. She rocked harder, her hips moving in delicious circles, rubbing her clit on the base of my cock.

I loved that she chased her own pleasure. That she wasn't afraid of letting go. Of learning me, revealing her, sharing what worked for us both.

"Christ, you feel good," I panted. "You feel so fucking good."

"You're mine, Penn. You always have been." Her lips found mine. We knotted ourselves into each other until I didn't know where my body ended and hers began.

The burn in my quads, spine, and cock smoldered until smoke and fire erupted. The irrefutable need to release came with agony laced with greed.

"Shit, I'm gonna come." I rode her harder, driving faster, turning sex into mania.

And Elle matched me.

The bed shifted, moving away from the wall with every thrust.

We had an agenda. An end goal. I arched my back, slamming into her soaked pussy, my muscles rigid with detonation.

She gasped, her fingernails scratching my spine. I loved the pinpricks of pain. The way her breath spurted in my ears, the seamless way my cock plunged into her body.

I fucked her with everything I had.

And when my release found me, it didn't fucking stop.

My thighs, ass, heart, every inch contracted with an all-consuming spurt. I sank deep, growling as euphoria shot from me and into this girl who'd given me my life back.

Elle let go too, her body quaking under mine, her pussy fisting me from root to tip as I filled her.

I chased the climax for as long as I could; shattering into tremors as the waves slowly grew weaker. I ceased holding my weight off Elle, slamming on top of her in a full-body embrace.

Her body was so hot. Radiating like an inferno.

Her pussy still rippled around me, sending delayed ricochets of bliss down my cock and into my legs.

"Damn, that felt good."

She giggled, kissing my cheek. "I agree."

She went to move away, but I grabbed her wrists, pinning them above her head. "Ah ah, you're not leaving."

"I'm not?" Her cute button nose wrinkled.

"Nope."

"Why?" Her gaze flickered to the bathroom. "A shower together would be nice…oh, we could take a bath. Spend hours relaxing."

Images of sliding my hands over Elle's nakedness definitely sounded like a great plan. But I couldn't admit I wasn't ready to let her go yet. I wasn't ready to withdraw and no longer feel her wet heat.

This wasn't about coming.

This was about connection, and hell, I needed it.

Her hips rolled in perfect circles, pressing her clit against me. "If you're going to restrain me, I might have to come again."

I raised an eyebrow. "Could you?"

"Not sure. Never gone for three before." Her smirk was the devil herself. "But I'm open to trying."

I nuzzled her hair, pumping slowly into her, already feeling myself grow hard again. "In that case, let's see what you're capable of. And then I'm washing you for hours, feeding you, and then we're taking a walk around Central Park."

"We are?"

"We are."

"But why Central Park? That's where you were stolen from me the first time."

"Because from now on, you're going to explore every inch of this city with me. I'm going to show you were I slept; I'll reveal my bolt holes, my food stashes, my emergency funds buried in people's gardens. This city has not been kind to me,

Elle, and the itch to leave is building. Last time Larry freed me, I moved to LA to get away. It helped."

I kissed her nose as stress etched her eyes. "But—you can't leave. My work…it's here." Tears sparkled.

"I'm not leaving. That's why I need you to replace bad memories with good. With you, I can learn to love this city again, but only with you by my side."

A tear rolled down her cheek. "I'll go to every street corner, every park, every bench. I'll go wherever you want me to, Penn. You'll never be alone again."

CHAPTER FORTY-TWO

ELLE

WE DID ALL those things.

After a second round when Penn flipped me onto my hands and knees, and a quickie turned into kinky playtime, we soaked in his bath before catching a taxi to Central Park and walking the same path we'd sprinted from the security guards.

We followed the chain link fence of the baseball field where we'd shared our first kiss and watched an evening game where men trampled the home diamond where Penn shared his chocolate bar.

We kissed in the same bushes where we were arrested and bought cinnamon-sugared churros from a street van as we strolled a few blocks of New York.

Penn didn't say much. His eyes turned more active, his entire body on high alert. The ruthless businessman I'd given my virginity to faded into the wild creature I'd met in the alley.

He sniffed the air as if he could smell a threat. He narrowed his gaze at a group of men coming toward us. He moved as a predator and prey all at once.

I took his hand.

He froze then relaxed. His eyes met mine. His lips turned from scowl to smile. And we made our way back to his apartment in harmony.

When we got back, I expected to climb into bed and either repeat what we'd done before or sleep. It'd been a long day and an even longer five months, but Penn ordered takeout from a local Thai place, and we snuggled on his couch while watching TV.

We laughed and snickered at jokes on the screen.

We licked our fingers free from curry puffs and slurped Pad Thai.

We shared normalcy and made it magic.

Like any normal couple.

Like a boy and girl in love.

It was the best day of my life.

CHAPTER FORTY-THREE

PENN

DEAR PENN,
I love many things in this world.
I love my company, my cat, my father, my financial security.
But I have to say, I love you more.
Watching you sleep this morning—you were soft for the first time.
Your forehead wasn't creased; your eyes weren't narrowed in suspicion
waiting for the next catastrophe. You trusted me to keep you safe while you
dreamed.
My heart is so full because of that.
And I hope you can forgive me for not waking you.
Belle Elle needs me, and I have to go to work. However, I've left you
a present. Call me when you're awake—sleep all afternoon if you want.
You deserve it. Then come find me at the office and perhaps take me over
my desk.
I'd like to put that particular fantasy into reality.
I love you.
See you soon,
Elle xx

I flopped onto my back, a ridiculous grin on my face.

The gift she'd mentioned was her lingerie. She'd left it neatly folded on the covers, proof that she'd gone to work naked beneath her clothes, thinking of me as I thought about her.

I grew hard picturing her bare and waiting for me.

I shouldn't get so caught up over a note on my pillow and her underwear on my bed, but I did.

It gave me peace of mind that this wasn't a dream.

This was real.

The second I woke, I'd had a panic attack thinking I was back in lock-up and the soreness in my body and slight dehydration from so much sex was all make-believe.

Then I'd stretched, and the crinkle of paper brought my mind instantly back to Elle.

She knew more than I'd wanted to show her. She knew how my temper and sharp need to protect worked against me and filled me with fear. She understood that the world I was from was full of danger and enemies, while happiness and friends padded hers.

It would take a while for me to relax and not search for disasters, but with her in my life, I had no doubt I could find the one thing I'd never been able to afford—no matter how much I stole or earned on the stock market.

Love.

Unable to fall back to sleep with her on my mind and lust in my heart, I showered, dressed, and headed into the kitchen to enjoy some caffeine before heading uptown to Belle Elle.

While the coffee brewed, I collected my laptop from the locked drawer in the sideboard, and for the first time in five months, opened the internet.

Not having regular visitors or phone calls in jail was hard. Not having access to daily news, stock prices, and portfolio updates was torture.

Logging into my charity, I noticed the offsite staff I'd hired had been busy with a local food bank, lunch day, and a temporary tent city where the council had let us do a trial for homeless people.

I had no doubt Larry would've kept it running. I had so much to repay him for.

Perhaps, before I headed to Elle's, I'd take him to lunch and show him in a woefully understated way how much I valued his friendship and support.

Opening the local news, I grabbed a cup of freshly brewed coffee and prepared to spend the next fifteen minutes perusing the disarray the world had once again fallen into.

Only…my coffee cup slammed onto the table, spilling brown steaming liquid everywhere. My heart stopped. My fingers scrabbled at the screen to jerk the technology closer.

After the happiness of last night…this couldn't be happening.

NOELLE CHARLSTON SHACKED UP WITH A HOMELESS CRIMINAL?

In terms of New York royalty, none come as close as the Charlston family—the owners and creators of the Belle Elle department stores. Not only have their clothes, toys, and household appliances graced our homes for decades, the Charlstons have regularly been noted for their impeccable social standing and unblemished record at avoiding scandal.

When Noelle's mother died, the country rallied in support and records showed florists in the New York area all had at least three deliveries a day to the Charlston family in condolences.

However, recent events have made the public doubt the Charlstons are as pure as they led us to believe.

Protesters were photographed yesterday outside their flagship store, boycotting their clothing line. Speaking to one protestor, they said they wouldn't dress in apparel provided by a company involved with criminals.

It brings up questions as to their own moral code and what they have been involved in over the years while painting the perfect family to the New York people.

Penn Everett is the man hiding in Belle Elle's shadow. Recently released from prison on an incorrect accusation, it's been said that his

previous arrests are in discussion by local lawyer Larry Barns, pointing
fingers at our very own chief of police, Arnold Twig.

Chief Twig states Penn is one of the most violent offenders out there,
and it's a disaster to see the justice system fail the American people.

In a personal interview earlier today, Chief Twig also said he feared
for his son, Sean, now that Everett was free. According to him, Everett
has always been jealous of Sean Twig and there's history to show Everett
places the blame for his crimes onto the innocent young man.

Neither Joseph Charlston or Noelle were prepared to make a
statement.

My elbows planted on the table either side of the damning article.

Fuck.

My legs jittered on the chair leg, my heart filling with snow.

I'd known this would happen. I'd heard rumors in prison and had updates from Larry that Belle Elle was regularly mentioned alongside my name.

But to see it in black and white?

To have a prominent newspaper tear Elle's family legacy apart all because of me?

Shit, it dug a dagger into my heart and twisted until I couldn't breathe.

I loved her. I would do anything for her.

But they were right.

This was all my fault.

I'd gone after Elle because of my hate. I'd dragged her into my chaos because of my love. I'd ruined her business because of my selfishness.

The longer I was with her, the worse the lynch mob would become.

It didn't matter what I wanted or how much I cared for her.

Elle had sacrificed far too much for me. I couldn't let her sacrifice anymore.

I loved her too much to let all she'd worked for be stolen. Slamming the laptop closed, I grabbed my keys and left.

CHAPTER FORTY-FOUR

ELLE

"ELLE, CAN YOU come in here, please?" Dad's voice came from his office.

I'd arrived early—before most staff—to finally get stuck into my mountain of work that I hadn't mentally been able to cope with over the past five months.

I'd kept the company ticking along—mainly thanks to Dad taking on more responsibility and Fleur's help—but it was time I took the reins again now Penn was free.

I had finally settled my debt with him. I was unbelievably happy. And the rest of life would work itself out like it was supposed to.

Striding into my father's office, I smiled. He wore a simple black suit with a gray waistcoat and maroon shirt. He sat behind his desk where he'd given me Sage all those years ago.

He read a newspaper with a grimace. "Can you explain this?"

"Explain what?"

He tossed the article toward me, spinning it upside down

so I could read it clearly. The blaring headline said: *BELLE ELLE MAY HAVE A NEW CEO AND HE COMES WITH A CRIMINAL RECORD.*

I warred with the need to burn the stupid thing and assure my father not to upset his heart.

"You know what reporters are like. They'll say anything to sell copies."

Dad scrubbed his face. "How much of it is true, though?"

"None of it."

"Most of it, you mean?" He sighed. "Greg retracted his statement. He wouldn't have done that if you hadn't have meddled."

My shoulders straightened. "I didn't do anything illegal, Dad."

"I'm not so sure about that. And now, you're dating someone who has done illegal things."

Standing primly, I refrained my temper from lashing back. "Penn is a good person. Or are you forgetting your approval when he first arrived?"

"A criminal record changes things, Elle." He slouched. "I want you to be happy, but I don't want Belle Elle to be dragged into this sort of scandal."

"The company can handle it. Why does the public opinion have so much sway over my personal relationships?"

Dad stood, patrolling around his office, bypassing awards for best retail experience, best merchandise, and best charity donations to organizations who supported fair wages. We followed the law and did our part for the world in all things business. Belle Elle ran my life. I wouldn't let it rule my love life, too.

"Because the public is our business, Elle. If you continue to drag the company's good will through the muck of prison and criminals, then I fear what sort of future you'll leave your heir."

"My what?"

"Your children. Come on. Be smart about this. I'm only

trying to protect you, Elle."

I let him pace around me, holding my cool. Barely. "I'm not ending it with him. I'm in love with him."

"You barely know him."

"You were happy for me to marry him after four days. Now that I've been with him for five months, you say it's too soon?"

"Five months while he's been in jail."

"It doesn't matter. Not everyone is perfect. Those who make mistakes but learn from them are better than those who have made none. He makes me happy. That's all you need worry yourself with."

I didn't wait for his reply.

With my hands balled, I left his office and stalked into mine.

I loved my father, but I was done taking orders.

Penn is mine.

And he's going to stay that way.

* * * * *

"Visitor, Elle." Fleur knocked gently on my office door after lunch.

I hadn't stopped to eat. In fact, I hadn't stopped since I'd sat down and fully looked at the financial statements and future dated campaigns. Fleur had done a great job, but a few areas had slipped through our fastidious control.

"If it's my father again, tell him I'll come over tonight, and we can discuss it like adults. But nothing will change, so he might as well get used to it."

Fleur took a few steps over the threshold. "It's not your father." Her mouth tipped up into the biggest smile. "It's your fiancé."

Instantly, I leaped from my chair and crossed the large space. Sage meowed from her basket, wondering if I was leaving or not.

Before I could assure her I wasn't going anywhere, Penn appeared, dressed in low-slung dark jeans and a black untucked shirt. He looked carefree and reckless and just as delicious.

The itch of having him last night wasn't sated, and my mouth watered to taste him again. To finish what he'd started last time he was here and be wicked together with orgasm-related fun.

"Hi." My cheeks pinked, picturing him inside me. How sexy he was. How lucky *I* was.

Only, he didn't wrap an arm around me and whisper hello in his raspy lustful voice.

He didn't smile.

In fact, he took a step back, holding up his hand. "Elle…don't."

Icebergs slithered down my spine. "Don't what? What is it?"

Fleur left, leaving us alone.

What the hell could've changed since I left him a few hours ago until now? His eyes tightened with pain. Pain matched inside me the longer he stared. "I—I have something to give you."

I rubbed my arms, my hands squeaking over the fabric of my wardrobe. The silver sundress with black panels over the chest that Fleur had picked out was a nod to the night we'd gone to his charity gala. My own way of telling him whatever happened that night was over because the lies were gone and we were together. "Give me what?"

A rap sounded on my door. Before I could snap for whoever it was to leave us alone, Dad popped his head in.

His gaze instantly latched onto Penn. "Ah, I thought I saw you." Moving into the room, he closed the door ominously behind him.

Goosebumps erupted full of fear.

I had no idea what was going on, but it hurt like hell already.

Dad held out his hand, trying to hide his thoughts (unsuccessfully) about the ridiculous news articles and slight inconvenience Penn's background was causing.

Penn swallowed back his own emotions, shaking Dad's hand. "Mr. Charlston."

Dad smiled. "Congratulations on being acquitted. I'm so glad." His voice lowered with sincerity. "I know I wasn't exactly supportive while you were locked up, but I want you to know, I never stopped being grateful to you for saving Elle." His soft gray eyes met mine. "She means everything to me. I get a little protective when anything tries to hurt her—reporters included."

Penn dropped his hand, shoving it into his pocket. "I understand."

Unlike last night when I got on my knees and sucked him, he wasn't doing it to hold himself back. He stood protective of himself—a safety thing to keep himself rigid and firm to do whatever it was he'd come to do.

Don't let him.

I had no idea what had changed, but every instinct screamed to stop him...before it was too late.

Striding to his side, I slinked an arm around his waist and kissed his cheek. "Do you want to grab some lunch? Maybe take a quick walk and get some fresh air?"

Penn shivered at my closeness then stiffened. Never looking at me, he clenched his jaw and sidestepped out of my embrace.

He didn't answer my question, sticking to his script, giving me no way to stop him. "There's something I came to do."

I trembled in terror, wishing I could grab the hands of a clock and shoot us back to last night when everything had been so rosy and bright.

Dad frowned. "What is it you came to do, Mr. Everett?"

My heart sank. It didn't escape my notice or Penn's that Dad had gone from calling him son back to his formal address. Just like Penn had called him Mr. Charlston.

This is all so wrong.

Penn needed to be welcomed—to feel as if he belonged because he did. Just because it would be rough for the next few months in the tabloids didn't mean Dad had to be cruel.

"Dad, Penn saved me. He deserves—"

"Don't, Elle." Penn pulled one hand out of his pocket and pinched the bridge of his nose. "It's best if your father is here to hear this." His voice stayed calm and focused, but his muscles tensed, his back going overly straight.

"Hear what?" I locked my knees from sudden quaking.

"About our fake engagement." He looked at the carpet, his voice bitter and sharp, his body broken and sad. "I think it's time to call it off." He exhaled in a rush, the raw agony in his eyes a bleeding wound.

"What?"

Dad interrupted. "What do you mean?"

"I mean, I think it's best—for everyone involved—if we go our separate ways."

I stumbled. "You can't be serious."

Dad held up his hand. "What are you saying?"

Penn's face turned black. "I'm saying I have too much shit in my life to smear your perfection. I have a chief of police about to come after me, a criminal record, and a whole bunch of other issues. I saw how you being associated with me is already affecting your business. I never wanted that. I never wanted to make things worse for Elle, especially knowing how hard she works."

I gulped. "Penn, stop. It's over. You're free. The rumors will fade, and life will go back to normal."

"No." Dad held up his finger. "He's right. It won't. These sort of things last forever, Elle. Sure, it will fade in favor of other gossip, but the next time Belle Elle has a lawsuit or some nasty reporter has a grudge, they'll drag this story out all over again. We'll never be free of it."

"Exactly." Penn nodded curtly. "You'd never be free of me and the turmoil I'd cause."

Dad puffed his chest even as his confidence faded. His mood switched from corporate to apologetic. "Look, I'm sorry, Penn. I genuinely like you, and you make my daughter happy.

You saved her, and you'll forever have my gratitude, but Elle isn't a normal girl. She comes with a company that has been a part of our family for generations. I can't let her jeopardize that."

Penn stood to his full height, hiding his wince. "Sometimes, love isn't enough. It doesn't conquer everything."

I flinched, holding my broken pieces together. "That's ridiculous. How can you say love isn't enough?" The dirty disbelief in my voice made me snarl. "You want me, Penn. I want you. Don't do something as stupid as—"

"I'm not being stupid, Elle. I'm being smart."

"No, you're being a raging moron." Stomping toward him, I placed my hand over his thumping heart. "Tell me you love me. Tell me what you told me last night. Tell my dad so he can hear what an idiot you are."

Penn gritted his teeth, moving away from my touch. "I'm not an idiot for trying to protect you, Elle. Why can you do so much for me and I can't do the same for you?"

"I didn't hurt you and call it helping!"

"You don't think I'm not hurting? That this isn't fucking killing me?"

My cheeks burned with terror that I wouldn't be able to talk him out of this. To stop this lunacy. "Then don't do it! It's a silly newspaper."

"It's in black and white!" He bared his teeth. "It's damaging. I know how awful the mob mentality can be, Elle. It can fucking ruin everything you love."

"Can you really stand there and talk about love even while breaking my heart?" I wrapped my arms around my waist, hugging hard. "I chose you, Penn. You're worth whatever silly stories they make up about us. Admit you love me and stop trying to be a martyr."

His lips remained stubbornly locked together.

He couldn't tell me that he loved me.

He wouldn't.

He believed he was doing the right thing.

It's not.

It's not the right thing!

"As much as I agree with you," Dad said. "Are you sure about this? You seem to care deeply—"

Penn tore at his hair. "Of course, I care deeply. I love your daughter—" His eyes flared, noticing his admittance. He waved it away as if it wasn't the point. As if it didn't matter. When it was the *only* thing that mattered.

His eyes met mine, but he spoke to my dad. "It's because I love her that I'm doing this. I can't stand by and be the reason for Elle's future to be at stake."

Dad crossed his arms. "That's a noble reason." His gaze turned calm, assessing Penn in a way he hadn't. Seeing him like I saw him—past the angry features and stuck-up confidence. Finally noticing the man who protected everyone he cared about by keeping them as far away from him as possible.

He was noble.

He was stupid.

He was so selfless, he was willing to cut out his heart and walk away as some misguided attempt to save me.

Couldn't he see I couldn't care less about reporters or phony tales?

Couldn't he understand I didn't want Belle Elle anymore if I couldn't have him?

Penn might not understand, but Dad did.

He shook his head, pinning his gaze on Penn, finally believing in the affection between us—recognizing its truth.

Not that it would help me win this fight with this stubborn ass determined on destroying me, all in the name of honor.

Screw honor!

"Penn…we'll fight this together. Just like we fought your sentence."

His body flinched with grief. "You've already done too much for me, Elle. I can't ask for anymore."

"Penn, perhaps you should sit down. Let's talk about this—" Dad pointed at the couch, his shoulders falling the longer he witnessed the life-splintering argument. "I'm sure we can work this out."

I waved my arms. "There, you see? Even Dad, who is adamant about protecting Belle Elle from controversy, is willing to discuss—"

"Just because he doesn't want to see you hurting doesn't mean he agrees that it's the right choice." Penn shook his head, his eyes black with agony. "I've already caused you more stress than you should ever have to live through. Don't ask me to make you live through more."

"I'm not asking you. I'm *telling* you." I stormed forward, desperate to touch him. "You don't have the right to walk away when I want you to stay, Penn. Don't punish me for loving you."

His jaw locked. He swallowed hard. He looked over my head. "I can't do this anymore."

"Anymore? We've been together one night!"

"And you were alone for five months to *earn* that one night. That's not a life you deserve, Elle." He suddenly exploded. "I've already taken far too much from you."

"No, you haven't."

He snorted. "Haven't I? What about the countless nights I gave you? The constant worry? The deliberating stress? I've cost you so much, and I refuse to take anymore."

"I paid that willingly. You're free. That's all in the past."

"Until the next fuck up."

Dad cleared his throat. "How about we all take a breather? It might be as simple as keeping your relationship quiet for now—until this all blows over."

Penn laughed coldly. "You know as well as I do that that won't happen. This is what has to happen. It's for the best."

"No!" My temper overflowed, but I battled it down. "Look, let's be rational. Did you forget everything we promised last night? All the love we shared?"

Turning to look at my father, I added, "Dad, you practically threw me together with Penn that night at the

Weeping Willow. We're finally together. You can see what exists between us. Don't let him be ridiculous."

It was a low ball playing my father against Penn, but Dad was on my side now. If Penn needed fatherly approval—he had it.

Penn clenched his hands. "Not ridiculous, Elle. Smart." He smiled sadly. "I didn't come here to argue with you." His shoulders bunched as he pulled his other hand from his pocket. "Before I say goodbye, I need to do something."

"You don't get to say goodbye, Penn. Not after I waited for you in prison. Not after I fell in love—"

He planted a hand on my mouth, his eyes guarded and unreadable.

But I didn't need to read them. I knew how much he was breaking under his ironclad façade.

He howled just as much as I did.

Why is he doing this then?

He'd swiped away my foundations and made the world shake like an earthquake.

"This belongs to you." He held up his hand, and the necklace that'd started this catastrophe dangled from his fingers.

When I didn't move, he took my hand, turned it upright, and dribbled the chain into my palm.

With a harsh breath, he closed my fingers over it. "Stewie and Gio agree you should have it back. I should've given it to you years ago when I came to find you that night." He kissed me so soft, I barely tasted his lips. "I'm so sorry, Elle."

Dad coughed, but I ignored him, fighting my tears. My heart cracked open, dying, gasping. "Why are you doing this?"

Penn touched my cheekbone reverently. "Because for the first time in my life, I need to do the right thing. You helped me so much, Elle. Let me help you by not ruining your future."

I sniffed back a sob, hating the necklace locked in my hand. "I don't know what to say."

"Say you forgive me."

"Forgive you?" I cupped his cheek, mirroring his hold on me with the hand not holding the necklace. "The only thing to forgive is this. You're hurting me, Penn. I don't care about the newspapers or what the chief of police will do. All I care about is *you*." Tears rolled unbidden. "Don't do this."

He bent and brushed his lips once again over mine, licking away a tear at the corner of my mouth. "I'm sorry for dragging you into my mess, Elle. But your father is right. I'll never be free of my past, and you'll forever belong to Belle Elle. There is no place for us." He stepped backward, once again jamming his hands into his pockets. "I'm going away for a while. Let the scandal blow over." He shrugged. "Let me go, Elle."

Dad came to my side. "Look, Penn. Perhaps, I've been too hasty. Stay. Let's talk—"

Penn shuddered, squeezing his eyes before opening them again, full of wavering agony. "I can't."

My tears morphed into a shout. "You can. Who put you in charge about what is best for me or what I want? I know what's best, and I want *you*, Penn."

"And you'll always have me." He back stepped toward the door. "I'll never stop loving you, but we can't be together. I won't hurt you anymore. Goodbye, Elle." Hiding his pain behind a sharp cough, he opened the door and disappeared.

The moment he was gone, I fell to my knees.

"Elle!" Dad squatted beside me in horror. "Are you okay?"

I let loose, tears becoming sobs when before I'd been so damn happy. "Am I okay? No, I'm not okay."

Dad rubbed my back like he did when I was a child and I felt sick or had a nightmare. Before, his comfort would work. This time, it only made me miss another man more. "He can't do this, Dad. I love him."

Sage crawled into my lap, mewing sadly. I dropped the sapphire star onto the carpet and grabbed her, cuddling her close, using her as a tissue to wipe away my sadness. She let me. She purred in encouragement, letting me cry.

With tear-fogged vision, I noticed Dad pick up the necklace he'd bought me for my nineteenth birthday. He spun the star in his fingers, his forehead furrowing. Slowly, his spine straightened as he looked at the door where Penn had vanished and back to me in pieces on the floor.

"Right, that's it." Standing stiffly, he bent down and hauled me to my feet. "I've been a stupid old fool."

I sniffed, hugging Sage closer.

Patting my cheek, wiping away my tears, he said, "That boy loves you."

My heart squeezed all over again. A fresh wave of tears threatened.

"And you love him."

I bit my lip, doing my best to stop the torrent. "I do."

"I'm an idiot. He's an idiot. We're all stupid idiots." Pushing me toward the door, he scooped Sage from my arms and gave me the sapphire star instead. "Go after him."

I froze. "What?"

He laughed abruptly, rolling his eyes as if it was the most obvious thing after being dumped. "He's only breaking up with you because he thinks it's the right thing to do. I must admit I played my part in encouraging that. But that was before I saw how much he adores you. How much he put you first and himself second even though he's obviously going to pieces without you. I liked him before, Elle, but he just showed a noble, honorable side that is so damn rare."

He kissed my cheek as he opened the door. "Who cares about journalists and stories? We're solid. Our business is thriving. And even it if wasn't, it doesn't matter."

His eyes took on that whimsical glow he got whenever he thought of Mom. "I loved truly, and there wasn't a day that went by that I wished I didn't. Every morning, I was thankful. Every evening, I was grateful. No amount of money or good publicity can replace true love, Elle. And I'm a moron that I've fought for you to find that exact connection only to do whatever I could to break you apart when you found it."

His face fell. "I hope you can forgive your old fool of a father."

My tears dried.

Should I chase after him? What would I say?

But I had no choice.

Dad was right. I didn't care about Belle Elle's reputation. If we believed a few online articles could tear us down, then we didn't belong at the head of the chain. And if we sacrificed our own happiness for material things, then we didn't deserve to find love.

And I *had* found love.

I wouldn't let it walk away.

"I won't let him go." The oath landed by my feet before I noticed I'd spoken.

Dad hugged me with Sage scrambling between us. "That's my girl. Now go and knock some sense into that boy like he knocked sense into me. Tell him he's part of this family, whether he likes it or not."

With tear-slicked cheeks and racing heartbeat, I tore from my office.

Fleur asked where I was going.

Sage meowed.

Dad whooped.

And I flew on wings to claim Penn once and for all.

CHAPTER FORTY-FIVE

PENN

I COULDN'T STAY in New York.

Not after this.

The moment I'd gone to Larry's to collect the sapphire star Stewie had been keeping for Gio, he'd known things were about to get sad.

He hadn't grilled me, but he had told me to call him when I got to whatever destination I would run to.

The reporters wanted to slander Elle and her company? Well, they couldn't fucking use me because I wouldn't be in town. By distancing myself, I was protecting Elle.

It hurt like hell.

But it was the best thing for everyone.

Arnold wouldn't be able to drag her into my chaos. Greg would remain locked up. My connection to the Charlstons would fade, and Elle could remain the perfect princess who so many people relied on for work and income.

Throwing a duffel bag onto my bed, I didn't pay much attention as I threw pants, shirts, and underwear into the general vicinity.

Everything fucking hurt.

My chest, my eyes, my motherfucking heart.

I hated myself for hurting Elle.

I despised myself for leaving her in tears.

But it was for the best.

The only way I could think of to protect her.

"You know, you should really lock your front door."

What the—

I spun from shoving socks into the side pockets of the duffel, my mouth falling wide. "What the hell are you doing here?"

Elle leaned against my doorframe, the sapphire necklace dangling from her finger as she cocked her hip. "Getting you back, of course."

My hands curled. "I told you. I won't put you through any more stress and ridicule."

She merely smiled. Her eyes bright and tear-free; her body poised and confident. "I want you to do something for me…" Her attention fell to my half-packed bag. "Before you go. Can you do that?"

I narrowed my eyes, searching for a trap, but she remained open and kind.

I nodded slowly. "Okay…"

"Great." Pushing from the doorframe, she came toward me with a sexy sway in her hips.

My cock instantly reacted against my will. I gulped as she planted herself in front of me.

"You did all the talking in my office. Here, it's my turn."

I didn't like it, but I nodded. "Fine."

"Good." She swung the necklace like a pendulum. "First, this no longer belongs to me. It belongs to the hooded hero who saved me. I told him that three years ago. I distinctly remember mentioning that if I *had* remembered to ask for it back, I would've given it to my rescuer in payment for saving me and walking me home."

I couldn't help myself. "And I distinctly remember telling

you there was no way in hell I'd take it."

She smirked. "Yes, I remember that too." Tossing the necklace into my bag, she muttered, "Too bad, it's yours. I don't want it back. Know what else I don't want back?"

I stood frozen, not falling into her trap.

The longer she stood in my room, smelling so goddamn delicious and being so brave, the more I wanted to kiss her until I passed out from oxygen deprivation and took back everything I'd said.

I was an idiot.

Worse than an idiot.

I deserved to be lonely after throwing her away all because I didn't want to hurt her.

Eventually, I'd hurt her—either through my direct actions or indirect. It would happen. Could I afford to take that chance?

She means too much to me.

When I didn't answer, she beamed. "My heart, Penn. I don't want that back, either. It's yours. So you might else well carve it from my chest and stuff it into that bag of yours because you're not leaving without it."

"Elle," I growled. "Don't be so—"

"What? Dramatic? Immature? Literal?" She stabbed my sternum. "Listen here, Mr. Everett, and listen good. I didn't pick you. You didn't pick me. Fate picked us, and there's nothing we can do about it. The reporters can't change it. Life can't break it. And you most certainly cannot walk away from it."

I sucked in a breath to argue, but she planted a hand on my mouth just as I'd done to her.

"I don't care about anything else. I'm not going to worry about what may or may not happen. I've been fighting to deserve you ever since the night you were taken in Central Park. Do you know how much guilt I've carried since that night? How terrible I felt? The debt I endured to pay back?" Her bottom lip wobbled.

I crumpled inside for hurting her. I had no idea she suffered the way I had. Her with guilt, me with misplaced hate.

If only I'd told her my name from the very beginning.

But if I had, who knew if we would be here right now. About to do something stupid and reckless but so right. I couldn't breathe with the thought of not claiming her. Walking from her office showed me how much I adored her. How utterly real this was.

It wasn't a fling. It wasn't short-term.

It was forever.

And if I stood by and acted like a dick—thinking I could keep her safe while abandoning her to the wolves—then I didn't fucking deserve her.

It was my job to keep her safe.

I thought that meant from myself.

But I'd rather keep her safe from other assholes and screw my fears about not being the man she deserved.

She'd leashed me to her the moment she'd appeared in my doorway. Her cute little argument turned me on until I throbbed in my pants for her tirade to end so I could show her just how much I'd never let her go.

Today had started off blissful and slid into terrible, but now, it was exactly where it should be.

Acceptance.

This was real. So fucking real.

"So you listen here, Penn. I don't care what argument you try. I'm not—"

"Elle..." I put a finger over her lips, silencing her with my stare. "Okay."

"Okay?" Her lips brushed over my touch, making me shudder with desire.

"You win." I leaned forward, my self-control at its end. Capturing her mouth with mine, I kissed her with every yes and apology I could. "I'm a fucking idiot, but I'm yours. I'm not going anywhere."

It took a second for my vow to travel from her ears to her

brain to her heart.

But when it did, she bounced into my arms as if she'd always belonged there.

"Truly?"

I chuckled. "Truly."

She peppered my jaw with kisses. "You're an ass. You know that, right?"

"I do know that. That was why I was trying to remove myself from your life."

"Well, you tried and failed. Don't you ever try again."

I nodded. "Yes, ma'am."

"And don't call me ma'am."

"What do you want me to call you?"

"Something dirty while you take off my clothes and have your wicked way with me."

My eyebrows rose. "In that case, turn around, Ms. Charlston. I suddenly have the overwhelming need to bend you over and stick my cock inside you."

She trembled. "I thought you'd never ask."

I swatted her ass, marching her to the bed. "Oh, I didn't ask. You've been a naughty girl, going against my wishes and making me keep you. You need to be punished."

Her laughter made my entire fucking galaxy blaze bright.

CHAPTER FORTY-SIX

ELLE

"MARRY ME."

My eyes flew wide. "What?"

Penn spun me around, shoved his clothes-strewn bag off the bed, and tossed me onto the mattress. "Marry me. Make our fake engagement real."

"I—wow."

"Wow isn't the answer I want." His voice was a seductive rasp. "Try again. Marry me?"

A shiver darted down my spine, loving his authoritative kinky tone.

I knew my answer, but I bit my bottom lip. "Um, how long can I think about it?"

I gasped as he pressed me onto my back, then hoisted up the silver dress and revealed my nakedness. I'd left him the gift of my underwear this morning and hadn't replaced them.

He groaned. "God, you're going to kill me." He sank a finger inside me, burying his face into my hair. "Yes or no, Elle. Put me out of my misery." Hunger poured off him, infecting me until I squirmed with starvation. He was so much bigger than me, so much stronger, so damn beautiful, yet with one little word, I had the power to break him into smithereens.

Just like he'd broken me.

I toyed with the idea of saying no. To give him a taste of his own medicine, but he withdrew his touch and rolled onto his side.

"You're all I want, Elle. I was a jackass." He kissed me reverently then contradicted it with sudden aggression. "It fucking destroyed me to go over there. To tell you to leave me. Feeling that god-crushing emptiness of having everything I ever wanted then giving it all away again. It hurt so fucking much."

More tears sprang to my eyes at his confession and soul-bearing honesty. He cut me open, leaving me to bleed in his arms.

"I want you more than I've ever wanted anyone. More than I ever wanted a dry place to sleep. More than food even after two days of none." A cocky smirk twisted his lips. "That's the truth, but the one you truly need to know is I'm crazy in love with you, and you're not leaving my bed until you say yes."

"Is that a threat?"

"Do you want it to be?"

My eyes hooded. "Maybe."

"I don't mind spending decades convincing you." Undoing his belt and zipper, he pushed his jeans and boxer-briefs down to mid-thigh. His erection sprang thick and hard.

My legs spread in invitation. "Good because I think I need convincing."

Pressing over me, his body vibrated with tension. His arousal soaked from his skin to mine as he found my entrance.

His lips moved against mine, hot and wet. We devoured each other, turning wilder and more in lust every second. Bites and licks and the incessant urge to join, to mate.

His cock throbbed at my core, tormenting me, making me heavy and achy with need.

"I'll be miserable without you, Elle. Please don't make me be miserable."

"You're making me miserable." I rocked against him, begging him to fill me. My senses were drenched in him—his scent and taste. I needed him to finish what he started before I went completely out of my mind.

"You want me?" He angled himself, mounting me in every sense. "You have me." He plunged inside.

"Oh, God." My eyes blacked out. The room spun.

A groan splashed from both of us. I couldn't stop my hips grinding into him as he thrust inch by savage inch.

"Is this enough convincing?" He captured my mouth as his hips flexed into mine, driving me hard against the bed.

"Not…quite…" I patted myself on the back for even attempting to speak with him fucking me, drugging me.

"More?"

I moaned when he sucked on my tongue.

His kisses came wrapped in apologizes and screw-ups. His nips were loaded with passion and love.

He held nothing back. Giving me everything he had left to give.

But I was greedy.

"More, definitely more." I sank my fingernails into his ass, pulling him harder, making him fill me deeper. He completed me.

I wanted him. I wanted him inside me. I wanted him for all eternity.

His breath came out in a shudder as our rhythm picked up, going from teasing to committed.

His mouth locked on mine again. One hand in my hair and the other on my chin, his lips taught mine a violent dance. His tongue thrust into my mouth at the same tempo as his cock plunged into my pussy.

My teeth sank into his lower lip as I arched into his hold. I was pinned by him. Held hostage by sex while he waited for an answer to his unconventional marriage proposal.

"You said yes to the fake one," he growled, thrusting faster. "Say yes to a real one."

I drank air like liquid. "I never said yes to the first one. I remember saying no multiple times."

He flattened me into the bed. "I didn't let you say no then. And I won't let you say no now." His passion overflowed. His fist landed in my hair, tugging hard enough to remind me I was completely at his mercy.

I slept with him in utmost trust that he'd never use his strength to hurt me.

"You can't make me say yes by fucking me, Penn."

"I can't?" He surged into me, making the familiar fireworks grab a lighter and hold a flame to their fuses.

I glued my lips together, holding back my moan as my body prepared to spindle and shoot into euphoric abandon.

"Do you trust me?" he whispered, his tongue tracing my ear.

Even swept away, so close to coming, I nodded, grabbing his shoulders with my nails. "Unequivocally."

"In that case. Say yes."

His gaze searched mine, his features turning brittle and sharp with his desire to come. "You put me through hell because I love you so fucking much, and I put you through hell because I come with baggage. But I'm willing to fight together, Elle. Are you?"

His hands found my hair again, holding me in place as he undid me with desperate kisses. "Marry me. Goddammit, Elle."

He thrust into me, switching the spark for annihilation.

I threw my head back and screamed as my body waked around his. My pussy fisted his cock, and every orgasm bubble popped down my legs.

His black chuckle brought me back to earth where he chased me off the cliff.

His fingertips brushed across my cheek. "Fuck, I love watching you come." He drove deeper into me. "It makes me so hard." *Thrust.* "I can't fucking control myself." *Plunge.* "Christ, Elle." His wickedly sexy mouth brushed over mine, feeding me his growl as the splashes of his cum filled me.

His eyes snapped closed as his body jerked.

Holding him while he came down from his high, keeping him safe, threading our lives into one, I murmured, "Yes. Yes, I'll marry you, Nameless."

EPILOGUE

PENN

SIX MONTHS OF fucking heaven.

Six months of waking up with Elle in my arms.

Six months of being hissed at by Sage for crowding Elle on the couch at night after a long day at work.

Six months of working out of an office at Belle Elle, running my charity, and trading the penny stocks I'd become so fond of.

Six wonderfully happy months where Elle's father welcomed me wholeheartedly into the family, Larry finalized the adoption on Stewie, and life settled into a full, joyful world rather than an empty, lonely one.

A few months ago, I'd taken Elle to Fishkill to see Gio.

At the start, she'd been cold and standoffish—which I understood seeing as the last time she'd seen him he'd been yelling abuse and physically hurting her.

But just like Larry always said, *Thieves can become saints. Saints can become thieves. Most of us deserve a second chance.'* Gio had changed. We'd celebrated with him over the phone when Stewie's adoption finally came through and he no longer carried hate caused by being in Sean's pocket.

He'd started a building course in prison, and in four years' time—when he was due to be released—he'd be a fully-fledged carpenter ready to trade a skill for money.

We'd already arranged he'd work for me building shelters and renovating apartments for those in need. He'd never be homeless again and had a readymade family who knew how to forgive and help rather than judge and ridicule.

The reporters never fully went away.

Arnold Twig ensured their tattletales and slander were given new details. Larry fought for me in another trial—this one with only judges presiding, not a jury. The evidence had three overseers, not just one.

I had the opportunity to stand and reveal everything that I'd endured. I looked Arnold Twig in the eye and buried him under details, evidence, and the long years I'd served incorrectly.

I was no longer a kid and afraid of him.

He was afraid of me.

And despite Arnold's rebuttal and lies, even marching Sean in front of the public as the perfect role model, the newspapers actually did a good turn for once and uncovered Sean's old juvie record for deliberately maiming a local dog.

That scrap of juicy detail encouraged more reporters to dig into the not-so-innocent world of Sean Twig.

Slowly, women came forward to issue statements that they'd been touched inappropriately at school and been sworn to secrecy by him. Even a female teacher swore under oath that Sean had raped her on the last day of senior year.

She hadn't reported it because she was afraid she'd be the one prosecuted for a teacher sleeping with a student.

The day Sean was officially arrested for more crimes than I could ever have done, Arnold Twig lost his position as chief of police and was detained, just like his son. His bail was set high enough that it would've hurt him in the wallet as well as his livelihood.

Despite knowing both would be sentenced for their crimes and would spend years paying for what they'd done to me, vengeance wasn't entirely sweet. It felt as if they got off too easy. That evil had won in some small way.

At least, I had one small victory. Sean had been sentenced last week. Due to the multiple charges and heinous felonies he'd committed, he earned twenty years with no chance of parole.

Hopefully, in another few months, Larry would have a verdict, Arnold Twig would be sentenced, and my records would be expunged forever.

That would be the day Elle and I would agree to an interview by the press constantly hounding us for our tale. That day I would be vindicated, and I'd tell the world everything. Finally proud enough and untainted by lies to stand beside Elle, not as a thieving shadow on her empire, but as her equal.

I couldn't wait.

All our loose ends were tying up neatly.

Greg finally went to trial, and Elle testified. However, our happiness meant she struggled to hold onto ill will, especially after seeing how changed Gio was. She hoped the same would happen to Greg.

She told the truth in court, the chains and cuffs that David had saved as evidence were revealed, the bank statements purchasing a second car, the diamond engagement ring he'd forced on her—every shred of premeditation Greg had done.

The jury oohed and aahed over her treatment. They glared at Greg and plotted his punishment even before the trial concluded.

Elle had full opportunity to push for a harsher sentence when the judge asked her what she wanted to see happen. However, she didn't get nasty. She didn't glower or beg for a harsh sentence.

She merely stated the facts and left—leaving the verdict up to the court.

It wasn't until a few weeks later, after he was sentenced to eight years, two months—which I thought was exceedingly short—a large donation in Greg's name appeared in my charity's bank account.

That night, Elle told me about the deal she'd made with Greg to give him twenty million for my freedom.

She'd paid him, as she was loyal to her bargains.

But the more she became involved with projects around town and traded Belle Elle's glitzy hallways for canvas tents and soup kitchens—helping those like me—she decided the bribery could be better used elsewhere.

Greg had done something unforgivable, and Elle took it into her own hands to make him redeemable. Fearing it would reflect badly on her character, she didn't take it all. But she did transfer seventeen million from his name into the charity's, leaving him with only three.

Only three.

It was a lot more than he fucking deserved.

The reporters noticed, as all charity donations had to be logged with the record service, and in the end, Elle's final zing at Greg turned out to paint his misdemeanors in a better light.

Who knew? Maybe she set him on a righteous path. He was interviewed and written about as the most generous criminal in history—not an idiot who was greedy.

At least, his father, Steve, had peace of mind. His son wasn't all bad. Belle Elle avoided more scandal about an attempted rapist who'd worked in their ranks for years. And I fell more in fucking love with the woman who was mine.

In a twist of fate, Sean was put into the same prison population as Greg and from rumors supplied to us thanks to Gio, Greg had earned his fair share of karma.

Unable to get to me, Sean took his frustration out on Greg. A broken arm and few other prison scuffles occurred. As much as I hated Sean for using me as his scape goat, I was kind of glad that Greg hadn't gotten off completely scot-free.

He'd suffered some bodily pain for what he'd done to Elle.

It was fitting.

Our fake engagement turned real engagement was celebrated only by the special people we invited. We kept it small, understated, but the ring I bought her was anything but.

The diamond glittered with rubies on either side, perfectly elegant and locked on her finger for eternity.

Her sapphire star necklace was fixed from Gio ripping the chain off her neck, and it hung in our walk-in wardrobe like a talisman, reminding us to keep fighting, because sometimes, even the bad guys turned out to be the good ones.

Without Gio and Sean, I might never have heard Elle scream and never have ventured into the alley to save the day. She would've walked around New York and returned to her tower, never knowing I existed.

The tragedy of that never failed to steal my breath at the thought of growing old without her by my side.

Her apartment had become my apartment when we moved into together two days after I was freed from jail. With me not living in my building, builders were free to move in, tear out stairs, rip out kitchens, and blitz the entire building in one go rather than piece by piece.

It was finished two months before I'd hoped, ready for new low-income renters who needed a break.

Everything we'd endured and survived had finally given us the benefit of the doubt.

We'd been tested to see if we deserved the greatest gift of all.

And luckily, we'd been found worthy.

Elle was my happily ever after.

And I was hers.

And who knew? Maybe in the future, we'd give her father and Larry what they wanted and deliver a new Belle Elle heir or heiress.

But for now…she was mine. I was hers, and we were having far too much fun practicing.

Speaking of which.

Elle padded out of the bathroom with a towel on her head and another wrapped around her stunning body. Sage trotted by her heels as she always did when it was dinnertime.

I stayed where I was on the couch, flicking through a magazine on investment opportunities in Africa.

I waited until Elle gave the gray feline her ration of freshly cooked chicken then watched as she unwound her long blonde hair and tossed it over her shoulder.

Hoisting the towel higher around her breasts, she moved back toward the bedroom to continue dressing for the charity gala I was hosting with Larry.

I already wore the gold tux that was this evening's color of choice.

Elle had yet to dress.

Checking my watch, I cracked a smile.

I was the host. I shouldn't be late.

But I had a fiancée who was too delectable.

Tossing the magazine away, I followed her into the bedroom, grabbed her wrist, and spun her around. I yanked at the towel.

"Hey." She swatted me as the fabric tumbled to the floor. Her eyes glittered; her love that I'd never get used to or tired of seeing shone so damn bright. "If you kiss me, who knows how long we'll be."

I smirked. "I plan on doing a lot more than just kissing you, Elle." Biting her ear, I growled, "Get on the bed."

With a grin, she obeyed instantly, spreading her legs, acting coy and shy all at once.

The perfect woman.

My perfect woman.

Undoing my belt, I fell to my knees to worship her.

We'd get to the charity event.

Eventually.

In the meantime, we'd be together.

Just us.

We'd love. We'd argue. We'd protect. We'd evolve.

We were a family.
And that was all that fucking mattered.

ACKNOWLEDGMENTS

I'd like to thank my beta readers for their tireless energy on helping me get this book out in time. Melissa, Amy, Yaya, Vickie, Melissa, and Tamicka. There is no way in hell I would've been able to do this without you. Same with every book I write. I'm honored to have you in my corner and hope you never leave me.

Thank you so much to all the bloggers and reviewers who helped spread the word about this duet and for all your mega support throughout the years. Again, I hope you never leave me because I could never do this without you.

Thank you to my international publishers who have taken my work and translated it into so many exotic, wonderful languages.

Thank you to Kylie and Eric for recording the audio so fast and so brilliantly.

Thank you to my long suffering husband who didn't like me working such long hours on this book (he got lonely). I think February 2017 will go down in history for the most hours worked versus lack of sleep. I know I'm going to coma and wonder what a day off is once I press publish.

I hate acknowledgements as I know I'm going to forget someone (hence why some of my books have them, and some don't). So thank you to everyone who I talk to on a regular basis online. Thank you to fellow authors for their wisdom and insight, and thank you to the friends I've made off-line who keep me sane with a horse ride or two.

You all mean so much to me.

Until the next book, be safe and kind and once again, THANK YOU.

OTHER WORK BY PEPPER WINTERS

Pepper Winters is a multiple New York Times, Wall Street Journal, and USA Today International Bestseller.

DARK ROMANCE
New York Times Bestseller 'Monsters in the Dark' Trilogy
"Voted Best Dark Romance, Best Dark Hero, #1 Erotic Romance"
Start the Trilogy with
Tears of Tess (Monsters in the Dark #1)

Multiple New York Times Bestseller 'Indebted' Series
"Voted Vintagely Dark & Delicious. A true twist on Romeo & Juliet"
Start the Series **FREE** with
Debt Inheritance (Indebted #1)

GRAY ROMANCE
USA Today Bestseller 'Destroyed'
"Voted Best Tear-Jerker, #1 Romantic Suspense"

SURVIVAL CONTEMPORARY ROMANCE
USA Today Bestseller 'Unseen Messages' *"Voted Best Epic Survival Romance 2016, Castaway meets The Notebook"*

MOTORCYCLE CLUB ROMANCE
Multiple USA Today Bestseller 'Pure Corruption' Duology
"Sinful & Suspenseful, an Amnesia Tale full of Alphas and Heart"
Start the Duology with:
Ruin & Rule (Pure Corruption #1)

SINFUL ROMANCE
Multiple USA Today Bestseller 'Dollar' Series
"Elder Prest will steal your heart. A captive love-story with salvation at its core."
Start this series for only **99c** with
Pennies (Dollar Series #1)

EROTIC ROMANCE
Brand New Release 'Truth & Lies' Duet
Start this duet with
Crown of Lies (Truth & Lies #1)

ROMANTIC COMEDY written as TESS HUNTER
#1 Romantic Comedy Bestseller 'Can't Touch This'
"Voted Best Rom Com of 2016. Pets, love, and chemistry."

UPCOMING RELEASES
For 2017 and beyond titles please visit
www.pepperwinters.com

SOCIAL MEDIA & WEBSITE
Facebook: Peppers Books
Instagram: @pepperwinters
Facebook Group: Peppers Playgound
Website: www.pepperwinters.com

ABOUT THE AUTHOR

After chasing her dreams to become a full-time writer, Pepper has earned recognition with awards for best Dark Romance, best BDSM Series, and best Hero. She's an multiple #1 iBooks bestseller, along with #1 in Erotic Romance, Romantic Suspense, Contemporary, and Erotica Thriller. With 19 books currently published, she has hit the bestseller charts twenty-seven times in three years.

Pepper is a Hybrid Author of both Traditional and Self-published work. Her Pure Corruption Series was released by Grand Central, Hachette. She signed with Trident Media and her books have sold in multiple languages and audio around the world.

On a personal note, Pepper has recently returned to horse riding after a sixteen year break and now owns a magnificent black gelding called Sonny. He's an ex-pacer standardbred who has been retrained into a happy hacking, dressage, and show jumping pony. If she's not writing, she's riding.

The other man in her life is her best-friend and hubby who she fell in love with at first sight. He never proposed and they ended up married as part of a bet, but after eleven years and countless adventures and fun, she's a sucker for romance as she lives the fairy-tale herself.

For more information on Pepper and her work please follow:

Facebook: Peppers Books
Instagram: @Pepperwinters
Facebook Group: Peppers Playgound
Website: www.pepperwinters.com